COURAGE FOR THE CLARKS FACTORY GIRLS

MAY ELLIS

Boldwood

This edition first published in Great Britain in 2024 by Boldwood Books Ltd.

Copyright © May Ellis, 2024

Cover Design by Colin Thomas

Cover Photography: Colin Thomas

The moral right of May Ellis to be identified as the author of this work has been asserted in accordance with the Copyright, Designs and Patents Act 1988.

Every effort has been made to obtain the necessary permissions with reference to copyright material, both illustrative and quoted. We apologise for any omissions in this respect and will be pleased to make the appropriate acknowledgements in any future edition.

A CIP catalogue record for this book is available from the British Library.

Paperback ISBN 978-1-83533-030-2

Large Print ISBN 978-1-83533-029-6

Hardback ISBN 978-1-83533-028-9

Ebook ISBN 978-1-83533-031-9

Kindle ISBN 978-1-83533-032-6

Audio CD ISBN 978-1-83533-023-4

MP3 CD ISBN 978-1-83533-024-1

Digital audio download ISBN 978-1-83533-025-8

Boldwood Books Ltd
23 Bowerdean Street
London SW6 3TN
www.boldwoodbooks.com

This story is dedicated to everyone affected by conflict in this world, whether in war or in their home lives. May peace return to you and never leave again.

1

SEPTEMBER 1915

Louisa smiled as she ran a loving hand over the crisp, cotton bedsheets that she had just placed in her bottom drawer. In the weeks since her sweetheart Mattie had been away fighting in France, she had been working hard, adding to her collection of household items so that when he came home, they would be ready to start married life together.

Her smile turned to a grin as she remembered him teasing her about the first things she'd bought. 'I've got a nice tea set, some pillowcases and a tin-opener so far,' she'd told him.

Mattie had burst out laughing.

'What's so funny?' she had asked.

He had shaken his head, still chuckling. 'Nothing at all, love. I'm just thinking that at least we can have a cuppa, open a tin of sardines and then have somewhere to rest our heads. I can't wait to use them.'

'Oh, you,' she had giggled, poking him in the ribs. 'My ma always said you need to be able to feed and water your man, then he'll need his rest.'

'Sensible woman, your ma.'

Now she had sheets and blankets as well as the pillowcases. She felt her blood warm as she imagined them lying together in their marriage bed.

'Oh, Mattie,' she sighed. 'I miss you so, my love. I wish this awful war would end.'

She tucked his latest letter into the beribboned bundle she kept in the drawer with their treasures. He had kept his promise, writing to her most days, even though it sometimes took a while for them to reach her. His letters were full of love and their plans for the future, interspersed with funny stories about army life. She knew he was playing down the hardships of life in the trenches, not wanting her to worry – although how could she not? She suspected that making things seem amusing helped him to cope with the harsh realities of war as well.

Her own responses to him were written in the same vein – silly stories about life working at the Clarks shoe factory and outings with her friends, Kate and Jeannie. She tried not to mention her parents and their disapproval of her relationship with Mattie on account of their different religions. She was still convinced that it was her Anglican father's influence that had persuaded Mattie, a Quaker, to enlist. It still made her stomach churn when she thought of it.

She took a calming breath and closed the drawer. It was nearly time for church. She would pray to God to keep Mattie safe and bring him and all the other lads home soon.

As she left her room and walked downstairs, there was a knock at the front door.

'Whoever can that be at this time on a Sunday morning?' muttered her mother as she went to open it.

As Louisa reached the hall, she recognised the voice of Peg Searle – Kate's sister.

'Good morning, Mrs Clements,' she said. 'Would it be possible for me to have a word with Louisa, please?'

Before her ma could say anything, Louisa stepped forward. The moment she set eyes on Peg, she knew something was wrong. Her face was chalk white and her eyes red-rimmed.

'Peg,' she said, dread filling her. 'What is it? Has something happened to Kate?'

Her friend had taken many a beating from her drunken pa. Louisa and Jeannie worried about her, especially since her ma's recent death.

Peg shook her head, not looking directly at Louisa. 'No, Kate's fine.' She addressed her mother. 'Can I come in, please?'

Not wanting to give Ma the chance to refuse, Louisa reached for Peg's hand and drew her inside. Her fingers were ice cold, despite the mild morning, and she was shaking.

'What is it?' she asked again, not at all sure she wanted to hear the answer.

Peg blinked back tears and swallowed hard.

'Take your guest into the parlour, Louisa,' said Ma. 'I'll put the kettle on.'

Louisa glanced at her mother as she turned away. She was confused. Her parents disapproved of Peg almost more than they did Mattie on account of her leaving Holy Trinity Church to become a Quaker Friend when she had married Mattie's brother Will. Why wasn't she complaining they'd be late for church?

She turned her attention back to Peg. Her heart was racing. If it wasn't Kate who had Peg so upset, it had to be Mattie. 'Just tell me,' she said. 'Has Mattie been hurt? Are they sending him home?'

'No.' Peg shook her head. Louisa let out a sigh of relief. She'd got it wrong. It wasn't Mattie. It must be his ma. Maybe she'd taken poorly?

'Not hurt,' Peg choked out before she could ask, finally looking directly at Louisa. The pity in her eyes filled her with dread. 'I'm so sorry, Louisa. The family wanted you to hear it from us and not... He's gone, love. An artillery shell landed in his trench. None of them survived.'

For a moment, it seemed as though the whole world had halted on its axis. She fought for breath as her heart faltered. She took a step back and shook her head.

'No, you're wrong,' she said. 'He's not dead; I'd know. I got a letter from him only yesterday. They must have made a mistake.' When Peg said nothing, just looking at her with the saddest expression Louisa had ever seen in her life, she shook her head again. 'No. Please, not my Mattie!'

'I'm so sorry,' Peg said again, her tears running freely now. 'His ma got the letter late yesterday. She's in an awful state. Will too. He's... he's gone to tell Lucas.' Jeannie's brother, Lucas, was Mattie's best friend.

Louisa barely registered the heavy tread of her father's boots on the stairs. Her mind was spinning as she tried to focus on Peg's words. It couldn't be true.

'Louisa?' he said. 'What's this?'

She couldn't answer. It was still hard to breathe. It didn't make any sense. It couldn't be right. She kept shaking her head in denial.

Peg turned to Pa. 'I'm sorry to intrude, sir. I'm Peg Searle, Mattie's sister-in-law. I... I've had to tell Louisa some bad news.'

'About Matthew?' he asked.

Peg nodded, putting a hand to her mouth as a sob escaped her lips. 'Lost, sir.'

Her father's hand touched Louisa's arm as he murmured his condolences to Peg. His fingers felt scalding hot against her cold skin.

Her mother bustled out of the kitchen holding a tea tray.

'Louisa, lass, what are you still doing by the front door? Come into the parlour.'

Louisa continued to shake her head, never taking her eyes off Peg. 'It's not true,' she whispered. 'Tell me it's not true,' she demanded, her voice rising. 'How do they know it was Mattie? He says it's chaos there most of the time. He could've been somewhere else.'

Her father's grip on her arm tightened and she tried to shake him off. His touch was burning her.

'Peg, please!' she begged. 'Tell me it's not true! He promised me he'd stay safe, that we'd be married when he got home.'

Peg closed her eyes, tears continuing to flow down her pale cheeks. 'I'm so sorry, Louisa,' she sobbed.

Louisa hadn't been aware of her mother moving, of the rattle of the tea tray as she'd put it down. But then Ma was at her other side and her parents were holding her up as her legs gave out from under her. She wailed as the awful truth finally hit her. Mattie was never coming home.

2

Louisa blinked. The low winter sun was shining straight through the high windows of the Machine Room at the Clarks shoe factory, into her eyes. The sharp light made her head throb in time with the hum of the machinery that vibrated through her body and the high-pitched chatter of her workmates around her. She already felt ill. The smells of the machine oil and leather and stale air that pervaded the vast room, and the racket created 300 women and girls, all working at their sewing machines, were overwhelming her this morning.

She should be used to it. She'd been working for Clarks since she was almost fifteen and she was eighteen now. She'd started at the same time as her friends Jeannie and Kate, who were working on either side of her on a long bench. Their job was to sew together the drill cotton vamp and counter lining pieces that would then be attached inside the leather uppers of the shoes, which other women and girls were making at the other end of the room. It was simple work, but easy to make a mistake if you didn't concentrate. Messing up meant wasted thread for which she would be charged, reducing her wages if she wasn't careful. Louisa was usually a fast, accurate worker, hardly ever making silly mistakes. But today, she couldn't concentrate. The noise and the smells and the dust from the cotton were conspiring together against her, making her light-headed. She could feel the throbbing vibrations of the machinery through her feet and her hands, adding to her nausea. Her hands weren't as quick as they usually were and she had narrowly missed piercing her fingers with the swift, sharp machine needle more than once in the past hour. It left her shaky and ready to weep.

The news of the past few days had left her sick with grief and hopelessness. What had once been a happy working place now held no joy for her. *Mattie is gone. I won't ever see him again.* Her whole body ached from the effort of trying to keep going when it was all she could think of. She wanted to lie down and die.

Just months ago, he would have been waiting outside her house in Somerton Road every morning to walk her through the village of Street to the Clarks factory, where they both worked. She would catch glimpses of him through the day as he moved carts filled with cut leather parts for boots and shoes from one department to the next and he would wave and blow her a kiss. He was always there at the end of the day to walk her home after work.

'One day, I'm going to marry you, Louisa Clements,' he'd say. 'Then I won't have to leave you at the door. We'll have our own house and we can shut the world out and live our lives how we want to.' And she had believed him.

Then, out of the blue, he had enlisted, determined to go and fight in the war raging in Europe. Louisa had begged him not to. She'd heard such terrible things about this awful conflict. He didn't even have to fight because he was a Quaker, like their employers, the Clark family, and could have refused to take up arms on account of his pacifist religion. But he'd said it was his duty and asked whether they could marry before he went away. She'd been ready and willing, but her father had refused to allow it, insisting they wait until he returned. Then he was gone, coming home for just a few days between the end of his training and being shipped overseas. Within weeks, he was in the trenches. And now... he was gone forever.

She thought the shock and the grief would kill her. She still wanted to die. To be with Mattie in the hereafter was preferable to staying here, without him. She could barely eat, never slept and was plagued with constant nausea.

As though her body was listening to her thoughts, her stomach revolted and she clutched at her mouth, breathing deeply through her nose in an effort to stem the growing feeling. But the inhalation of oil-and-leather-tainted air made it worse and she quickly stepped away from her machine and ran for the privy, praying she'd make it there before she was sick.

* * *

Kate and Jeannie stared after their friend as she ran from the Machine Room.

'Should we go after her?' mouthed Kate to Jeannie over the rattle of the machinery.

Jeannie shook her head, inclining her head slightly towards the supervisor, Mr Briars, who watched Louisa's escape with a disapproving frown. Both girls turned back to their work as he approached them.

'What's wrong with her?' he asked. 'She's been like a wet rag for days.'

'She's had some bad news, sir,' said Jeannie. 'Her sweetheart was killed in battle.'

'Matthew Searle? Betty Searle's lad?'

Jeannie nodded. Mattie's ma worked in the Trimmings Department.

'That's right, sir. She's taken it really hard.'

'Well, I'm sorry for her loss. He was a fine lad from a good family. But she must pull herself together and get on with her work. She's not getting paid to rush off and leave her post every five minutes. If she's ill, she should go home. She won't get paid, mind.'

'I'm sure she'll be all right, sir,' she said.

'We'll help her catch up, sir,' said Kate.

Jeannie nodded. Although she didn't know how they'd manage to complete their work and Louisa's as well before their shift ended. They were already working as fast as they could. Being on piecework meant they had to produce linings by the dozen, all to an acceptable standard, and fewer completed pieces meant less money in their pay packets. It would be a struggle to produce extras to cover for what their friend couldn't manage today, but she knew they would try. She and Louisa had done the same for Kate when her ma was dying.

'Well, see you do.'

When Louisa hadn't returned five minutes later, Mr Briars sent Kate to find her.

'Lou? Are you here?' she called out as she entered the women's privy. 'What's taking you so long? Mr Briars is having a fit. You'd better get back or he'll be docking your pay.'

Kate frowned into the silence. 'Come on, Lou. Where are you?' When there was still no answer, she turned to go back to the Machine Room. Maybe she'd missed Louisa and she was already back at her place?

A soft groan had her turning again and searching the cubicles more thoroughly. Behind a door at the end, she found her friend, crumpled on the cold, concrete floor.

'Good heavens, Lou, whatever's happened?'

As Kate tried to sit her up, Louisa groaned again but didn't open her eyes. She had a bruise blossoming on her cheek where she must have hit her face on the floor as she'd fallen. Kate realised she wouldn't be able to lift her friend while she was in a dead faint, but she didn't want to leave her to summon help.

'Help!' Kate yelled as loud as she could, her voice echoing around the walls. 'Someone help us!'

* * *

Louisa slowly became aware of her surroundings as she was carried from the privy by her father.

'Pa?' she said, her voice raw and painful. 'What happened?'

Her father looked down at her, his expression grim. 'You fainted, lass. Young Kate found you, yelled blue murder and someone came and got me.'

Louisa closed her eyes, wishing Kate had just left her there. 'I'm all right, Pa. You can put me down. I've got to get back to work.'

'Don't be daft, girl. I've to take you to the ambulance room to see a first aider. You can't go back in there if you're going to drop where you stand. You've hit your face on the floor. You're in no fit state to work. You'll end up with more than bruises if you lose your concentration on a machine.' He paused outside the nurse's room. 'You've not been eating,' he said softly. 'I know you've had a shock over young Mattie and I'm sorrier than I can say that he's gone. He was a fine boy. But you're young and you've got your whole life ahead of you. You've got to take care of yourself, Louisa.'

Louisa blinked back tears and buried her head in her father's shoulder. 'It's so hard, Pa. He was everything to me.'

'I know, love. But he wouldn't want you to hurt yourself like this. Now, let's get someone to see to you, then I'll have to ask for permission to take you home to your mother. I just hope they don't dock both our wages. The Clarks are fair people. They do what they can for folks who need help but they expect us to get on with our work and do a decent job. You can't be slacking, not even when you're grieving, lass. Why, Matthew's own ma was back in the Trimmings Department after only a day away, even though management told her she could take more time if she wanted to.'

Louisa had seen the older woman, pale from her own grief, on the way into the factory that morning. 'I've had to get back to work,' she had told Louisa. 'Else I shall fall apart. It was the same after his father died. The thought of never seeing them again is too much to bear. It breaks my heart we can't even bring my beautiful boy home, but they said he'll have a Christian burial near where he fell. We need to keep busy, lass. Mattie wouldn't want us losing our jobs because we gave up. Lord knows, without my boy, I've got to work to keep food on the table and a roof over my head. I'm only thankful that I still have one son left and he's settled with a good wife. But I won't be a burden to them.'

'I'm sorry, Pa,' Louisa said now, feeling weak and feeble compared to Mattie's ma. She wanted to say that if they gave her a few minutes, she was sure she could sort herself out. But she felt so sore and heart-sick that she didn't have the energy. She wasn't as strong as Mrs Searle. She couldn't just carry on. If it meant losing her job at Clarks, she would be sorry, but she couldn't bring herself to worry about it. Not yet. Not when the pain was so raw.

'Hush now.' He kissed her hair then knocked on the ambulance room door.

* * *

Jeannie had moved over to sit at Louisa's machine so that she could carry on working while Kate told her what had happened when she'd been sent to find what was keeping Louisa.

'I've never been so scared in my life,' said Kate. 'When I saw her there on the floor, she looked so deathly pale, I thought she was dead.'

'Oh, lord. So she just fainted and hit her head?'

'Looks like it. She'd been sick as well. I saw some fresh blood in the vomit. That's serious, isn't it? She could be real poorly.'

'Let's hope not,' said Jeannie. 'The poor love's been through so much lately. I still can't believe Mattie's gone. He was Lucas's best friend.'

Kate nodded. Lucas was the eldest of Jeannie's three brothers. 'How's he taking the news?'

Jeannie frowned. 'I don't know. He's gone quiet. Really quiet. If you try to talk to him about it, he just gets up and walks away.'

Mr Briars approached their benches. 'Less gossiping, more working, please, ladies.'

'Sorry, sir,' the girls chorused.

'We're just so worried about poor Louisa,' said Jeannie.

The foreman nodded. 'I'm sure you are. But there's work to do and we're a girl down, so save your chattering until your break time.'

* * *

Louisa's father was given permission to take her home. As soon as they got there, he left her mother to fuss over her and rushed back to work.

'What have you done to yourself?' her mother asked as she tucked her up in bed. 'This has got to stop, Louisa. I know you're grieving, lass. But you have to eat or you'll be making yourself really ill.'

Louisa felt her nausea rising again. She felt so awful. Why couldn't her mother see that, without her Mattie, nothing mattered? But she said nothing. She couldn't. She knew that both of her parents were worried about her because they loved her. She turned her face into the pillow, welcoming the pain from her bruised cheek as it rested on the cool, feather-lined cotton. She wished that pain was all she could feel, but now she felt fear, too. Not for her job – that was the least of her worries.

No, the fear that was threatening to overwhelm her related to something the nurse had said to her father.

'I expect it's her monthlies,' she'd said. 'You'd be surprised how many girls faint dead away on a regular basis. A good plate of liver will build her blood up and she'll be as right as rain.'

It had only been then that Louisa had realised she couldn't remember the last time she'd bled.

3

When Louisa didn't return to work the next day, Jeannie and Kate had no answers to the questions their workmates kept asking them as the machines shut down for the lunch break.

'What's up with her?' one of the other girls asked.

'If it was just a faint, she should've been back before the end of her shift,' said Mrs Howard, one of the older women, looking like she wanted to say a lot more.

'She banged her head,' said Kate, staring the woman down, knowing she was a horrible gossip, always doing people down. 'And she'd chucked up blood, so I think it's a bit more serious than *just a faint*.'

'She was sick as well?' another woman asked. 'Oh my, the poor love. She must be really poorly if she's bringing up blood.'

'I hope it ain't anything catching,' said the first girl, shivering and putting her arms around her body.

'Mmm,' said Mrs Howard. 'So long as she didn't do anything daft with that young Matthew Searle before he shipped off to Flanders.'

'What do you mean?' asked Jeannie, looking confused.

The older woman smirked. 'She wouldn't be the first stupid girl to end up carrying a soldier's bastard.'

Jeannie gasped, her eyes wide with shock. 'Louisa's not like that,' she said.

'No,' Kate agreed. 'She's not. She's ill. She's lost the man she loves and has hardly eaten or slept since he went to fight. Of course she's ill. So don't you go telling people otherwise.' She glared at Mrs Howard. 'I doubt her father would appreciate you spreading nasty lies like that about his daughter.' As Louisa's pa was a foreman in the Clicking Department – the leather cutting room – where Mr Howard worked as a clicker alongside Kate's pa and her brother, Fred, and Jeannie's brother Lucas, she knew that Mrs Howard would be cautious about what she said. Foremen held a certain amount of sway at the factory. If this old hag started spreading dirt about his daughter, he could make life difficult for her and her husband.

She shrugged, her ample bosom shaking as she did so. 'I'm just saying. Plenty of girls have got themselves in trouble since this war started. She wouldn't be the first, or the last, I'm sure.'

The back-to-work hooter sounded from the clock tower at the entrance to the factory, saving the girls from having to respond to her comment. Everyone turned back towards the Machine Room, knowing they had to be working again within five minutes or they'd face the wrath of Mr Briars.

'That witch,' hissed Kate as she linked arms with Jeannie and they hurried up the three flights of stone steps towards the Machine Room. 'Fancy saying that about our Lou.'

'I know,' said Jeannie. 'I just hope to God she's just being her usual nasty self and it's not true.'

Kate's steps faltered. 'You can't believe it, Jeannie. Not Louisa.'

Jeannie tugged her friend along. 'I know. It's just old Ma

Howard stirring, as usual. Once Lou's back at work and clearly not expecting, she'll find someone else to pick on.'

'So long as it ain't either of us,' said Kate with a sigh. 'I've had enough of that at home.'

Jeannie frowned. 'What's your pa done now?'

They reached the door to the Machine Room. Kate shrugged. 'Same as always. Still drinking and being a nasty brute. I'd hoped he might soften a bit after Ma died.' Her darling ma had passed away a few months ago, succumbing to an illness that had weakened her over several months. As the youngest and only unmarried child in the family, it had fallen to Kate to take on the caring for her ma as well as keeping on top of the housework and putting meals on the table for her pa. 'But if anything he's getting worse, always on the cider,' she sighed. 'Anyway. I'll tell you about it later. We'd better get on.'

* * *

The girls decided to pop over to Louisa's house on the way home from work. But they had barely left the factory when they bumped into their friend's father going in the same direction.

'Evening, Mr Clements,' said Jeannie. 'We're going your way to see how Louisa is. Do you think she'll be back at work tomorrow?'

He shook his head, slowing his pace. 'If you don't mind, girls, could you give her another day before you knock on our door? Her poor face is covered in bruises and the nurse said she might feel the effects of hitting her head for a while. Her mother's taking care of her. I don't think she'll be in any fit state for visitors now.'

Kate felt a wave of pity for her friend. 'Poor Louisa. She's had such bad luck lately. Give her our love, won't you?'

'Yes, do, Mr Clements,' said Jeannie. 'Tell her we miss her.'

He nodded, looking tired. 'I will. She's lucky to have such good friends. Thank you, girls.'

They watched as he strode away homeward. 'He's worried about her,' said Jeannie.

'Well, of course he is. She's not been herself since Mattie joined up, has she? Now he's gone for good and she's collapsing with grief. Any *decent* man would worry about his daughter in that state.'

Jeannie gave her a narrow-eyed look as Kate turned away and began walking. 'Why did you say it like that?' she asked, following her.

Kate sighed as she felt Jeannie link arms with her, forcing her to slow down and look at her friend. 'You know I've been trying to get Pa to sort out a headstone for Ma's grave?'

Jeannie nodded.

'Well, he said he's got better things to spend his money on.'

Kate looked away as Jeannie's eyes filled with sympathy. She couldn't bear it that her friend pitied her.

'But... oh, Kate. I don't know what to say, love. Can you change his mind?'

She laughed, a rough, raw sound. 'Like hell I can. I've been trying for weeks now. But he's made up his mind.'

'What do your brothers and sister have to say about it?'

'They've tried to talk to him, but he won't listen. He yells at us all to mind our own business and if we want a bloody stone we'll have to pay for it ourselves.' She felt tears of frustration welling up. She took a deep breath, blinking rapidly to try to stop them falling. She knew that if she started crying, she might never stop and she'd end up as lost and ill as poor Louisa. 'But my brothers have got their own kids to feed and Peg and her husband are moving across the country for his new job, so none of them has any spare cash, and Pa takes all my wages and barely gives me anything back, so how can I pay for it? She was his wife, for God's sake. She put up with him for so many years, cooking and cleaning and bringing up his children, all the while running round after him to keep him happy. She never even complained that he spent so much time at the Street Inn, drinking. How can he treat her memory so foul?'

Jeannie squeezed her arm. 'Let's face it, Kate. He was never very nice to her, was he? You always said he didn't deserve her.'

Kate nodded. 'He didn't. I hoped when she died that he'd see the error of his ways and maybe guilt would make him try to change a little – be a bit kinder, maybe. But, if anything, he's got worse.' She swiped angrily at the moisture on her cheeks. She would not cry over that man. 'What scares me is, seeing as how I'm the only one of his children still living at home, he expects me to do everything my mother did but still work all hours at the factory for the rest of my days.'

'You'll get married one day and you can leave him behind.'

She knew Jeannie was trying to comfort her, but it didn't make her feel any better. 'I'll not let any man rule my life like he has,' she said, almost shaking with anger at the thought of it. 'I'd rather die an old maid. Just so long as I don't have to stay at home with *him*, that is.' She stopped, looking up at the sky. The starlings were flying, wheeling through the air, dancing together in the early-evening sun. She watched them, wishing she could fly free like a bird. She wanted to lose herself in the flock, safe from harm in the middle of the whirling mass of creatures.

'I thought that maybe you and Ted Jackson...' Jeannie began.

Kate shook her head. She'd gone out with Ted for a few months and they'd got along fine, or so she'd thought. But then his brother was killed in France and the other lost his mind and Ted had enlisted. He'd told Kate he was going and he didn't want to have any ties calling him back. If he survived the war, he intended to make a life for himself somewhere else – where he could be something other than a shoe-factory worker. Then he was gone, and neither Kate nor any of their friends had heard from Ted since.

'Don't,' she said. 'He made his choice. Me and this place aren't good enough for him, so I'll not waste any energy thinking about him.' She spoke with resolve, but deep down, she still missed him and prayed every day that he was safe.

'I know. I can't understand it because I was sure he was sweet on you. His cutting himself off from you still doesn't make sense to me. But you're right. You've enough on your plate with your pa. What will you do?'

'Jeannie,' she whispered. 'I think I might end up leaving Street, maybe even Somerset altogether.'

'But where will you go?' Jeannie asked gently. 'With no money...'

'I know, that's the problem. I thought about going to join the war effort.'

'What do you mean? You can't be a soldier!'

'Of course I can't and I wouldn't want to be. But I heard Miss Alice Clark talking to Mr Briars about someone going off to train to be a nurse. With so many wounded soldiers, they need as many women as possible to learn how to take care of them.'

'Oh, Kate, love. Don't go, please. I can't imagine the horrors you'd have to face. And you'd miss your brothers and sister. Can't one of them take you in?'

Kate shook her head, sighing. 'They've all got more than enough to deal with without having an extra mouth to feed. None of them has any room for me. But anyway, I can't leave Clarks, so don't get your knickers in a twist. I went to the recruitment office and asked about the nursing, but they said if I didn't have the training already, I'd have to go to something they're calling VADs – Voluntary Aid Detachments. But if you want to do that, you've got to pay your own way and supply your own uniforms and the like. I can't go and train as a proper nurse without Pa's permission either. So I'm trapped here, aren't I? Because I work all hours but still haven't got a penny to my name.'

'Well, I'm sorry you don't have your own money, love, but grateful you'll be staying, at least. I couldn't bear it if you left here. Please don't do anything rash like leaving the village,' Jeannie begged. 'If it gets too bad at home, come to our house. We haven't got a lot of room, but we'd find some space for you if you needed it. Mother wouldn't mind.'

Kate smiled, even though she felt so sad, she ached with it. 'You're a good friend, just like Mr Clements said. I don't know what I'd do without you.'

'All the more reason not to rush off,' said Jeannie. 'Give yourself time to grieve for your ma. Who knows? A miracle might happen and your pa might soften.'

Again, Kate gave that harsh little laugh. 'The only miracle I pray for is for him to drop dead. But I doubt I'd be that lucky. If there is a god, he certainly didn't hear all my prayers for my poor dear ma.'

'Maybe God decided your ma had suffered enough,' Jeannie suggested gently. 'At least now she's out of pain and at peace.'

Kate closed her eyes, acknowledging the truth of that. 'But now I'm left with him on my own and I don't think I'm as strong as she was.'

'Don't give up, Kate, love. You're stronger than you think.'

Kate hoped so. 'I hope Louisa is as well,' she said.

4

'You stupid, stupid girl!' The slap that accompanied her mother's angry words took Louisa by surprise, because up until this moment, she had never raised a hand to her in all her eighteen years. 'Your life is ruined. No decent man will ever want you now!'

She placed her hand to her stinging cheek and stared open-mouthed. As though she was looking at herself from outside of her own body, she registered that at least her mother had hit the uninjured side of her face, although its sting echoed around her whole head. But the physical pain was nothing compared to the wrenching pain in her heart. She had no one to turn to. If the woman who had given birth to her wouldn't stand by her, she doubted her father would either.

'Ma, please.'

'No, Louisa. I don't want to hear a word from you. You will listen to me. I *told you* what to expect – that young men heading to war would try to seduce you, to persuade you to give them what should be saved for the marriage bed. I suppose it was Matthew? At least give me the consolation of that. I could not bear it if you had been ruined by some other lad who you barely knew.'

Louisa sobbed as a fresh wave of grief rolled over her. 'Of course it was Mattie. Oh, Mother, how could you imagine otherwise?'

Her mother ignored her tears and sighed. 'And now he's dead in France just weeks after he left you and you're bearing a bastard. Soon everyone will see your shame and will know that you're a whore.'

Louisa's knees gave way and she crumpled to the floor. 'I'm not a whore!' she cried. 'There could never be anyone else for me but Matthew. I loved him. We were to be married, you know we were. You said there wasn't time before he was posted. You and Pa said we should wait.'

'Yes, and for good reason. You are both still young and in the passion of war is never a good time to choose your lifelong partner.'

Louisa gasped. 'How can you say that when we've been courting these past long months?'

Her mother waved a dismissive hand. 'It seems that God has chosen that Matthew was not to make old bones. Who knows how many other young men will suffer the same fate before the Kaiser is stopped? That's the nature of war. Yet, even though I told you not to, you still defied me and chose to anticipate your wedding night.' Her face twisted with disappointment and disgust. 'And now you've brought shame to this house.' She shook her head. 'Lord knows what your father will say. You know the pain his own sister's fall caused him. We are seeing history repeat itself with our own daughter.'

Still on her knees, Louisa tried to make sense of what she was saying. 'I know Aunt Clara died young.'

Her mother leaned close, her face cold and hard. 'She died at the hands of an abortionist after she gave her favours to a soldier. The beast went off to fight the Boers and stayed in South Africa afterwards, making his fortune, not caring that your aunt died a horrible, shameful death.'

Louisa hung her head, her mind reeling. She had not known that. She felt awful for the poor aunt who she had never met. 'Mattie would not have abandoned me,' she said. 'I know he wouldn't.'

She was aware of her mother straightening and stepping away from her. 'But he has,' she said, her voice flat. 'It matters not that he might not have been intending to. He's lying dead in Flanders Fields, never to return. Oh, Louisa. Why could you not have waited?'

Louisa looked up, willing her mother to understand. 'I love... loved him. I've always loved him. I couldn't bear for him to leave for war without knowing how much.'

Her mother closed her eyes and shook her head. 'Much good will it do you now. You won't even have the honour of calling yourself a widow. And what of the child? It will forever carry the stigma of being fatherless.'

'My child had a father who would have married me if you'd allowed it. A fine man who died a hero.'

'Pah! You were both too young to know your own minds. And he was but a boy who had barely fired a shot before being mown down. There was little time for him to be a hero. He dishonoured you in such a way that every other man will know your shame. You will never be married now, not with a bastard child.'

'I want no other man. I shall devote my life to my child – Mattie's child. I will make sure it knows what a good man his father was.'

Her mother shook her head, her expression grim. 'You cannot keep it. You must get rid of it.'

Louisa gasped, wrapping her arms around her still slim body.

'You would have me die at the hands of an abortionist like my aunt?'

For a moment, she thought that her mother would agree. She did not recognise the angry woman staring down at her. But then her demeanour changed, her face crumpled and her shoulders slumped. She pulled a chair from beside the table and sat on it beside Louisa, who was still on her knees on the cold stone floor. Yet still she did not touch her daughter. Louisa yearned for the easy affection and hugs from her mother that she had taken for granted all her life.

'No, of course not,' she said, her face reflecting her tumult of emotions. 'But can't you see, child? You cannot keep this baby. You must give it up or it will ruin you and the child as well. In keeping it, you would condemn it and yourself to a life of shame.'

'But it's Matthew's child! A part of him. I cannot be parted from it,' she sobbed.

'You can and you must,' she said. 'Or you will never be able to live here. Your shame will ruin your father. He's in a position of respect in Clarks. You'll make him a laughing stock. Would you do that to him?'

She closed her eyes and hung her head again, her arms still tight around her body. Despair descended on her, weighing her down. What was she to do?

'Could I not go away and have my baby and wait awhile? We could pretend I wed another and lost him too. I could live as a widow with my child.'

At last, her mother touched her – just a gentle hand on her head, like a benediction, then it was gone. 'No. Folk are not so stupid as to believe it. They would know when Matthew was here and that it was his child. If you try to fool them, it would be even worse. You cannot live a lie. You must do what is right and give up the child. No one must know of this, Louisa. No one, not even your friends, do you hear me? You must go away. I shall arrange it. You will stay away until after the child is born. Then you must come back without it.'

Louisa shook her head, her tears falling faster. 'Please, Mother, I beg you. Don't make me give up my child. It's all I have of him.'

'It will be better off with a proper family – a mother and father who will give it a good life. Think on it. Would Matthew want you and his child to be shunned all your lives? No, he would not.'

She grasped at the only thing she could think of to say. 'But surely his mother would want to see her grandchild grow? She has lost her beloved son. How can you deny her the knowledge that he lives on in my child?'

Her mother's chair scraped against the stone floor of the kitchen as she stood. 'You think she will want you to stain the name of her son – a so-called hero now in everyone's eyes by virtue of dying in battle? Would she have people know he seduced you? I think not. Now get up and wipe your tears. Your father will be home soon and I will not have him upset.'

5

'Lucas, you cannot go. It will kill our mother.' Jeannie wanted to shake her older brother. 'You promised her you would not enlist.'

'I should have gone with Mattie. If I had, he might still be alive.'

Jeannie wanted to weep at the reminder of their dear friend, dead so soon. There had been a time, not so long ago, when she had dreamed of being Matthew's sweetheart. But he had only had eyes for Louisa, and now the poor girl was sick with grief.

'Or you would be dead alongside him. Is this what you want? To throw your life away on his funeral pyre? I know you loved him like a brother but sacrificing yourself will not bring him back. You're not a warrior, Lucas. You've been the man of this house since Pa died. We need you here.'

He sighed, staring down at the bowl of stew she had put before him in the moments before he had announced his intention to join up. He had missed the family meal with their mother and younger brothers. They were all in bed now. Jeannie had waited up for him, worrying that he was so late.

'You must eat,' she said, sitting opposite him.

'I'm not hungry.'

'Fine. Starve yourself to death. It can't be more painful that being shot, or gassed, or blown to pieces. I hear some poor souls are even drowning in the mud.'

He glared at her before picking up his spoon and taking a mouthful. Jeannie knew it was good – thick and tasty. But she realised that he might as well have been eating mud for all the good it would do him in this state of mind. He swallowed it down then dropped his spoon, as though he had no energy to hold it.

'Where were you this evening?' Jeannie asked.

'You know I was at a meeting at the Friends' Meeting House.'

'But that ended hours ago.'

'I went for a walk after. I needed to think.'

'Well, you need to think some more, brother, because your thoughts at the moment are as stupid as they are dangerous. Have you thought of your job? Your family? Have you not heard the stories of how the men in the trenches are suffering?'

'I've thought about it all, Jeannie. I still have to go.'

'I don't understand. You embrace our Quaker life, attend the gatherings, and yet you plan on becoming a soldier? You know that war is not the answer. You know that the government hasn't even made conscription compulsory yet and has already acknowledged that Quakers are to be granted exemption from taking up arms on the grounds of our beliefs and Peace Testimony if they did. You don't have to do this, Lucas.'

He closed his eyes and took a deep breath. 'I do. I cannot stand by and watch my friends go to fight and die alone. I am not a coward.'

'Of course you're not.'

He opened his eyes and stared at her. Jeannie felt her heart shatter at the pain she saw there.

'Mrs Jackson was waiting outside the Meeting House. She gave us all white feathers.' This was the mother of Ted, Kate's sweetheart until he'd broken up with her and gone off to fight. Mrs Jackson had joined the White Feather Movement and was active around the village and surrounding area, pressuring young men to enlist.

Jeannie gasped. 'How dare she! She knows full well that it's against our faith to fight.'

He shrugged, looking away.

'Everyone knows young men from her church have joined ours,' she went on.

'That's as may be, but the others have joined up, including her three sons. Now one is dead, they say one is in an asylum having lost his mind and the other hasn't been heard from for months.'

'And yet she torments you to chase the same fate?' Jeannie was torn between anger and fear. 'How can she do that? She should be campaigning for peace, not recruiting more boys as cannon fodder to prolong this horrible war. Will it never end?' She covered her face with her hands, unable to stop her tears.

'Don't cry, Jeannie, please.' Lucas put a hand on her shoulder. 'Try to understand. I need to go.'

'No, you don't. If you go, what will become of us?'

'You'll be fine. The twins are working now, and I'll arrange for Ma to receive the separation allowance from my wages from the army.'

Jeannie knew that the wives and mothers of serving men could receive this allowance from the soldiers' wages. Some of the married women in the Machine Room were getting it. It helped keep food on the table at home while the main breadwinner was away from home, but it didn't compensate for not having their men around, which was why many wives had gone back to work.

'You have a good job here. Good prospects. Do you think Clarks will take you back if you go off to fight?'

He laughed. It was a harsh, humourless sound. 'They will be

obliged to. Times are changing, Jeannie. They say they'll bring in conscription soon. We'll all have to go or face the consequences. Even Mr Frank Clark's son Hugh has already gone to fight.' He had left for France in April, driving his own vehicle that had been converted into an ambulance.

'He's an officer, in an Ambulance Unit behind the lines,' she scoffed. 'He's trying to save lives, not trying to kill men. If conscription comes in, you can apply to the tribunal. They were talking about it at work. You can be exempted from bearing arms. Lots of local men who attend our Meeting House will be applying. You know they are.'

'And as many more are accepting that we must go and fight. Don't worry about my job after the war. Clarks can't afford to turn us away. If they refused to employ every returning soldier, they would soon be left with nothing but old men and girls to make their shoes. Not that there's much future in staying here in Street, anyway. The shoemakers in Northampton won the contracts to make boots for the army. They were more competitive than Clarks, who dragged their feet about war contracts, just like they did during the Crimean War. Clarks are on their way out, mark my words. If I survive this, I'll not be looking to stay around here. There's nothing for me here any more.'

Rage and despair filled her and she picked up his abandoned spoon and smacked him with it. The blow caught him on the chin.

'Ow!' he yelped, putting a hand to where she'd hit him. 'What did you do that for?'

'Nothing here? Nothing here? Do we mean so little to you? It's not your wages I was thinking of, you stupid boy!' She was shrieking now, heedless of anyone who might hear her. 'Your leaving will kill Ma, you know it will. And then the twins will be desperate to enlist. They might even lie about their age to sign up sooner, because they adore you and want to be just like you. How will I go on then, when you're all dead?'

'Hush, Jeannie. You'll wake Ma and the boys.' He stood up, pulling her out of her chair and into his arms.

She fought against him, slamming her fists against his chest. 'I can't believe you would be so selfish,' she hissed, heeding his warning and not wanting to wake Ma, even though she was still burning with rage and fear. 'Turning your back on everything, and for what? To avenge your friend who would hate that you felt that way. So go on then, go and kill a German. Do it for Mattie. Do you honestly think that will make you feel better to leave another mother without her son? That it will bring Mrs Jackson's sons back to her? They're never coming back. Not Mattie, not the Jackson boys, not hundreds of other lads who rushed off to fight.'

'Stop it, Jeannie. You're hysterical. That's enough.' He shook her, his expression fierce.

The fight drained out of her and she slumped against him, weeping. 'Please, Lucas, I beg you. Don't go.'

'I can't stay, Jeannie. I'm sorry. I just can't.'

'What's the matter with Jeannie?' John, one of the twins, stood in the doorway to the stairs, rubbing his eyes.

'Nothing. Go back to bed,' Lucas told him. 'She's just having women's problems.' He winked at his younger brother.

'Huh. I'm never getting married,' he muttered as he turned and went back upstairs, leaving a deathly silence behind him.

* * *

Lucas stayed up long after Jeannie went to bed. He was sorry that she was so upset and he dreaded Ma's reaction. But he couldn't turn back now. His mind was made up.

If only he hadn't confessed his feelings for Mattie that morning after their meeting for worship at the Friends' Meeting House. He had been upset that Mattie was so set on getting Louisa's father to agree to their marriage that they'd argued. Mattie had accused him of not understanding a powerful love, goading Lucas into finally admitting that he not only understood it, but that Mattie was the one he loved. Within a week, Mattie was on his way to basic training, telling Louisa he was determined to prove to her father that he was a man worthy of her.

But that wasn't the real reason, Lucas was sure of it. It was *his* fault that Mattie had enlisted, so this was his penance, doing the same.

6

On Sunday afternoon, Kate sat on the cool grass next to the grave, staring at the crude, bare wooden cross that marked her mother's final resting place in the churchyard. Her father claimed he had no money for a stone. It was the last insult to the woman who had spent her life trying to please a man who was never satisfied.

Her mind was whirling with memories of her mother, each one overwhelmed by the knowledge that her father had ruled the family with no mind to his wife's happiness or comfort. Her heart ached with regret for the times she had shown contempt for her mother when she was growing up, accusing her of being weak when she refused to stand against her husband, even when his decisions had been cruel and unjust.

'I shall erect a stone for you, Ma,' she whispered. 'I'll pay for the finest. I'll find a way, even if it takes me years. It's what you deserve for putting up with *him* all this time.' *And when he dies*, she thought, *I shall dance on his grave and make sure nothing marks its location.*

The earth was bare, save for the small bunch of violets that Kate had brought with her and a few tufts of new grass. Autumn was slowing nature's growth. Kate and her siblings had come regularly to keep it tidy and to lay flowers when they could. She knew for a fact that her father hadn't been back since the funeral.

The churchyard gate squeaked and she looked up. Louisa came through. Her gaze was downcast, not looking up as she walked towards the church.

'Louisa!' Kate called out, standing up, resting a final touch of her fingers on the cross before leaving the grave behind. She brushed down her skirts and walked towards the other girl, pleased to see her. She hadn't been back to work for the past three days. 'What are you doing here?'

Louisa jumped as Kate approached. She looked round in a panic.

'I'm sorry,' said Kate, putting a hand on her arm. 'I didn't mean to startle you.'

'It's all right. I... I didn't see you,' she said, looking away as though shy. 'How are you, Kate?' She glanced over at the grave. 'I'm so sorry. I've been meaning to come and see how you're getting on. I know you're missing your ma. But...'

Kate touched her friend's hand. 'It's all right. I was going to say the same to you. We did try to come and visit, but your pa said it was best to leave you be. I know you've been poorly. We've been so worried about you and missed you at work this week. Are you better? Did your parents get the doctor? I was so worried when I saw you'd sicked up blood. Please tell me you're all right. You look very pale, but at least the bruises on your face are fading.'

Louisa didn't answer her questions. She looked at the closed church door. 'I'm all right. I'm not ill. I was coming to light a candle for Mattie,' she said, her eyes filling. 'I miss him so much.'

'Oh, Lou.' Kate put an arm around her shoulders, realising as she did so how frail her friend felt. 'We're all desperately sorry about Mattie. It must be so hard for you.'

She looked around. 'Kate, it's been so awful. I have to talk to someone. Can we go somewhere?'

'What about in the church? You can light your candle and we can talk. There's no one around at this time of the day.'

As she said it, the gate squeaked open again and an old woman came into the churchyard. She pulled her shawl around her and nodded to the girls before she walked around them and entered the church.

'Not in there,' said Louisa. 'Somewhere private. Please. I've got a secret, Kate. Will you promise not to tell anyone?'

'Not even Jeannie?'

Louisa looked torn. 'I don't know. I'm not supposed to tell anyone. My mother will be so angry if this gets out. But I swear, if I don't tell you, I will die.'

Kate frowned. 'Then you must tell me. You can decide whether Jeannie can know later. You can trust both of us. You know that, don't you?'

'You may feel differently about me when you know what it is,' she whispered, her voice full of tears.

'We all have secrets, Lou,' said Kate, her heart heavy with her own secrets as she led her through the gate and away from the village. 'Come on, we'll sit by the river and you can tell me yours and I'll tell you mine.'

* * *

Louisa was silent on the walk to the River Brue and for several minutes when they found a shady spot under a weeping willow tree where they couldn't be easily seen. Rather than badger the poor girl, Kate decided to tell her friend the terrible truth that she had uncovered.

'My father has a fancy woman,' she said, staring out over the water.

'Oh! Goodness, that was quick. I mean—'

'I know exactly what you mean. My mother's barely cold in the ground. But it's even worse than that.' She took a deep breath. 'He's been carrying on with her for a long time and he might even be the father of her children.'

'No! Who is she? How can she have a married man's children and no one knows?'

'She lives in Glastonbury. I think she had a husband once, but he's long gone, sick of her lies, no doubt.' Kate looked at Louisa, barely able to contain her anger and outrage. 'Now he says he's moving her into our home and telling me to call her Mother. Well, I won't. I shan't even speak to her or her brats. If I could leave, I would. But where would I go?'

'Oh, Kate. That's awful. I'm so sorry. Maybe you could find some lodgings? Will your wages at the factory be enough for you to live on?'

'I don't know. I'm not even allowed to pick up my wage packet. He collects it with his own on pay day and then I must wait for him to dole out some pocket money when it pleases him, which isn't often.' She could no longer stop the tears that filled her eyes. 'He takes all my money, yet he wouldn't spend a penny on trying to help Ma get well, and now he won't even mark her grave with a decent stone and he's moving another woman into my mother's home. I hate him, Lou. I really, really hate him.'

'You cannot be expected to live like that. There must be something we can do. I wish I could speak to my father about it for you, but... he keeps so busy these days,' Louisa said. Her voice caught on a sob and she turned away. 'I can't bear it. Why are we so at the mercy of our parents? Oh, Kate, I think I'm going to die from the cruelty my mother is imposing on me, I really do.'

Kate scrubbed at her face, blinking away her tears to look at Louisa. Guilt made her stomach roil. 'Don't upset yourself, Lou, please. You've been poorly. I shouldn't have told you. You'll make yourself ill again.'

'That's the point,' she cried quietly. 'I'm not ill, Kate. I'm expecting, and my mother is sending me away and says I must give Mattie's baby away or I can never come home again.'

Kate's mouth dropped open. She knew old Mrs Howard had hinted at it, but she truly hadn't thought it was possible. But of course, Louisa and Matthew had been deeply in love, and he had been leaving to go to war... *How did I not realise?* 'Are you sure?'

'Yes. My mother realised when I fainted that I'd stopped asking for rags for my monthlies. You know I've been sick, too. Some days, I can hardly keep anything down.'

She looked so wretched that Kate felt awful for her friend. Everyone had known that Louisa and Matthew were sweethearts and would one day be married. But now he was dead and she was left with the shame of carrying his child.

'I expect you think I'm as bad as your father's fancy woman.'

Louisa's sad expression made Kate feel even worse.

'No. You're nothing like her. She's been carrying on all this time with someone else's husband. You and Mattie, well, he only had eyes for you. He loved you.'

'And I loved him,' she whispered. 'So much.'

'What are you going to do?'

'Mother is taking me to her sister's in Exeter. I'm to have the baby there and she says it's to be given away to a family of strangers and I'm to return here and act as though nothing has happened. They'll say I was sick with grief and needed a change of air.'

'Maybe it will be for the best, Lou,' Kate said, gently wiping her friend's tears. 'Your baby will have a good life, I'm sure. And you can start again. Maybe one day, you'll fall in love again and have more babies.'

She shook her head. 'I won't. I'm never going to marry now. And I'll never forgive myself or my mother if I'm made to give away mine and Mattie's child.' She rested her forehead against Kate's. 'I've thought about this a lot these past few days and I can't do it, Kate. I can't abandon my baby to strangers. I'm going to have to run away.'

'No, Lou, don't. How will you manage? You won't be able to work with a child and people will be horrible to you, just because you don't have a husband to protect you.'

'But there'll be countless widows thanks to this awful war. I won't even have to invent a dead husband. I'll tell them about Mattie. As far as I'm concerned, I *was* his wife. We would have wed before he left if my parents had let us.'

Kate took Louisa's face in her hands. 'There must be a better way. What does your father say?'

'He won't speak to me. He can barely look at me. His sister... I shouldn't say...'

'I won't tell a soul, I swear.'

'She was seduced by a soldier who abandoned her and died at the hands of an abortionist.'

Kate felt her words like a kick to her gut. 'That poor girl!'

'I know. I thought Mother was going to send me to the same fate.' Her tears began again. 'She is so changed by this, Kate. My dear, sweet mother has turned into a monster. There's no reasoning with her. When I suggested Mattie's ma would want to see her grandchild grow, she forbade me from telling her, saying I would forever taint her memories of her son by foisting his bastard on her.'

Kate gathered the weeping girl into her arms and held her as she cried. She felt almost overcome by the terrible situation her friend found herself in. It was so unfair. But... something occurred to her.

Would it work? Could it be the solution?

'Louisa,' she said, pulling back a little to look at her friend. 'Listen. I think I may have a solution.'

She looked up, hope shining in her eyes. 'Really?'

Kate hesitated. She hated to kill that hope. 'It's not perfect. I'm afraid you still won't be able to keep your baby, I'm sorry.'

Louisa closed her eyes.

'But you would know that the child is well-loved and its grandmother – Mattie's ma, that is – would know him or her. That's got to be better than giving your baby away to strangers, hasn't it?'

When she opened her eyes, the pain and defeat in Louisa's expression made Kate want to weep again. 'What are you suggesting?'

Unsure whether she was right to say it, Kate touched Louisa's cheek. 'You know my sister Peg is married to Mattie's brother, Will?'

Louisa nodded. She had shared many happy times with Mattie and his family and seen Peg there with his brother. Peg also worked in the Machine Room, although she worked on leather uppers at the other end of the vast workroom. And, of course, it was Peg who'd brought her the news of Mattie's death.

'They're moving to Lincolnshire,' Kate went on. 'Will is to work for a company that makes something called the Little Willie tanks – a machine they say will change the course of the war. He promised his ma he wouldn't enlist, and wanted to make sure he would definitely get exemption from conscription when they bring it in – which, let's face it, will be soon, won't it? Anyway, I think we should go and see them.'

'Why?'

'Because they've been married three years now and have no

children of their own yet. Peg told me in confidence they're desperate to start a family but it hasn't happened. They're so tired of people asking when they're going to have a baby because they would love one and it hurts every time. Don't you see, Lou? They're your baby's uncle and aunt. What if they were to bring up Mattie's child as their own?'

'But—'

'Please, think about it,' she said again. 'Why, I'll be an aunt to the baby if you were to agree to this. I promise you, I will love it with all my heart and will be able to reassure you of the child's happiness and progress. Our Peg is really kind and will be a fine mother. Will is as good a man as Mattie, and he has the same blood. If the child is like his father, he may even look like Will. Mattie's ma will have her grandchild and be none the wiser.'

'It would certainly be better than losing my baby to a stranger. But what if they are angry about me expecting? Peg might resent that I fell so easily and she hasn't.'

'Peg is a good woman. She joined the Quakers when she married Will, seeing as how his family was always more devout than most of our family, apart from our mother, and Ma didn't mind because Mrs Searle is a good friend of hers. Peg won't judge you for loving her brother-in-law. They both loved Mattie and are feeling his loss. I'm sure they'll both see this baby as the gift that it is.'

'Are you sure? If she does judge me... she could tell everyone. My mother would never forgive me for the shame it would bring to our door.' She wrung her hands, fear in her gaze.

'Louisa.' Kate became stern, not willing to let her friend descend into despair again without at least considering it. 'I have faith in my sister. She will not betray you, I'm sure of it. In fact, I believe this is a perfect solution – you know that they're moving to Lincolnshire soon. If you were to go with them, it would stop your parents taking your baby from you, wouldn't it? You'd be safe.'

'I don't feel safe,' she confessed. 'I feel as though my whole world has been turned upside down. I've lost Mattie, my parents act like they hate me. The thought of losing my child to someone I don't know, who might not be kind to my baby... Oh, Kate, if Peg and Will could rescue us... I'm almost afraid to hope.'

'Let's talk to her. What have you got to lose?'

'Nothing. But if my mother finds out...' Louisa frowned. 'Yet, if I fall in with her plan, I'll have to leave Somerset before the end of next week and my choices will be taken away from me.' She thought for a few moments before nodding. 'You're right. I truly have nothing more to lose. Either Peg will be a loving mother to my baby, or I will lose him or her anyway. At least this way, Mattie's family will have the chance to look after our child as one of their own.'

Kate nodded, satisfied that this was a good plan. Her sister would get the child she craved and Louisa could rest easy that she had at least placed her baby within the heart of its father's family.

'Will you speak to her?' Louisa asked. 'I'm so afraid, I can't bear to see her turn away from me in disgust as my mother has.'

Kate couldn't imagine how awful it must be for Louisa. The fear and despair in her friend's eyes were terrible to see.

'I'll go there now. You should come with me. I'm sure she'll be kind to you.'

The church bells rang the hour. Louisa shook her head. 'I can't. My mother will be wondering where I am.' She got up, brushing the grass from her skirts. 'How will I know what she says? Mother has refused to let me see my friends. It took me ages to persuade her to let me walk to the church today.'

'I'll think of something. If I must, I can still climb up the drain-pipe to your bedroom window like I did when we were younger.

I've never been caught, have I? Your parents won't know I'm there. Just be in your room or, if you can't, leave the window on the latch and I'll sneak in and leave you a note under your pillow.'

'All right. I've been spending most of my time in my room anyway, so they won't be suspicious.'

Kate got up and took her friend's hand. 'I promise, I'll do everything I can to make sure your baby is brought up by its own blood, even if you are denied the chance to do it yourself.'

'Thank you, Kate.' She wiped the remains of her tears from her face. 'You're a good friend. You've given me hope for the first time since I heard that my darling wouldn't be coming home. I know Peg will be a good mother, and Mattie always looked up to Will.'

'Be strong, Lou. I'll do my best for you.'

The two girls walked back towards the village, separating with heartfelt hugs.

As Louisa returned to her parents' cottage, Kate headed for her sister's home, hoping she hadn't misjudged the situation and that she could fulfil her promise to Louisa to keep her baby safe within its father's family.

7

Louisa insisted on going back to work at the Clarks factory on Monday, despite her parents' disapproval. It took most of Sunday evening to persuade them that she was well enough and would keep her secret to ensure that they weren't shamed by her.

The news from Kate had finally dragged her out of the fog of despair that had been weighing her down, leaving her unable to fight against her fate.

'Are you sure?' she had whispered to Kate when she had climbed through her bedroom window just an hour after they'd parted.

'Yes. I spoke to Peg and then we explained everything to Will. They understand. They said to tell you they're so sorry that Mattie didn't live to be a father to your baby, but they will do everything they can to make sure the child would know about him, even if only as an uncle. And they'll love it as their own.'

It still broke her heart that she would have to give up her baby, but she knew that giving him to Mattie's brother was the right thing to do. At least it would allow her to follow her child's life from afar while Mattie's family brought the baby up. She would rather the pain of that than spending the rest of her life wondering what had become of the child born of her and Mattie's love.

She walked through the village towards the factory, her father at her side. She held her head high, enjoying the crisp, autumn air, thankful that after a few days' rest and eating whatever her mother put in front of her, the sickness had eased. She still emptied her stomach as soon as she woke in the morning, but then the nausea left her and she was confident she could get through the rest of the day without disgracing herself again.

'Remember what we said, Louisa,' said her father, keeping his voice low as they approached the factory entrance. 'You will tell no one. I'll be reporting to the office that you're moving to Exeter so this will be your last week.'

Without asking Louisa's opinion, her parents had decided to tell everyone that she needed a fresh start away from all her memories of her dead sweetheart.

'Yes, Pa,' she agreed, keeping her tone meek. She had no intention of going to Exeter, but it would be too dangerous to show her hand yet. She would be making her plans with Peg in the quiet moments they could manage at work.

Jeannie and Kate were waiting for her at the door to the Machine Room. She smiled and let her friends hug her and kiss her cheek.

'It's so good to have you back,' said Jeannie. 'We've missed you so much.' She studied her face with concern. 'Are you sure you're better? I swear you feel thinner than ever.'

Louisa touched Jeannie's cheek. 'I'm much better, thank you. You mustn't worry about me.'

She felt a twinge of regret that she'd told Kate not to tell Jeannie. But she had thought long and hard and decided that, for the time being at least, it would be better that no one else knew about what was going to happen. She knew that if her parents questioned Jeannie about her whereabouts when she escaped to Lincolnshire, she might well give her away – because Jeannie, bless her, could not lie. Kate, on the other hand, would keep her secret to her last breath. After all, she was protecting both Louisa and her own sister in this plot.

'Of course I worry about you,' said Jeannie. 'How can I not when you're having such a time of it?'

'Leave her be,' said Kate, her tone brisk. 'She's back and we've got work to do.'

Jeannie frowned at her but said nothing as Mrs Howard passed them.

'So you finally dragged yourself out of bed, lass,' she said to Louisa. 'Some folk were starting to think you might be off for a good few months yet.'

Louisa paled, her vision blurring as panic overwhelmed her. *Does she know? How can she know? Oh, lord, what will I do? What will Ma and Pa say?*

Kate stepped in front of her before she could react, shoulders back, head high as she confronted the older woman. 'No folk but you thought that, Mrs H,' she said loudly so everyone around could hear. 'And you've no right to go saying things like that about a decent girl who's been sick with grief. It's wicked and nasty.'

The older woman bristled as others nodded and murmured their agreement, but was silenced when Mr Briars came to stand in the doorway.

'Are you ladies intending to work today? Because if you are, I suggest you get to your machines and get on with it. We're not paying you to stand around gossiping.'

With a huff, Mrs Howard turned away from the girls and bustled past the foreman. Louisa took a deep breath, trying to calm her shattered nerves.

'Just coming, sir,' said Jeannie, linking an arm with Louisa. 'We were coming in when Mrs Howard stopped for a word with Lou.'

'I heard.' Mr Briars nodded his head towards the Machine Room, not giving them any clue as to what he thought of it. 'Get on with you now.'

As they passed, he put a hand on Louisa's shoulder, stopping her while he waved the other girls through the door. 'How are you, lass?'

'I'm much better, thank you, sir. I'm sorry I couldn't finish my work last week.' She took another calming breath. 'But I need to tell you, Pa's putting my notice into the office this morning. I'm moving to Exeter to stay with my aunt next week. Mother thinks I've more chance of getting over... over losing Mattie if I'm not surrounded by memories all the time. So this is my last week in the Machine Room for the time being.'

'I'm sorry to hear that, lass. You're a good worker. But I'm sure your parents are right. A change of air will do you good. There's a job for you here when you come back.'

Louisa nodded, her throat felt full and locked tight with the lies she was forced to tell. She had no idea what her future held. But she had just a few days to get through and she needed to make sure no one guessed her secret – not if she ever wanted to return to Street. 'Thank you,' she said.

'Right, off you go then, lass. Time's a wasting.'

* * *

There was no chance to talk as they worked and Jeannie was frustrated at being unable to check that Louisa was all right. She still looked so pale and wan. She hadn't been the same since Mattie had left to fight. Then, her usual sunny demeanour had disappeared and she had gone quiet, no doubt missing him and worried for her sweetheart. When the news of his death had arrived, Jeannie had seen all hope drain out of her friend as her heart broke.

This morning, she seemed better – a little stronger in spirit if not in body. Jeannie knew it would be a long time before the poor girl could look forward to life with any sign of enjoyment, but hoped she would soon start to come to terms with her loss.

As Jeannie worked, she kept sending glances to Lou, wanting her to know she was there to help her if she needed it. But she didn't look up from her work at all – focusing on it as though her life depended on it. Jeannie finished another lining and put it in her basket and reached for another pair of vamp and counter lining pieces and lined them up on the machine. She flexed her fingers, knowing they would feel stiff and painful by the end of the day after working dozens of linings through the machine.

I expect Lou needs to keep her mind off Mattie. Lord knows, I need to think of anything but Lucas taking himself off to the recruitment office this evening.

She hadn't told their mother, or the younger boys, hoping against hope that he would change his mind, or that they would reject him. *If only he had a squint or a weak chest*, she thought. But he was strong and healthy, so it was unlikely.

She shook her head, trying to shake her worries away. Instead, with another swift glance at Louisa, she turned back to her work. She would talk to them in their lunch break, tell her and Kate about Lucas... *Or maybe I shouldn't mention it to Lou – it might upset her. I'll see what Kate thinks first.*

But when the hooter went, Louisa rushed off after Peg, Kate's older sister.

'Where's she going?' Jeannie asked Kate as they watched Peg talking earnestly to Louisa.

'Oh, Peg wanted to talk to her about Mattie,' she replied. 'He was her brother-in-law, after all. The family thought she could offer Lou some comfort. They want to include her when they remember him.'

'That's nice,' she said. 'It must be so hard for all of them. I'm sure they can all help each other get through this.'

'If Mattie hadn't been so stupid as to rush off to fight, they wouldn't have to,' said Kate, looking cross. 'I think he was selfish. His poor ma is broken. He was her golden boy. Thank God Will's got more sense. At least she still has one son.'

The girls ate their lunches in silence for a while, although Jeannie wasn't really hungry and after a couple of bites of bread, she gave up.

'What's up, Jeannie?' asked Kate, eyeing her half-eaten food. 'You're not sickening for something, are you?'

Jeannie shook her head. 'No, but I'm heart-sick, Kate. Lucas is set on enlisting and nothing I can say will dissuade him.'

Kate frowned. 'But why?'

She sighed. 'Someone gave him a white feather and he's convinced himself Mattie wouldn't have died if he'd gone with him.'

Kate rolled her eyes. 'God save us from stupid men. More like he'd be dead alongside him.'

Jeannie closed her eyes, willing her threatening tears not to fall. 'I know. I think he knows it as well. But he feels guilty that he let Mattie go on his own. Honestly, Kate, I'm at my wits' end. He didn't even know Mattie was signing up, so how he can blame himself, I'll never know.'

'He certainly kept it quiet,' said Kate. 'Peg said he didn't tell his mother until the night before he left. She didn't have time to get Will round to talk him out of it. If he'd wanted to do something for the war, he could have got a job in Lincolnshire with his brother. He didn't need to go and fight.'

'And poor Lou didn't know until it was too late, either. What was he thinking? One minute, he was talking about marrying her, the next he was getting on the train and leaving her behind.' Jeannie wrapped up her bread and put it back in her bag. When the days got a bit colder, she'd buy some hot food from the staff canteen, but for now, she was glad she hadn't wasted a good meal. She could use the bread in a bread pudding. 'I don't know how Mother is going to cope without Lucas. She's not been strong since Pa died. Lucas has been her mainstay. With him gone, I'm worried she'll give up.'

Kate grimaced. 'Everyone's leaving,' she said. 'Mattie's gone, my ma's gone, Peg and Will are off in a few days.' *Ted, too.* But she wasn't going to think about him.

'And now Lucas is going.'

Louisa came over to them and sat down just as Jeannie spoke. 'Where's Lucas going?' she asked.

Jeannie glanced at Kate, who shrugged as if to say, *What can you do but tell her the truth?* 'He's enlisting,' she said.

Louisa stilled, closing her eyes. 'Can't you talk him out of it?'

She shook her head. 'God knows I've tried,' she said. 'Nothing I can say makes any difference.'

Louisa touched Jeannie's shoulder. 'I'm so sorry. Men are so stubborn sometimes. I wish...' She shook her head and looked away.

'I was just telling Jeannie that Peg and Will are off soon as well,' said Kate. 'But at least they'll be safe in Lincolnshire. Let's hope those machines Will is going to be making help end this war soon.'

Louisa nodded. 'I'm off as well,' she announced.

Jeannie noticed that Kate didn't seem surprised, while she felt her heart skip a beat at the shock of her friend's words. 'What? Where are you going?'

'To my aunt's in Exeter. Ma and Pa think I need a change to

help me get over Mattie.' She pulled a face, her feelings about that clear.

Jeannie shook her head, hardly believing it. As if Lou would ever get over him. She'd loved that lad with all her heart. 'Is that what you want?' she asked gently.

The short, harsh laugh that burst out of Louisa, who was usually so calm and serene, caught them all by surprise. 'Of course not,' she said. 'But they're set on sending me away, so go I must.' She took a deep breath and blew it out again. 'Although, in truth, things aren't well at home and I'll be glad to get away from the house. They just don't understand. I'll never forget Mattie, never get over losing him. They seem to think I'll spend a few months away and then come back and marry someone else. But I won't. There's no one but Mattie for me. To be frank, I need to get away from Ma and Pa for a while or I'll go mad.'

Jeannie couldn't have been more surprised. 'But you get on so well with your parents,' she exclaimed.

Louisa shrugged, her expression grim. 'Not any more.'

'But—'

The hooter rang out over the factory site, calling them back to work. Louisa and Kate stood up immediately as Jeannie cast her confused gaze between them.

'Come on, lazybones,' Kate teased. 'Better get back. We don't want to get in trouble for gossiping again, do we?'

She got up and followed them back to the Machine Room, wondering what she was missing. Something was going on between her two friends that she couldn't work out. It bothered her because they had always shared everything and, for the first time, she felt that they were keeping something from her.

Louisa slowed, turning to wait for Jeannie to catch up. She linked an arm into hers as Jeannie joined her.

'I'll try and talk to Lucas, if you like?' she said. 'We don't want him to end up like my Mattie. If I can persuade him not to go, I will, I promise.'

Jeannie felt awful in the light of her friend's generosity. Even in her grief, she was willing to try to help Jeannie keep her brother home safe. 'Thank you,' she said. 'I'm going to miss you.'

Louisa nodded, squeezing her arm. 'I'll miss you, too.'

8

———————

Louisa managed to get out of the factory before her father, so she was able to make her own way home. She was glad of the chance to be alone as she walked through the village. Apart from her walk to the churchyard on Sunday afternoon, she hadn't been out alone since she had fainted.

She kept her head down until the crowds of workers leaving the factory thinned, not wanting to talk to anyone, afraid that someone might guess her secret. Her conversation with Peg at lunchtime had reassured her that she and Mattie's brother didn't think badly of her and that they were willing to help her but she doubted anyone else would treat her so kindly. Will was making plans so that Louisa could slip away and go with them to Lincolnshire without anyone knowing; they were even bringing forward their departure by a couple of days so that they could leave before Louisa was due to go to Exeter. But she had a lot to think about in the meantime.

She knew that her parents would be angry and concerned when she disappeared. She just needed to work out how she could let them know that she was all right without giving away where she was. She didn't want them coming after her and forcing her to give up her baby to a stranger.

She was deep in thought when she realised that the young man walking ahead of her along the lane was Jeannie's brother, Lucas. She remembered that she'd promised to try to talk to him, so she quickened her pace until she drew level with him.

'Lucas,' she said, startling him out of his own thoughts. They couldn't have been happy ones – his shoulders were slumped and he looked tired and dispirited.

'Louisa,' he said, coming to a halt. 'How are you? Jeannie told me you've been ill.'

She was tempted to tell him the truth, to share her grief and desperation because she knew that Lucas was grieving Mattie's loss too and might understand how she felt. But, as she hadn't even told Jeannie, she knew she couldn't. Instead, she lifted her chin and tried to sound convincing when she replied, 'I'm fine, thank you. Well, as fine as you can be with a broken heart.' She blinked against the sudden onset of tears. 'I still can't believe that I'll never see my Mattie again.'

He nodded, looking away. 'I miss him too.'

'Of course you do. You were his best friend. It's awful, isn't it? I've never felt pain like it before. I can't bear it. I hate this damned war.' She swiped at the tears that had escaped and were making their way down her cheeks.

Lucas took a deep breath, scrubbing at his own eyes with the heels of his hands. 'He shouldn't have gone,' he said. 'Or if he was so set on it, he should have told me so that I could've gone with him.'

'Is that why you're enlisting now?' she asked, her voice gentle as she placed a hand on his arm. 'Because you know Mattie wouldn't want you to do that, don't you? I don't even know why he felt the need to go – he always said fighting wasn't the answer. But he changed his mind and went off so suddenly, we didn't have the chance to talk him out of it.'

He glanced at her hand and then away again. Louisa thought he was going to push her hand away but he didn't move. She wondered why he wouldn't look at her face.

'I know,' he said. 'If I'd had the chance, I'd have stopped him. I feel like it's my fault. I—'

'Oh, Lucas, don't think that, please. I've spent hours and hours wondering if it was my fault, too – if he thought I was pressuring him to get married and settle down, so that maybe he went off to fight to get away and experience a different life before he was tied down. Then I blamed my parents for making him feel like he had to prove something to them before they'd accept him. But Pa said the only person who knows the real reason he went was Mattie, and he's taken it to the grave with him. If we try to take the blame, we're only hurting ourselves and diminishing the man that he was by implying he wasn't capable of making his own decisions for his own reasons.'

'But Louisa, you don't understand,' he said, his pain evident in his tortured expression.

She squeezed his arm. 'Yes, I do, Lucas. If you're signing up because you feel guilty about Mattie, you're making a mistake. It won't bring him back, no matter how much we both want that. Please, Lucas, think again. Jeannie's in a terrible state, worrying about you. She's frightened to tell your ma for fear it will kill her.'

He pulled his arm away. 'Jeannie worries too much. I'll be all right, and so will our mother.'

Louisa narrowed her eyes at his tone. He had always been pleasant and polite to her before. She didn't recognise the surly young man glaring at her now.

'How can a sister who loves you worry *too much*?' she asked. 'You're set on going off to die like Mattie and Jeannie will be left to cope with your grieving mother and your young brothers – who will no doubt repeat the same mistake and rush off to fight the moment they can with the foolish notion of avenging you, leaving your mother without any of her boys, just like Mrs Jackson.'

'Jeannie's trying to run my life and I won't have it,' he said, his voice rising. 'I need to do this.'

'For what? For Mattie?' Her angry tones matched his.

'Yes, for Mattie!' he shouted, stepping back as though he couldn't bear to be anywhere near her. 'You of all people should understand. You loved him too. I can't just stay here and do nothing.'

'It's too late for Mattie. But you've got a chance to follow another path, Lucas Musgrove, and you're a fool if you don't see that.' She lowered her voice. 'I understand your grief, of course I do. But this isn't the way to deal with it. Mattie wouldn't...' She hesitated, a feeling of hopelessness overwhelming her. 'Please, Lucas. Don't go.' She began to cry in earnest as he stood frozen, staring down the lane, saying nothing. 'I have to leave Street... My parents want me to get over my grief and forget him but I can't and I won't. I'm being sent to my aunt's. She didn't even know Mattie and won't want to talk about him. I need you, Lucas. You were his best pal – you knew him better than anyone. I want to be able to talk to you about Mattie, to keep his memory alive. But if you go and get yourself shot or blown up, who will talk to me about him?'

'They're sending you away?' He frowned, looking at her again. His expression softened slightly when he saw her distress.

She nodded, scrubbing again at the tears running down her face. 'To Exeter. At the end of the week. Mother says I need to get away from the memory of him. But it won't work. I'll never forget him.'

He nodded, his anger gone, replaced by a sad look of sympathy, which she hated. 'How long will you be away for?' he asked.

'I don't know,' she said, looking away, not wanting him to guess her secret. 'A few months perhaps. Maybe I'll never come back.'

He rubbed the back of his neck. 'I'm sorry, Louisa. I didn't realise.'

She wondered whether he would feel so sorry for her if he knew about the child that grew in her belly. For a brief moment, she felt a flash of anger at Mattie for leaving her like this. How selfish he had been to risk his life while he left behind another life to grow inside her. No doubt Lucas's sympathy would turn to disgust if he knew.

Disgusted with herself and her wildly fluctuating emotions, she shrugged. 'Well, I hope the people who love you never have to go through what you and I are feeling right now, Lucas, because I don't think I could bear to see Jeannie suffer like this. I think you're mightily selfish to do this to her. She's not trying to run your life. She just wants to keep you safe. You know she'll not rest easy until you come home and if you don't...' She shook her head, unable to say any more.

'Please,' he said, his face twisted with pain. 'Don't.'

She took a deep, shaky breath, recognising that he wasn't going to be swayed. 'Think on it, Lucas Musgrove. You have a family that loves you and needs you. You don't have to fight. As a Quaker, you can get exemption. If you must go, why not go into the ambulance service? Or you can do what Mattie's brother Will has done and go and work in a reserved occupation. Don't go and get yourself killed, Lucas, please. I'm begging you. Mattie would hate it.'

He raised his gaze, looking over Louisa's head. 'Your pa's coming,' he said.

Her shoulders slumped as she realised her brief moment of freedom was over. 'Think on it,' she said again softly.

He shrugged. She didn't know whether that meant he would or

that his mind was made up, but with her father approaching, she
didn't have time to ask him.

'Can I write to you while you're at your aunt's?' he asked
quietly. 'To talk about Mattie?' he said when she frowned. 'Like you
said, me and you knew him better than anyone. It might... I don't
know, maybe like you said, it will comfort both of us to share our
memories.'

'Louisa,' her father's stern voice rang out. 'You should be home
by now, lass. Your mother will be worrying.'

She was torn between defying her father and confessing to
Lucas that she wouldn't be at her aunt's if her plan worked. But she
knew it certainly wouldn't if she showed her hand now in front of
her father.

'All right,' she whispered, wiping away the last of her tears
before turning towards her father. 'I'll send the address to Jeannie
when I'm settled. Pa.' She raised her voice. 'I was just talking with
Lucas, telling him how I'm to go to my aunt's next week.'

Lucas nodded. 'Hello, Mr Clements. I'm sure a change of air
will help Louisa feel much better.'

Louisa's father stared at them with suspicion. She knew he was
no doubt trying to work out whether she'd revealed her shame to
the young man. She stared back, her gaze defiant. She loved her
father, but she was beginning to hate him for the way he had
treated her since her mother had told him about Mattie's baby.

'I was just telling Louisa that my ma would like to see her
before she goes. Maybe she could come home with Jeannie after
work tomorrow or the day after and have some tea with us?'

Louisa sent him a brief smile at the invitation, but she could
tell from her father's expression that he wasn't likely to agree.

'We'll see,' he said. 'Her mother doesn't want her to overdo
things and make herself ill again.'

'Of course, sir. I promise we'll look after her. I could walk her home to make sure she gets there safe and sound.' He turned to Louisa. 'See what your ma thinks and let Jeannie know,' he said.

She nodded, not saying anything.

'Well, I'll be off,' said Lucas. 'Nice to see you, Mr Clements. My regards to Mrs Clements.' With a wave, he was gone – not in the direction of his home, Louisa realised, but towards Glastonbury, where the recruitment office was based.

9

Kate went to Peg's house before she went home. The plans to rescue Louisa were coming along apace. If all went well, she would be out of Street and safe with Peg and Will before Mr and Mrs Clements knew she'd gone.

When she reached home, Kate immediately wished she was escaping with her friend. Her father was raging.

'Where the hell have you been, girl? I want my dinner.'

'I was helping Peg pack up ready for her move, Pa. I told you last night that's where I'd be. I left some cold meat and bread for you.'

He frowned. No doubt he'd been too far into his cider jug to remember what she'd said. 'You never told me,' he denied. 'I'd not have allowed it if I'd known. A man's entitled to expect a hot meal on the table after a day's work.'

'I've been at work too, Pa,' she pointed out, sick of being expected to do everything at home after putting in the same hours as her father.

'Don't you cheek me, lass, or you'll be feeling the back of my hand.'

She took a step back as she heard a woman's laugh from behind him. 'Who's that?' she asked.

Her heart sank as her father stepped aside and she saw a woman watching them with a smirk.

'Is this her? The only one who's left?' she asked. 'She's a bit skinny, ain't she?'

Kate glared at the woman, matching her rude regard with her own inspection of the creature who had turned her father into an adulterer. She was much younger than Pa – a few years older than Peg, she'd heard – but she looked a lot older than her sister with her painted face and over-blown bosoms. She wore her clothes tighter than any decent woman would, showing off her curves in a way that had Kate's father staring at her with ill-disguised lust.

He grunted. 'This is Beryl,' he told Kate. 'Her and her littluns are moving in. You'll call her Mother.'

'I will not!' Kate snapped. 'My mother is in the churchyard, waiting for her husband of thirty years to erect a stone for her.'

Beryl pursed her lips. 'Are you going to let her talk to you like that, Reggie, darlin'?'

'No, I ain't,' he snarled, stepping forward and grabbing Kate's arm. She yelped in pain as he pulled her towards him. 'You'll keep a civil tongue in your head, lass, or you'll pay for it. Your ma's dead. She ain't going to notice whether she lies under a stone or not. No point in wasting good money.'

'You tell her, my love,' cooed Beryl. 'We don't want the littluns upset by such a rude girl. If she can't be nice, she'll have to go.'

Kate glared at the woman. 'I speak as I find in my own home,' she said. 'It's not up to you.'

She didn't see her father's free hand until it swung up and slapped her hard.

'I told you to watch your tongue,' he shouted. 'This is my

house, not yours. Now apologise to your new mother and then get our dinner sorted.'

Kate stumbled as he pushed her away. She landed painfully on her backside on the stone floor. Beryl burst out laughing.

'Look at her,' she sneered. 'Pathetic.'

Kate scrambled to her feet, unwilling to remain within range of her father's boots. The slap had been enough for one night; she could do without a kicking as well. She turned away from them, not wanting them to see the tears that threatened to spill.

'I'll see to your dinner, Pa,' she said, shaking with anger and helplessness.

'And Beryl's,' he said.

'There's not enough for three,' she said. 'Unless she's brought something for the pot.' She raised her chin, ignoring her stinging cheek as she turned back, her tears forgotten, challenging her father's fancy woman.

Beryl stared back, her eyes cold. 'I'm bringing plenty,' she said. 'I'm bringing your poor father the love and comfort he deserves while you, young lady, clearly bring him nothing but insolence and disobedience.' She turned to him. 'Oh, Reggie,' she sighed. 'You said it was bad, but I had no idea how dreadful things were. If she were my daughter, I'd have shown her back my belt regular, I can tell you. What an ungrateful little wretch she is.' She ran a finger down Reggie's cheek, making him drool as she leaned closer. 'Well, don't you worry, my love. I'll soon whip her into shape. You won't be kept waiting for your dinner on my watch.'

Kate wanted to scream and launch herself at the woman and slap her silly. *How dare she talk about me like that? How dare she act like this in my mother's house?* But she knew she would come off worse if she did, so she bit her tongue. Instead, she kept her voice calm and low. 'So you're going to do the cooking while I'm at work, are you? That'll be nice.'

The other woman's throaty laugh sent chills down Kate's spine. 'Oh, no. Not me. I've got the children to take care of, haven't I, Reggie?'

'That's right,' he said. 'Don't you go thinking Beryl will be running round after you, lass. She'll be busy.'

She couldn't keep the words back. 'Ma managed to look after four children and you and cook and clean with no trouble.'

Another slap caught her unawares again. She managed to keep her feet this time, but only just.

'Enough!' roared her father. 'You will not mention your mother in this house again, d'you hear me?'

Kate stared at him, silently begging him to take it back – to see what a witch this woman was, how she was deliberately baiting him to get him to punish Kate. She could see clearly what her intention was – to move into this house, to take her mother's place and to push Kate out of the door. *Or to use me as a skivvy so that she doesn't have to work up a sweat.* But her father turned away, his hungry eyes roving over Beryl's bosoms again. It made Kate feel sick, seeing him act like a lustful fool over this scheming trollop.

'Now get in the kitchen and do as you're told before I give you another wallop.'

Beryl's laughter followed her as she left the room.

Kate mixed the cold meat and bread she'd left for her pa's supper with some eggs to make some rissoles. She quickly put potatoes, carrots and parsnips on to boil, all the while seething as she heard the Floozy's laughter and her father's answering chuckles in the other room.

The back door opened as she was turning the rissoles in hot lard in the frying pan and two children entered. The boy was taller

than the girl but no more than about seven. They were dirty and
their clothes were scruffy, but it didn't take Kate any time at all to
recognise them. They had their mother's colouring and beady
eyes, but the rest of their features unmistakably declared them as
her own father's offspring.

'Are you our new skivvy?' the boy asked.

Kate slammed down the spatula on the counter. 'No, I'm not,'
she snarled. 'It seems I'm your big sister, although Pa kept you his
dirty little secret while my ma was alive. Don't you dare call me a
skivvy.'

'But Ma said you was gonna be our...'

She held up her hand, her anger boiling over. 'I don't care what
your bloody ma said. I am not your servant. Now get back outside
to the outhouse and wash the filth off your hands and face.' When
the boy opened his mouth to speak, she snapped, 'Do as you're told
and mind your tongue or I'll wash your mouth out with soap. And
when you come back, leave your muddy boots by the door. I've got
enough to do without having to scrub the floor again.'

The children fled. Kate took a deep breath, trying to calm her
nerves. She was in such a state, she didn't know what to do or
think. She ached for her mother. She wanted to weep to think that
that poor woman had been faithful to her father even when he
treated her like dirt and carried on with that woman behind her
back. She wanted to rant and rage at the evidence of his unfaithful-
ness and lies. *All these years... that floozy must have been about my age
when they started carrying on... poor Ma... I hate him... I hate her... I
can't stay.*

She swiped at her angry tears, blinking more away before the
children came back into the kitchen. She barely glanced at them,
not wanting them to see her distress. Instead, she pointed towards
the parlour. 'Your ma's in there. Go and tell her dinner's ready.'

They ran off as Kate began dishing up. She realised the children probably needed feeding as well. With a sigh, she got out a fourth plate and slapped the food on, dividing her portion between the two children, hoping they all choked on it. She slammed them down onto the table, not even bothering to get out the cutlery or salt and pepper, and turned to leave. Her father stood in the doorway.

'It's ready,' she said. 'You didn't tell me the children needed feeding as well.'

'I told you they was moving in,' he said.

She shrugged. 'Well, I didn't know they were already here, did I? I'll leave you and your family to get on with your meal.'

He frowned. 'You being funny?'

She closed her eyes, knowing she was in for another slap if she spoke, but she couldn't keep the words in. She opened her eyes and stared at him. 'No, Pa, I'm not intending to be funny. But anyone can see they're yours. Give it a day or two and the whole village will know, if they don't already.' She felt sick, wondering if she ever really knew him. She'd always accepted her mother's view that he was a good man under his gruff exterior, but now she knew different. 'How could you do that to Ma? She loved you.'

He looked away. She wondered whether he actually felt ashamed at last. But he was simply looking over his shoulder at Beryl and the children as they followed him into the kitchen. Kate's heart broke as she realised he didn't care – had probably never cared.

'Only four plates?' said Beryl.

'I'm not hungry,' said Kate. 'Something's made me feel sick.'

Beryl shrugged. 'More for us then,' she said. 'Come on, my darlings.' She ushered her children in, forcing Kate to step back to let them get to the table. 'Let's hope Kitty-Kat is in a better mood tomorrow.'

Kate bristled at the nickname while the others, including her father, laughed. She kept her expression neutral, not wanting to let the Floozy know it bothered her. As she headed towards the stairs to escape to her room, Beryl's voice stopped her again.

'We've moved your things into the attic room. You're out at work all day so you don't need so much space. My darlings will be sleeping in your old room from now on.'

Kate didn't look round. She knew that if she did, she would scream out her pain and frustration. Instead, she walked up the stairs and opened her old bedroom door. Inside, there were baskets and sacks piled on the floor and the bed. There was nothing that Kate recognised as her own. She closed the door and passed the main bedroom – her mother's room, where Kate and her siblings had been born and where her beloved Ma had spent her married life. The door was open and evidence of the Floozy's occupation could already be seen in the clothes and shoes scattered about. The bed that Kate had made for her father that morning was rumpled, the covers turned back and the sheets pulled in all directions. She wanted to vomit when she realised her pa and that woman had probably had sex in there while the children were out playing. The laughter floating up the stairs from the kitchen mocked her.

She closed the door, vowing never to enter that room again. It had been defiled. She just thanked God her mother wasn't here to witness her father's shameful behaviour. No doubt the neighbours would already be gossiping and she'd have to bear their knowing glances from now on.

She climbed the steps up to the attic. There were two rooms here. One was unusable because of the hole in the roof that her father had said he intended to repair but he never did. Kate came up here most days to check that the bucket under the leak wasn't overflowing with rainwater. She had intended to ask one of her brothers to fix it if Pa wouldn't, but now she would leave it. She might even forget to check the bucket. If it overflowed, it would leak down into the main bedroom. Her face creased into a grim smile. *That would put a stop to their carryings-on. I hope the whole ceiling falls in on them.*

She opened the other door. The room was gloomy in the early-evening light and there were no gas lights up here. With a sigh, she noted her things heaped onto the bare mattress. She would have to go downstairs to find some sheets and blankets and a pillow from the linen chest. *But not now. I can't face any of them tonight.* Instead, she nipped down to her old bedroom and grabbed the quilted bedspread. It had been made for her by her mother. She wasn't going to let those brats have it.

Back up in the attic, she began to pick up her clothes, folding them and putting them on the only shelf in the room. She didn't have much, so she tended to look after her things. It made her angry all over again to see how they had just thrown her belongings onto the mattress like that. Her few books hadn't fared any better and her meagre supply of cosmetics had disappeared, as had her best stockings. She would look for them tomorrow but she suspected the Floozy and her children were thieves as well as interlopers and her things would never be recovered. She touched the thin silver chain under her blouse, glad that she always wore the cross that her mother had given her. If they took that, she wouldn't be held responsible for her actions. It was all she had left of her mother now and she would never trust her father again.

She lay down on the bare mattress, pulling the bedspread around her, not bothering to get undressed, and stared up at the grubby skylight above her as night closed in. With no covering on the window, she would be woken by the dawn. She would leave the house early and not come home until she absolutely had to. If she could leave, she would. But with no money, where could she go? It looked as though she was destined to become a real-life Cinderella. Only her chances of being rescued by a handsome prince like the girl in the fairy story were non-existent.

'Oh, Ma,' she sighed. 'Help me.'

10

As the three girls arrived for work at Clarks on Saturday morning, Jeannie realised she hadn't had a chance to talk to either of her friends for more than a passing moment over the past few days. She'd been so wrapped up in trying to calm her mother, who had taken to her bed once Lucas had announced he had enlisted, and making sure that the things he needed to take with him were clean and in good repair, that she'd barely had time to think.

'Oh, Louisa, we never did get you round for a farewell tea,' she said, feeling awful that she'd neglected her friend. 'Lucas said he'd invited you. Can you come this afternoon? Mother would love to see you and we'll have the chance for a proper natter before your train on Monday.'

Lou looked like she was going to burst into tears, but she seemed to give herself a little shake, lifted her chin and put a smile on her face. 'No need,' she said. 'I hate goodbyes. How about we just plan on writing to each other? I don't have my aunt's address right now, but I'll send you a note as soon as I'm settled.'

'Good idea,' said Kate. 'I'm going to be heartily sick of bloody goodbyes this weekend.' She looked at Jeannie. 'I suppose you'll be at the station tomorrow to see Lucas off?'

Jeannie nodded, feeling the weight of the world on her shoulders.

'I'm sorry, Jeannie,' said Louisa. 'I did try to talk him out of it. But he's as stubborn as my father. Nothing will change their minds. I'll pray for him every day, I promise. With any luck, this horrible war will be over by Christmas and you'll get him home safe and sound before he even gets the chance to fight.'

She wasn't so sure. The newspapers were positive, but their view of the war didn't seem to match with the rumours of thousands of lads dying or being gassed and maimed. If poor Mattie and the Jackson boys were an example of what was happening, Jeannie feared she might never see her brother again. Or, if she did, he would never be the same carefree, loving boy. But she couldn't think on that right now.

'And who's going to pray for you, stuck down in Exeter with your aunt?' she said instead. 'Do you even know her? I've never heard you mention her before. It's your ma's sister, isn't it?'

Lou nodded, her expression grim again. 'Yes. I've only met her a couple of times and she's not the most cheerful woman as far as I can remember, so yes, I'd welcome prayers as well as letters.'

'We're going to miss you,' she said. 'I wish that, just once, things would go our way for a change. I don't think I can bear much more of this.'

Kate snorted. 'We've all got our crosses to bear,' she said. 'I'm just trying not to lose my rag at those brats the Floozy brought with her. I swear I'll swing for 'em one of these days.'

'So we'll all pray for each other and write lots of letters to stop ourselves from going mad,' said Jeannie.

'Agreed,' said the others.

The hooter sounded, cutting short any further conversation as the girls rushed to their places.

* * *

They worked hard all morning. Jeannie knew it was daft, but she found comfort in the noise and vibrations from the rumbling machines and the oil and leather smells that permeated the vast Machine Room, and even the repetitive, pressured work that left her aching by the end of the shift, even though it was a half day. At least here she knew what she was doing. She had so many pieces to finish sewing every day, so many hours to work, and if her quality slipped, Mr Briars would be sure to let her know, docking her pay and charging her for wasted thread. So she focused on the linings, making sure they were just right. She couldn't afford a drop in pay now that Lucas was going away and Ma was incapable of earning on account of her nerves and her arthritis. The twins were only on day work rates, which wasn't much at their age and she had no idea how much of Lucas's army pay would make up the separation allowance that would be sent to Ma.

Once the shift was over, she needed to pick up some groceries on the way home and get on with cooking a meal as Ma wasn't up to it at the moment. The twins would be ravenous as usual and she needed to make sure that both Ma and Lucas got a decent meal inside them today. If Ma stopped eating, she'd make herself worse and only the lord knew when Lucas would get a decent, home-cooked meal again after he got on that train tomorrow. She needed to eat, too, to keep up her strength. Even though Lucas was telling Peter and John that they were the men of the house in his absence, she knew they were too young and daft to be any use. They were more interested in football to bother with helping out at home.

They handed over half their wages like she and Lucas did, but that was the extent of their usefulness.

She would have to make sure they collected the coal for the fire and helped her on wash days. She couldn't manage it all on her own. Jeannie and Lucas had been helping Ma for as long as she could remember – even before Pa died. It was about time the twins did their share as well.

She resolved to buy a good-sized rabbit on the way home as well as the sausages she was planning to cook tonight with some mash. She could make a pie and Lucas could take a piece with him on the train.

* * *

Saturday's lunchtime hooter was also the end of the day's work and a signal to queue up to collect their wages. As usual, Kate held back, knowing her pa would have collected hers with his own when the wages trolley went through the Cutting Room where he worked as a skilled 'clicker' or leather cutter. They were called that because of the clicking noise their blades made as they sliced through the skins, cutting as many pieces as possible from each hide of leather. Although, judging by Kate's comments about her pa's drinking, it was a miracle that he could cut straight these days.

Jeannie felt so sorry for Kate. Her pa hardly ever bothered to give his daughter any of her hard-earned money. Today, Kate looked even more fed up than usual.

'You all right, Kate?' she asked, hanging back with her friend even though she knew she should get a move on. 'I know it's bad at home right now, but surely it's about time he let you collect your own wages.'

Kate turned away, but not before Jeannie saw the utter despair on her friend's face. 'You'd think so, wouldn't you?' she muttered.

'And now Peg and Lou are off and you're busy with your ma and I'm reduced to being a bloody skivvy in my own home.' Kate looked up at the high ceiling of the Machine Room. 'I'm starting to wish I could pretend to be a lad and sign up. Anything would be better than staying here.'

'Oh, no, Kate, please don't you go off to war as well. Don't leave me all alone.' She looked around for Louisa, hoping she'd help her persuade Kate against it. She was nowhere to be seen. 'Where's Lou?'

Kate shrugged, still not looking at her. 'Gone to the privy, I expect. Anyway, don't fret about me. I wouldn't really do it. I'm not that daft. I'm still stuck here.' She blew out a breath. 'Look, I'm going to head home. With any luck, they'll be at the tavern and the brats will be out playing somewhere. Probably scrumping some-one's apples, knowing them.'

'All right. When are Peg and William leaving?'

'Erm, not sure. Monday, I think. Will doesn't have to start his new job until next week, so they're going to take their time setting up their new place and getting to know the area.'

'It's a shame you couldn't go with them,' she said.

'Yeah, well, Peg hasn't got herself a job yet so they'll be relying on Will's wages for now. They can't afford another mouth to feed. So I haven't told them how bad it is. I don't want to worry her. But if she gets a job and there's a chance of one for me, I'll be off, first chance I get.'

Jeannie nodded, wishing she could suggest something else to help Kate. She really needed to get away from the situation with her pa; it wasn't doing her any good. She'd lost weight and she seemed so sad all the time lately. So did Louisa. They'd both lost people they loved and it was killing her to watch them suffer. Just as it was killing her to see her own ma falling back into the deep chasm of grief she'd fallen into after Jeannie's father had died. It worried her that she'd never climb out of it this time, especially if anything happened to Lucas.

'I was going to ask Ma if you could have Lucas's room, but Peter's already claimed it, saying he can't stand John's snoring at night. But if you need it, I'm sure...'

Kate shook her head. 'No, leave them be. I'm so grateful you thought of it, but I can't impose. Not when Pa keeps my wages. I couldn't even pay my way.' She gathered up her things and tilted her head towards the door. 'It looks like Lou must've gone home. You'd better get your wages before they run out,' she smiled, although her eyes remained sad. 'D'you want me to come with you to see Lucas off tomorrow?'

'Would you?' she asked, feeling a rush of relief. 'I know you hate goodbyes, but I could do with someone to help if Ma collapses. She insists she'll be there, but she's not eating and she's crying all the time. I'm sure she'll faint dead away, if only to try and persuade Lucas not to go.'

Kate gave her a hug and kissed her cheek. 'I'm sure your ma is stronger than she lets on. But I'll be there to help if need be. No doubt the twins will scarper if your ma has a turn on the station platform.'

'They will, the little beggars,' she said, frowning. 'Though the lord only knows why I call them little. They're growing like beanstalks. Anyway, I'd best get on. I'll try to pop round to Louisa's later to say goodbye.'

'No, don't!' Kate looked alarmed.

'Why ever not?'

'She said she hates goodbyes, remember? I think we should leave well alone. Her parents aren't exactly welcoming these days, are they? Her pa warned us off the day she fainted and her ma was really off when we tried to call on her the other day, wasn't she?'

Jeannie frowned. 'I suppose so. But I'm sure it's just that they're worrying about Louisa since Mattie went away.'

'They've got a funny way of showing it,' Kate muttered before she raised her voice and said, 'Anyway, I've got to get going. I'll see you tomorrow.'

They made arrangements to meet and Jeannie headed off to join the end of the line at the wages trolley to get her pay. She couldn't shake that feeling that something was off with her friends. It wasn't like Louisa to rush off without saying goodbye and she worried that things were a lot worse at home than Kate was letting on. But her own situation filled her thoughts as she contemplated the changes that Lucas's departure would bring.

Louisa hurried away from the factory, praying that her father was too busy with the end of the last shift of the week to come looking for her. She'd been one of the first girls to collect her wages, which she slipped into her purse as she rushed to leave before her father caught up with her. She caught a glimpse of Peg in the queue for her final wages as well. Peg gave her a quick wink before looking away. They didn't want anyone knowing they were in cahoots. When Louisa disappeared, she didn't want her father coming to Lincolnshire looking for her or causing trouble for those left behind in Street. Peg and Kate's brother Fred worked in the Clicking Department under her pa, so it was important he didn't make the connection and make life difficult for Fred. Lucas also worked there, so Louisa was glad she hadn't involved him or Jeannie in her escape plan.

She went out through the gates, turned left and walked briskly down the High Street towards The Cross amongst the crowds leaving the factory. She sighed with relief when she saw the lorry parked up behind the Street Inn. The man standing by the cab, reading a newspaper, was Peg and Kate's other brother, George. She was nervous about him knowing about her escape with Peg and Will, but they and Kate had assured her that he wouldn't betray her. He didn't know about the baby, but he knew she needed to get away and didn't want to go to Exeter. She hoped they were right about him. He was quite a bit older than Kate, so Louisa didn't know him very well, other than he worked for his father-in-law, a haulier, and had been given permission to borrow the lorry over the weekend to help his sister and brother-in-law to move.

As she approached, he glanced up and winked at her just like Peg had before he opened the door. Without a word, she felt his hands on her waist and he boosted her up into the cab. She didn't have time to worry about whether anyone walking by could have seen and might tell her pa.

'Will says get in the footwell and cover yourself with the blanket there. Him and Peg won't be long,' he told her quietly. As soon as she was inside, he closed the door again. She could hear him whistling as he went back to reading his paper. No one approached, so she assumed no one had seen her.

Louisa was shaking as she lay down in the footwell and pulled the blanket over herself. She was hot from rushing but didn't dare push the covering away. It didn't help that she was wearing extra clothes in order to fool her parents so they wouldn't know she'd smuggled out some of her belongings. It had been Peg's idea. From Tuesday until Friday, she'd dressed in double layers and slipped off the extras in the privy, folding them up tightly and stuffing them in a bag which Kate had passed to her sister so that she wouldn't have to run away with just the clothes on her back. There hadn't been time to shed today's extra layer, so she felt heavy and overheated. But at least she wouldn't have to beg for clothes in her new home, at least until she started getting bigger.

She'd also brought her life savings with her. It wasn't much, but she'd saved as much as she could of her pay after she'd given her parents her keep ever since she started work three years ago, intending to have a little nest egg for when she got married. She wouldn't need it for that purpose now, so it would help her pay Peg and Will for her keep while she stayed with them. Of course, they were paid a week in arrears (and in fact, her pay packet had been from the previous week which she hadn't been there to collect) so her wages from this week would go to her parents next week. But she didn't care. It was a small price to pay.

After what seemed like an age but was probably only a few minutes, the door opened again and she heard a woman laugh as George boosted Peg onto the seat, closing it behind her as he called out to Will to get a move on.

'You there, Louisa?' asked Peg softly.

'Yes. My pa's not out there, is he?'

'No, love. I heard someone got one of the cutting machines jammed and he's sorting it out.'

Louisa blinked as she heard the laughter under Peg's words. 'How did you...?'

'Will's good at winding people up,' she chuckled. 'Made a bet that he'd finish his last shift with the most machine-cut pieces. He knew at least one of the lads would try to best him and end up buggering up their machine. He wasn't wrong. Sounds like he got the timing just right.'

Louisa relaxed a little, knowing that her father was going to be kept busy. But that didn't mean she could take anything for granted. Until they were well away from Street, she wouldn't feel safe at all. If her parents found her before she got away, they wouldn't let her out of their sight and she'd be forced to do their bidding whether she wanted to or not.

'You all right down there, love?' Peg asked.

'I'm scared,' she whispered.

She felt Peg's warm hand on her back. 'I know. But don't you fret. Will and me will keep you safe, I promise. The lorry's all packed up and we'll be off in a minute. We've said our goodbyes so no one is going to stop us now.'

In the darkness under the blanket, she heard Peg winding down the window.

'Come on, lads,' she called. 'It's time to go.'

Louisa heard them mumble in response, then the doors opened.

'Scoot up,' she heard Will tell Peg. She fidgeted when she felt the poke of Will's boot on her back. 'Sorry, lass,' he said.

'It's all right,' she said as the engine cranked into life.

'Stay down for a bit. As soon as we're past Glastonbury, you can get up. No one will recognise you past there,' he told her.

'I hope you girls have had a wee,' said George as the lorry began to move. ''Cause I ain't planning on stopping every five minutes. We need to get to Lincolnshire tonight and it will be a late one. Then we'll have to unload pretty sharpish first thing so I can head back here by tomorrow night.'

Louisa wondered how on earth they would manage to drive over two hundred miles in one day in this slow, heavy vehicle. It was already lunch time. And then poor George had to turn around and drive all the way back tomorrow.

'You're a good brother, George,' said Peg, her voice full of affection.

'That I am,' he replied cheerfully, changing gear and picking up speed. 'Remember that when I'm a miserable sod after I've been driving for hours on end. I'll be expecting a couple of pints of cider as a reward.'

'Already taken care of,' said Will. 'There's some bottles in the back. Just be careful how you drive. We don't need all our stuff covered in spilt cider.'

In the warm cocoon of her layers of clothes and thick blanket, Louisa began to smile as it finally dawned on her that she had escaped. Her biggest regret was that she had left without properly saying goodbye to Kate and Jeannie. She knew Kate understood, but Jeannie had no idea what she had planned and might well be hurt that they hadn't let her in on the secret. But Louisa's first priority now was keeping Mattie's baby safe and ensuring their child had a good life.

11

Jeannie could hear the shouting inside Kate's father's house from the street. Worried for her friend, she rushed to the door and knocked on it. The yelling continued, this time punctuated by a child's high-pitched scream. Jeannie knocked again, louder this time, sure that no one had heard her the first time over all that noise.

There was a brief lull in the commotion before it resumed. About to bang on the door again, she stepped back in surprise when it opened and a sullen-looking boy peered out.

'What you want?' he asked.

'Is Kate in?'

He sneered. 'Yeah, and she's getting a walloping.'

'What are you talking about?' Jeannie demanded. 'Where is she?' She pushed past the boy. 'Kate?'

In the front room, she saw Kate's father. He was in his shirt-sleeves, the belt on his trousers undone. As he moved, she spotted Kate, her back against the wall, held there by a larger woman who had an arm across her friend's throat.

'Who's this?' snarled the woman, turning to study Jeannie with cold eyes, still pinning Kate in place. 'One of her little friends, are you, eh? You ain't been invited, young miss, so I'll thank you to turn around and get out.'

Jeannie glanced at Kate's father. He had the grace to look embarrassed before he turned away.

'I need a piss,' he muttered, walking away.

Jeannie couldn't believe he would leave his own daughter to this woman's mercy. 'Let her go,' she said, ashamed that her voice shook. 'Let her go at once,' she tried again, forcing some strength into her words.

'Or what?' The woman laughed, not moving. 'I could take both of you skinny mares with one hand tied behind my back. Now get out, before I show you.'

Kate closed her eyes. She was pale and looked as though she was at breaking point. She was clinging onto the woman's arm, no doubt trying to stop her from completely blocking off her air supply. Jeannie wondered what else had been going on since the Floozy, as Kate called her, had moved in. No wonder Kate had been quiet these past few days.

'No,' she said, stepping closer. 'If you don't leave her alone, I'm going straight to the constable to report you.'

The Floozy laughed. 'Oh, you will, will you? And what's he going to do? I'm merely teaching my new *daughter* a lesson in respect. That ain't no crime. Now get out or I'll have you for trespass.'

Kate still hadn't opened her eyes. Jeannie couldn't leave her like this. 'Oh, yeah?' she mimicked the woman's tone. 'Go ahead. I'll stand before the magistrate and tell them I saw you trying to kill Kate while her father did nothing.'

'No one will believe you.'

Jeannie noticed the narrowing of the woman's eyes as she sneered at her. She wasn't as sure of herself as she pretended. It gave Jeannie a bit more courage. 'No? Are you willing to take that chance? After all, you're the woman from Glastonbury who had relations with a married man behind his dying wife's back, and I'm a respectable working woman who's lived in this village all my life and worships alongside the Clark family every Sunday. I've never been in trouble before.' She paused, looking the woman up and down, pretending she knew more about her than she actually did. She had no idea how she had the nerve, given the woman's violent hostility, but she needed to try or she might well do Kate serious injury. 'Who do you think the magistrate will believe, eh?'

Kate cried out as the Floozy grabbed her hair with her free hand.

'What did you tell her, you little bitch?' she snarled.

'Nothing,' Kate rasped as she gasped for air.

'She didn't need to,' Jeannie said, her anger and panic rising in equal measures. She wanted to jump on the woman's back and pull her hair the way she was pulling Kate's. 'One look at your littluns and it's obvious you've been sniffing around a married man for years. You're the talk of the whole village. No woman trusts you near their men. I think the magistrate will have heard about you by now as well. Now *let her go!*'

As she shouted, Kate's father walked back in, concentrating on buttoning up his fly. At her words, he looked up.

'What the hell's going on?' he demanded. 'Why is Jean Musgrove shouting in my house?'

'Reggie, darling,' the Floozy whined, batted her eyelashes at him. 'This little cow is threatening me.'

'What?' He turned to stare at Jeannie, his hands on his hips. 'That right, young Jean?'

She wanted to run. Kate's father was a big man and fierce with it. But she wouldn't leave until Kate was safe. 'Yes, Mr Davis,' she said, raising her chin and making herself look him in the eye. 'I threatened to call the constable. She's hurting Kate, choking her and pulling her hair. And she threatened me, too.'

He looked at his lover. 'For God's sake, Beryl. Drop it.' He sounded fed up but not at all concerned about poor Kate.

Jeannie didn't think she was going to take any notice of him at first. The look she sent her left Jeannie feeling chilled to the bone.

'I mean it, Beryl. Leave her alone.'

With a huff that expanded the woman's huge bosom even more, the Floozy stepped back but not before leaning against Kate's throat until her eyes bulged. As she turned away, Kate dropped to the floor. Jeannie rushed over to help her friend, ignoring the angry woman who began shouting at Mr Davis.

'I'm telling you, Reggie, you sort her out. I won't have her talking to me the way she does, and you heard how poor Olive screamed when she brushed her hair. She deliberately pulled it to hurt our little girl.'

'I did not,' Kate rasped. 'She pulled away. Then she kicked me.'

''Cause you're a bitch, like Ma says,' whined the girl, who had been sitting in the corner, watching her mother assault Kate. 'You hurt me, cow.'

Jeannie was horrified that a child so young could be so coarse and rude.

Kate was still lying on the floor. She sighed and held out a hand to Jeannie, silently asking for help to get up. As she did so, she groaned, then coughed, gasping for breath. When she was upright, she looked at the girl. 'If you ever bothered to brush your hair like you should, it wouldn't be full of knots and God knows what else. I'm surprised the school nurse hasn't sent you home with a note about nits and ringworm.'

'Don't you dare talk to her like that!' The Floozy stepped forward, her hand raised.

Jeannie quickly stepped in front of Kate, who didn't move.

'If you hit me, I'll definitely get the constable to arrest you for assault and battery,' Jeannie declared. 'It'll be all round the village before the day's out. I'll make sure of it.'

She had no idea whether the constable would even bother to get involved, but she had to try. She kept her gaze steady, trying not to blink or twitch. Never in all her days had she ever had to stand up anyone like the Floozy. She only hoped the woman thought she was shaking with anger and not the fear that was threatening to overwhelm her.

The woman's eyes narrowed as she pushed her face close to Jeannie's. She smelt of cheap perfume and stale sweat. Her bleached hair was immaculate. Jeannie thought it was a shame she didn't pay as much attention to her own daughter's untidy locks. As Kate had pointed out, the child's hair was a mess of tangles. Even the gentlest hands couldn't sort that out without a lot of tugging and combing.

'*Enough!*' Kate's father's bellow made them all jump.

The Floozy's cold expression dissolved into theatrical tears. 'Oh, Reggie, don't be like that. I'm trying so hard to make us a proper family like we should be, but her...' She tipped her head in Kate's direction. 'She's doing everything she can to break us up. She's rude to you and me. She's nasty to the children. Why, she even took the bedspread off their bed the other day. I wasn't going to tell you, but...'

'It was my bedspread,' said Kate, her voice still strained. She put a hand to her throat and swallowed hard before continuing. 'My mother made it for me. I needed it because no one put any sheets or blankets on the mattress in the attic.'

Jeannie gasped, outraged. 'You can't sleep on a bare mattress!'

'Oh, don't give me that,' Beryl sneered. 'She knew where the linens were. She just couldn't be bothered to make up the bed. She's not hard done by. She's just lazy.'

Kate's father put his hands over his ears. 'I said enough!' he said, his voice less loud but no less angry. 'I'll not have our family business conducted in front of a stranger.' Jeannie shrank a little as he glared at her. 'I think it's time you went home, Jean. And I'll thank you to mind your own business. If I hear you've been talking about us behind my back, I'll have words with your mother.'

She wanted to argue – to stay and make sure Kate was all right. She knew her ma would understand and would defend her against Mr Davis. It wasn't right that someone could be treated so in her own home, especially when Kate worked so hard. But before she could open her mouth, Kate put a hand on her arm and shook her head.

'I'll see you out, love,' she said, still raspy. She turned to her father. 'Jeannie won't say anything, Pa. But if she keeps on yelling like a banshee all the time,' she tilted her head towards the Floozy, 'you won't need anyone else to let everyone know what's going on in this house.'

Jeannie nodded. 'I heard it down the street,' she confirmed.

'Don't exaggerate!' snapped the Floozy.

'I'm not.' Jeannie copied Kate's calm demeanour, even as she was still shaking inside. 'I saw some of your neighbours looking out of their windows. One asked me where the racket was coming from.'

Kate's father growled, making Jeannie blink. She might be able to stand up to the Floozy, but Kate's pa frightened her.

'Bloody nosy parkers,' he muttered. 'Ain't they got anything better to do?'

There was a knock at the door. Jeannie hoped someone had called the constable. She could see the bruises already starting to bloom on Kate's neck and, despite believing that everyone should have a chance to repent and follow the path of peace, she really,

really wanted to see that bully of a woman carted off to the lock-up and put away for a long, long time.

With a scowl on his face, Mr Davis wrenched open the door. 'What?' he snapped, before taking a step back at the sight of Louisa's father – and his boss – standing on the threshold.

* * *

Kate didn't think the day could get any worse after what Jeannie had just witnessed, but having Louisa's pa turn up managed to make it so. She put her hand to her throat, hoping to cover any marks that had been left by the Floozy's arm. Out of the corner of her eye, she saw Beryl signal to her children and they silently disappeared in the direction of the kitchen, almost as though they were used to running from figures of authority. Their mother didn't leave, though. Instead, she patted her hair and stuck out her bosoms and went to stand next to her lover.

'Reggie, dear. Who's this handsome gentleman?' she cooed, smiling at Mr Clements.

'His boss,' said Kate softly, enjoying Beryl's alarm as she registered what Kate had said.

She quickly recovered, her smile widening. 'I'm so pleased to meet you, sir,' she said, holding out her hand. 'I'm Beryl, soon to be Reggie's wife.'

If Kate hadn't known what he was there for, she'd have enjoyed seeing poor Mr Clements trying to retrieve his hand from hers after a brief, polite shake. But Beryl had other ideas and covered their linked hands with her free one and moved closer until her bosoms were an indecently short distance from his arm. She was so focused on the visitor that she completely ignored the look of surprise on Kate's pa's face.

'I thought you was still married to that other fellow,' he

muttered under his breath before he remembered who their guest was. 'Everything all right, Mr Clements? Not a problem at the factory, is there? That son-in-law of mine didn't thieve anything, did he?'

Mr Clements finally managed to step away from the Floozy, forcing her to let him go. He stood with his hands behind his back, looking even more stern than usual. 'Certainly not,' he said, his frown deepening. 'William was one of my best workers and will be sorely missed. I hope he'll come back to Clarks when the war is over.'

'Huh,' her pa muttered. 'Might be a good worker, but he's a lousy son-in-law. Didn't even let my Peg come and see her old dad before they left.'

Kate nearly did laugh at that. In truth, Peg had come round to see him last week and he'd been so wrapped up in the Floozy that he'd barely noticed she was there. It wasn't Will who stopped her coming back; it was Peg's choice. Neither George nor their brother Fred had been around either, so great was their disgust at the situation.

Mr Clements ignored him. 'No, it was Kate I came to see.'

Kate's pa looked around to where she was standing with Jeannie. Mr Clements followed his gaze.

'Oh, no,' sighed Beryl, feigning concern while her eyes gleamed with malice. She made sure her bosoms moved as she took a deep breath. 'What's she done now? I swear, Mr Clements, we can't control her. She never listens to Reggie and she's running us ragged. I'm trying to be a good mother to her, but she just won't do as she's told. Have you come to sack her?'

Kate looked up at the tobacco-stained ceiling as Jeannie gasped in outrage. She squeezed her friend's arm, giving her a slight shake of her head. The last thing they needed right now was to set off another row.

'Of course not. I have no control over the women in the Machine Room. As far as I'm aware, Kate is innocent of any wrong-doing there,' he said. 'I simply wanted a private word with her, if I may – and young Jeannie, as she's here. It's about Louisa.'

'Oh, is she at home now, Mr Clements?' asked Jeannie, looking hopeful. 'I popped round before I came here but no one was home. I was hoping to get the chance to say a proper goodbye before she goes away tomorrow. I missed her at the end of our shift.'

Kate's heart sank. She knew that Louisa wasn't home. With any luck, she'd be well on her way to Lincolnshire now. She tried to keep her expression innocent, aware of all the eyes on her at the moment. She'd promised Lou and Peg and Will that she wouldn't let them down. She didn't want Mr Clements guessing she knew what was going on.

'Me too,' she said. 'Shall we come with you now, Mr Clements? Is Louisa excited about the trip? I've never been on the train, have you, Jeannie?'

Jeannie shuddered. 'I was on that Clarks day trip to Weston a couple of years ago – you know, when the train derailed? I've never been so scared in my life. Then we had to wait for hours until they got a new train to take us all home. I won't be rushing to get another train, thank you very much.'

'Oh, yeah, I remember. It was a miracle no one was hurt.' Kate wanted to kiss her friend. She had no idea how she was helping to distract everyone.

Mr Clements frowned, glancing at Reggie and Beryl, who were listening and showing no signs of leaving them to talk in private. 'Reg, I'll walk with the girls if you can spare Kate.'

Beryl opened her mouth to say something but her lover nudged her with his elbow. She hissed as it hit her bosom but didn't say anything.

'Of course, Mr Clements. I hope your girl appreciates you

giving her the chance to spread her wings like this.' He shook his head, sending a baleful look in Kate's direction. 'I wouldn't trust this one in a place like Exeter, that's for sure.'

Louisa's pa didn't comment. He simply nodded and stepped back, waiting for the girls to join him. Kate's hand was still on Jeannie's arm so she pulled her with her, grabbing her coat and scarf, and slipping on her shoes as she went. She wrapped the scarf around her neck, not wanting Mr Clements to know about the Floozy's attack.

As soon as they were out of the door, it was slammed behind them. Kate and Jeannie both jumped but didn't stop as they followed Mr Clements. He strode down Silver Road in the opposite direction to his own house on Somerton Road, not even checking to see if they were following. If Jeannie noticed, she didn't say anything, but hurried after him with Kate. Once they turned into Goswell Road and were out of the sight of Kate's house, he stopped suddenly and turned towards them.

The girls halted, Jeannie letting out a little squeal of surprise when she just stopped herself from careering into him. Kate tried to look startled as well, not wanting him to suspect anything.

'Is everything all right, Mr Clements?' she asked, her voice still a bit raspy. 'Did you forget something?'

He shook his head, glancing around before he spoke. 'Can I trust you girls to be honest with me?'

'Of course, sir,' they said together. Kate crossed her fingers behind her back.

'I don't want to hear that you've been telling anyone about what I'm about to tell you. Do I make myself clear?'

Kate looked at Jeannie and then back to Mr Clements. 'Yes, sir,' she said. 'Me and Jeannie don't gossip.'

Jeannie nodded, looking confused. 'Aren't we going to see Louisa, sir?' she asked.

'Did she tell you what she planned?' he demanded.

'I'm not sure what you mean, sir,' said Kate. She held his gaze, trying not to let him intimidate her.

'Me neither,' said Jeannie. 'What plan, Mr Clements? To go to Exeter to stay with her aunt?'

'Is Louisa all right, sir?' asked Kate, keeping her eyes on him and her expression open. 'I know she's been quite poorly lately, hasn't she? Mattie's death hit her hard, the poor love.'

He looked away, giving Kate a little respite from the tension. 'My daughter didn't come home from work today. Do you have any idea where she might be?'

'Maybe she's gone to see Mattie's ma,' Kate suggested. 'I know she was asking if Louisa would visit. She thinks it will comfort them both to be able to talk about Mattie.'

'She won't be going there. I told her not to. We don't think that's a good idea,' he dismissed. 'The sooner she forgets the boy, the sooner she can get on with her life.'

Jeannie looked upset but didn't say anything. Kate wanted to argue, to tell him he was being cruel and was doing both his daughter and Mattie's ma a disservice by dismissing the dead lad like that. But she held her tongue. It wasn't worth the risk.

'Do you want me to pop over and check, Mr Clements? Just in case she went there anyway. I'm related to Mrs Searle on account of my sister being married to her other son. Unless you wanted to go yourself?'

She could see that he was struggling to decide what to do. If he turned up at Mattie's ma's house looking for Louisa, word would soon get out that he didn't know where his daughter was and it was clear he didn't want anyone to know she'd gone missing. Louisa had predicted her parents would want to keep it quiet.

'Can I rely on you to be discreet? I don't want the whole world to know my business.'

'Of course, sir. As I said, our Peg's married to her William, so I'm practically family. I'll just nip in for a quick chat. See how she's getting on.' It would be better for Kate to go anyway as Betty Searle might mention Peg and Will's move and Mr Clements was smart enough to put two and two together and work out where Louisa had gone. 'I'll come round to yours and let you know when I find her, shall I?'

'When you find her, you send her straight home, thank you very much.'

'Yes, sir,' she said, turning towards Jeannie. 'Are you coming, Jeannie? If she's not there, we can check if she's gone to your house. She might be having a cuppa with your ma, waiting for you to get home.'

'All right,' said Jeannie, her expression thoughtful. 'Bye, Mr Clements. We'll send her straight home when we find her.'

Kate hoped to God her friend didn't guess how much she had been involved in all this. Louisa had made it clear she didn't want Jeannie knowing the truth because she was too honest for her own good. If she'd known what was going on, she'd never have been able to fool Mr Clements.

Kate linked her arm with Jeannie's and strode off towards Betty Searle's house in The Mead. She didn't mind popping in there to make sure Mattie and Will's mum was all right. The poor love would be feeling so sad today, what with one lad being gone for ever and the other moving across the country. She only had the two boys – her husband had died a few years ago – so she'd be all on her own now.

'I'm surprised Mrs Searle hasn't gone with Will and Peg,' Jeannie mused. 'Do you think she'll follow them?'

'What?'

'Mrs Searle – you know – Mattie and Will's mum. She'll probably want to move to Lincolnshire now Will's working there, what with Mattie never coming home.'

Kate shook her head as though to clear her thoughts. She slowed her pace, forcing Jeannie to slow down as well. 'I doubt it. She's got a good job in the Trimmings Department and has lived here all her life. Anyway, Peg says they're only going to Lincolnshire while the war's on. They'll be back here the moment peace is declared. I'm more worried about finding Lou than wondering what Mrs Searle will do.'

'And I'm even more worried about you, Kate. What on earth was going on back there? I thought she was going to kill you.'

Kate looked away, burning with shame that her friend had seen that. 'I'm all right. She's just kicking off, staking her claim, that's all. She'll soon learn I won't take any notice of her and she's wasting her time.' She gave a short, sharp laugh. 'Either that or Pa will get sick of her demands and her kids' whining and he'll kick her out.'

'Do you think he will?' she asked.

Kate shrugged. In truth, she didn't think he would. Not while he was getting plenty of sex – which he certainly was, judging by the noise coming from the bedroom night after night. It was no wonder that her pa was so short-tempered. The Floozy wasn't giving him much chance to sleep at night. Kate hoped the neighbours couldn't hear it. That would be so embarrassing. It was bad enough that they were the talk of the village. If it got out that they were going at it like rabbits all the time, Kate would die. She got enough pitying looks when she walked down the street as it was.

Jeannie gently touched Kate's throat where her scarf had come loose. 'She's bruised you.'

Kate flinched back. 'She ain't likely to apologise, that's for sure.'

'Oh, Kate, what will you do? You can't stay there.'

She knew that. 'But what can I do? I want to go but I can't leave because Pa collects my wages and I'm lucky if he throws me the odd few pennies of my own money when he's in a good mood. I don't even see any housekeeping money now *she's* there. He gives it to her to buy the food. Only she spends as much of it on cider as she does on meat and veg. There's not enough food in the house for a decent meal tomorrow and you can bet she'll find a way to blame me for that.'

She was so angry and frustrated by the whole situation that she wanted to weep. But she wouldn't break down in the street. It wouldn't do her any good either, so she would just have to make the best of it. She'd thought she was doing the right thing – a good thing – by offering to brush the Floozy's daughter's hair. It was such a mess and she thought the child might look quite pretty if she was tidied up a bit. But the moment she'd started, the Floozy had come into the parlour, shouting at Kate about the state of the kitchen (which had been fine when Kate had left for work that morning). As her mother had yelled, the girl had screamed the place down, accusing Kate of pulling her hair. It was nonsense, of course. The child had shifted in her seat, startled by her mother's shouts, and the brush had caught in her tangled hair. Kate hadn't pulled anything; the girl had. But the intention hadn't mattered. Before she'd had a chance to gather her wits, the Floozy had pinned her up against the wall by her throat and Jeannie had walked in to witness Kate's humiliation.

'If I leave,' she said, 'I'll be on the streets. I swear Pa's so caught up with his filthy lust for this woman he won't care about what happens to me. He'll carry on collecting my pay and leave me to starve in a ditch.'

Jeannie looked ready to cry for her. Kate hoped she didn't because that would set her off. If she started, she thought she might not be able to stop.

'There must be someone who can help you,' she cried. 'What about your vicar?'

Kate laughed again, though nothing was funny. 'Pa never goes to church. My brothers had to march him down there for Ma's funeral. He'd have gone to the pub if they hadn't made him. He's not likely to listen to the vicar.'

'Mr Clements, then. He respects him.'

She shook her head. She didn't want to have to talk to Mr Clements any more than she had to. Not while she was keeping his own daughter's whereabouts from him. 'It won't do any good,' she sighed. 'Pa's decided he's entitled to my money because I'm his daughter and I owe him for bringing me into this world.'

'But your sister and brothers all left home.'

'I know, which is why he's making me stay. He did the same to them until they left home to get married. Between all of us, he's had a pretty penny over the years. Now I'm the last, he doesn't want to lose what I earn, at least not until those brats are old enough to work. Which is why he won't let the Floozy kill me and why he'll never throw me out.'

She could see it clearly. The Floozy might want Kate gone, but Pa wanted her earnings, so he'd make her stay no matter what. It wasn't like Beryl was bringing anything into the home but three more mouths to feed. *And at the rate Pa and her are going at it every night, there'll be more mouths to feed soon enough.*

Jeannie huffed, her usually sweet face creased by a frown. 'There must be something we can do.'

Kate leaned close and kissed Jeannie's cheek. 'Bless you for caring, love. But it is what it is. Now let's go and see how Betty is, then I'll walk with you back to your house.'

'Louisa might be at Mattie's ma's,' said Jeannie.

'She'll certainly get more comfort there than with her own ma,' said Kate, unable to look Jeannie in the eye.

12

The next morning, Jeannie stood on the platform at Glastonbury Station, wishing she could be anywhere else on that cold Sunday. The place was heaving with folks – young lads in their Sunday best, a few belongings packed in a duffle bag, eager to be off to fight the Hun and prove their manhood; weeping sweethearts; proud fathers and worried mothers. *And scared sisters*, she thought as she handed her mother a fresh handkerchief.

'Ma, please,' she said. 'We have to be brave for Lucas.'

'I can't help it,' her ma sobbed. 'What if he doesn't come back? How will I be able to live without my boy?'

Jeannie felt the same, but nothing she'd said had changed her brother's mind. 'We must pray for him every day and if it's God's will, he'll come back to us,' she said, quoting the words one of the elders at the Friends' Meeting House had said to her when she'd expressed her fears for her brother. She'd wanted the elder to try to talk Lucas out of going. But, as sympathetic as he was, he had declined to interfere, saying that every man had to look within himself for divine guidance. Now it was too late. The recruiting officers were at the station, clipboards in hand, waiting to shepherd

Lucas and the other lads onto the train as soon as it arrived. It was due in a few minutes.

Lucas stood a few feet away, speaking earnestly to Peter and John. The twins listened intently, nodding occasionally. They adored Lucas and were so proud that he was going to fight. They scoffed at Jeannie and their ma's fears, refusing to imagine for a single moment that their brother might be hurt or even killed. Jeannie was only grateful that they were too young to enlist. Lucas was old enough at nineteen to be sent overseas. With any luck, the war would be over before the twins were old enough to fight. She couldn't bear it if they rushed off to the trenches as well.

The shrill whistle of the approaching train chilled Jeannie's blood. She felt her mother sag beside her and quickly put an arm around her waist to hold her up.

'We must be strong, Ma. For Lucas. Let him go with the memory of our smiling faces, not our useless tears.'

Her mother let out a sob before making a visible effort to pull herself together. 'You're right, Jeannie, lass. If this is the last time he sees us, we must make the effort.' She wiped her eyes and blew her nose before she faced her son as he approached. Her smile was weak, but Jeannie could see that Lucas appreciated the effort it took for Ma not to cling to him and weep all over his chest.

'Not long now, Ma,' he said. 'I've told the twins they're the men of the house while I'm away and they're to mind you and take care of you and Jeannie. They'll do the lifting and carrying like I did, so you make sure to let them, all right?'

Jeannie rolled her eyes and tutted at the thought of Peter and John taking on the jobs that Lucas had done without complaint. She hoped they did, but she knew they'd all been soft on the boys all their lives. They'd been so tiny when they were born and sickly for a lot of their early years, so she supposed it was only natural that they'd been allowed to get away with a lot more than Lucas and Jeannie had. She only hoped that now that Lucas was leaving, they would step up and do their bit.

The train pulled into the station, slowing to a halt with a wheeze of steam. The recruiting officer called for attention and told the lads they had five minutes to say their goodbyes and get on the train. As soon as he'd finished his announcement, there was a mad scramble of hugs, kisses, laughter among the soon-to-be soldiers, accompanied by equal parts of back-slapping, cheering and sobbing from their loved ones.

Jeannie stood frozen with dread and misery as Lucas embraced Ma and ruffled the twins' hair before he turned to pull her into a bear hug.

'It'll be all right, sis, I promise. I'll come back.'

'You mind you do,' she said through her tears, unable to heed her own words about sending him off with a smile.

He stepped back and nodded. He picked up his bag and turned, only to turn back again. 'Oh, I nearly forgot. I said I'd write to Louisa. But I don't know her aunt's address. Will you send it to me?'

She nodded, not wanting to tell him that it looked like Louisa had run away. She hadn't been at Mrs Searle's house, and Ma said she hadn't been to theirs. She'd wanted to go to tell Mr and Mrs Clements and ask if they'd found her, but Kate had said she'd do it and she'd had so much to do to get ready for Lucas's departure, she had let her get on with it.

She'd been expecting Kate to meet her here at the station. She'd said she would come to say goodbye to Lucas. But she was nowhere to be seen. Jeannie hoped Kate hadn't been attacked by that awful woman again.

It seemed as though all three of the girls had their trials at the moment. Jeannie had never felt so alone in all her life. The responsibility of caring for the family while Lucas was at war weighed heavily on her and she wasn't sure if she was strong enough to bear it.

Someone jostled Jeannie and she was forced to step back to let a lad pass. All around her was noise and rush and before she could catch her breath, Lucas blew her a kiss and got onto the train. Several others pushed on behind him, so he was lost to sight almost immediately.

'Lucas! Where's he gone?' Ma cried.

'He'll be in the carriage, finding a seat,' said John, running along the train trying to catch a glimpse of him. 'There he is!' he yelled above the babble of voices, the hiss of steam and the shrill whistle from the guard.

Jeannie left Peter with Ma and rushed to where John stood. Lucas pulled down the window and leaned out. 'Remember what I said, Johnnie. You take care now. I'll be back before you know it.'

'Go and kill some Jerries, Lucas. Make us proud.'

Jeannie wanted to slap John around his head for saying such ungodly things. If any of their church elders were here, they'd be disgusted. War and killing were not the answers. There was no pride in taking the life of any of God's people.

'I'll do my best,' Lucas replied, his voice low so they could barely hear him. 'Although I'll settle for dodging their bullets in truth.'

'Keep your head down and don't try to be a hero,' said Jeannie.

Another whistle sounded as doors slammed and the order was given for the men to settle down. The train began to move slowly away. Jeannie kept her eyes on Lucas, her vision blurring as her tears fell. She blinked them away, determined to keep him in her sight for as long as possible. He waved as a cheer rose inside the train.

Those stupid lads, she thought, her tears welling again. *Cheering their journey to destruction. Why is no one stopping them? Do they not care about the weeping women they've left behind on the platform?*

When she could no longer see him, she turned away. Peter was cradling Ma in his arms as she leaned against him and sobbed.

'Don't cry, Ma,' he said, his voice cracking as he tried to soothe her. 'He'll be all right, you'll see. And we'll look after you, won't we, Jeannie?'

'Yes,' she said. 'We will. Now, let's get you home, Ma. No point in standing around in the cold, is there? You can write a nice letter to Lucas and I'll post it in the morning. It'll be good for him to hear from home so soon.'

'Keep it cheerful, though,' said John, joining them. 'Got to keep morale up for our lads in the trenches.'

Jeannie glared at him. 'He's going to basic training. He won't be in the trenches for weeks yet.'

'Thirteen weeks,' said Peter. 'Then he can have a few days' leave before being posted.'

'Well, there you are, Ma,' said Jeannie, trying to sound cheerful. 'He could be home for Christmas. Won't that be lovely? We'll knit him some warm socks and feed him up and we can make sure it's a happy time, can't we?'

The crowd was beginning to thin now that the train had gone. She hadn't taken a lot of notice before, but now she saw people she recognised from around the village and the factory but no one was in the mood to stop and talk. She linked arms with her mother, guiding her gently towards the exit. The weeping woman kept looking back along the train tracks, as though she might catch one more glimpse of Lucas.

Jeannie was so busy trying to lead her mother out of the station that she almost collided with Kate as she rushed inside.

'Am I too late?' she gasped, trying to catch her breath. 'Oh, God,

I'm so sorry. I couldn't get away. I ran all the way here. Did they get away all right?'

Jeannie closed her eyes as her mother let out another sob. She really didn't need Kate to remind her of why they were there. 'Yes,' she said, her voice cool. 'Now I need to get Ma home.'

'Oh. All right. I'm sorry, Jeannie. I really wanted to be here but Pa and the Fl—' She stopped, no doubt realising that calling her pa's new woman a floozy in public could earn her another walloping. 'Pa was out and I had to look after the children,' she said.

She still sounded quite raspy under the breathlessness. Jeannie wondered whether the Floozy had damaged her friend's throat in her attack yesterday. She wore a bandana around her neck, no doubt hiding her bruises. Jeannie would have asked Kate, but not now. Now, her priority was her ma. She couldn't be doing with anyone else's problems right now.

'It can't be helped,' she dismissed Kate's apology. 'We've got to go.'

'Oh.' Kate looked surprised, as well she might be. It wasn't like Jeannie to be so cool and indifferent. But today, things were different. 'Do you want me to come and help?'

'No, it's all right,' she said. 'The twins will help me.'

'But we promised our friends we'd go and play football,' protested John.

'Not today you're not,' Jeannie said briskly. 'Ma needs all of us. And we missed our meeting at the Friends' House this morning so we ought to go this evening.'

'Oh, yes,' said Ma, still tearful. 'We must go and pray for your brother. Every chance we get.'

'Don't need to go to a meeting to pray,' muttered John, kicking a stone across the road.

'Today, you do,' snapped Jeannie. 'Did you not listen to anything Lucas told you?'

John glared at her. 'I did. He said we were the men of the house now. So I'm not taking orders from you no more.'

If she hadn't been supporting her mother, Jeannie would have grabbed the boy and boxed his ears for his cheek. 'That is not what he meant and you know it.'

Peter, who'd been on the other side of Ma, frowned at his brother. 'We can get Ma home and settled first before we go and play,' he said, always the voice of reason.

'We'll see,' said Jeannie. 'Ma needs us. If she feels better once she's settled at home, maybe you can pop out for half an hour later.'

'But the lads are waiting for us,' John protested.

Kate stepped forward. 'Come on, Johnnie,' she said with a smile. 'They won't mind. They know your brother's going today. Anyway, I hear you and Petey are the best footballers in the village. They'll want you on their team even if you miss today's kickabout.'

Jeannie wanted to stay irritated with Kate for being late, but she was grateful for her help in placating the twins.

'You heard that, did you?' Peter grinned. 'We are pretty good.'

'But we won't be if we let the lads down and don't practise,' said John. He turned to Jeannie. 'Why can't Kate help you?'

It was Ma who answered, her voice a little firmer. 'Kate's welcome, of course. But I want you to take me home, boys. I need you with me today.'

Jeannie was glad her mother had spoken. On any other day, she might well have given in to her brothers and welcomed the chance to spend time with Kate. But today she felt unlike herself. She felt like her world had been knocked off kilter. Lucas was gone. The twins were playing up already. Ma was fragile with grief at just the fact that her firstborn had gone off for his basic training. *Lord knows how she'll cope when he's sent overseas.* And, on top of all that, Louisa had disappeared and there was nothing she could do about it, or about that horrible woman who had moved in with Kate's pa. Everything was changing, and not for the better.

13

A new girl arrived to work at Louisa's machine on Monday morning, but Kate soon told her to swap places with her. She didn't want a stranger between her and Jeannie. The girl moved without complaint and settled down at Kate's old machine.

'You used one of these before?' she asked her.

The girl shook her head. 'This is my first day at work. My ma wanted me to stay on at school and maybe one day be a teacher. But then my pa had an accident – he worked on the railway and his leg got crushed while he was uncoupling a loco. So now he can't work and...' She blinked rapidly. 'Me and my brother started here today.'

Kate didn't want to feel sorry for the girl, but she knew what it was like, wanting something better, only to have to go to work to help put food on the table at home. 'What's your name?' she asked.

'Sally. Sally Harper.'

'Well, Sally, I'm sorry about your pa. But we all have to do our bit for our families, don't we? Now, let me show you how this works...' She spent half an hour showing Sally the ropes. Mr Briars popped over to check what they were doing – and probably to make sure they weren't just gossiping. He nodded his approval and left them to it. Kate hoped the supervisor would take into account the time she was spending helping the new girl when he checked Kate's work tally at the end of the day.

Jeannie was quiet this morning. Apart from wishing Kate and Sally good morning, she got on with her work.

'I think I've got the hang of it,' said Sally. 'Thanks ever so much, Kate.'

Kate nodded. 'Just take it steady. If you get it wrong and have to re-do it, you'll have to pay for the wasted thread. And mind your hands. You don't want to catch a finger under that needle. It hurts something awful. You won't be as fast as the rest of us for a while. Concentrate on getting it right, though, or Mr Briars won't be happy.'

She left Sally to work alone and got on with her own. She would have to keep her head down if she was going to make up what she'd missed while showing Sally the ropes.

Beside her, Jeannie carried on as though Kate wasn't there. She wondered whether she was still upset that she'd missed seeing Lucas off at the station. She felt bad about it, but after all the drama on Saturday, Pa and the Floozy had decided to go out drinking, leaving her with strict instructions to stay with the children until they got back. What they didn't tell her was that they weren't going to return until Sunday, still drunk from the night before. She hadn't bothered asking where they'd been before running all the way to Glastonbury Station, but she'd still been too late.

She'd tried to explain all this to Jeannie, but she had been preoccupied with her ma and the twins and in the end, Kate had given up and left them to it, telling Jeannie she'd see her at work. But now Jeannie didn't seem to want to talk – not even a quick word while they worked.

By lunchtime, Kate was fed up. She had enough aggravation at home without her best friend sulking alongside her all day. She was starting to wish she hadn't made Sally swap places. It might have been less noticeable that Jeannie wasn't talking to her if there was someone sitting between them. She wished Louisa was still there. She missed her already. Lou was the glue that kept the three of them together – making them laugh, keeping everyone's spirits up. At least, she had been until Mattie had enlisted. She'd perked up a bit when he'd come home for a few days' leave before being posted, but after that it was like the light had gone dim inside her. The news of his death, so soon after he'd landed in France, extinguished that light completely.

At last, the dinnertime hooter sounded. With a sigh of relief, Kate switched off her machine. A friend came over to greet Sally and took her off to eat lunch together. Kate turned to Jeannie.

'The new girl seems all right,' she said. 'A bit slow, but that's to be expected. We were all like that on our first day.'

Jeannie nodded but didn't say anything. Kate sighed.

'Jeannie, I said I'm sorry about yesterday. Please don't sulk.'

Jeannie frowned. 'What? I'm not sulking. What made you think that?'

Kate rolled her eyes. 'Maybe the fact that you haven't said a word to me all morning.'

'You were dealing with Sally.'

'Not all morning.'

'It's too noisy to talk while we're working. You know that.'

'It's never stopped us before. I'm working right next to you now. You haven't even looked my way.'

Jeannie bowed her head and sighed. 'I'm sorry, Kate. It's just hard, with Louisa not here. I keep thinking that, if Mattie hadn't enlisted, she wouldn't have gone away, and then I start thinking about how Mattie dying meant Lucas felt he had to go too and I get all upset and... then I think about Saturday and feel ashamed I didn't do more to help you when that awful woman—'

Kate put a hand on her arm. 'You did plenty. You stopped her and got her worried about whether you'd call the constable. I didn't get round to thanking you at the time, but I am grateful.'

Jeannie shrugged. 'I wish I'd hit her,' she confessed. 'I've never felt like that before. She made me so angry. How dare she treat you like that!'

This time, it was Kate who shrugged. She wished she could fight back, but as she didn't have her pa's support, the Floozy would always win, no matter what. 'Who knows with a woman like that?' she said. 'She hates me because she wants Pa to herself. But she wants to be a woman of leisure, so she expects me to be her skivvy. And, of course, Pa controls my wages, so he won't let me leave. So I'm stuck between a rock and a hard place – being hated but needed at the same time.' She sighed. 'At least I can get away from them at work. Come on, let's go and have something to eat before the hooter goes to call us back.' She hoped Jeannie didn't notice that she only had a couple of pieces of dry bread with her for her lunch because the Floozy's children had eaten everything else in the pantry. If their mother didn't go and get some groceries today, there'd be nothing for supper tonight.

As they left the Machine Room, Jeannie leaned close. 'There's Louisa's pa. Should we ask if he's found her?'

Mr Clements was walking across the yard towards the offices, his head down as though deep in thought.

'Best not disturb him,' said Kate. The last thing she needed was another interrogation from him. She'd seen George briefly on her way to work that morning as he drove past in his lorry. He hadn't stopped, but he'd smiled and nodded when he'd seen her, so she took that to mean that Louisa was now safe in Lincolnshire. 'He told us to keep it to ourselves, didn't he? He doesn't want anyone knowing she's run away. We can't go running over to him, asking questions, can we?'

'I suppose you're right. I'm just so worried about poor Lou. I hope she's all right. I can't bear the thought that something awful has happened to her.'

Something did, Kate thought. *She lost the love of her life and her parents tried to steal her baby away from her and give it to strangers.* But she couldn't tell Jeannie that. Instead, she said, 'Lou's a sensible girl. If she's run away, she'll have made plans. I'm sure she's fine. We'll probably hear from her any day now.'

'I hope so. I wish she'd told us what she was doing.'

Kate laughed and nudged her shoulder. 'And have us give her away? Come on, Jeannie, you know you wouldn't be able to lie to her pa. If you knew where she was, you'd have had to tell him when he asked, wouldn't you?'

Jeannie frowned. 'I don't know. I don't know why she felt the need to run away. After all, spending a few weeks in Exeter isn't exactly a hardship, is it? It might have been a nice holiday for her. I'm sure that's what Mr and Mrs Clements thought.'

'But, Jeannie, you know Lou didn't want to go. She hardly knows her aunt and sending her away wasn't going to make her forget Mattie, was it? I think her parents were being cruel to her.' She wished she could tell Jeannie the whole story, but Louisa had made her promise not to. If Jeannie knew about the baby, she might see their friend's escape in a different light and stop trying to defend her parents' decision. 'I don't blame her for running away,' she declared. 'I wish I could do the same.'

They reached the canteen and joined the other women at the long tables. Some had brought their own food; others were tucking into a hot meal they bought for sixpence. Kate's mouth watered at the sight and smell of their meals but she ignored them and got out her bread. There was no more opportunity for a private discussion with so many ears on the alert for new gossip. Instead, they ate their lunches and listened to the chatter around them.

One woman was gloating that her son had been turned down by the army on medical grounds, on account of him having a weak chest, even though everyone knew he was as fit as a butcher's dog so he had clearly pulled the wool over the doctor's eyes.

The conversation got louder as some of the women tried to defend the lad and others called him a coward. Still others – the Quaker women – argued that war wasn't the answer and no man should be called to fight against his will. Jeannie agreed with those speaking out against the war, but she also felt the lad was deceitful and was jealous that he'd found a way to get out of fighting while her brother, a lifelong pacifist, felt obliged to fight. Not that she said anything. It was clear that the different groups weren't about to agree on this. These discussions had been going on since the war had been declared back in 1914 and only got more heated as time went on and more local men went away to fight.

Kate was only grateful that her brothers were older and both married with children, so they weren't being expected to enlist yet. No doubt they would be, if the war went on much longer. But everyone said it would be over soon, so with any luck, they wouldn't be called to fight.

Tired of the arguing, Kate signalled to Jeannie that she was leaving. She headed over to the privy before going back to her machine. She was hard at work, trying to catch up, when the hooter went and the others came rushing back.

* * *

Jeannie got back to work, her mind wandering as she fed the drill cotton through the sewing machine. The pieces she stitched together would end up in a lady's pair of shoes, but she rarely got to see the finished product. She simply did her part in the production process by joining the lining pieces, which were then moved to another station where someone would take them to the next stage. The finished uppers and linings would meet the soles, heels and trimmings in another part of the factory before being shipped out to shops all over the world.

She wondered how Lucas was getting on, whether he'd had a decent night's sleep in the barracks and if he'd had some decent grub to eat. She had no idea where he was, although the rumours were that all the local recruits ended up somewhere on Salisbury Plain for their basic training. She hoped they heard from him soon. Ma had been in an awful state all day yesterday, and Jeannie was sure she hadn't slept last night. Maybe if she heard from Lucas, Ma would feel a bit better.

She glanced briefly at Kate, who was working hard, no doubt trying to catch up after spending time showing Sally the ropes this morning. The new girl looked up and gave Jeannie a shy smile before turning back to her work. Jeannie tried not to resent the girl for taking Louisa's place – it wasn't her fault, after all – but it was hard. She should try to be nice to her. She wished she knew where Lou had got to. It wasn't like her at all to worry her parents like that. She'd always been a good girl. But losing Matthew had changed her and Jeannie could honestly say that she didn't have a clue what was going on in her friend's mind lately. The poor girl had been so mired in grief that she couldn't be comforted. She only hoped that she wasn't mentally ill. The thought that she might have had a breakdown and taken herself off to do herself harm was a real fear for Jeannie. Louisa had seemed so frail lately. She didn't want to think like that, but she couldn't help it. Until she knew Lou was safe, she could only think the worst.

It bothered her that Kate didn't seem to be as worried about Lou as she was. *But then Kate's having a time of it, as well. Fancy having to put up with that horrible woman and her awful children. I should hate it.* She wished she could do something about it but, as Kate pointed out, if Mr Davis kept all his daughter's wages, she couldn't afford to lodge anywhere. Even though she'd like to offer her sanctuary at her house – and she knew Ma would understand and agree – they couldn't afford to have another mouth to feed in the house if they didn't bring some money with them.

She looked up at the steel beams above their heads, wishing life wasn't quite so hard. She put the last of her finished pieces in the basket by her machine and got up to go and get a new batch. As she returned to her seat, a movement in the yard outside the window caught her eye. One of Kate's brothers – Fred, she thought – went by with a couple of lads, pushing a cart laden with hides no doubt destined for the Cutting Room. Fred was a clicker like his pa and Lucas, working for Louisa's pa.

Maybe I should talk to him? she thought. *But I don't know him very well. What if he's like his pa? Kate doesn't mention her family much, other than Peg. Fred's a lot older than the girls. I don't want to make things worse for her.* It was a shame that Peg had moved away because Jeannie knew that she was close to Kate. *If only I could contact Peg... she might know what to do for the best.* She would have to think on it and maybe discuss it with Ma. She couldn't sit back and do nothing when Kate was being so poorly treated. But then she thought back to when Kate's ma had been ill and had made Kate promise not to tell her siblings. Not being tied to the promise Kate had made, Jeannie and Louisa had told Peg and Kate's then sweetheart, Ted, had told Fred. All the Davis siblings had swept into action, including Fred, getting a doctor to examine their ma. Jeannie remembered that Fred's wife had helped look after Mrs Davis during the day while Kate was at work.

Of course she could talk to Fred. He would want to know how

poorly his sister was being treated. She would have to think of a way to approach him.

Jeannie had popped to the Meeting House, which was next to the factory, with a note for the Warden before she headed home from work. As she headed back past the factory, she encountered Louisa's father. She hoped he wouldn't see her as he seemed deep in thought, but she wasn't so lucky and he beckoned her over.

'Hello, Mr Clements,' she said. 'Any news of Louisa?'

He scowled and looked about them. 'I specifically told you not to discuss my daughter, yet here we are in the middle of the street and you're calling out her name.'

Jeannie took a step back, startled by his angry words. After all, he'd been the one to call her over. She glanced around. There was no one within earshot. 'I... I'm sorry, sir. I didn't mean any harm. I'm just worried about her, disappearing like that.'

'Well, you can stop spreading untruths. She's not missing. She's on her way to Exeter with her mother, as planned.'

Jeannie blew out a relieved breath. 'Oh, good. You found her, then? I was sure she wouldn't have run away. Not Lou... er, I mean Louisa.' She felt her cheeks warm as he glared at her use of his daughter's nickname.

'Of course she wouldn't,' he snapped. 'She'd just gone for a long walk and forgot the time. Now, I must be on my way. I'll thank you not to discuss my daughter with anyone from now on. She's been through a terrible loss and is taking time with her aunt in Exeter to deal with her grief and get on with her life.'

'Yes, sir,' she said to his back as he strode away.

Jeannie felt so sorry for Lou. She wished she'd had the chance to see her before she left. She'd have to get the address and write to her, let her know she was thinking of her even when she was all the way down in Exeter. She thought to ask Mr Clements, but then decided against it, given the mood he was in at the moment. She'd have to pop over to see Mrs Clements when she got back next week, if she hadn't heard from Louisa by then.

Her thoughts turned to her brother. Lucas had been friends with Mattie all his life and had been just as devastated by his death as Louisa. She hoped that his decision to enlist hadn't been some awful wish to join his dearest friend in the hereafter. She didn't think that was the case, but he'd been very down since they'd got the news. *Please, God,* she prayed. *Make sure he keeps his head down on the battlefield and bring him home to us in one piece.*

14

Mr Clements strode up the Somerton Road towards his empty house. He'd been proud to move into the semi-detached cottage a couple of years ago when he'd been promoted to foreman in the Cutting Room. A man needed to provide for his family and he knew he'd done his wife and daughter proud. But today, he approached his home with a heavy heart. He had lied to Louisa's friend. His girl – the apple of his eye – was still missing and he didn't know if he'd ever see her again.

His wife had found the letter when she'd gone through Louisa's things, trying to find a clue as to where she might have gone.

Dear Mother and Father,

By the time you find this, I shall be gone.

I am sorry, but I cannot accept the plans you have made for me, so I have made my own arrangements to leave this place to ensure a better future for my baby, who I already love with all my heart, just as I love its father and will do so for the rest of my days.

You mustn't worry, I will not bring you shame. No one knows what I am doing. You can tell everyone I am with my aunt. I will write to you when I am settled so that you will know that I am safe. I will prove to you that I can take care of myself. I hope that you will forgive me one day, although my only sin was to love a man who loved me.

Please don't try to find me. Let me do this my way. I am sorry that we have been such a disappointment to each other, and I pray that we will one day be reconciled. But for now, I must do what my conscience tells me is right for my child, just as you have tried to do for me. Please trust me. It is for the best.

I remain your daughter, who loves you,

Louisa

The words had all but broken his wife. She begged him to find her, but he'd found no trace. He'd hoped her friends would tell him where she'd gone but it was clear the Musgrove girl hadn't a clue and the Davis girl kept her own counsel. She said she didn't know where Louisa had gone, but he was sure she knew more than she was telling him. But, short of trying to beat it out of the girl – and though he'd been sorely tempted, he didn't hold with any man laying a violent hand on a female – he couldn't persuade her to talk.

He let himself into the cottage and lit a lamp to dispel the gloom. He'd put his wife on the Exeter train that morning before work. She would stay with her sister for a week and then come back. As far as the rest of the world was concerned, Louisa had gone with her mother and would remain with her aunt for the foreseeable future. They would keep up the pretence for now and pray the girl would come to her senses before it was too late.

Of one thing he was sure – if she chose to keep the child, she would not be welcome in this house again. He would not allow her to bring such shame to his family.

He cursed the day his daughter had met Matthew Searle. He wasn't even a member of their church, but rather a Quaker. If the Clarks themselves weren't members of that congregation, he had no doubt the so-called Friends in Street would be shunned for their un-Christian practices of worship. Why, they simply sat in silence – no hymns, prayers or sermons, not even a cross or an altar to gaze upon as they worshipped. Who was to say they were thinking about the lord while they sat there? What man could be trusted to guide his own worship? It wasn't right and he didn't want a Quaker for his daughter's husband. Why, if he didn't rely on the Clarks for his livelihood, he'd give them short shrift. He refused to believe they were truly Christian, no matter how well they served the community. He sighed, feelings of grief, anger and frustration making his chest ache.

If... *no, when* Louisa returned, he would ensure that she had nothing to do with the Quakers, including that friend of hers, Jeannie Musgrove. He would make sure she made a decent match with an Anglican lad and pray that her husband never became aware of her shame.

15

Jeannie had been keen to tell Kate what Louisa's pa had told her as soon as they got to the factory the next day.

'He's lying,' said Kate without hesitation.

Jeannie gasped. 'He wouldn't. Not Mr Clements. He's a foreman and he goes to church, regular.'

'Huh!' Kate scoffed. 'Going to church don't always mean you live a truly Christian life, does it? Come on, Jeannie. We've known plenty of people who turn up every Sunday and say all the right things to the parson or the elders. But as soon as they walk out of the church or the Meeting House, they're as mean-spirited and untruthful as they've always been. He's lying, I tell you.'

'Why on earth would you say that, Kate?' She narrowed her eyes. 'What aren't you telling me?'

Kate looked away, immediately regretting her response. She hadn't meant to say that, but it had just come out. Now Jeannie was suspicious. *What can I tell her?*

'You know where she is, don't you?' Jeannie said.

Kate's heart sank. She hated lying to her, but she'd promised Lou. With her father still suspicious of them, she didn't dare tell

Jeannie anything that she might give away to him. She took a deep breath. 'Please don't ask me,' she said.

'But—'

'Time to work, ladies,' called Mr Briars, giving them both the evil eye.

Kate immediately turned on her machine, glad that young Sally had only just arrived, rushing to get to her machine just as the hooter sounded.

'Sorry I'm late,' she gasped.

'No skin off my nose,' shrugged Kate. 'But Mr Briars notices these things, so you'd better make sure you're on time from now on. If you're not at your machine, ready to work the moment the shift starts, he'll know. Plus, you're on day rates for now, aren't you?'

Sally nodded. New staff began as day workers, earning a basic rate, until they were deemed competent to go onto piecework rates.

'Well, bear in mind, if you clock in a minute late, you'll lose a full quarter of an hour's money.'

Sally's eyes widened. 'Oh, no! I'll be on time tomorrow, I promise.'

Kate gave her a vague smile before focusing on her work. She didn't dare look at Jeannie.

* * *

By dinner time, Jeannie had built up a head of steam and was ready to start in on Kate.

'You lied to me,' she hissed, pulling her friend back from the throng of women and girls heading out of the Machine Room. 'Where is she?'

Kate shook her head. 'Not here, for God's sake,' she whispered. 'Do you want the whole world to hear? Mr Clements'll be down here like a shot.'

'So you don't deny it,' she said, keeping her voice low. 'I expected better of you, Kate Davis. I thought we were friends.'

'We *are*,' she insisted. 'But Lou is my friend too, and she made me promise not to say anything to anyone.'

Jeannie couldn't believe this. She put her hands on her hips and glared at Kate. 'So now she's not here, you're blaming her, is that it? Well, it's not good enough. I can't believe you've been lying to me.'

'I haven't lied,' said Kate through gritted teeth. 'I just haven't told you.'

'Same thing,' Jeannie muttered, aware that some of the women were looking over their shoulders to see what was going on. As most of the women had mastered the art of lip-reading over their years of working in the noisy factory, she turned her back on them so they couldn't see what she was saying. 'You acted like you didn't know where Lou is, but you do, don't you? You know and you haven't even told her parents. In fact, you downright lied to Mr Clements.'

Kate rolled her eyes and looked at the stragglers by the door who were no doubt keen for some new gossip. She turned her head and leaned closer towards Jeannie. 'It's her parents I'm protecting her from,' she whispered. 'Can't you see?'

'No, I can't. Mr Clements is beside himself. I expect her ma is even worse. You should tell them where she is.'

Kate snorted and turned away. 'I'm not discussing this here. But you're wrong, Jeannie Musgrove. Which is probably why she confided in me and not you.'

Jeannie watched, stunned by the pain her friend's words had evoked, as Kate stalked away to join the others heading down the stone stairs to the courtyard. With so many people around, she couldn't go after her and demand to know what on earth was going on. The thought that Louisa had indeed run away shocked her and the realisation that her two best friends had conspired without including her left her feeling hurt and alone. She'd always thought she could rely on them both, but judging by Kate's words, they hadn't thought the same of her. She'd assumed Louisa had a close, happy relationship with her parents, being their only child. She'd even envied her sometimes when the responsibility of caring for her ma and brothers got too much. Mr and Mrs Clements might have been a bit demanding, expecting a lot from their only child, she supposed, and she knew that things had been strained in the Clementses' household since Mattie had died – or even before that, when Louisa and he had started courting – but she'd assumed it was because Lou was grieving and her parents were trying to chivvy her out of her low spirits. It must have been painful for them to watch her suffer – a bit like it felt for Jeannie, watching her mother in so much distress about Lucas going to war. That was why Jeannie felt she understood how worried Mr and Mrs Clements were about Louisa. Their actions came from a place of love for her. She couldn't believe her friend would choose to run away from that and that both she and Kate had kept it from her. It didn't make any sense.

Still confused, Jeannie grabbed her lunch and ate it with some of the older women, ignoring Kate, who was happily chatting to the new girl, Sally.

'You two had a falling out?' asked one of the women, tilting her head towards Kate. 'I thought you was joined at the hip.'

A couple of the others laughed, all of them watching Jeannie's reaction to the teasing with gleaming eyes.

'We're friends, not Siamese twins,' she shrugged, trying to look as though she didn't care. 'I thought it'd be nice to sit with you ladies today for a change, but if I'm not welcome...' She went to stand up.

'Oh, sit down, lass. Don't take on so. You can sit where you like.'

She sank down onto her seat again and concentrated on eating.

'I hear that trollop what moved in with Reggie Davis is making a right fool of him,' someone commented. 'No wonder young Kate is looking so sour these days.'

Jeannie frowned, saying nothing. She wanted to tell them about the scene she'd witnessed and the awful things Kate had told her about the situation at home, but she hesitated. Kate would hate everyone knowing her business. She might fight back as best she could at home, but she wasn't one to share her dirty laundry in public. And she would hate to be pitied by anyone.

But maybe someone here could help her if I told them?

Jeannie dismissed the thought as soon as it formed. Kate wouldn't ever forgive her for sharing her humiliation with all and sundry. No, she would have to think of a better way to help her, like telling Fred, for instance, even if Kate had lied to her about Louisa. Even though the realisation had left her feeling hurt and badly let down, Jeannie wasn't one to be petty and she tried to live by the moral standards of the Friends. If someone needed help, even someone who had lied and who she believed was doing something terribly wrong by not telling the Clementses where Louisa could be found, Jeannie felt it was her duty to offer it, no matter her personal feelings. She had to have faith that Kate would do the right thing in the end.

Her companions all had an opinion about Reggie Davis's new woman – including that she wasn't that new, given that her children were the spitting image of Kate's pa. Some expressed sympathy for Kate, while others were outraged by the Floozy's blatant behaviour. One or two thought it was hilarious and claimed to have always known about Reggie Davis's philandering ways. Jeannie kept her head down, refusing to be drawn into the gossip, feeling bad for Kate that folk had been gossiping about her family even before poor Mrs Davis had taken ill and died.

She was relieved when it was time to go back to work and she quickly headed back to her machine.

'Are you still speaking to me?' Kate asked as she sat down beside her.

Jeannie pursed her lips. She wanted to demand to know where Louisa was, but she could tell from Kate's belligerent expression that she wouldn't get anything out of her right now. She sighed. She supposed it wasn't the time nor the place for the conversation she desperately wanted to have with Kate. It hadn't escaped her notice that her friend had been looking tired and drawn these past few days. Maybe she'd intended to tell Jeannie some time, but with all the shenanigans at the Davis house, it probably hadn't seemed important to Kate. Much as she hated being kept in the dark, Jeannie could see that. She just wished she hadn't discovered that Kate knew more than she was telling. She'd much rather have been kept in blissful ignorance, thinking Louisa was safe and sound in Exeter.

'Yes, I'm still speaking to you,' she said, feeling unutterably sad. She leaned closer to Kate. 'Just tell me this. Is Lou all right?'

Kate nodded, putting an arm around her shoulders. 'Yes. She's safe and being well looked after. But that's all I'm going to tell you for now. And if I hear you've said a word to her ma or pa, I'll knock your block off, d'you hear?'

Jeannie gave her a sideways glance. 'I hear you.'

'Good. 'Cause Lou needs some time and space to work her life out.'

'But she'll be coming back, won't she?'

When Kate hesitated, Jeannie's heart sank.

'I hope so,' said Kate. 'We'll just have to wait and see.'

16

It was a week before Kate heard from Louisa in response to the hurried letter she'd sent her, asking her what she could tell Jeannie. As luck would have it, she met the postie as she left the house to go to work, so no one at home knew she'd got a letter. She'd worried about that – whether Pa or the Floozy would demand to know who was writing to her. The last thing she wanted was for either of them to know where Louisa was. She hated to think what they'd do with the information.

She thanked the postie and tucked the letter into her pocket until she was out of sight of the house. But she couldn't wait any longer, so as soon as she turned the corner, she opened the envelope and began to read.

> *Dear Kate,*
> *Thank you for your letter.*

Kate grinned as she read that. It was typical of Lou to write in such a formal manner.

The journey here was long and tiring, I cried most of the way, then we had to stop so I could be sick, but we made it at last and are settling in well. Will has started work and I'm helping Peg unpack and get the house in order.

She went on to describe the small cottage that had been allocated to them by the factory and how people were arriving from all over the country to work there.

I don't have the words to tell you how much I appreciate your help in getting away, Kate. I would have rather died than go along with my parents' plans for me. I know from a letter Will got from his ma that my father has been telling people I'm in Exeter with Ma. She doesn't know I'm here yet, of course, so she couldn't say otherwise. I expect Ma is spending her time cursing me with her sister, but I don't care. They should have listened to me.

Kate nodded in agreement as she walked and read. But she also knew that parents were a law unto themselves and there wasn't much you could do about it but keep your head down and hope you could escape sometime. Despite the awful situation Louisa found herself in, Kate couldn't help but envy her friend. She wished she could escape, too, but she couldn't see how, unless she could get accepted for training as a nurse. But even then, she suspected her pa would stop her going by refusing to let her give up her job.

I'm sorry things have been so awkward with Jeannie. The last thing I want is for my two dearest friends in the whole world to fall out. I've talked to Peg about it and we think we've come up with a solution. She's writing to Will's ma while I'm writing this.

She's telling her she's found out she's expecting and wanted to share her good news. She's told her she's having a hard time of it and heard from you that Louisa is looking for a new start and so she's saying she has written to me in Exeter to ask if I'll go to Lincolnshire to help her prepare for the baby. Mrs Searle will accept that as she knows Peg and Will have been trying for a baby for so long that they won't want to take any chances of losing it. We know my parents will realise straight away that Peg helped me escape, but what can they do? As far as everyone is concerned, I'm just helping a friend who's having a baby, so that should placate my parents. I'm not bringing any shame to their door, especially as Mrs Searle doesn't know the truth of it.

Kate couldn't help but admire the speed with which they'd come up with this plan. It did her heart good to know that she'd been right to think Peg and Will would help when Lou had confided in her.

I can't pretend that I'm not bitter about what I've been forced into. If they'd allowed me and Mattie to marry when we wanted, none of this would have been necessary and I could have brought up our child without any shame. But what's done is done. I won't ever trust my parents again, that's for sure, and I doubt if they will trust me either. I don't know if I'll ever be able to return to Street, which breaks my heart.

Kate felt her heart sink at the thought of Lou not coming back. She would miss her a lot.

Anyway, regarding Jeannie, I'm sorry to ask you to keep on carrying my secret. I can't risk it getting out. It wouldn't be fair to Peg and Will after all their kindness to me. It didn't take me long to realise that they will be the best parents for mine and Mattie's child if we couldn't fulfil that role ourselves. But, now that Mrs Searle will know I'm here, I'm happy for you to tell Jeannie the same story Peg has told her. Would that be all right?

She breathed a sigh of relief. Yes, that would do the trick. She hated to keep more than she had to from Jeannie. She knew she was weighed down with worry at the moment – about Lucas, about her ma, about Louisa and even about Kate herself after the fuss with the Floozy the other week. If she could at least put her friend's mind at rest about Lou, then that would have to do for now.

The High Street was busy with workers heading for the factory. Kate tucked the letter back into her pocket. She decided she would burn it as soon as she had a chance. She couldn't risk anyone finding it and reading it.

* * *

As she expected, as soon as she managed to have a quiet word with Jeannie and tell her what Louisa had asked her to, her friend was all smiles.

'I'm so pleased for Peg,' she said. 'It must have been so hard, wanting a baby and it not happening. Just think, Kate – new house, new baby! And I'm so relieved Lou is all right. Why on earth didn't you say she'd gone with Peg and Will? I've been so worried about her.'

'I know, I'm sorry. But Lou was really worried that her ma and pa would stop her going. They've been so over-protective since Mattie...' She almost choked on the words. In truth, she thought they'd been monsters to their only child. But her loyalty to Louisa wouldn't let her give voice to her real opinion. 'Anyway, she's been feeling suffocated and needed to get away.'

Jeannie nodded. 'I expect she wants to start fresh. D'you think she'll stay in Lincolnshire?'

Kate shrugged. 'Who knows? But anyway, Will's ma knows about the baby now, but I don't think Peg wants it spread about too much – you know, in case anything goes wrong. So please don't say anything to anyone yet.'

Jeannie looked pained. 'Poor Peg. It must be such a worry. I'm glad Louisa's there to help her. It's the perfect solution for both of them.'

'Yeah. And Will has been able to start his new job without worrying about Peg being on her own without any family or friends around. If things had been different, Lou would have been his sister-in-law, so she's the perfect choice.'

'But you're Peg's sister. Why didn't you go with them? It would have been the perfect excuse to get away from home.'

Kate shrugged, looking away. 'I haven't told Peg the truth of it. I didn't want to worry her. But anyway, I'm glad Lou went with them. She needed to escape more than I did.'

Jeannie looked at her, frowning. 'But—'

'Shh! Here comes Mr B,' Kate hissed, turning back to her machine.

They got on with their work. The repetitive tasks, the rumble and roar of the machines, the smell of leather, cotton and machine oil, the dust motes floating in the air all surrounded Kate with reassurance. It might be hell at home, but in the Machine Room, she had her place, her friend and the knowledge that she wasn't going to be belittled or battered. For now, it would have to be enough.

17

Street, Somerset
1 October 1915

Dear Lou,

I'm so relieved I can tell Jeannie something. It's been hard – missing you and having to keep her in the dark. It's just as well we did, though, because she was so keen to help your pa find you. I'd decided that, if she got too close to doing that, I'd have to confess all to her as that would be the only way she would understand why we shouldn't tell your pa where you are.

Peg's idea about telling Mrs S seems to have done the trick with your parents. I popped round to see her and she said she saw your pa in the village and told him how grateful she was to Louisa for agreeing to go to Lincolnshire to help Peg through her pregnancy. I haven't seen your parents, but I heard someone say they'd seen your ma this morning and she'd told them you'd had a little break with her in Exeter and have now gone to help Peg in Lincolnshire. No one suspects a thing and your parents can't say anything without giving the game away. So you can rest easy.

Things aren't so good at home. The Floozy is making my life a misery, knowing I can't leave because of Pa keeping all my wages, although I don't doubt she'd happily see me living in a ditch if she could still steal my money. Thank goodness, I found a few coppers I'd hidden in my clothes from last time Pa bothered to give me anything, so I can afford a stamp for this letter at least.

By the way, I managed to meet the postie in the morning and got your letter from him before they see it, then I burnt it after I've read it so no one could see it. But I'm scared one of them will find one of your letters before I can get to it, so do you think you could write to me care of Jeannie from now on? It would be a weight off my mind. I'd hate for them to find out your secret.

Did Jeannie send you the address for Lucas? She's hoping he'll be able to come home on leave for Christmas as his training ends then and they should get some time off before being shipped overseas. Her ma is holding up at the moment, but we don't think she'll cope very well when he goes to fight. The twins are getting a bit too big for their boots now that Lucas is away, which is really vexing poor Jeannie. She's usually so placid, but I know she's sorely tempted to bang their heads together!

Anyway, I must go. Pa and the Floozy have gone out drinking again, so I've to keep an eye on the children. They're a bit too quiet for my liking right now, so I'd better go and see what mischief they're up to!

Write soon, lots of love,

Kate

Kate sealed the letter and put it in her pocket under her apron before she went to find her half-siblings. When she saw they were playing with their ma's cosmetics and cheap, flashy costume jewellery, she laughed softly and left them to it. No doubt the Floozy would blame her, but she didn't care.

* * *

Lincolnshire
4 October 1915

Dear Lucas,

I hope this finds you without too much trouble. I got this address from Jeannie. I know that no one is allowed to know where you are, even while you are doing your basic training, but I hear that the postal system is working wonders for the army, making sure letters get to the soldiers, so with any luck, it will not take too long for this to reach you.

How are you? Is the training rough? I have to confess that, like Jeannie and the rest of your family, I pray that peace will be declared soon and you won't have to fight at all.

I have another confession. You may already have guessed from the address at the top of this letter, but I am not where you thought I would be! As you know, I never wanted to go to Exeter – that was Ma's idea and I wasn't happy about it at all. So instead, I have moved to Lincolnshire! I am staying with Will and Peg Searle. Peg is expecting and needs some help around the house as she's having a hard time of it. I will be here for at least until after the baby is born (it is due in March, I think), so please reply to me at this address.

I do hope you meant what you said about us writing to each other. You were Mattie's very best friend. I miss him so much and it will mean a lot to me to be able to stay in touch with you. It is so very hard, being without him. Sometimes, I catch a glimpse of Will in a certain light and my heart skips a beat, thinking it is my Mattie. But then he moves and I realise it is his brother and I grieve all over again. He and Peg are being so kind, even when I burst into tears, which was often during the first few days. They lost him too, of course, so they understand my grief. It is getting a little easier as I notice more differences than similarities now between Will and his brother. I realise that they are very different men, even if they do – or rather did – look alike. But I still can't get used to thinking that Mattie is gone forever. I don't know if I ever shall.

Peg is very kind and reminds me so much of Kate, who I miss a lot. I miss Jeannie, too. But we're all writing to each other and so it is not so bad. I hope that I will get to see them again one day. I expect Jeannie is writing to you every day. She loves her big brother very much!

Lincolnshire is quite nice. I am sure I shall get along very well here. Better than if I had gone to Exeter. I do miss Street and working with the girls at Clarks, although I am not sure whether it is the place I miss or just the people, in particular Mattie, you, Kate and Jeannie. I wondered whether you had seen or heard about Ted Jackson as well? No one seems to have heard from him since he enlisted. But I suppose as we get older, we all have to find our own place in the world and cannot expect things to always stay the same.

Please write back to me, Lucas. Even though we are both a long way from Street, I feel as though we can send each other a little piece of home through our letters.

Yours sincerely,
Louisa Clements

Louisa folded the letter and tucked it into the envelope that she had already addressed as Jeannie had told her. It had been hard, having to tell her lies again. She hated it. But the die had been cast and she had to maintain the falsehood that it was Peg and not Louisa who was expecting. She also realised that she couldn't bear the thought of Lucas thinking badly of her or of Mattie. She didn't think he would – he was as tolerant and understanding as his sister. But just in case... no, she could never tell him.

Not everything she had written had been a lie. She *did* burst into tears at the oddest moments. Being around Mattie's brother was far harder than she had imagined.

But she was also learning fast that he was as good a man as Mattie had been. That gave her some comfort, knowing that the reality of her situation was that – whether she wanted it or not (and she really did not) – she would have to hand her and Mattie's child over to Peg and Will and walk away. She tried not to think about it, but she knew that it would have to happen.

It's the right thing to do, she told herself as she sealed the envelope. *Our baby will be brought up in a good family – his father's family (for I've a feeling it will be a boy), his blood kin. He'll be loved and have a good life, better than I can offer him without Mattie.*

With a sigh, she got up and fetched her coat. She would walk to the post box and send the letter. As she did, she sent a little prayer for peace and Lucas's safety, just as she'd told him she would.

* * *

Location Classified Confidential
7 October 1915

Dear Louisa,

Thank you for your letter, which arrived safely. As you say, our post office is doing a grand job, making sure all the Tommies get news from home. My ma has already sent an apple cake for me to share with my mates. No doubt the twins will have been complaining but I expect Ma will have made one for them as well. The cake I got has made me mighty popular amongst the lads and I only managed to eat one slice before it was all gone. I don't mind, so long as they share their care packages with me when they get them.

Training isn't so bad. I suppose working at the factory kept me fit, so I'm not struggling as much as some of the others. I can't tell you any more about it. I'm sure you understand.

I was surprised to learn that you went to Lincolnshire with Will and his wife, but I can see that you might prefer that to staying with your aunt. I hope it will help you, Louisa. I know how hard it has been since we lost Mattie. I miss him too. I should never have let him go off on his own and for that I am heartily sorry.

Please congratulate them on the baby news. Mattie would have been so proud to be an uncle!

As you guessed, Jeannie has written every day, as has Ma. The twins aren't so regular, though I've had a brief note or two from them enclosed with Ma or Jeannie's letters. I expect they were scolded into it. So long as they do as they promised me and look after the family, I don't mind if they don't get round to writing.

I am happy to write to you, Louisa. As you say, we offer each other a little slice of home. Perhaps while we're both away from Street, we can tell each other things that we might not be able to tell the folks back home. I'm thinking about how much we both miss Mattie. If I said that to anyone else, they would tell me to stop dwelling on what I can't change. I expect they've said the same to you. But I don't want to forget him, and I know you don't want to either.

Look after yourself. I'll try to reply to your letters as soon as I get them, but please forgive me if it takes a day or two. They're working us hard to make sure we're fighting fit and ready to do our bit when we finally get to France.

Thank you for your prayers. I think we all need them.

From your friend,

Lucas

As she finished reading the letter that had arrived this morning, Louisa breathed a sigh of relief. She had half-expected Lucas to decide he didn't want to write to her after all. She'd been afraid he might feel he couldn't bear to have her reminding him of his lost friend, especially now he was in the army and making new friends in his regiment.

But, as comforting as it was to hear from him, she knew she couldn't share her deepest secret with him – not about the additional, shattering grief she bore of knowing that she would have to give up Mattie's child. She couldn't share that with anyone. Instead, she would be as faithful a friend to him as he had been to Mattie. She would send him cheerful letters, share their best memories of Mattie and keep him in her prayers until he returned to his family, safe and sound.

18

Three weeks later, Jeannie finished reading her latest letter from Lucas and breathed a sigh of relief. In her last letter she'd told him about what was happening to poor Kate. She felt bad writing about it, but had been desperate to tell her brother something other than how difficult things were at home. He already knew how hard his going away was on Ma, but he didn't need to know the twins were acting up without him being there to keep them in line. If she told him that, he'd write to Peter and John and tell them off, which would make them more resentful of her for being a tell-tale-tit. So instead, she'd poured out her worries about Kate and how she felt helpless to do anything to help as her friend got paler and thinner and less like her usual strong, cheerful self. She'd tried to get a chance to talk to Fred, but had chickened out at the last minute. It was difficult for a girl to approach a married man she wasn't related to at the factory or in the village, where anyone could see and comment, even if it was no one else's business. But after she'd written to Lucas, she still worried that she shouldn't have told anyone her friend's business.

She was glad she had now, though, because when he replied,

Lucas had suggested something she hadn't thought of. She just hoped he was right and it would work. She quickly wrote another letter and added it to the pile to post on the way to work in the morning.

'Jeannie, love, where are you?'

She sighed at the sound of her mother's tremulous call. 'I'm here, Ma,' she said, getting up from the kitchen table where she'd been writing. 'What do you need?'

Ma came into the room clutching Lucas's most recent letter. He'd only been gone a few weeks and was still training, but as far as she was concerned, he was already in grave danger. 'He said some of the recruits have influenza. What if he gets it?'

Jeannie went over to her and put an arm around her frail shoulders. She silently cursed Lucas for giving Ma another thing to worry about. 'He's as strong as an ox, Ma. A dose of flu won't hurt him. But they might have to delay sending them out to France if too many of them get it. I don't suppose they'll want it to spread through the trenches. So it might be a blessing in disguise.'

Ma thought about it for a moment then nodded. 'You're right, Jeannie. We must hope it's a blessing in disguise. Maybe the answer to our prayers.' She looked at the small pile of letters on the table. 'I must write back to him straight away. Will you post it with yours?'

'Of course I will. I always do, don't I?'

She nodded again. She always seemed to agree to anything Jeannie said these days, even when she'd asked Ma if she would mind her slipping a couple of postage stamps to Kate when she didn't have the money to buy her own. She never argued or corrected, and leaned on Jeannie more and more to make decisions for her. It was as though she'd lost any sense of herself and simply existed rather than really lived, leaving her daughter to adopt the role of parent. Jeannie had seen her like this before –

after her pa had died ten years ago. It had been ages before she started to take an interest in life again and to become just a shadow of the woman they'd known before she'd been widowed. It broke Jeannie's heart to see her slide back into her grief, even when Ma knew that Lucas was safe and sound in a training camp somewhere. It made her fear the day they would hear he was finally being sent to fight. She didn't think Ma could bear the worry of it. And if anything happened to Lucas, it would be the end of her, Jeannie just knew it.

For a brief moment, her anger at her brother rose again. He was so selfish, going off like that, leaving her alone to cope with Ma and the twins. The boys had been less than useless – hardly ever doing any chores at home, rushing off to play football with their friends the minute they got in from work. Then they came home whenever it suited them and demanded supper. Jeannie was sick and tired of trying to do everything as well as having to keep their meals warm when they didn't turn up when it was ready to eat. In that moment, she resolved to leave their plates to go cold if they weren't home in time to join her and Ma round the table. That would teach the beggars.

'You've written a lot of letters, lass,' Ma commented.

'Only three, Ma. One for Lucas, one for Louisa, and I thought I'd send a note to Peg Searle.'

'That's Kate's sister, isn't it? Didn't you say Louisa is living with her in Lincolnshire?'

'That's her.' Jeannie gently guided her ma to the table and encouraged her to sit down. 'Let's have a cuppa, shall we?'

'All right,' she agreed, her tone listless. 'Are the boys playing football again? I saw you brought the coal in for the range. Lucas said they would do that for you.'

Jeannie pulled a face as she checked the kettle on the range.

'Ma, if I waited for them to do it, the fire would go out and we'd freeze to death.'

'But Lucas said—'

'We all know what he told them,' she interrupted. 'But he's not here to make sure they do it, and they won't take any notice of me, so all I get are arguments. I can't be bothered, Ma. It's easier to get on with it myself.'

'They've got to learn, love,' Ma said quietly. 'If their brother doesn't come back…'

'He will,' she said, not allowing herself to believe anything different. 'And when he does, I'll give him a piece of my mind, I can tell you. What was he thinking, telling the twins they were the men of the house now, eh? The idiot. Now they think they're in charge. They don't accept that with rights come responsibilities. You know John tried to cut what he gives for housekeeping out of his wages, don't you? I told him if he did that, I wouldn't feed him.'

'Oh, I'm sure he didn't mean it.' Ma looked uncertain in the face of Jeannie's irritation. 'He's just testing, that's all. Lucas did the same at that age when he got a notion to buy a bicycle.'

'I never did,' said Jeannie. 'And I doubt that Lucas meant to keep money from you week after week.' *Or that he'd use his wages on cider instead of a useful thing like a bicycle.* She remembered he'd wanted to get it so he could cycle out of the village to pick up odd jobs on the farms at weekends. 'We've always known how tight things are, just as John does. Well, I'm not letting him get away with it. I mean it, Ma. If he don't pay up, he don't eat. He's got to learn that actions have consequences.'

'But you can't starve the poor boy. He works hard.'

'I don't know whether he works hard or not when he's at the factory. It's not like working in the carton workshop is difficult, is it? I know I work hard and it's more skilled. When he's on piece-work and doing a skilled job, he might have a bit more say. But until then, he can shut up and do as he's told. He does nothing here and still expects his meals on the table and his laundry done. You have to tell him, Ma. He's got to pay his way and do his chores. Because if he gets away with it, he'll encourage Peter and then we'll all starve. It's not like they're left short. They only hand over half their wages. Why, Kate doesn't see a penny of hers.'

Ma frowned. 'What? Nothing?'

Jeannie shook her head as she put the tea in the pot and poured in hot water. 'That's why I gave her some of our stamps, so she could write to Peg and Louisa. She saves by putting their letters in the same envelope, but still needs help to post them. When her ma was alive, she'd get some pocket money from her, but I'm beginning to suspect it came out of her housekeeping allowance. Since she passed, Kate's had to beg her pa for every few coppers and nine times out of ten, he won't give it to her. He won't even let her collect her own wage packet.'

'Oh, that's terrible. That poor girl. Her ma must be spinning in her grave, especially with that woman from Glastonbury moving in with her children.'

'I know. Things have been a lot worse since she turned up. She's awful to Kate and she does nothing round the house, leaving it all for Kate to do.' Jeannie scowled. 'And those children are little beasts. Don't tell anyone, Ma, but that's why I'm writing to Peg. I don't know Kate's brothers well enough to speak to them, but Lucas suggested I tell Peg what's happening.'

'I don't suppose there's much she can do from Lincolnshire, lass,' said Ma, shaking her head. 'But I'm proud of you for doing something. No young woman deserves to be treated so shabbily by her own father. Tell her to come round here any time she needs to get away.'

She nodded in agreement. She poured the tea and sat with her mother to drink it. Ma sipped her drink while she wrote back to Lucas.

Jeannie hoped Peg would be able to do something for Kate – maybe she would have Kate come and live with her and Will instead of Louisa? She didn't think they had room for both of them once the baby arrived. But she was sure that Lou's parents would have got the message that she wouldn't be forced into moving to her aunt's. She'd proved to them she could make her own decisions and move on with her life after Mattie's death. So maybe Lou could come home now. The trouble was, judging by what she said in her letters, Louisa was content in Lincolnshire and only referred to her parents in the bitterest of tones. She might not want to come back.

Jeannie hated that both of her closest friends had fallen out with their families and might leave Street altogether. In an ideal world – Jeannie's ideal world, that was – both of the girls would be there. Lord knows, Jeannie could do with having them both around right now. They would let her complain about her brothers and lend a shoulder to cry on when she needed it. But with Louisa gone as well as Lucas being away and maybe Kate being forced to leave, she'd have no one.

I mustn't be selfish, though. Kate can't possibly stay in that house when they treat her so badly. It's my Christian duty to help her, even if it means losing my remaining friend to pastures new.

With fresh resolve but a heavy heart, she finished her tea before taking the letters to the post box. A few people were out strolling. She smiled and said hello to those she knew. Some girls were on the arms of their sweethearts. It gave Jeannie pause to think that it had been months since she'd discovered Douglas canoodling with another girl when he was supposed to be courting her. For the first time in her life, she had lost her temper and poured drinks over the pair of them in front of everyone at the

Crispin Hall dance. No one had bothered asking her out since then.

She sighed as she dropped the letters into the box and turned for home. She didn't miss Douglas. In fact, it had been a relief to know he wasn't for her and to cut her ties with him. But it had been nice to walk out on the arm of a lad, to be part of a couple. She missed that. But what with people gossiping about the incident at the dance, and so many lads enlisting, there wasn't much chance of her finding another sweetheart any time soon. Not that she had the time for courting at the moment. And if Lucas didn't come home and if the twins didn't grow up and do their share around the house, she'd never have the time nor the energy for love. She'd die an old maid, lonely and miserable.

19

Lincolnshire
7 November 1915

Dear Lucas,

Happy Birthday! Yes, I remember that your birthday is exactly two days after Mattie's. We used to call you his twin, remember? Peg and Will send their best wishes as well.

I hope that you have a nice day, although I suspect you won't get any special treatment while you're in the middle of training. Anyway, I made the enclosed card for you, which we've all signed. I hope you like it. It had been a long time since I did any painting – probably since I left the board school and went to work at Clarks. But then Mattie bought me some art supplies for my last birthday and I've rediscovered my interest in it. I thought you'd appreciate a view of home. Do you recognise Glastonbury Tor? I painted it from the memory of the view from the banks of the River Brue on the edge of the village, where we used to go swimming in the summer. I wonder when either of us will see it again? Or swim in the river? In some ways, I miss it; in others, I hope to never set eyes on the Tor again.

Mattie's birthday was hard for me. I spent most of it in tears. I can't believe that he never got to see twenty. But I'm not going to dwell on it now on your special day. I'm simply going to say, have the best day you can, my friend. I wish you many, many more and continue to pray that peace will be declared before you have to go off to fight.

From your friend, Louisa

* * *

Location Classified Confidential
10 November 1915

Dear Louisa,

Thank you for your letter and card. It was a lovely surprise. It was kind of you to remember me. Please thank Will and Peg for their good wishes as well. Like you, I remembered Mattie on his birthday. I miss him more than I can tell you. It's hard to imagine never celebrating our birthdays together again, or growing old without him. I didn't tell anyone here it was my birthday, but then I got cards from you and my family and Ma sent a fruit cake and Jeannie sent socks and gloves she'd knitted and the word got out. I had a beer with the lads (although only one as I know Ma and Jeannie wouldn't approve) but didn't feel much like celebrating without Mattie.

Regarding your painting, I stand in awe of your artistic talent! I recognised the Tor straight away. I've put it inside my locker, so I see it every time I open it. I will take it with me when we're posted, so I'll always have a view of home. I don't know if I'll see it again in real life, but I hope I do.

It seems strange to think I'm over halfway through my training already. The time has gone quickly and I'm learning a lot. In my first week, I thought I'd never get the hang of everything, but now I'm a good shot and can strip down my gun and clean it then put it back together in no time at all. My sergeant says my years of heavy work at the factory has given me the strength to put a lot of force behind a bayonet thrust, although I'm not sure how I'll feel if I ever have to use it on another man rather than the scarecrows we've been practising on.

I realise you probably don't want to hear things like that. I apologise. But I don't want to spoil the look of this letter by crossing it all out, and I don't have time to start writing a fresh one before I have to be on parade. I hope you'll forgive me.

Anyway, thank you for my card. I will cherish the painting and dream of one day meeting you again within sight of Glastonbury Tor.

Your friend, Lucas

20

Kate took her time shutting down her machine and tidying around it as the other women joined the rush to collect their wages from the trolley that had been wheeled into the Machine Room from the accounts office. There wasn't any point in following them. Her pa would collect her money with his own, as usual. *And I won't see a penny of it, as usual.* She could weep at the unfairness of it all. She was trapped. Things were terrible at home – the Floozy was evil and so were her children. They treated her like a slave, making her do all the cooking and cleaning, while sitting there, mocking her – when they weren't physically attacking her, that was. Pa did nothing to stop them. That hurt the worst.

'Kate, you coming, love?' asked Jeannie after she'd collected her pay packet.

She shook her head. 'I'll just finish up here. You go ahead.'

She turned away, not wanting Jeannie to see the utter despair on her face. *I've got to get away or I'll die. I'd go to Peg and sleep on her floor if I could – anything is better than staying at Pa's house. But I don't have the money for a train ticket.*

She dropped her chin to her chest, so tired she could weep.

The thought of going home filled her with dread. She didn't know how much more she could take before she went stark raving mad. *That might be my way out – a one-way ticket to the asylum. At least I'll be safe from the Floozy and her spawn there. And I might get a decent meal as well.*

A hand on her shoulder startled her. With a stifled shriek, she turned, half-expecting Beryl to be there, ready to torment her. But it was Jeannie.

'Oh, Jeannie,' she said, clutching a hand to her chest. She thought her heart would burst out of it. 'You frightened the life out of me. I thought you'd gone.'

'You've got to come with me,' she said, her expression earnest. 'I promised your brother.'

'What are you talking about? What brother?' For a horrible moment, she thought she meant that snivelling little brat at home.

'Fred,' she said. 'And George is waiting for you as well. I just saw him walk across the yard.'

'What? Why on earth...?' Kate couldn't understand what Jeannie was saying. 'Oh, God, has something happened? One of their wives? Are their children all right?'

Jeannie shook her head. She put her hands on Kate's shoulders. 'Listen to me. They're waiting outside to confront your pa and make sure you get your money.'

Kate felt herself start to shake. 'What have you done?'

Jeannie lifted her chin, her face set with determination. 'What any decent-minded person would do. I wrote to Peg, told her what you're having to put up with at home and she told your brothers.'

'You had no right,' whispered Kate, shame flooding through her.

'Someone had to. Look at you! You've lost weight. You're exhausted. I've seen the bruises you've tried to hide. They're killing you, Kate. It's got to stop.'

'And you think telling Peg and my brothers is going to stop it?' She let out a harsh bark of laughter. 'You idiot! Now it'll be ten times worse.'

Jeannie swallowed, doubt clouding her expression for a moment before she shook her head and stood taller. 'No, it won't. Because your brothers aren't just helping you get the money you've worked for. They've promised to make sure you're never treated like this again.'

Kate looked up at the ceiling, wondering briefly why she didn't just get herself a noose and hang herself from the beams. 'You don't get it, do you? The minute I get home, they'll rip that money out of my hands and Pa will probably take his belt to me for getting my brothers involved.'

Jeannie squeezed her shoulders. 'No, they won't. Trust me, Kate. Trust your brothers. What have you got to lose?'

My bleeding life, she thought. But she said nothing.

'Come on. It'll be all right. I promise. They've got it all worked out.'

Kate sighed, too weary to argue any more. *What's the point? None of them understand. Pa's never going to change. They're just making things worse.* 'Just make sure you bury me with Ma after he kills me,' she muttered, her empty stomach clenching with dread.

'He is not going to kill you,' said Jeannie. 'Now come on. It's going to be all right. I promise.'

Kate was shaking, but she let Jeannie loop her arm in hers and lead her out of the Machine Room, down the stone stairs and through the factory yard towards the front gates. Before they even came in sight of them, she could hear her pa yelling.

'Oh, lord,' she whispered as they drew nearer and she saw her two brothers holding their father by his arms. It was a bit of shock to realise that George and Fred were now taller and broader than Pa. Kate had taken after their ma and was the smallest of the family, so Pa always seemed to be a huge mountain of a man in her eyes. Now he looked... less, diminished in size and power compared to her grown brothers.

'Let me go, you young bastards,' Pa yelled. 'Treat your own pa like this, would you?'

Someone came out of the office as he struggled against their restraint. Kate's fear spiked as she realised it was Mr Roger Clark, the company secretary. 'What's going on here?' he asked, frowning. 'Why are you holding that man?'

Pa looked slyly triumphant, no doubt expecting them to let him go, but when they didn't, he tried to appeal to Mr Clark. 'My own sons have turned on me, sir. Tell 'em to leave me alone. They're after stealing my wages. They're determined to part me from me own hard-earned money.'

'Is this true?' Mr Clark asked Fred and George. 'Because if it is, I shall call the constable.'

'No, sir,' said Fred. 'It's the opposite. We don't want his money; we earn our own. But he's been taking our sister's wages and not letting her have a penny of it and treating her something terrible. We want to put a stop to it. The poor girl's being robbed by her own father. Search him. You'll see. He's got her wage packet in his pocket along with his own.'

Kate's shaking increased. She closed her eyes, shamefully aware of the crowd of workers who were watching and listening. Jeannie pulled her close, letting her lean against her as her knees weakened. If her friend hadn't been holding her up, she'd have fallen onto the cobbled ground for sure.

'He's letting his fancy woman mistreat her at home as well, sir,' said George. 'If the constable needs to see anyone, it's them. As soon as we found out, we came here to put a stop to it.'

Mr Clark took in the crowd witnessing the proceedings with avid interest. 'If you have finished your shifts,' he addressed them, his firm voice echoing around the courtyard, 'I suggest you go home straight away,' he called out. 'Everyone but the parties involved in this dispute can go. This isn't a circus.'

The crowd dispersed, some casting sympathetic looks towards Kate, others laughing with delight at the latest scandal. Kate didn't doubt she'd be the talk of the factory – and probably the whole village and beyond for months to come. She wanted to curl up on the ground and weep at the unfairness of it all, but she couldn't – not after the risk her brothers were taking on her behalf. Instead, she lifted her chin and waited. Either Mr Clark's intervention would save her, or would result in her brothers being hauled before a magistrate and they would all be doomed.

Mr Clark look round and saw her and Jeannie. Kate thought he was going to tell them off for not leaving.

'That's our sister Kate, sir,' said Fred before he could comment. 'And her friend, Jeannie.'

'If it wasn't for Jeannie, we'd never have known what this monster was doing,' said George.

Mr Clark studied her. 'You're the Musgrove girl – a Friend. Am I right?'

Kate felt Jeannie stand a little straighter. 'That's right, sir,' she said. 'And I swear, I've seen Kate being attacked in her own home for no good reason with my own eyes. She's got bruises, sir.'

'She's lying,' snarled Pa. 'If she's got bruises, it's because she's a clumsy mare.'

Hearing her father accuse her sweet, loyal and honest friend of lying finally broke something within Kate. She stepped forward, her back straight, legs strong. 'No, Pa. Jeannie's as honest as the day is long. You're the one who's lying. You know full well where I got my bruises. At the hands of your fancy woman, who treats me like a slave and beats me while you do nothing, apart from denying me my wages from the factory.'

'I put a roof over your head, you ungrateful little bitch!' he snapped. He turned to Mr Clark. 'See what I have to put up with, sir? A man's entitled to some housekeeping money from his children when they're working.'

'But you take all of it,' she cried, unable to stop the rage pouring out of her. 'Every penny. I've not a farthing in my purse. Not even enough to buy anything from the canteen at dinner time while she sits at home drinking cider paid for with my wages.'

'You don't deserve any money, you useless cow. Beryl's right. You're a sodding waste of space. Oof!' He doubled over as George punched him in the gut.

'That's enough!' the normally calm and collected Mr Clark roared. 'Watch your tongue, man. I will not tolerate such profanity here.' He pointed at George. 'Nor will I tolerate violence. Do you work here?'

George shook his head. 'No, sir. I came to help my brother protect our sister from him.' He tilted his head towards his groaning father. 'You see what he's like. He don't care who hears his filth. If he talks to her like that again, I'll give him another wallop.'

'Not on Clarks premises you won't,' Mr Clark said firmly. He looked around, his gaze alighting on Jeannie, who stood a little behind Kate. 'Miss Musgrove. Please go into the office and tell them I want some assistance out here immediately.'

Kate took a deep breath as Jeannie ran to do his bidding. 'Please, sir,' she said. 'My brothers don't mean no harm; they're just trying to help me. Don't sack us or call the constable. We work hard. We'd never let you down. I'm sorry about...' She lifted a hand towards her pa, still held by his arms as he wheezed and struggled against his sons' restraining hands.

Mr Clark's stern features softened for a moment before tightening again as he observed her pa. 'Calm yourself,' was all he said.

Kate felt her tears gather as she saw the worry on Fred's face. If he lost his job because of her, she'd never forgive herself. None of this was worth that. She'd hand over her wages willingly and be the Floozy's skivvy for the rest of her life if it meant Fred could keep his job and feed his family. She couldn't stop a sob escaping as she covered her face and wept.

A woman's voice cut through the silence that followed. 'Whatever's the matter?'

Kate turned towards the sound to see Miss Alice Clark approaching. A stern-looking Mr Clements was striding behind her, followed by a scared-looking Jeannie. Kate felt her shame increase as Miss Clark came to stand by her brother Roger. Now two of the Clarks directors were witnessing her humiliation. She was more upset about Miss Clark, the manager in charge of the Machine Room, being there. The lady had smiled at Kate occasionally as she'd inspected the operations while they worked, but she had never had much to do with her as Mr Briars oversaw Jeannie and Kate's section.

'Ah, Alice,' said Mr Clark, pointing towards Kate. 'I believe this young woman works in the Machine Room?'

'Yes, that's right. It's Kate Davis, isn't it? Mr Briars speaks very highly of you. Are you all right, dear?'

Kate felt her mouth drop open in shock as Miss Clark addressed her directly. She had thought the woman didn't even know her. After all, there were 300 women and girls in the Machine Room. She had no idea Mr Briars had discussed her with Miss Alice.

'She's upset, Miss Clark,' said Jeannie, putting her arm around Kate.

Her squeeze of Kate's arm brought her out of her shock and she found her voice again. 'I don't mean no trouble, Miss Clark,' she sobbed, so scared they were all going to lose their jobs she couldn't think straight. 'I'm a good girl. Really I am. I work hard and do what I'm told.'

Miss Clark looked confused. 'I'm sure you do.' She looked at Mr Clark. 'Is she in trouble, Roger?'

'I don't believe so. But I would appreciate it if you would kindly take her and her friend for a cup of tea and ask them to tell you their side of this story.'

'Yes, of course. Right away. Come along, girls.'

Kate felt a strong arm around her waist and heard Miss Clark's gentle voice as she urged her to move. 'Come on now, Kate. Let's get a nice cup of tea and get to the bottom of this, eh?'

As she was led away, she heard Mr Clark tell Mr Clements that he needed him to be a witness and take notes while he talked to the others. When her pa tried to protest, he was cut short.

'You shall have your say, man,' said Mr Clark. 'But so shall your children. I will know the truth of this. Lying, profanity and violence will not be tolerated. Do I make myself clear?'

Kate didn't hear their responses before Miss Clark led the girls into Mr Clark's office, known to everyone as the Number One Office, and called for someone to bring some sweet tea.

* * *

Over the next half an hour, Alice Clark gently got the whole story from Kate, with encouragement from Jeannie. Now, the girls were left in the room, sipping their tea while Miss Clark went off to report to her brother.

'Do you want one of these biscuits?' asked Jeannie, pointing to the plate that had been brought in on the tea tray.

Kate shook her head, but her stomach rumbled. Jeannie tutted and pushed the plate towards her. 'Eat one,' she ordered. 'I'll bet you haven't eaten all day, have you?'

She shrugged as she gave in and reached for a biscuit. 'There wasn't a crust in the house this morning,' she admitted. 'The Floozy said she didn't have money for food until Pa got paid. She had enough to buy a jug of cider last night, though, the cow.' She tried to mind her manners, but she couldn't help stuffing the biscuit into her mouth and reaching for another one before she'd even swallowed it. 'Oh, that tastes so nice,' she said, spraying crumbs as she talked with her mouth full. She winced and brushed the crumbs off her chest and the table, hoping Miss Clark wouldn't notice when she came back.

'Want another?' asked Jeannie.

'No. I'm all right,' she said, her mouth empty again. 'I'm so scared, I might be sick if I have any more.' She pushed the plate away. On the wall opposite the stained writing table they were sitting around, a stern portrait of William S Clark stared down at them, as did the sepia photographs of the company's founders, brothers Cyrus and James Clark. They all looked very serious and Kate fidgeted in her seat, wishing to be anywhere but here in the Number One Office. It wasn't her place. 'What if we're all sacked?' she whispered, wishing the images of the Clark men didn't seem to be judging her for being there. She looked away from them, looking to her friend for reassurance. 'Well, me and Fred. Not you, Jeannie. You've done nothing wrong.'

'Neither have you,' she said. 'None of this is your fault.'

Kate shrugged. Jeannie no doubt thought she was pathetic, letting things get like this without standing up for herself. She didn't understand how hard it was to stand up to her pa, especially now that the Floozy was there, egging him on. He'd never been a loving father, but he hadn't been so bad when her ma was alive. Ma had protected Kate from the worst of it, she realised now.

'If Pa's sacked, he'll kill me, for sure.'

'Your brothers won't let him.'

'But they might sack Fred as well. He's got a wife and children to support. How will he cope? And what if Mr Clark contacts George's boss and gets him sacked? His missus is expecting again. Oh, lord, they'll all have to leave Somerset.' She stood up, her chair clattering to the floor behind her. 'The Clarks will make sure no one will give them a job and it's all my fault!'

Jeannie stood and pulled her round to face her, holding her firmly by her shoulders. She gave her a little shake. 'Stop it, Kate. You're getting hysterical. The Clarks aren't like that. They're fair people, and anyway, you know George works for his father-in-law. He's never going to sack him.'

She couldn't respond – couldn't breathe. Jeannie gave her another shake, stronger this time. 'Calm down. You mustn't take on so. Getting in a state isn't going to make anything any better.'

Kate finally managed to take a deep, shaky breath. Jeannie was right. It wouldn't help anyone if she was a hysterical mess when Miss Clark came back in. 'Sorry,' she said, taking another breath and trying to stop the shaking.

'It's going to be all right, Kate. You have to have faith. You've been honest with Miss Alice and your brothers will make sure Mr Roger knows what's what, I'm sure.' She pulled Kate into a hug. 'If this mess is anyone's fault, it's mine, isn't it? I'm the one who interfered and wrote to Peg. I'm so sorry, Kate. I never for a moment thought it would end up like this. I know how you hate anyone knowing your business.'

Kate had buried her tear-stained face into Jeannie's shoulder, but now she looked up at her friend. Jeannie had shed tears while they were talking to Miss Alice as well. 'I know you meant well,' she said, touching her cheek. 'You're such a good friend. But… what happens when I get home? Pa's already spitting mad. If he's had a telling-off from Mr Clark as well as a beating from George, he's sure to take it out on me.'

Jeannie looked worried for a moment, but then her face cleared and she shook her head. 'No. Your brothers promised he wouldn't be able to. They've got a plan. I'm sure of it. Peg won't have let them just pile in and make things worse, I know she wouldn't.'

Kate was doubtful. She didn't know her brothers that well these days, not since they left home when they married, which was years ago, when she was still at school. Oh, she saw them when they'd popped round to see Ma, especially during her last illness, and she'd visited them and their families sometimes – usually taking round something from Ma that Pa didn't know about, like something she'd knitted for one of the children, or a pie when they had a glut of apples, or some bramble jam. They were nice enough, but she wasn't as close to them as she was to Peg.

'What I don't understand,' Jeannie went on, 'was why you didn't tell Peg what was going on. She'd have helped you.'

Kate sighed. She knew she could have told Peg. But she had enough going on in her life and if she and Will had taken Kate with them to Lincolnshire, they wouldn't have had room for Louisa as well. As Peg was going to raise their friend's baby as her own, it was more important for Lou to be there than Kate. But she couldn't tell Jeannie all that without giving away a secret that wasn't hers to tell. Instead, she sighed again and shook her head.

'I didn't want to worry Peg, not while... the baby, you know?'

Jeannie looked stricken. 'Oh, no, Kate. I didn't think. I should have thought. I was just so worried about you and I was sure Peg would want to know. I'm so sorry. I hope I haven't made things difficult for her.'

This time, it was Kate who hugged Jeannie. 'It's all right. What's done is done. I'm sure Peg will be all right. I just couldn't see what she could do all that way away, so I didn't see the point in bothering her. Come on, I expect Miss Alice will be back soon. I might have another one of those biscuits.' The lord only knew when she'd get to eat again. She picked up her tumbled chair and sat down.

She'd just finished eating her third biscuit when Miss Clark returned. She smiled when she saw their worried faces. 'I'm pleased to say the matter has been resolved to everyone's satisfaction,' she announced, placing a brown envelope on the table in front of Kate. 'Your wages, dear.'

Kate stared at it, afraid to touch it.

'Now, I understand that your father has agreed that you shall collect your own wages from now on and the wages department has been informed of this.' She sat down opposite Kate, nudging the envelope towards her. 'It's all right. Take it. You've earned it.'

Kate blinked back tears as she touched it, feeling the outline of some coins inside. But she still didn't pick it up. 'Thank you, Miss Clark. But I'll have to hand it over the minute I get indoors anyway,' she whispered.

'Ah, well. About that,' she said. 'It appears that your brothers were aware that might be the case and they have informed us that you won't be living at your father's house from now on. I'm told your father agreed.'

Kate looked up, her eyes going wide. 'He's throwing me out?'

Miss Clark looked sympathetic. 'Not quite, my dear. I get the impression that your brothers made other arrangements for you before he had the opportunity to do so.'

'What other arrangements? Neither of them have got any room.'

'So I understand. But I'm told that your sister's mother-in-law is in need of a companion now that her remaining son has moved to Lincolnshire to work. She has agreed that you will lodge with her at her cottage in The Mead.'

'Oh, my word,' Jeannie said, smiling. 'Of course! Mrs Searle will see you right, Kate. She'll love you like one of her own.'

'I'm going to live with Betty?' she asked, looking from one to the other, barely able to understand what they were saying.

Miss Clark nodded. 'That's right. You'll have to pay your way, of course. But be reassured, my dear, your new landlady is a good woman who will not seek to profit from you as your own father did. I can vouch for her. I am acquainted with the lady; she worships at the Friends' Meeting House. You'll be welcomed in her home and will have your own money at last, without fear of abuse.'

Kate nodded, fresh tears falling, only this time they were tears of relief and happiness. 'I know her. She's lovely.' She scrubbed at her face. 'I'll be able to save up and buy Ma a headstone,' she said. 'Oh, thank you, Miss Clark. You don't know what this means to me. I'll work so hard for you, I promise.'

Miss Clark smiled. 'You already do, my dear. I may not have the opportunity to speak to everyone in the Machine Room, but I am aware of you and your supervisor keeps me up to date with your progress. Just keep on doing the good work you already do and I shall be satisfied.' She stood up. 'Now, your brothers have escorted your father home and will be collecting your belongings for you. They didn't think you would want to go back to a place where you have been so mistreated.'

Kate blew out a relieved breath. 'I don't,' she agreed.

'Then I suggest that you go directly to Mrs Searle's residence.'

'I'll go with her, Miss Clark,' said Jeannie, putting an arm around Kate's shoulders. 'Don't forget your pay packet, love.' She pointed to the envelope on the table.

Kate picked it up, almost bursting into tears again at the reassuring weight of it. 'Thank you, Miss Clark,' she said. 'And thank you, Jeannie. If you hadn't...' She shook her head as Jeannie kissed her cheek.

'You'd do the same for me,' she said. 'Now come on. We've taken up enough of Miss Clark's time. Thank you for the tea and biscuits, ma'am.'

'You're welcome. Now off you go. I wish you well in your new home, Kate. I'm thankful that you have such a good friend and siblings who love you. I shall pray for you all.'

21

At Betty Searle's modest cottage in The Mead, Kate was greeted like a long-lost daughter and swept into a hug.

'Come on in, my lovely girl. Oh, you've been in the wars, haven't you? If I'd known before now, I'd have given that pa of yours a piece of my mind. He's always been a shifty one, that one – I told your ma not to marry him, but he sweet-talked her into it and then she'd made her bed.' She shook her head. 'She was a wonderful friend and she had such a time of it with him. But she always said her children made it all worthwhile.' The older woman touched her cheek. 'She loved you so much and you gave her such joy, Katie, girl. Now, you're not to worry about a thing. You're welcome to call this your home for as long as you want, you hear me? I loved your ma like a sister, so that would make me your auntie, wouldn't it?'

Kate, nodded, smiling through her tears. 'Can I call you Auntie?' she asked.

'If you want to, lass, I'd be honoured to answer to that. Although I won't be offended if you call me Betty. Just don't go bothering with addressing me as Mrs Searle, eh?'

She ushered both girls into the cottage, where George's pregnant wife Ada waited. She was sitting in a chair by the range, her feet on a footstool.

'Ada,' said Kate. 'Are you all right?'

'I'm fine, love. Betty has been spoiling me while we waited for you. My ankles are a little swollen, so she insisted on me putting me feet up.' She sighed. 'I don't get much chance with little Georgie running around all the time. But he's off with Fred's missus, Vi, at their place. We thought you'd appreciate some peace and quiet when you got here.' She studied Kate's face. 'Was it really bad?'

Kate sank down on to her knees beside her sister-in-law while Jeannie followed Mrs Searle's – or rather *Auntie Betty's* – directions and sat at the table. 'It was awful,' she confessed. 'I thought we was going to get the sack. Pa was horrible and George hit him in front of Roger Clark.'

Ada groaned. 'The idiot. Has he been carted off to jail? If he has, I'll kill him.'

Jeannie giggled. 'No, he's all right, Ada.'

'Oh, my word,' said Auntie Betty. 'What a to-do. I don't suppose Mr Clark took kindly to any of that.'

Jeannie fanned her hands in front of her face. 'It's been a time of it, I can tell you. But Miss Alice came and was so kind, wasn't she, Kate?'

Kate nodded, still finding it hard to believe the events of the past hour.

'It sounds like it,' said Ada, looking worried. 'So long as my George didn't make it any worse.'

'He didn't,' said Kate, smiling up at her. Now that she was away from it all, she was beginning to feel better and thankful that her brothers had turned up. 'Him and Fred were heroes. I'd never have had the nerve to stand up to Pa without them.' She frowned as she thought of something. 'I just hope Pa's not causing trouble with them now. You know, since they left the factory. He didn't dare really kick off with Mr Roger and Mr Clements there, but you know what he can be like. He'll be gunning for a fight.'

'They'll be fine, lass,' said Auntie Betty. 'Reggie Davis is a coward around real men. Those boys of his are all grown up now and more than capable of bringing him down a peg or two. They haven't before out of deference to your blessed ma. Now she's not here to act as peacemaker, he wouldn't dare kick off.'

There was a knock at the door.

'That'll be them now. Jeannie, love, will you let them in?'

Her brothers came in, each carrying a pillowcase stuffed with Kate's belongings. 'I think we got it all, Katie,' said Fred. 'But if not, let me know and me and George'll go back round there and collect anything that's missing.'

'Thanks so much, lads,' said Kate, getting tearful again as she stood up and took the pillowcases from them. She touched the silver cross on a chain around her neck. 'But this'll do. So long as I've got Ma's necklace and a change of clothes, I don't care about anything else. Most of it is old and past its best anyway.'

He nodded. 'We're only sorry we didn't do something earlier, lass. We knew he'd moved his fancy woman and her little beggars in. We should've made sure you were all right.'

'Yeah,' said George. 'Sorry, sis. I was so disgusted by it all, I swore never to go round there again. I should've, though, to check on you.'

Kate waved their apologies away, although it filled her poor, empty heart with warmth to hear them say so. After weeks of feeling worthless and unloved, she realised her brothers had always loved her. They just hadn't known how to show her. She smiled at them.

'You weren't to know. I didn't want to tell anyone. Jeannie only found out 'cause she came round one day and caught the Floozy throttling me.'

'That madam!' snapped Ada, almost leaping out of her chair in her outrage as Kate's brothers scowled and Betty gasped and touched her own throat. 'How dare she? I've a mind to go round there and give her a taste of her own medicine.'

George stopped his wife from getting up by placing a firm hand on her shoulder. 'Calm down, woman. You're in no condition to be starting a cat fight.'

'No, she's not,' said Betty, crossing her arms over her substantial bosom. 'But rest assured, if I ever see that woman, I shall call her out and tell her what I think of her. I'll not stay quiet and I won't care who hears me. I'm not so old that I can't give that trollop a good slap.'

Kate didn't know whether to laugh or cry. 'Please don't, Auntie,' she said. 'Or you, Ada. She's not worth it. You got me away and I don't have to deal with her again, and that's all I wanted.' She gave a rueful smile. 'And anyway, *she* might be glad to see the back of me, but when Pa realises she's not going to lift a finger at home while her children run riot and make an awful mess, that'll be punishment enough for him.'

Fred laughed. 'It surely will. I don't suppose he ever appreciated anything you did for him. I'd like to be a fly on the wall when he's looking for his supper and she's polishing off his cider instead – like she was when we turned up today.' His smile slipped. 'But if she comes anywhere near you again, I'll make sure she regrets it, Kate. I swear. Same for Pa. That old beggar will rot in hell for what he's done to you and to Ma.'

Kate put her things down in the corner out of everyone's way and went to him, hugging him for the first time she could remember. After a moment of surprise, he returned her embrace.

'Thanks, Fred,' she said, kissing his cheek before turning to

George and hugging him as well. He squeezed her tight as she kissed him too. 'Thanks, George.'

Fred coughed as George let her go. Kate could see that he was getting choked up. She didn't want to embarrass him, so she didn't comment on it.

'Don't you fret now, lads,' said Auntie Betty. 'I'll take care of her. She'll be safe here.'

'It's so kind of you,' said Kate. 'I hate to be such a nuisance.'

'Nonsense, lass. I've been mighty lonely since my Will and Peg went off to Lincolnshire. I'm grateful for the company. Your ma was a good friend to me all her life. Why, she was the first to come round after my dear husband died. Fed me and my boys and helped make the funeral arrangements when I wasn't capable of doing a blessed thing. So her daughter is more than welcome here. And, of course, you're my dear daughter-in-law's sister, so you really are family. This is your home now, Kate, and I'm sure you and I shall get along fine.'

'Well, we'd better be off,' said Ada, rubbing her swollen belly. 'We've got to pick up little Georgie from Vi. He'll be driving her and his cousins round the bend by now.'

George grinned. 'That's my boy,' he said, making them all laugh. 'Thanks ever so much, Mrs S. If you need anything, you must let us know, all right?'

'I will, lad. Thank you. Your ma would be proud of both of you boys today. I know I am.'

George shrugged, looking pleased but a little embarrassed by the older woman's praise. He helped Ada up and she came over to kiss Kate. 'Like George says, if you need anything, you must let us know,' she said. 'We're family, Kate. You can always rely on us, I promise.'

Kate nodded, too full of emotion to speak.

'I'd better be off as well,' said Jeannie. 'Ma will be wondering where I am. Although someone will have told her about the shenanigans, I'm sure.'

After everyone had gone, Kate suddenly felt shy in front of Auntie Betty. She reached into her pocket and brought out her wage packet.

'I have to give you my keep,' she said. 'I don't know how much you want,' She offered her the unopened envelope. 'I don't even know how much is in there.'

Betty looked at the proffered wage packet, her smile gentle. 'How about you spend some of what's in there on a fish supper for both of us tonight and we'll see how we get along over the next few days before we work out how much you pay me, eh? I hear you haven't been eating, so you'll have a proper breakfast with me every day before we both go off to work.' Betty was a deputy to Florrie Bond, the forewoman in the Trimmings Department at Clarks, overseeing the attachment of the buckles, buttons and bows that adorned the fine shoes the company sold. 'You can buy yourself something hot in the canteen for your dinner now you've got your money, and we'll make supper together when we get home. We'll soon get some meat on your bones, lass.' She pinched Kate's cheek lightly and smiled. 'And before you know it, you'll have a line of young men out the door wanting to court you.'

Kate shuddered at the thought. 'I hope not,' she said. 'I've just got my freedom. I'll not be handing it over to another man any time soon.'

Betty nodded, her soft gaze understanding. 'I'm pleased to hear it. But that doesn't mean you can't let a lad take you out dancing now and again.'

Kate thought about Ted and the fun they'd had together before his brother had been killed in the trenches and her ma had died due to her pa's callous neglect. But he'd left her, too. She shook her head, trying to dispel the hurt she always felt when Ted popped into her thoughts.

'Now,' Auntie Betty went on. 'I'll work out how much it costs me to feed you and we'll come to an agreement. But for the first week, I'm regarding you as a welcome guest and I won't take a penny from you – other than that fish supper, of course.' She winked at Kate, smiling. 'How does that sound, love?'

'That sounds like heaven, Auntie,' Kate smiled. 'But then you must tell me what I can do around the house. We're both working, so it's only fair we share the chores at home.'

The older woman gave her a thoughtful look. 'I'm not used to sharing the house with a woman. Apart from fetching and carrying, I didn't let my lads do much. But I confess, splitting the housework and cooking between us will give us both more time to relax than we're used to.' She smiled. 'I rather like the sound of that.'

22

Dear Louisa,

I got your letter the same day that Jeannie wrote and told me about the goings-on with Mr Davis and Kate's brothers at the factory as well. I'd heard about the Floozy – as Jeannie calls his fancy woman – and I told Jeannie to let Peg and Will know what was going on. I'm mighty glad she took my advice and that it all worked out in Kate's favour. Lord, I hate men like Reggie Davis who break their marriage vows and mistreat women. I'm surprised he managed to keep his job, acting out in front of Mr Roger Clark, who hates violence and profanity. But I suppose it's better to keep him fully employed where he won't have a chance to cause trouble or be a burden on anyone else.

Training is getting harder, with more drills and trench-digging practice, day and night. So forgive me that this will be a brief note. But I wanted to let you know how pleased I am that Kate is now living with Mattie's ma. She's a very nice and kindly woman, isn't she? She will see Kate right.

I hope that you are well, and I promise to write a longer letter next time.

Your friend,

Lucas

* * *

Lincolnshire
20 November 1915

Dear Lucas,

Thank you for your note. I hope they're not working you too hard with everything they're making you do, but I suppose that, once you get to France (although I still pray every day that you won't be sent to fight), you'll need to be alert all the time, so I expect they must intend this to be good practice for you to be doing all these things at all hours now. Do try and get rest when you can. I so enjoy getting your letters, but I will understand if you're too busy to write. I'd rather you got the sleep you needed than you were over-tired because you were writing to me instead of getting your head down.

I'm so relieved that Kate has finally managed to escape her bully of a father. She tells me she's very happy with Mattie's ma and they get along like a house on fire. I'm also relieved that Mrs S has someone to keep her company. I know she's been mighty lonely since we lost Mattie, and of course, now that Will is working here in Lincolnshire, she hasn't had any family in Street. All three of us here write to her as often as we can, but it has been hard for her being on her own, we can tell. Now that Kate's there, she sounds more content, for which we're all grateful. I know I'm not related to her, but if things had been different, she would have been my mother-in-law. Anyway, I love her as though she was, because she's a kind and wonderful woman and Mattie loved her. I don't expect to ever have a mother-in-law now, and none would be as nice as she is, anyway.

All is well here. The cottage is looking cosy, and there's a big enough garden to grow a good crop of vegetables. Peg and I have been clearing the ground – it was full of weeds – and working out what seeds we need and when we should plant them. I can't tell you how satisfying it is! It's a shame that winter will soon be here and we won't be able to grow much until spring.

Will says that the machines he's building should shorten the war as the Hun will run off like headless chickens when they see what they can do. But in the meantime, the Kaiser continues to order his navy to sink our merchant ships, so we are facing shortages. Peg says growing our own vegetables will at least mean we can put food on the table. They're thinking about building a chicken coop so we can have fresh eggs and meat as well.

I haven't heard from my parents, although I get little snippets of news from Jeannie, Kate and Mrs S. Apparently, my father helped Mr Roger Clark deal with Kate's pa. Fred told Peg that Pa warned Mr Davis that if he didn't leave Kate alone, he'd recommend to Mr Clark that he be sacked immediately. I'm quite proud of him for that.

Well now, you must get your rest, soldier! Take care, Lucas, and stay safe.

Your friend,

Louisa

23

———

The Machine Room was full of the rumble and whine of machines working at full capacity. In the lining maker's end, where Jeannie and Kate worked, the girls were rushing to get as many pieces stitched as they could before the end of the shift. Jeannie knew that if she could finish a few dozen more, her next payday would be really good. But she had to get her numbers checked and approved by Mr Briars before the chits were sent to the wages office after the hooter went at a quarter to six.

But even as she rushed, she made sure to concentrate and get it just right. Any mistakes, and her work would be rejected, she wouldn't get the numbers, she'd be paying for wasted thread, and she'd be in Mr Briars's bad books as well. She really wanted the extra money so she could get Lucas a few little treats. His training was nearly over – just a couple of weeks to go, now. She still prayed night and day for peace to be declared so that he could come home without having to fight. But, if he had to go, she wanted him to go with loving thoughts of home and family to sustain him – to make him remember what he'd left behind so that he would do every-thing he could to make sure he came back to them.

She glanced sideways at Kate on the machine next to hers for a moment as she pulled a completed lining from her machine and reached for the next set of pieces to stitch together. Her friend was also putting in the effort. Since she had started managing her own money, she was delighted by the weight of her weekly pay packet. It did Jeannie's heart good to see her friend flourish now that she was no longer dependent on her selfish pa. Kate looked up as she, too, finished a liner and caught Jeannie's eye. They both grinned and turned back to their work.

They both left the Machine Room with a spring in their step when the shift ended. Jeannie linked arms with Kate as they set off down the High Street towards The Cross. Jeannie was going in the same direction for just a few steps because she had persuaded her ma to go to the Friends' Meeting House this afternoon with their elderly neighbour. Folk who could get there were gathered to pray for peace. She'd promised to meet them there and walk them home.

'I got my best numbers yet today,' said Kate, all smiles.

Jeannie squeezed her arm as they halted by the gate to the Meeting House. 'And you can spend it all,' she said, making Kate laugh. She was relieved to see her friend happy again. She was so glad that Lucas had suggested she write to Peg so that Kate could be rescued from her awful situation. 'We should go to the picture house in Glastonbury tomorrow night. We could both do with a treat.'

'Good idea,' said Kate, her eyes sparkling. 'Oi,' she called out to the crowd around her, all making their way home from Clarks and the late-autumn twilight. 'Anyone know what's showing at the picture house?'

'Charlie Chaplin,' someone replied.

Jeannie clapped her hands. 'Oh, yes, that'll do. I could do with a giggle.'

A lad who'd worked in the Cutting Room with Lucas sidled up next to the girls. 'I'll take you, Jeannie, and my mate can take your friend.'

Jeannie laughed. It wasn't the first time he'd tried his luck. Much as she longed for a sweetheart, this lad wasn't for her. She wanted a true love to marry and have children with and he wasn't the sort of fellow she would want to spend time with. 'I don't think so, Sid. Lucas warned me about you.'

'Aw, come on, Jeannie. You know what big brothers are like. I'm a good catch, y'know.' He winked, sending Jeannie into fits of giggles.

Sid was the older brother of Doris, the girl who she'd caught canoodling with her then sweetheart Douglas at a dance at the Crispin Hall a few months back. It had been the end of that romance, that was for sure. The idea that Jeannie might now have any interest in Doris's brother was laughable. She could just imagine his sister's reaction if she did.

'I'm sure you are,' she said when she'd stopped laughing. 'But I promised him I wouldn't let you sweet talk me the minute his back was turned.'

He shrugged and turned to Kate. 'What about you, then, gorgeous? Want to go with me?'

Jeannie huffed out her indignation at the ease at which he'd changed his focus to her friend. It just went to show he wasn't the kind of chap she would want to get involved with.

Kate looked him up and down then shook her head. 'Sorry. Not interested.'

He frowned. 'Why not?' he demanded, puffing out his chest. 'Like I said, I'm a good catch, me.'

Jeannie knew that Kate had sworn off men. She didn't want to find herself beholden to someone who could take her wages and mistreat her like her pa had done. She also suspected she was still hurting from Ted's sudden disappearance. Jeannie had no doubt some girls would find Sid handsome, with his slicked-back, dark hair and broad shoulders, although she didn't think he was that attractive. But he was on a hiding to nothing with Kate. Jeannie was glad – he wasn't as much of a catch as he claimed and she didn't fancy him at all. He was far too cocky for her liking. Lucas said he was a braggart – telling anyone who would listen in the Cutting Room which girls he'd kissed. To her mind, handsome is as handsome does, and being indiscreet like that was bordering on downright ugly. No, he was definitely not going to take her or Kate to the pictures and then tell all and sundry that she was easy.

Kate shrugged. 'I don't need a boy to take me to the pictures. I can pay my own way.'

Jeannie heard the pride in her friend's voice and smiled.

'You'd probably end up paying for him as well,' called one of the girls as she walked past them. 'Sid's not known for his generosity.'

The younger folks around them laughed while a couple of the older ones muttered their disapproval. Sid's good-natured grin dissolved into a scowl as he glared at the girl who'd spoken.

'I might have been more generous if you hadn't been such a cold fish,' he snapped.

Jeannie gasped at his tone. 'Sid Lambert! I never knew what a rude beggar you were. No wonder my brother warned me off you. That's a horrible way to talk to a girl.'

'I might have been a cold fish,' the girl called over her shoulder, 'but you were clinging onto me like a wet limpet. No wonder you can't find a girlfriend.'

As people laughed at him, Sid went red. 'Blooming women,' he muttered. 'I was only being nice. Don't want to watch stupid films anyway. You're all miserable mares, that's for sure.'

'You're not helping your cause, Sid,' said Kate with a smirk. 'Girls want to be wooed, not slobbered over and insulted.'

'Bugger off,' he snapped and walked away, his laughing friend following behind.

Jeannie giggled. 'His chum is going to rib him for that performance.'

'Good,' said Kate. 'Stupid fool. Thinks he's God's gift. Even I've heard about that one.'

'I'd better see how Ma is getting on,' said Jeannie, gesturing towards the Meeting House. 'I'll tell her we're off out tomorrow.'

'She won't mind you leaving her for the evening?'

Jeannie sighed. 'Probably. But it's about time the twins took a turn keeping her company. They've been out with their pals every night this week. I need a break.'

'What have they been doing? It must be too dark to play football.'

'Lord knows,' she shrugged. 'Just hanging around and gossiping like girls, I reckon.' She frowned. 'I think they might have been drinking cider while they're out, although they swear they haven't. I told them, if I catch them doing it, I'll bash them just like Lucas would. They know Ma is dead against drinking.'

Kate looked sympathetic. 'Well, let's hope you're wrong. There's nothing worse than drunks, I can tell you. Pa was never so bad as when he was in his cups. And don't get me started about that Floozy. She was vicious when she'd had a few.'

Jeannie shuddered. 'You're well rid of them, love.'

'I know. I thank God every day for sending me to Auntie Betty,' she smiled. 'Anyway, you see to your ma and we'll go out tomorrow. We'd better go straight from work or we won't get in.'

'Good idea.'

* * *

In the end, they barely made it to the picture house in Glastonbury in time for the first feature. Jeannie had had a blazing row with the twins when she got home, all carried out in hissing whispers so that Ma didn't realise they were fighting. She'd only managed to get them to agree to stay with Ma the next evening by threatening to tell Lucas exactly how little they did round the house since he'd gone away. She'd meant it too. She was heartily sick of asking them to do things and then having to end up doing it all herself because they'd sneaked off and Ma was too poorly to deal with it.

The double feature of Charlie Chaplin films was just what she needed. She couldn't remember the last time she'd laughed so much her stomach hurt. As they left the picture house in the Town Hall building, the two friends linked arms and started striding down Magdalene Street towards Street Road. It was only a couple of miles' walk back to the village, but the evening had turned cold and the dark night was only illuminated by the moon when it took the trouble to occasionally peek out from behind the clouds, so she wasn't looking forward to it. But she supposed it was the price they had to pay for a night out. There were a few others walking the same way. She noticed that Sid wasn't amongst them.

Kate was still giggling over the films. 'That was hilarious,' she said. 'I'm so glad we came.'

'Me too,' said Jeannie. 'I don't know how he does it.'

'Me neither. When he climbed the outside of that building to rescue that girl from the fire... oh, my lord, my heart was beating like a drum.'

The crowd leaving the picture house thinned as they left Glastonbury town behind and the high, red-brick walls of the Morlands sheepskin factory came into view, the hulking, stinking buildings looming over the road in the dark. The girls hurried past, trying not to breathe in the stench of urine and chemicals that hung around the place. They talked about the films they'd watched, giggling over Chaplin's antics.

'I'm glad we didn't go with any boys,' said Kate. 'That Sid would probably have talked all the way through the film, bragging and strutting like a peacock.'

'I know. He'd probably be right handsy as well. Thinks he's a card, that one. But Lucas told me he's a nasty piece of work. Lazy, too.' She shuddered. 'I'd hate to have him kiss me. I keep thinking about what that girl said.'

Kate laughed. 'Yeah. A wet limpet. It sounds revolting.'

'It certainly does.'

They crossed Pomparles Bridge over the River Brue. They could see the lights from the cottages on the edge of Street village now.

'Lou would have loved this evening,' said Jeannie. 'I miss her.'

Kate sighed. 'Yeah. Me too. But she's better off with Peg and Will.'

'But is she?' Jeannie asked. 'I can't help thinking it's time she came home and got on with her life. Mattie wouldn't want her to mourn him forever, would he? I mean, what if she ended up like the old queen, forever in black and miserable?'

'It's not been that long. She's entitled to grieve for a while yet, isn't she? Anyway, she promised to stay and help Peg until after the baby's born.'

'When is it due?'

'March, I think. So I'm thinking she won't be back before Easter.'

'She'll miss Christmas and the wassail in January.' Although Jeannie's Quaker family never made much of Christmas, the three girls had always enjoyed the wassailing celebrations in the orchards, when the community took part in ancient ceremonies to wake up the apple trees. Lou in particular had loved it. 'It won't be the same without her.'

Kate squeezed her arm. 'She'll be back for next time. We need to let her do what she has to do.'

Jeannie frowned into the darkness. She felt as though something was off, but she couldn't put her finger on it. Kate always seemed to get a bit tense whenever Lou was mentioned. 'She is all right, though, isn't she? Her letters are... I don't know. She seems to be trying too hard to convince me she's content – like she's trying to convince herself.'

Kate sighed again. 'I don't know, Jeannie,' she said. 'I don't think she's particularly happy, but how else is she going to be? She needs time, and being away from here and the pressure her parents were putting her under. I hope she'll be all right eventually. But it will take a long time. Mattie was everything to her. It can't be easy. But in the meantime, Peg and Will are looking after her, don't you fret.'

They reached on the edge of Street and the turn-off for The Mead. Kate hugged Jeannie and kissed her cheek. 'Try not to worry about her. It will all work out, I'm sure. Now, do you want me to walk with you to your house?' The Musgrove family home was at West End, at the other end of the long High Street.

'No, I'll be all right. It's not far and there's the street lamps all along the High Street now. I'll see you tomorrow.'

Kate turned towards Betty Searle's cottage as Jeannie walked along Glastonbury Road towards The Cross. She hoped Kate was right about Louisa. She also hoped that Louisa would come home soon. It was November now, so Easter seemed a long way away. She sighed. She supposed she was fretting about Lou as a way of trying not to fret about Lucas, but it wasn't working. She missed them both and wished with all her heart that they could both come home now and stay there.

The Cross came in sight. Jeannie, keen to distract herself from her gloomy thoughts, focused on it. She had always thought it was funny that it was called that, because it wasn't a cross – it was a lamp post in the middle of a junction, surrounded by a stone horse trough. She supposed there might have been an ancient cross there long ago, or that the junction was originally called The Crossroads considering it was where the Glastonbury Road met the High Street and Somerton Road crossed it to become Grange Road. She wouldn't be surprised if that was it and the locals had shortened it to The Cross. She wondered who might know the truth of it?

She was so deep in thought that she didn't notice Sid Lambert until he stepped out from the shadow of the Street Inn on the corner. She didn't have time to step back before he grabbed her upper arms.

'Sid! What are you doing?'

'Waiting for you, missy.' He squeezed her arms, bringing his face close to hers. She could smell the sweet cider and stale tobacco on his breath. He must have been drinking in the Street Inn all evening. 'Think you're too good for me, don't you?'

She turned her head to the side, not wanting to breathe in his rank breath. 'Of course not. I'm just not looking to walk out with anyone at the moment. I'm too busy, what with Lucas being away and my ma being poorly.'

'You didn't have to embarrass me, though, did you? Did you and that Kate Davis have a good laugh at my expense? Every other beggar who heard you did.'

She tried to step back, half nervous, half irritated by his boorish behaviour, but he held her fast. 'I'm... I'm sorry if you thought that,' she said. 'I just spoke the truth.'

He shook her, his hands hurting her arms. 'You damn well laughed at me!' he shouted. 'You and your stuck-up friend.'

Jeannie yelped, struggling to get away. But he was too strong for her.

'Made me look a right fool, you did. You should show a man more respect. Don't know what you've got to be so proud of. Them brothers of yours ain't no saints, you know. What would your mother think if she knew, eh?'

'I don't know what you mean. Let me go!'

He laughed, shaking her again. Her arms would surely be bruised, his grip was so tight and painful. She looked around, wishing someone could come out of the inn to save her, but afraid that anyone who frequented the place would be just like Sid and would make matters worse for her. What if it was Mr Davis who came out?

'Not until you've paid for making me look like a fool,' he snarled. 'I reckon a few kisses will do for now. Be sure to tell your brother Lucas. I hope he eats a bullet, like that Mattie Searle did.'

Jeannie wanted to scream, but if no one had come to see what was going on with Sid yelling, she didn't think it would do any good. *Oh, God, why isn't Lucas here to protect me?*

As the thought slipped from her terrified mind and Sid's face got closer to hers, she turned her head again and closed her eyes tight. In that moment, she realised that Lucas *had* made sure she was protected. He'd told her exactly what to do in situations like this. Behind her closed eyelids, she could see his face, hear his voice telling her what she had to do. But could she do it? The heat of Sid's cider-laden breath on her cheek decided it for her.

She forced her body to go limp so that Sid had to hold her up or let her fall. As she'd been fighting against him since he'd grabbed her, this confused him, just as Lucas had said it would.

He raised his head and pulled back a little to get a better look at her in the faint light coming from the inn's windows. As soon as she had enough room, she brought her knee up, as hard as she could, hitting him in the privates.

Lucas hadn't told her what would happen then. Sid let out a howl that nearly burst her eardrums as his grip on her loosened. She stumbled back, landing on her backside as he dropped to the floor, curling up in a ball as he gasped and cursed.

The door of the inn opened and a man came out. Jeannie caught a glimpse of his face in the light of the doorway. She recognised him.

'What's going on?' he asked, his voice deep and firm.

If he hadn't just come out of the inn, Jeannie might have been relieved to see him. But seeing him there made her realise that he was another drinker.

'She bloody...' Sid gasped for breath, still cradling himself. 'Me knackers,' he hissed.

Jeannie scrambled to her feet as the man approached, ignoring his outstretched hand. She didn't want anyone touching her right now. She just wanted to get home to Ma. But she wasn't about to let Sid get away with accusing her of anything.

'I told him to let me go and he wouldn't,' she said, her voice high and breathless, tears not far from the surface. 'I had to knee him to get him to leave me alone and I'd do it again if he comes near me.'

The man frowned. 'Are you all right?' he asked her.

'Bugger her,' snapped Sid, his voice whiny. 'She bloody attacked me! I'm the one who's not all right.'

The man looked at the drunken lad on the ground. Jeannie couldn't see his expression, but his voice was laced with contempt. 'Watch your mouth. Looks like self-defence to me. You should have let her go when she told you.'

'She was asking for it!' he yelled, rolling to his knees and groaning as he tried to straighten up. 'Bitch.' He looked up at Jeannie, his face contorted with pain and anger. 'You're going to pay for this. I'll get you, Jeannie Musgrove, see if I don't.'

'Do you want to call the constable?' the man asked her, standing between Sid and Jeannie. 'I'm Thomas, by the way. Tom,' he said quietly, his voice gentle. 'I've seen you in the Machine Room.'

She nodded. She'd seen him too, repairing machines. She was tempted to let him call the constable. Sid had hurt her and frightened her. But Ma would be worried if she didn't get home soon, and anyway, if she reported this to the law, it would be round the village in no time. She shook her head.

'No. I—'

'Yes,' Sid yelled. 'Get the copper. I want her done for assault and battery.'

Tom turned to Sid. 'Really? You want to tell the constable that you were floored by a girl after she told you to leave her alone? All right. If you want to end up sleeping it off in a cell, that's fine by me.'

Sid, who had been struggling to his feet, froze. He looked up at Tom, who was a good few inches taller than him, and blinked as his cider-soaked brain thought about what he'd said. Jeannie could see that he hadn't considered that the constable might take Jeannie's side against him.

'Bloody constable don't like me,' he muttered. He winced as he straightened a little more. 'But I reckon I'll take my chance. I've been attacked. You saw. I want her locked up.'

'The only one likely to get locked up is you, lad,' said Tom. 'What I see is a frightened woman who defended herself against a drunken brute and I'm happy to report that to the law. Better if you just apologise to the young lady and get yourself home to sleep it off.'

'I ain't apologising to her,' he sneered. 'She's no bleeding lady.'

'It wouldn't mean anything, anyway,' she said, still shaking with a mix of anger, fear and shame. 'Not coming from him. I just want to go home,' she said, not looking at either man. 'And for him to leave me alone.'

'Who are you, anyway?' Sid demanded, giving Tom a filthy look. 'You ain't from these parts. You from Glastonbury?' He spat on the floor, just missing Jeannie's shoes.

She jumped back, disgusted. Tom put out a hand to steady her, but dropped it when she immediately pulled away.

'Northampton,' he said. 'Started at the factory this week. Mechanics Department.'

Sid sneered. 'One of them spanners, are you? Well, you'd better learn not to mess with another man's business, or you'll be kicked back to Northampton sharpish.'

Tom actually smiled at that. Jeannie held her breath as she recognised the danger in his eyes as he observed Sid's strutting, which wasn't much, considering he was still cradling his privates. 'You and whose army? I'm not going anywhere,' he said. 'And if anyone's going to get kicked, it'll be you, lad. If I ever see you mistreat a woman again, I won't just stand by, d'you hear?'

He took a step forward and Sid stumbled back, alarmed. If Jeannie hadn't been so shaken up, she might have laughed at the look on Sid's face. The lad was obviously only brave enough to take on women, not real men. As it was, she just wanted to get away from there and forget this had ever happened.

Sid shrugged, like he wasn't at all rattled. 'I wouldn't touch that cow with a bargepole now. You have her. See if you can get a friendly kiss without her crushing your balls with her bony knees. Led me on, she did.'

'I did not!' gasped Jeannie. She felt her cheeks burn with shame. 'I never would.' She didn't dare look at Tom. No doubt he was thinking there was no smoke without fire. 'You're a filthy liar, Sid Lambert. You jumped out at me in the dark as I walked by. There was nothing friendly about the way you were manhandling me.'

Sid made a lunge for her and she shrieked and jumped back out of his reach. Luckily for her, he was slow on account of the pain he was still feeling – if the hissing and cursing he was doing was any indication – and Tom was right there to grab him by his collar and pull him away from her.

This time, it was Sid who yelped. Tom pushed him backwards until Sid was pinned against the stone trough in the middle of The Cross. 'Enough!' he roared. 'Stop this nonsense right now or I'll knock your block off and then cart you round to the constable myself.'

Jeannie's eyes were wide as she stood there, her arms protectively around her body as she watched this man intimidate Sid, the village braggart. Tom seemed to have grown a foot upwards and outwards in his rage, while Sid had shrunk against the trough, diminished.

She didn't move, paralysed by fear that he was going to beat the living daylights out of Sid. As if sensing her fear, Tom turned his head to look at her, eyes blazing. In that moment, she understood what people meant by the word *passion*. Underneath his quiet exterior, this new man in the village was full of it.

The emotions that swirled through her body as he held her gaze frightened her as much as Sid's heavy-handed assault had done, yet they thrilled her too. She couldn't breathe until he blinked and turned back to Sid and began to speak to him in low tones that she couldn't hear.

The moment she felt able to move, Jeannie took off, running for the safety of home.

It wasn't until she got inside and bolted the door behind her
that she realised she was crying. She was angry, too. At Sid for
manhandling her. At Tom for unnerving her with his passion. And
at Lucas for going away and leaving her vulnerable to men like
them.

24

Lincolnshire

18 December 1915

Dear Lucas,

I can't believe it is only a week until Christmas! In some ways, time drags so slowly, especially when I'm missing Mattie. But other times, it seems to rush past so quickly that I barely have time to catch my breath before another month has gone.

I finally heard from my mother. She sent me a letter saying how disappointed she and Pa are in me for going against their wishes, but that I could go home, although only if I was prepared to follow their rules. I have to confess, I was so happy to see Ma's handwriting, but then her words left me hurt, angry and feeling let down. I'm not sure it will be possible to repair my relationship with my parents. They are so set in their ways, not willing to understand. So I don't know whether I can return to their house. The world is changing and so am I. I feel as though I need to make my own way from now on.

I do want to go back to Street one day, though. I miss my

friends and yes, even working at Clarks! I always enjoyed my job in the Machine Room. It was hard, but the Clarks are fair employers and, from what I'm learning about other factories, the workers there are treated very well indeed. Will is finding it tough at the tank factory. It's not like Clarks at all. Peg says I should be able to get my old job back without any trouble when the time comes for me to return to Street. She's also going to ask Mrs Searle if I can lodge with her like Kate does if I can't reconcile with Ma and Pa. I think I would like that, although the thought of living in the house where Mattie grew up, without him, having to see his beloved mother every day might be more than I can bear. I just don't know if I'm strong enough.

But enough of that. I don't want to be sad when I write to you. Do you remember the performances put on by the Operatic Society? They were such fun. I never used to have the courage to take to the boards myself before, although remember when Jeannie and I helped with making costumes while you and Mattie helped with the scenery and props? Kate says she's thinking of joining the Society chorus and is trying to persuade Jeannie to go with her. It made me smile to think of it as Jeannie isn't one for showing off and would probably hate it, wouldn't she? I do think I might enjoy it now that I'm a little older and wiser, so long as I'm in the back row of the singers! It would be good to bring smiles to people's faces. Peg and I sing all the time, trying to remember old nursery rhymes and songs we sang as children, as well as some of the songs from the performances we've seen. She is going to be a splendid mother and the baby is going to be so well-loved. So when… if I go back to Clarks, I shall go with Kate (and Jeannie if she'll do it) and join the Operatic Society if they'll have me, and remember Peg and the baby every time I sing.

Your training finishes this week, doesn't it? Are you looking forward to going home for Christmas? I know that your ma is desperate to see you and so is Jeannie, who tells me she can't wait to see you. She's got a lot to tell you, I think.

This year will be hard for all of us. I am very grateful to Will and Peg for letting me stay with them. We're going to make the best of it here in this little cottage in Lincolnshire. Will has saved a bottle of his best cider to toast Christ's birthday, even though as a lifelong Quaker, he's never celebrated Christmas in the same way that Peg and I did at Holy Trinity. He said it will be a little taste of home. I know you won't be celebrating either, but I hope you manage to find some joy in the season and in seeing your family.

When you get to Street, be sure to give Jeannie a kiss from me and pass on my regards to your ma and brothers.

I am still praying for a Christmas miracle of peace and hope that you stay safe always.

Your friend, Louisa

* * *

Location Classified Confidential
20 December 1915

Dear Louisa,

Thank you for your letter. Your reminder about the Operatic Society performances had me laughing out loud, so I had to explain to the other lads about them, which made them chuckle as I told them about Mattie and me helping make the scenery. Do you remember that we made the bridge of a ship to represent HMS Pinafore? It was complete with a proper bridge and an enormous ship's wheel and sails hanging from the ceiling so that it looked from the audience as though the cast were on a real vessel. It looked very fine! What you might not know is that, during the dress rehearsal, the wheel fell off and nearly broke one performer's foot, then a sail dropped down over the chorus, knocking them down like skittles! Did Mattie tell you? They were both accidents, but Mattie and me could hardly breath for laughing. It was like watching one of those films by Charlie Chaplin. I'm laughing now as I think of it. We were up half the night with the other scenery makers, putting it right.

Thank you for making me laugh about something so inno-cent, Louisa. I'm afraid the humour here in the camp is rather dark and not something a woman would appreciate.

I do not think I'm going to get the chance to go home for Christmas. They say we may have to be shipped out just a day or so after our passing out parade. They need the fresh blood – sorry, that is the dark humour I was telling you about. I meant to say that they urgently need reinforcements at the front, so we might not get the usual five days' leave before we go. I'm writing to Ma and Jeannie today to warn them. On one hand, I'm heartily sorry that I won't be able to see them one last time before I have to leave for the front, but on the other hand, it might be for the best. It was hard enough, saying goodbye to them when I left for training. This time would be so much harder. I know they'll be upset but I hope that they will understand. Better to get out there and give the Hun a beating so that the war can be over sooner.

I'm sorry that you don't feel able to put things right with your parents. I always thought you were a very close and strong family. I'm not sure what has gone wrong between you, but I hope you'll find a way to get back to how things were before. We all need our families, especially now. But I suppose you have a different family of sorts around you now, with Mattie's brother and Kate's sister. I know Mattie would be pleased that Will and Peg are looking after you if your own ma and pa aren't.

Just two days until our passing out parade. I'm not sure how soon I'll be able to write to you again, especially if we are shipped out straight away. I promise I will write as soon as I can, even if I can't tell you where I am or much of what's going on. Please keep writing to me. The regiment will make sure I get your letters, even if it takes a while for them to get through.

Merry Christmas to you, Louisa, and to Peg and Will, and a Happy and Peaceful New Year.

Your friend, Lucas

* * *

Lincolnshire
22 December 1915

Dear Lucas,

I just got your letter saying you might not get home for Christmas. I promised not to say anything until now because I thought you'd go home and Jeannie could tell you everything herself. But now I feel as though I have to – just as Kate stepped in and helped me, and like Jeannie told Peg when Kate didn't want to worry her about her troubles. That's what friends do, isn't it? We try to help!

If you can get home, Lucas, even if just for a day or a few hours, please, please try to do it. Jeannie's been having an awful time of it. First, the twins won't lift a finger to help and they cheek her all the time. They're out playing football and drinking cider, leaving everything to poor Jeannie. They don't even go to the Meeting House with your ma any more. Jeannie won't write and tell you because she says there's nothing you can do and if *you write to them about it, they'll know she told you and it will make things worse. But, from what Kate tells me, it can't get much worse. Jeannie's exhausted and your ma is upset too. She's missing you so much, and her nerves have never been good, have they? I'm told she spends more and more time in her bed and there's only Jeannie to care for her, on top of her job at the factory, because the twins are always out gallivanting. Kate's doing what she can to help, but she can't persuade the twins to help, either.*

Not only that, but… and I hate to be the one to tell you this, but if you're not going home to find out for yourself, then I believe I owe it to both Jeannie and you to tell you. The fact is, Sid Lambert asked Jeannie out and she turned him down. That was no surprise to anyone. He's far too cocky and Jeannie would never want to walk out with a lad like him. Well, he didn't like it, so a few weeks ago, he waited for her when she was coming home from Glastonbury after a night out at the picture house with Kate. He grabbed her at The Cross after he'd been drinking at the Street Inn.

Now, don't worry. He frightened her good, but she held her own. Kate says Jeannie kneed him hard, just how you taught her to do if a lad wouldn't take no for an answer. Then one of the new engineers came along and restrained Sid while Jeannie got away. Jeannie hasn't said much about it, but Kate says everyone's saying Sid howled like a baby and it soon got round that he'd been bested by a girl. He was a laughing stock and could barely walk for a couple of days. The girls thought Jeannie was a heroine and keep asking her to show them how to do it. I must say, I was mighty proud of her when I heard!

The trouble is, Kate tells me that Sid is still angry about it, almost a month after it happened and is drinking a lot. He shouts and says horrible things to her if he sees her in the village. It's got so that Jeannie doesn't want to go out, apart from to work or to the Meeting House. Jeannie promises me that she's all right. She says she's just too busy looking after your ma to go out, but Kate thinks otherwise.

I'm so sorry to be the bearer of bad news, especially now. But I had thought you would see for yourself what was going on when you went home on leave, and that you'd be able to sort Sid out and make him leave Jeannie alone. I'm wondering whether there's someone at home who might be able to step in and help? If only my pa would talk to me, I'd ask him, but he hasn't answered any of my letters. I don't even know whether he reads them or just throws them on the fire. Kate wanted to ask her brothers, but Jeannie told her not to. Tom, the engineer I mentioned, has asked after Jeannie, according to Kate. He might be willing to help. But Jeannie is so embarrassed that he saw what happened that she won't have anything to do with him and runs off like a scared rabbit whenever she sees him.

I feel so helpless and frustrated. I know she'll be angry with me for telling you, but me and Kate have been counting the days until you went home and now you say you won't be going and I'm sorry... I just thought you should know. Me and Kate will do anything we can to help. But we think it needs a man to sort Sid out. If you can't get there, then I think it's time Kate got her brothers to help. They're mighty grateful to Jeannie for alerting them to Kate's troubles, so I'm sure they'd be more than happy to step in and do what's necessary. Just say the word.

I'm so sorry about this. It's the last thing I wanted to do. But I love Jeannie like a sister and can't bear that she's having such a time of it. I don't know what you can do, if anything, from where you are, but if anyone can find a way to sort this out, I know you can.

Take care and stay safe. I'm praying for you and for Jeannie,
day and night.
Your friend, Louisa

Lucas cursed as he folded the letter and put it back into its envelope. He was furious with the twins for playing up; with Jeannie and Ma for not telling him that they were; with himself for not realising the boys would do something like this. They'd always been spoilt since Pa died in the accident at the factory. He'd done his best to be a father-figure for them, setting the best example he could, but he'd only been a little lad himself when it had happened. He had thought they'd take on some responsibility now that he wasn't there. They weren't little kiddies any more. But, from what Louisa said, they had just gone wild without him being there to keep them in line.

He felt a wave of pain and guilt rush through him. At times like this, he'd turn to Mattie for advice. He'd know what to do. But he was gone. Lucas was on his own and a long way from home. He wished he could rush home and put things right. It was his fault. He shouldn't have left. He knew that now.

But he was stuck. Later today was the passing-out parade and the next day, they set sail for Europe as they were that short of men on the front line. He didn't know where he would end up. If he tried to get home now, he'd be arrested as a deserter.

He put his head in his hands, thinking hard. Then, with a resigned sigh, he pulled out his notepaper and an envelope and started to write.

25

Jeannie and Kate looked up as Sally let out a wail that could be heard above the rumble and clatter of all their machines. Kate rolled her eyes and mouthed, 'She's done it again.'

Jeannie sighed as Mr Briars rushed over to see what all the fuss was about. She only hoped the supervisor could put it right without calling someone from the Mechanics Department. It had been a few weeks now since the incident at The Cross and she'd managed to avoid coming face to face with Tom so far and wanted to keep it like that. He'd actually come to their cottage to ask after her, but she'd hidden in the outhouse so she wouldn't have to talk to him. Ma had scolded her for being so rude, but she couldn't help it. She had no desire to see the man again, knowing he had witnessed her shame that night.

She'd stayed away from Sid as well, although he seemed intent on seeking her out and hurling abuse at her whenever he spotted her. She never responded, not wanting to give him the satisfaction. But his behaviour had been noticed and people had asked questions. She'd told Kate about it the morning after Sid had grabbed her, but she wouldn't discuss it with anyone else.

Kate, bless her, had defended her stoutly when Sid had started spreading horrible rumours about her. Jeannie hadn't wanted to say anything, but Kate had insisted that they put the record straight.

'You don't need to say anything,' she'd said. 'I'll tell 'em he's a drunken beast who shouldn't be allowed out in decent company. You can maintain a dignified silence. Once people know your side of the story, they'll soon see what a lot of hot air and nonsense Sid is spouting.'

Jeannie had wanted to think that people would know her well enough to understand that anyway, but, of course, not everyone did, so she'd been getting some sideways glances from lads and unpleasant comments from the likes of Mrs Howard, the Machine Room's worst gossip, and her friends that made her very uncomfortable. So she'd let Kate tell people what Sid had done and Jeannie had remained above it all. It didn't stop her from feeling embarrassed and ashamed, though, sure that no decent man would want to associate with her now, which was why she didn't want to face Tom.

But her luck was running out. Mr Briars had sent Sally off to get an engineer and Tom was the man she brought back with her. Jeannie kept her head down, trying to focus on her stitching. The last thing she needed was to mess up her work and lose money by wasting thread or to get her finger caught under the needle. She'd done that once and it had hurt like the Devil. That didn't stop her from noticing his progress across the room towards Sally's machine out of the corner of her eye until he was standing just two steps away from her.

She was surprised to notice that he walked with a limp. It broke her concentration for a moment, causing her line of stitching to slip. With an exclamation, she took her foot off the treadle, lifted the needle and pulled the ruined pieces out. She'd have to unpick it and do it again, which was wasted time and thread. She huffed, annoyed with herself and with Tom for distracting her.

Even as she thought it, she realised she was being unfair. He was talking to Mr Briars and working on Sally's machine, taking no notice of Jeannie at all. Poor Sal was standing there, wringing her hands. She tried so hard, but she really hadn't got the hang of the work in the Machine Room. Jeannie suspected she'd be moved to another department soon, which would probably be for the best as the girl barely managed to get more than the minimum number of pieces day workers were expected to complete each shift. She just couldn't seem to speed up enough to switch to the better-paid piece-work rates – every time she tried, she managed to snag up the machine.

'All right, Jeannie?' asked Kate as she pulled a completed liner from her machine, snipping the thread and dropping the perfect piece into her basket with brisk efficiency.

She replied with a brief grimace. 'Missed the line,' she said as she unpicked her stitching.

'Bad luck.' Kate turned back to her work.

Jeannie got on with her work, determined to catch up. Any extra money she could earn was vital these days, as the twins weren't really earning much on day rates and the money Ma received from the army for Lucas wasn't as much as his regular wages at Clarks. He'd proved to be a good clicker, cutting out the leather pieces for the shoe uppers. He worked hard and fast, so his pay had reflected that. They should be spending less money on food without Lucas at home, but the twins seemed to be putting on a growth spurt and were eating them out of house and home. Jeannie was giving a bigger portion of her wages to Ma as a result.

With a sigh, she pushed those thoughts out of her mind. She was still aware of Tom as he bent over Sally's machine. Mr Briars had sent Sally off on an errand and was watching him with a grim expression. When he straightened, Jeannie looked up and saw him smile at the foreman and say, 'All done, sir.'

His smile made her blink rapidly as her pulse rate increased. He really was a nice-looking man, probably in his mid-twenties. But he was also, she reminded herself, the one who'd seen her on her backside in the middle of the road after Sid had tried it on. She felt herself redden as she turned away just as he caught her eye. She was relieved that he was immediately distracted by Mr Briars.

Jeannie had finished unpicking the crooked seam, so she set to, restitching it carefully and moving on to the next piece. She didn't look up until Tom was walking away. Again, she noticed the slight limp and wondered about it for a moment before she caught herself and turned her attention back to her work.

* * *

'Wasn't that chap who came to fix Sally's machine the one who rescued you from Sid?' asked Kate as they entered the canteen.

Jeannie sighed. She'd hoped Kate hadn't noticed, but she supposed it was too much to ask. Kate noticed everything. She was annoying like that.

'Yes,' she said. 'What of it?'

'He kept glancing your way,' she said with a smile.

'Did he? I wouldn't know. I was busy.'

Kate nudged her shoulder as they joined the line for hot food. 'Are you sure you didn't notice him? It's not like you to miss your line.'

Jeannie gave her friend one of her looks – the ones that no longer had any effect at all on the twins, much to her annoyance. 'I noticed his limp, that's all. It surprised me.'

Kate nodded. 'I heard he was injured in Flanders.'

'He's a soldier?'

'Not any more, obviously.'

Jeannie's heart hurt as she thought of the danger her brother was about to face. What if he was injured, like Tom? She said nothing as she selected her food and paid for it. She felt bad spending the money, but Ma had insisted she had a hot dinner to keep her strength up.

Kate seemed to read her mind, because as soon as they sat down, she said, 'Better to be injured but come home intact than end up like poor Mattie,' she said.

Jeannie glared at her. 'You're not helping. That doesn't make me feel any better at all.'

Kate had the decency to look regretful as she apologised. 'Sorry, love. Aren't you expecting Lucas home in a day or two?'

She sighed and shook her head, her appetite gone. 'He doesn't think he can get home now. They're talking of sending them to the front straight away. Ma's beside herself. I just keep praying that they at least give him a twenty-four-hour pass before they go.'

'Oh, no! I'm so sorry, Jeannie.' Kate put a hand over hers on the table. 'That's such a shame, especially as you'd hoped he'd be with you for Christmas Day.'

She shrugged. 'We'll just have to cope, somehow. Although I expect Ma will cry all day and I might just join her once I've cooked our dinner. The twins will be no use at all.'

Kate grimaced. 'I could slap them, I really could. Stupid boys. Don't they realise that real men look after their families rather than sit on their backsides and expect to be waited on?' She crossed her arms over her chest. 'That's why you won't ever catch me running round after a man. I'm going to be like Miss Alice Clark. Why, she's in her forties now and has no need of a man to make her life complete. I'll be like her – stay single and in control of my own life.'

Alice Clark was the only female director of the company –

appointed by her father alongside her brothers. These days, she was in overall charge of the 300 women and girls in the Machine Room, as well as the Trimmings and Turnshoe Departments and the Home Order Office. She was also active in the Quaker movement, so Jeannie saw a lot of her and other members of the Clark family at the Meeting House. While Jeannie admired Miss Clark, she had no desire to be like her. Jeannie couldn't stop hoping that one day, she'd meet a nice man and make a good marriage. But she didn't expect it to be any time soon, not with everything that had been going on. She was far too busy with Ma and the twins to think about courting. Nevertheless, she understood Kate's point of view. She'd been bullied in her own home for most of her life, then Ted had suddenly disappeared to foreign parts, never to be heard again, so why would she want to give another man the chance to let her down?

'Good for you, love,' she said. She picked up her fork. 'Anyway, I'm sure we'll manage without Lucas. When he gets married one day, he'll have his own house and we'll have to manage then, won't we? So this shouldn't be any different.' She wasn't sure whether she was trying to convince Kate or herself and she didn't dare give a voice to the fear that one day, she might be left at home, a dried-up spinster, with the sole responsibility of caring for their ma, any hope of love and a family of her own gone forever. She had hoped that the twins would grow up into decent men, and that their and Lucas's wives might lend a hand with Ma. But given their recent behaviour, she was beginning to doubt if they'd ever grow up, and no sensible girl would take them on. And if Lucas didn't come home from the war...

'Let's eat up, or we'll be late back.'

Walking back to the Machine Room from the canteen, the girls passed Tom. Jeannie hoped he wouldn't notice them as he walked along, hands in pockets, deep in thought. But Kate had other ideas.

'Good job this morning, Tom,' she called out.

He stopped and looked up at the sound of her voice. He recognised the two girls and gave them a polite smile. 'Just doing my job,' he said.

'We keep trying to help Sally, but she's a bit of a disaster on them machines,' Kate went on, stopping in front of him. 'Isn't she, Jeannie?'

Jeannie nodded. Too well-mannered to ignore him completely, she glanced up at him to find his gaze on hers. He had clear blue eyes that regarded her calmly. She'd always thought blue eyes were cold, but his seemed to radiate warmth, making her cheeks heat up.

'I heard Mr Briars telling her she was going to be moved to another job where she can do less damage,' Kate said cheerfully. 'I think Sally's quite relieved. I expect you will be too, not being called up to the Machine Room all the time.'

Kate's words distracted him and he looked away from Jeannie. She was relieved because she seemed to be paralysed whenever he looked at her. First back at The Cross, and now right in the middle of the factory grounds. She didn't like it. Not one little bit. She turned away, unwilling to look at him again.

'Come on, Kate,' she said. 'Or we'll be late back.'

'All right. Bye, Tom!'

Jeannie hurried back to the Machine Room with Kate close at her heels. She breathed a sigh of relief as they left Tom behind and she couldn't feel his intense gaze on her any more.

'I think he likes you,' sang Kate.

'Don't be daft,' she denied, pulling her apron on over her blouse and skirt and securing it with shaking hands.

'I'm not. He can barely keep his eyes off you.'

'Everyone's been staring at me lately,' she said, thinning her lips. 'I'm heartily sick of it.'

Kate shook her head. 'He's looking at you kindly, Jeannie,' she said gently. 'Not like the Sids of this world. And he's a lot finer to look at than Sid as well. A lot finer, indeed, with that good head of fair hair and those dreamy blue eyes.'

Jeannie rolled her own eyes and huffed as she sat at her machine. 'It sounds like you're sweet on him yourself. I have no idea why you're trying him push me towards him.'

Kate laughed. 'I told you. I'm not looking for a man, never will be. But you want it all, don't you? Love, marriage, babies. It strikes me that Tom is a good prospect.'

'Because he's got blue eyes?' she asked, her tone sceptical.

'Not just that – although what girl wouldn't want to stare into those? No, I'm thinking he's a mechanic and handy around machines, so he's always going to have well-paid work, isn't he?'

'So are shoe- and bootmakers. Everyone needs them.'

'I know. But more and more, we're relying on machines to help us make the shoes and boots, so without the Toms of this world, none of us could work, could we?' She pointed a finger at Jeannie. 'Mark my words. It's the mechanics who keep the world working these days. That's why they're paid better than the rest of us.'

'That's as may be, but I'm not going to make a fool of myself over Tom, all right?'

'Why do you think you'd look foolish?' Kate asked, her head to one side. 'It's not foolish if you both like each other. It's romantic. Why won't you give him a chance?'

Jeannie sighed. 'Lots of reasons. First, I don't have time for romance. I need all my energy for looking after Ma and trying to keep the twins in line at the moment. Second,' she counted on her fingers, 'he's not a Quaker.'

'Does that really matter?' asked Kate softly. 'It didn't stop you stepping out with Douglas, did it?' Jeannie glared at her. 'All right, that's not a good example, because he was trying to fool you and everyone into thinking he was a pacifist. But I'm not a Quaker either, and you've never held it against me, and Will said it didn't matter that Peg wasn't a Friend when he married her.'

'It does to me now,' she said. That nonsense with Douglas had left her feeling naïve and foolish. 'I want to marry a man who believes as I do. Don't pretend there weren't folk who were disapproving of Will and Peg's match. I know Auntie Betty said she just wanted her boys to be happy, but others weren't so tolerant and they were quick to point out the differences. Which brings me to the third reason. He's a drinker, not Temperance like me and Ma. I saw him with my own eyes coming out of the Street Inn, just like Sid.' Jeannie and her ma had taken the Temperance pledge never to drink alcohol.

Kate frowned. 'Are you sure about that?'

Jeannie nodded.

'Only I heard he was lodging there for just a few days until he got a room with Mr and Mrs Persey up Wilfred Road. He's moved in with them now. They wouldn't take in a drinker, would they? They're Temperance through and through.'

Jeannie frowned. They were indeed Temperance and Friends. 'Are you sure?'

'Yes. Auntie told me Mrs Persey herself told her he was their new lodger. Said he's a fine young man.'

'Oh!'

'Yeah, oh!' Her friend grinned. 'So maybe he's not such a devil after all.'

Jeannie looked away, her thoughts in a turmoil. 'It doesn't matter. I'm still not interested. He's not Quaker. I haven't seen him at meetings.' She'd have noticed him for sure. 'And after my encounters with the likes of Douglas and Sid, I'm sure there's not a lad within ten miles who'd want to have anything to do with me. Come on, Mr Briars is looking. We'd better get on.' She switched on her machine and bent to her work, the noise precluding any further conversation. They weren't in trouble – some of the others weren't even at their places and the hooter hadn't sounded yet – but she didn't want to carry on this conversation. Tom bothered her. Not just because she was ashamed of what he witnessed, or because he *was* as fine-looking as Kate said. No, what bothered her the most about him was the memory of the blazing passion in his eyes when he'd looked at her that night.

He'd been enraged by Sid's behaviour, leaping to her defence and threatening him with violence. It was that violence she sensed in him that was the root of the problem. When he'd looked at her, he looked almost desperate for her to give him permission to knock Sid's block off. *He'd wanted to hit him.* And, if he was a former soldier as Kate said, then he was capable of inflicting far more than a few bruises on a man.

No, he's not for me. When I marry, it will be to a man of God and peace. Not an angry soldier who was prepared to use violence against another man to solve a problem.

She thought briefly of Lucas, sending up a quick prayer that her brother wouldn't ever become like that. It didn't occur to her until much later to acknowledge that she herself had used violence against someone and that she had not one jot of remorse over it. In fact, she was glad she'd hurt Sid, for which she couldn't repent. She wondered whether she had really been frightened of Tom, or if what she'd felt had been excitement in the presence of his passion. That thought made her even more determined to stay away from him.

26

1916

The twins turned fifteen in January and the government announced compulsory conscription of all unmarried men aged between eighteen and forty-one. Kate was relieved that both of her brothers were married.

'Did the boys have a good birthday?' Kate asked Jeannie as they enjoyed their dinner in the girls' canteen at Clarks for a change. It was cosier than the general canteen and only the women and girls went in there. A bowl of hearty soup and a chunk of bread was just what they needed on a cold winter's day, and in recognition of the times when Jeannie had helped Kate out when she'd been without food, she paid for her friend's lunch as well.

Kate wrapped her hands round the warm bowl, her fingers aching from the cold and the repetitive clenching and pinching as she worked at her machine. She breathed in the lovely scent of the root vegetables and pearl barley in the soup, making her mouth water.

'I think so,' Jeannie replied, looking a bit puzzled before she took a mouthful of soup.

'Don't you know?'

Jeannie shrugged, swallowed her food and sighed. 'Not really. They've been acting mighty strange since just after Christmas.'

'Strange? How?'

'I don't know... Christmas was miserable, with Lucas not being there and Ma taking to her bed. They weren't keen on going to the Meeting House with me, but Ma made them promise, so they did. They moaned all the way there, mind. I was ready to tell them not to bother, but I'd promised Ma I'd make sure they went as well.'

Kate giggled. 'Sorry, love, but I can imagine it. I'd have wanted to clip their ears.'

'Not so easy to do these days. You know, they're both so tall all of a sudden. I swear they're going to be even taller than Lucas. Ma has been letting down the hems of their trousers, but she says we'll have to buy them larger sizes soon. At this rate, I wouldn't be able to reach their ears even if I wanted to clip them.' She shook her head. 'But it was after that, things got a bit odd.'

'Oh? How?' Kate tucked into her soup as Jeannie pulled her bread apart.

'Well, you know how keen the twins are on football, don't you?'

Kate rolled her eyes. 'I know. Like my brothers.'

'Well, that's the thing. On the walk home, we met your brother George coming home from church with his family. He called the twins over and they had a conversation.'

'What did he say?' Kate had a good idea, but she didn't want to let on to Jeannie.

She shrugged again. 'I don't know. I got distracted by Ada and the new baby.'

Kate beamed. 'Little Katherine – named for me and Ma. I'm so glad she had a girl. I was beginning to think I'd have nothing but nephews.'

Jeannie smiled. 'Ada let me have a cuddle. Ooh, I could eat her up! She is a little poppet. Even her brother, George junior, seems smitten.'

She laughed. 'I don't suppose that will last long, but we'll enjoy it while we can. Anyway, what happened with George and the twins?'

'Something to do with football, I think,' she said, taking a quick sip of soup. 'Doesn't Fred help run the factory team? I think George was passing on a message, because they were desperate to run straight round to Fred's house. I had to remind them it was a holy day for being with your families, not visiting, and that Ma was waiting for us at home. So we went home and I had to put up with them griping and moaning for the rest of the day when they weren't talking to each other about football. Poor Ma fell asleep, she was so bored with their chatter.' She dipped some bread in her soup and ate it.

Kate rolled her eyes. 'Boys and football, eh? I suppose it's better than war talk.'

'We don't allow any war talk in our house. It's too upsetting for Ma. She's terrified the twins will try to enlist.'

'But they're too young.'

'I know. But like I said, they're tall, their voices are as deep as Lucas's most of the time now – although they do squeak occasionally, which is amusing for me and Ma but not so much for them! They're starting to get facial hair as well – you know, that fluff that boys are so proud of? So they do look like they could be older, and I wouldn't put it past them to try it on and lie about their ages.' She paused a spoonful of soup held mid-air. 'Well, I thought they would. But I might have your brothers to thank for distracting them.'

'How?'

'They rushed round to Fred's the minute Ma said they could go, and he's offered them extra training so they can get onto the men's football team. Some of the best players are enlisting, so they're short of good men. Rather than accept older men who might be past their prime into the team, Fred's scouting among the younger lads.' She raised her hands. 'I don't know what he said to them, but the change in the twins is nothing short of miraculous.'

'Do tell,' said Kate, nudging her. 'What's happened?'

'I honestly don't know,' she confessed. 'They've been round to Fred's a couple of times since the New Year. Each time they come back, they lock themselves into their room and talk – well, sometimes it sounds like an argument, but they keep it low so as not to disturb Ma and so I can't hear what they're saying.'

She finished her soup, glancing up at the clock to make sure they weren't going to be late back to work. 'I haven't caught them on the cider since Christmas Eve, either. If I didn't know better, I'd think they'd taken the Temperance pledge and given up drinking alcohol,' she laughed. 'I don't suppose it'll last, but I'm mighty glad for the change for as long as it does.'

'That is good news,' Kate nodded, using her bread to mop up what was left of the thick vegetable soup. 'Are they helping at home as well?'

Jeannie snorted. 'Don't be daft!' She paused again, frowning. 'Although they have been a bit tidier. I haven't had to go round picking up after them so much. But they always disappear when there's work to do, the beggars. I had to carry the coal in this morning to make sure Ma could stay warm while we're at work. I asked both of them to do it, but they never did. Nearly made me late for work.'

'But Lucas said—' She stopped, putting a hand to her mouth as though to take the words back.

Jeannie narrowed her eyes. 'What has Lucas got to do with anything?' she asked, her voice low. Kate could see she was starting to realise the truth and wasn't happy about it. She sighed, wishing she'd kept her big mouth shut. Now she'd have to confess.

'Nothing, really,' she said, trying to keep her voice light and breezy and not laced with guilt. 'I told Lou about how the twins weren't helping you and she might have mentioned it to Lucas in one of her letters.'

'And how do you know this?' Jeannie crossed her arms, looking far from happy.

Kate wriggled in her seat, knowing Jeannie was going to be spitting mad. She hated anyone knowing her business, just as Kate did. But she couldn't lie to her. 'Lou mentioned she'd told him. Then Lucas wrote to Fred. You know they worked together, don't you? He asked him to take the twins under his wing and set them straight.'

Jeannie closed her eyes. 'I might have guessed. I'd hoped they were just growing up at last. But now it all makes sense. They'll listen to a man, but not their sister or even their own ma.' She opened her eyes and blinked rapidly. 'But why did Lou bother Lucas with it all? I deliberately didn't tell him because I didn't want him getting distracted by worries from home.'

Her words made Kate feel rotten. 'That's my fault,' she confessed. 'I was so worried about you that I told Lou. Well,' she defended when Jeannie glared at her. 'We're both used to telling Lou everything, aren't we? You told her about what was going on with Pa and the Floozy, didn't you? That worked out all right. So what's so wrong about me telling her about your troubles?'

Jeannie looked around before leaning closer. 'What else did you tell her that she couldn't help but write to Lucas about? Did you mention the incident with Sid?'

Kate looked away, guilt flooding through her. She nodded.

Jeannie was silent for a while. It made Kate nervous, so she glanced back at her friend to try to work out what she was thinking. 'I'm sorry, Jeannie. I didn't realise she was going to tell him – I told her you was going to tell him yourself when he came home, but then he didn't, so I suppose she thought someone ought to mention it to him.'

Jeannie stood up and took her dishes and cutlery to the hatch for the washer-uppers. Kate followed and they left the canteen in silence.

'Are you angry with me?' Kate asked when she couldn't stand it any longer.

Jeannie sighed and shook her head. 'No. Not really. Like you said, I did the same for you. I suppose I should be grateful.'

'But you're not.'

'No. I'm fed up. I know I said it was a miracle, but I actually thought that maybe the twins were starting to come round – to respect me like they do Lucas.' She gave a harsh laugh. 'I should've guessed they needed a man's hand to bring them in line.' She spun round to face her just before they reached the entrance to the Machine Room. 'Why didn't Lucas say anything to me? I've had a letter from him since then. Has he decided I'm so useless, I'm not worth consulting with? What else is he doing behind my back?'

Kate's heart sank. 'No, I'm sure it's nothing like that. I think he just wanted to spare you all the aggravation – to make your life easier. If anything, I think he's feeling guilty about going off and leaving it all to you.'

'And this thing with Sid,' Jeannie went on, getting herself worked up. 'What did Lucas do? And don't tell me nothing, because I've seen Sid twice this week and both times, he's turned tail and gone in the opposite direction the moment he sets eyes on me.'

Kate scratched her temple, not sure what to say.

'Kate,' Jeannie warned. 'Tell me.'

She blew out a breath with a huff. 'All right. He asked Fred to have words with Sid. Fred took George and a couple of other chaps with them. They confronted Sid and threatened to castrate him with a rusty knife if they ever saw him within twenty yards of you.'

Jeannie gasped and covered her burning cheeks with her hands.

'They wouldn't do it, of course,' said Kate, quickly. 'But Sid's too stupid to realise that, isn't he? And it's worked, hasn't it? They knew it would. Let's face it, he's one of those cowards who'll push women about but runs a mile when a real man challenges him. Have you seen him scurry off when he sees Tom? It's comical to watch.'

More women were returning to work, so the girls had to step out of the way. Jeannie wasn't looking at Kate as she lowered her hands and hurried to her machine. Her shoulders were shaking, filling Kate with panic.

'Jeannie, I'm sorry,' she whispered, aware that there were people taking notice. 'I know you hate violence. But someone like Sid needs to be threatened or he'll keep on doing what he tried with you. The next girl might not have the sense to do what you did.'

Still with her back to her, Jeannie shook her head. 'You don't understand.'

'What don't I understand? Talk to me, please.'

Jeannie's shoulders shook again. Kate put a hand on her arm, urging her friend to look at her. When she did, it was Kate's turn to gasp. Far from being in tears of distress as she thought, Jeannie's eyes were brimming with mirth and her shoulders were shaking as she tried to contain her laughter.

'You're not angry,' she said, eyes wide. 'I thought you'd be spitting mad.'

'Oh, I'm angry,' she said, taking out her handkerchief and wiping her eyes. 'I want to be cross with you and Lou, but I can't be because I know I'd do – have done – the same thing. I'm more angry at Lucas for going over my head and getting your brothers involved and I'm spitting mad at the twins for showing me so little respect but falling in line the minute they think they might get a place on the football team out of it.' She took a deep breath and gave Kate a narrow-eyed look. 'I'm annoyed with you for not telling me before now what was going on, and with your brothers for threatening violence because you know how I hate that. But...' She giggled and covered her mouth for a moment. 'I wish I'd been a fly on the wall and seen Sid's face when they did it.'

Kate burst out laughing, relieved that Jeannie could see the funny side of it all. 'George said he thought Sid was going to wet himself.'

That sent Jeannie into peals of laughter, drawing smiles from some of the girls and women around them and disapproving glances from others.

* * *

Kate hurried home to Auntie Betty's house after work, eager to write to Louisa tonight and tell her about Jeannie's reaction. She knew that Lou would be relieved as she'd been worried that Jeannie would hate her for telling Lucas what was going on. Poor Lou was convinced that everyone at home would hate her. Kate blamed her ma and pa for that. They were still being horrible to her. They just wouldn't accept that their daughter had made the right decision for herself and her baby.

Louisa was six months along now and Peg said she was blooming. It made Kate feel so sad that Mattie wouldn't see his child and that Louisa was being forced to give it up. But she was also happy for Peg and Will because it meant they'd have a child they'd always longed for but never managed to create for themselves. That Will was the baby's natural uncle and Auntie Betty was its natural grandma made it all seem so perfect. It was hard not to let on to Betty, though. She was still under the impression that it was Peg who was expecting and she had no idea of the sacrifice Louisa was planning to make. All Kate could do was to sympathise when Betty wished she could be closer to Will and Peg so that she could help them with the baby, knowing that she would be kept from seeing them until after the baby was born and Louisa was out of the picture.

She let herself into the cottage. 'I'm home, Auntie. Are you here?'

No answer. She wasn't worried, because the older woman walked more slowly than Kate, so she was probably still coming down the High Street. She sometimes went into the Friends' Meeting House on the way home to see her fellow Quakers. Kate had been thinking about going with her lately. She'd never been a great one for church, although she'd gone with her ma every Sunday. But she hadn't gone any further than the churchyard and Ma's grave much since they'd laid her there. She'd been a couple of times when Ted was there, but never since he'd gone away. George and Ada went, but Fred wasn't a regular. His wife Vi was a Methodist, so they sometimes went there. Peg was a Friend now, and she and Will attended Quaker meetings in Lincolnshire. She didn't know whether Lou went with them.

Auntie Betty didn't preach, but she did live her faith in her everyday life and talked about how the Friends helped her on spiritual matters, just as Jeannie did. Kate was slowly coming to the realisation that she wanted to find out more about being a Quaker because Betty and Jeannie seemed content with their faith and she knew that it suited Peg as well. Maybe she'd find some peace among the Friends at the Meeting House.

She lit the oil lamp, bringing a warm glow to the cosy room before she filled the kettle and put it on the range, stoking the embers of the coals they'd put in this morning and adding more fuel. Auntie would be ready for a cuppa when she got in. It was mighty cold outside and even the short walk from the factory was enough to chill your bones. She also checked the pot of rabbit stew that had been cooking slowly in the oven all day. It smelt delicious. She closed the oven door and put a couple of bowls on the top of the range to warm through while she laid the table.

That done, Kate sat in one of the chairs by the range, sighing with pleasure. For too long, she had been working all day at Clarks and the rest of her waking hours had been taken up with nursing her ma and cooking and cleaning at home. Then she'd endured the Floozy and her brats, working her fingers to the bone even though she only ever got abused and ridiculed for her trouble.

Now, she worked alongside Auntie Betty to prepare their meals and keep the house tidy. She could afford to come home and take a few minutes by the range to relax and let the aches and pains of the day melt away. The lovely smells of meals cooking and the beeswax polish Auntie used on the furniture that her late husband had built with his own hands replaced the stink of leather and oil that surrounded her all day, and the peace in the cottage calmed her after hours of noise and vibration in the Machine Room.

This is how it should be. No shouting, no pain, no drudgery. This is my life now and I love it.

She must have dozed off for a few minutes, but she awoke when she heard the latch on the front door to see the kettle was boiling. Yawning and scrubbing her eyes, Kate got up and set about making a pot of tea.

'Good day, Auntie?' she asked when Betty came in.

'Not bad, lass. I'll be glad when the spring comes, though. I'm tired of the winter chill.'

'Amen to that,' she said. 'Come and get warm by the range. Tea's in the pot.'

'Ah, bless you,' Betty smiled, groaning as she lowered herself into her chair opposite Kate's by the range. 'Ooh, my old bones. It's so good to sit and rest after a long shift.' She flexed her gnarled fingers. 'I swear if my eyes aren't letting me down these days, my hands are stiffening up and my back is aching from being hunched over all day.'

Kate nodded. 'You do such close, detailed work in Trimmings, don't you? I wouldn't have the patience.'

Betty shrugged. 'Trimmings is all I've done at Clarks since I was twelve years old and I'm gone fifty now. My fingers were nice and nimble then. I just hope I can carry on. I'm not ready for the scrapheap yet. It's easier now I'm helping to supervise – I tell others what to do rather than having to do so much of it myself. But I struggle with writing my reports for Miss Bond some days when these fingers don't want to hold a pen. Anyway,' she leaned forward and took Kate's hands in her own, 'come and sit for a minute while the tea's brewing, lass. I need to tell you something.'

For a moment, Kate couldn't breathe. Her first thought was that she was going to ask her to leave. She sank into the chair opposite the older woman, gripping Betty's hands as though she'd never let go. The urge to beg her not to send her away was overwhelming, but she was too nervous to say anything.

Betty must have seen the fear on her face, for her solemn expression softened. 'Nothing to fret about, lass,' she said. 'Just some news I heard that I thought you ought to know.'

'What about?'

'You know that woman who's living with your pa had a husband, don't you?'

Kate nodded. 'He left her, though, didn't he?'

'That's what she told people. But I just had a chat with a Friend from Glastonbury up at the Meeting House and she told me that he went up Bristol to work on the docks and saw he'd earn more

on the ships, so he joined the Merchant Navy with his wife's blessing. He's been at sea for these past two years and finally came
home to see his family a couple of days ago. You can imagine his
surprise when the neighbours told him she'd taken off to live with
a man in Street and there's a new family in his house. I hear he was
chased down by the landlord for unpaid rent as well. Seems she's
been taking the money he sent home and not paying her bills like
she was supposed to.'

'Oh, my lord,' said Kate. 'That woman has no shame.'

Betty nodded. 'I agree. Even after she moved in with your pa,
she's been going to the Post Office in Glastonbury and collecting
his letters and money. She's been writing to him as though nothing
was wrong, so you can imagine the poor man's surprise when he
turns up, thinking to give his wife a nice surprise.'

'He'll be furious.'

'Indeed. I'm told he's got a temper on him. That's what made
him leave Glastonbury, for a fresh start after he got into one too
many fights when he worked at Morlands, but he couldn't
persuade his missus to go with him. She said she needed to be
near her mother while he was at sea, but she hasn't spoken to the
woman in months.'

'Of course she wouldn't leave the area,' Kate scoffed. 'She's
been carrying on with Pa for years. Does her husband even know
the children aren't his?'

'If he doesn't yet, I expect he will soon. As soon as people saw
your pa with those littluns, it was obvious. Someone's bound to tell
him. If they don't, he'll see for himself as soon as he claps eyes on
your pa.'

Kate blew out a breath. 'I don't suppose the husband will just
go back to sea and forget about her?'

'That would be the sensible thing, wouldn't it? But it seems he's
still thinking those children are his. He told the neighbour he was

going to find her and bring her home, even though the landlord told him he couldn't have the house back. He said the new tenants are more reliable. Gave them a real fright it did when this angry sailor confronted them in their own home.'

Kate didn't know what to think. She'd been under the impression that the Floozy's husband had left her and wasn't likely to be back. She shook her head.

'I can imagine. Those poor people. And the husband must be beside himself. Fancy finding out his wife has left him and not even told him. It's just like her to still be taking the man's money. She's got no conscience, that one. If she did, she wouldn't have been carrying on with a married man and rushing to take over the house the minute Ma passed.'

'I know, love. No shame at all.'

Kate reluctantly let go of Auntie's hands and got up, busying herself pouring the tea. She handed the older woman a cup and saucer and sat back down with her own. She took a sip before she spoke again. 'You never know, Pa might be so sick of her by now, he might be glad to hand her back.'

'No doubt,' said Betty. 'She's not a patch on your lovely ma. But what man is going to want her back when the evidence that she's made a fool of him for years will be looking back at him? I expect there'll be an almighty row, then the husband will tell your pa he's welcome to her and the kiddies.'

'Shame,' sighed Kate. 'Pa was never the warmest of fathers, but we managed to rub along together somehow when Ma was well. That all changed once Ma was ill and even before the Floozy descended on us, of course. But if she stays, that'll definitely be the end of my relationship with him. He'll be beyond redemption.'

'Don't give me that, Kate Davis. Even as a Quaker who knows not to judge, I can see that he's already too far gone. There'll be no redemption for him either way. That man stole from you from the moment you started working at Clarks as a girl and did the same to his other children for as long as he could. He lied to everybody for years and didn't lift a finger to save his own sweet wife. We should be grateful your ma never knew the full horror of it all.'

Kate was a little surprised by Betty's angry words because she was usually so placid, but she couldn't argue. 'I suppose so,' she conceded. 'But he's my pa, you know? Don't we all want to think the best of our kin? That's what Ma taught me.'

Betty's expression softened. 'That we do, lass, and it's a measure of your good character that you can still look for the good in him after everything that's gone on.'

'Foolish, more like,' Kate said, shrugging as she felt the bone-deep hurt of it all again. She was silent for a moment, sipping her tea. 'I just don't understand how some men can be so daft when it comes to women. It's not like she's even pleasant.'

Betty gave a low chuckle. 'Some men aren't ruled by their heads when it comes to the fairer sex, lass. They see a pair of bosoms and they forget themselves. And let's face it, that woman has made the most of what God gave her. Your pa and her poor husband, no doubt, both lost their minds.'

'More fool them,' she declared, crossing her arms over her own chest. She'd never been comfortable with having bosoms. To her, they were a sign of a woman's weakness – an excuse for men to lord it over them. She would never dream of flaunting hers like the Floozy did.

'More fool them, indeed. I'd say your pa is going to regret his foolishness soon enough.'

'I think he already does.' Kate couldn't keep the bitterness out of her voice. 'A few people have told me they've seen Pa and the Floozy arguing – that's when they're not making a spectacle of themselves when they're in their cups. I'm so ashamed of him.'

Betty leaned over and patted her knee. 'Don't you be feeling ashamed, lass. It's him who should be ashamed. You had nothing to do with his sinful behaviour and none but himself can persuade him to follow that path or to repent and live a righteous life. Leave him be to sink or swim. You've managed to build an independent life and I'm proud to have such a good-hearted young woman as you in my home.' She heaved herself out of her chair. 'Now, how's that rabbit stew doing?'

Kate jumped up to help her, taking their cups, rinsing them and leaving them to dry on the wooden draining board while Betty dished up their supper. She was so grateful to the older woman for giving her a decent home and the love and care she should have been able to expect from her pa. But she couldn't help worrying what would happen when the Floozy's long-lost husband turned up to confront them.

Should I go round and warn them? she wondered. She considered it for a moment, but then realised that they wouldn't thank her even if she did, and it certainly wouldn't persuade them to do anything different. So it was probably better if she just stayed out of it.

She resolved to at least tell her brothers what she'd heard, but she doubted whether they would be interested. Pa had burned his boats when it came to his legitimate children. The hurt he had inflicted ran too deep to be forgotten.

No. He's on his own with his Floozy. Let them sort this mess out themselves.

27

Location Classified Confidential
15 February 1916

Dear Louisa,

I hope this finds you well. I am still in one piece, although it truly is a miracle. I had no idea what real war would be like. I have seen things I never imagined before and hope to never see again. I cannot tell you anything because of the danger of the Hun getting hold of information if they manage to intercept our letters, so all I will say is that it is cold, muddy and grim here.

Some of the lads here have received Valentine's greetings from their sweethearts. A few are cock-a-hoop about that. For others, it's bittersweet. They miss their loves a lot and fear they'll never see them again – or that some chap will turn the girls' hearts against them while they're away. I'm grateful that I don't have a sweetheart but rather have good friends like you and my family praying for me at home. I regret that I've put you all through so much worry, but I felt that coming to fight was the thing to do. Now that I'm here, I aim to do my duty as best I can.

I saw two ambulance units the other day, one of which had been donated by the Friends and another from the Boot and Shoemakers Union. I don't envy those chaps their work; it is truly awful. But seeing the names on the sides of the ambulances made me think of home. How I wish I was back in Street with Ma and Jeannie and the boys, and working in the Clicking Room at Clarks! I couldn't wait to get away, but now I can't wait to get home. They say that you never appreciate what you have until it is gone and that is true for me. It strengthened my resolve to fight as hard as I can to help end this war with a victory over the Hun, so that I can go home safe in the knowledge that my family and friends will be able to live in peace.

I hear that things are better at home. The twins are benefitting from the influence of Fred and George Davis and not causing so many headaches for Ma and Jeannie. Fred wrote to tell me that Sid and his ilk who frequent the Street Inn have been met with ladies handing them white feathers every time they show their faces in public, but they have managed to dodge the recruitment officer so far, although they won't get away with it for much longer, I'm sure. Much as I hate it here, I think the discipline of being a soldier will do that crowd good.

How are Peg and Will getting along? It can't be long now before their child is born. Will is a sound chap and Peg is a good woman, so I am sure they will be very good parents. Do give them my best wishes and let me know when there's news of the baby. Mattie would have loved to have been an uncle, wouldn't he? He often talked of you and him having lots of children. I think it came from there only being him and Will after their pa died so young. Mattie often said he wished their family was bigger. He envied me that, even though I didn't appreciate it at the time.

I must apologise if you don't hear from me for a little while.

Things can get quite busy here, as I'm sure you'll understand. But I do enjoy receiving your letters and will try to reply to you as soon as I can.

Your friend, Lucas

* * *

Lincolnshire
20 February 1916

Dear Lucas,

Thank you for your letter. I confess I always breathe a sigh of relief when I get one from you because it means you are all right. I pray every day that you stay safe and well. I couldn't bear for you to be lost like Mattie. Sometimes, I get so angry with him for going off like that. I know that Jeannie gets angry with you, too. You must make sure when you get home to make it up to her. She worries so because she loves you.

I'm sure you do not appreciate hearing things like that, so I will change the subject. I am sending you some wool socks, gloves and a scarf with this letter, which I hope will help keep out the cold. It has been freezing here, with thick frost every morning and sometimes snow. We are getting through a lot of coal, trying to keep warm. I fret that if it is as cold where you are, you'll not have the chance to sit by a fire, so you must wrap up warm. Peg and I are both knitting every day – gloves and socks for soldiers as well as clothes and blankets for the baby.

With the weather being so cold, we don't go out a lot for fear of falling when there's ice on the ground, so we are like a pair of old ladies, knitting by the fire and talking about the old days back in Street, where the weather was milder. We both agree we miss working at Clarks and all our friends there. We even miss the smell of leather and machine oil, but not the noise in the Machine Room! I am sure that Peg and Will shall go back to Somerset when the war is over and Will's job here is no longer necessary. I am not so sure what I should do. Once the baby arrives, there will be less room here and I feel I should take my leave of them so that they can concentrate on parenthood. I will only be in the way. But I am still estranged from my parents and do not imagine that we shall ever get back to the loving relationship we had in the past. Peg still says I should lodge with Mrs Searle and Kate. I do sometimes think I might like that, but she might not wish to be reminded of her loss. Every time she saw me, she would remember Mattie, just as she would remind me of my beloved whenever my glance strayed in her direction. I'm not sure whether I'm strong enough to bear that again. It has taken me a while to get used to seeing Will every day, which has been hard, even though he is kind and understanding (as his ma would be, I'm sure). Yet nor do I feel strong enough to try and start a new life alone in a strange town once the time comes for me to leave Peg and Will's home, so I really don't know what the future holds for me.

Are you getting the gossip from home? Did you hear about the fuss over Kate's pa and his fancy woman? The woman is a liar and a cheat and her husband is just discovering the full extent of it.

Kate has tried to stay out of it, but she says the whole village knows there was a terrible row when the husband finally tracked down his unfaithful wife. The neighbours fetched the constable because the Floozy, as Kate calls her, was screaming blue murder. We all knew that her children bear an uncanny resemblance to Mr Davis, but it seems the husband had no idea that his wife had been passing off another man's children as his until he saw them together. By all accounts, he flew into a rage and *knocked Mr Davis over and started beating his wife, only stopping when the constable pulled him off her and arrested him.*

I cannot help but feel sorry for the man. He thought he had a loving wife and children, worked hard to support his family, only to find that everything was a lie. The magistrate showed some sympathy and imposed a small fine and ordered him back to his ship. His wife seems to have gotten away with her life, but her already rotten reputation is even worse now and Mr Davis is a laughing stock for he claims he had no idea she was lying about her husband. He swears she never told him she had money coming in and made him pay for everything. Kate says the neighbours keep reporting that the lovers argue all the time now and the children are even wilder than before, but she says her pa has made his bed, she has no sympathy for him at all. I thought Kate might have some sympathy for the children, but she says they are too much like their mother in temperament for anyone to feel sorry for them.

Peg has just lit the lamps as the winter evening is drawing in, so I must stop and help her prepare Will's supper before he gets home.

As always, please stay safe, my friend, and write to me when you get the chance.

Your friend, Louisa

Location Classified Confidential
2 March 1916

Dear Louisa,

Thank you for the socks, gloves and scarf! They were all very welcome as it is indeed very cold here. If the ground isn't frozen solid, it becomes a muddy quagmire which makes life even more miserable. Having extra socks, provided we can keep them dry, helps to keep our feet from rotting. They're calling it 'Trench Foot' and a lot of men are suffering with it. Some have lost toes and their flesh smells something awful. I've been spared so far and pray that will continue. I'm wrapping the scarf round my body over my vest and under my uniform, which is helping keep the wind out, and your gloves fit snuggly under my heavy leather gauntlets, keeping my fingers cosy and in good working order. Ma sent me some sheepskin gaiters to wrap around my shins. The other lads are quite jealous and want to know how to get some for themselves. For my part, I'll never complain about the stink from Morlands sheepskin factory ever again.

I had to smile at the picture you paint of you and Peg knitting by the fire. I hope that Peg is well and that she doesn't have too long to wait before her baby arrives.

I think you should definitely return to Street rather than end up amongst strangers. Peg's suggestion that you lodge with Mrs Searle is a good one. She is a kind soul and I am sure that, even though you will remind each other of Mattie, you will also find comfort in each other because you have his loss in common. I know that Mattie would rest easy if you were to live with his ma. But it must be your choice, so I'll say no more – other than to say I would miss you if I went home and you were not there.

Jeannie tells me things are settling down at home with the twins, although she says she is angry with me for interfering. But I'm glad I did. She has enough to deal with without the twins or even Sid Lambert making life difficult for her.

As for the gossip, I had heard a little of what went on with Kate's pa, but I confess I hadn't thought about it from the husband's point of view until I read your telling of it. I should *hate to be cuckolded like that, especially as the man was serving his country and still supporting his faithless wife. No wonder he went berserk when he learned that the children he believed to be his were fathered by another man. I do not think I could forgive such lies. As Kate says, her pa has made his bed. It sounds as though it is not a pleasant one, but he should do the decent thing now and take responsibility for the children, even though their mother is a lying ~~bi~~ baggage (I confess I nearly used a stronger word there – the language used here in the trenches is rather riper than you are accustomed to and I almost used a phrase I've heard here, but thought better of it). I do feel sorry for the children. Their parents have shamed them, and now everyone knows that they were not truly born in wedlock. They will no doubt have to live with that stigma for the rest of their days.*

I know I've already said it, but do I hope you do go back home to Street, Louisa. I don't like to think of you so far away from everything that is familiar to you. I know that Mattie would be glad that you are with his brother and sister-in-law when they need you, but if you cannot stay there, then your friends, including Jeannie and my ma, will welcome you home.

God willing, spring will be here soon and we can look forward to new life and the return of the sun into our lives.

Look after yourself and give my regards to Will and Peg.

Your friend, Lucas

Louisa sighed as she put the letter back into its envelope. She rubbed her swollen belly as the child within shifted. She smiled sadly, cherishing these moments as they would be all she would be able to keep of her beloved Mattie's baby. It was hard, pretending to Lucas that it was Peg who was bearing this child. She had thought of telling him; she hoped he might understand. But his views of the Floozy and her children gave her pause. He was an honourable man. He might think badly of Mattie for anticipating their wedding vows and leaving her in this situation. She couldn't bear it if he turned against his memory. Nor could she bear it if he should think of her in the same way that he regarded the Floozy.

Of course, that was the real reason why she was reluctant to agree to live with Mrs Searle. How could she bear to hear about the woman's grandchild as it grew, knowing that it was her own child – one that she had no choice but to give up to ensure that her baby didn't grow up stigmatised by the circumstances of his or her birth, like Kate's half-siblings were now going to face? Keeping the secret from Betty Searle would surely kill Louisa. Yet... at other times, she considered that though it would be bittersweet, it would be the only way she could ensure that she would have news of her child as it grew.

Sometimes, she hoped that she might die in childbirth. At least that way, she might hope to be reunited in death with her beloved and wouldn't have to live with the guilt and regret of having to give up Mattie's baby. She prayed for it, even as she feared that God might well be angry for her wanting to give up her life. It frightened her to think she might end up in hell while Mattie was surely in heaven.

28

Jeannie found little solace in the early signs of spring as they began to emerge in Street. Letters from Lucas were becoming sparse and the information he could give them did nothing to reassure her. He tried to keep a cheerful tone, but she could read between the lines and could tell that her brother was suffering as men and boys around him were maimed or killed. He didn't say much about it, but had occasionally mentioned names of local lads, asking Jeannie to pass on his condolences to their families. Every time that happened, her blood ran cold. Would another local lad send the same message home for Lucas one day? She couldn't bear to think of it.

They were short of people at work so the machine next to Kate had remained unused for a couple of weeks.

'Maybe Lou can have her old machine back when she comes home?' said Jeannie, raising her voice over the noise of the machines. 'I miss her a lot, don't you? You said she should be home by Easter, after Peg has her baby. Any news about that?'

Kate shook her head, frowning. 'No news yet,' she said, concentrating on her work. Jeannie wondered whether Kate was worrying about her sister giving birth. It was always a concern. She decided not to mention it, in case her friend hadn't been thinking that. She didn't want to worry her unnecessarily.

She finished another lining and put it aside, flexing her aching fingers as she did so. She worried sometimes that she'd end up with arthritis in her hands like the older women who worked in the Machine Room. Ma had succumbed to it after working so many years, trying to support her family after Jeannie's pa had died in the accident at the factory. Now she could barely lift anything without crying in pain, leaving Jeannie to do all the lifting and carrying at home.

The constant repetition of the work left Jeannie's hands sore and stiff by the end of the day. Some nights, she bound her wrists firmly so she could sleep without waking in the darkness in pain, and she rubbed her fingers and knuckles every day, trying to keep them supple.

Both girls sighed with relief when the dinner hooter went and they could have a break.

'You know,' Kate said as they walked to the canteen. 'I'm not sure whether Lou will come back.'

'Because of her parents?' Jeannie asked. 'Surely they'll come round after all this time, won't they? They must miss her terribly. She's their only child.'

Kate sighed. 'I know. But I think that's half the trouble. They set such high standards for her, they were never going to be satisfied, no matter what she did.'

Jeannie frowned. 'What are you talking about? Until Mattie died, I thought they all got on fairly well. It was only that they wanted her to get over Mattie when she'd barely had time to grieve that drove a wedge between them.'

Kate shrugged, not looking at her. 'I think things were getting difficult before then,' she said. 'Remember – she wanted to marry

Mattie before he went to war and they wouldn't hear of it. I think Lou is finding it hard to forgive them that.'

'Poor Lou,' said Jeannie, feeling the familiar sadness in her heart at the thought of what her friend had gone through. 'But I suppose it doesn't make any difference, does it? Mattie still died, so she'd have lost him anyway.'

Kate winced. 'It makes a difference to Louisa.'

They decided to go to the main canteen rather than the smaller girls' one this time for a change, and joined the queue for food. There was some teasing going on of one of the younger lads in front of them. Jeannie recognised him as a friend of the twins. He was red as a beetroot, the poor lad, as the others around him mocked him about a girl he was sweet on.

'She ain't ever going to look at you,' said one of them. 'She likes a man who washes his neck.' He flicked the lad's nape with his fingers. 'When was the last time you used soap on that?' he asked to the amusement of his pals.

The object of their teasing shrugged him off. 'I wash,' he insisted. 'But I work hard, too. Not like you beggars, hiding out and smoking every chance you get.'

'That's 'cause we're proper men,' said one, puffing out his chest.

'Is that right?' asked Kate, drawing their attention away from the boy. 'Seems to me, the real man is one who gets on with his job, not the lazy toads looking to leave it to their friends to make up the numbers. And most girls prefer a decent worker over a peacock.'

'That's right,' said Jeannie. She couldn't bear cocky fellows who thought it was a joke to do as little as possible while expecting a decent pay packet. 'And using tobacco isn't attractive either. Look at the stains on your fingers.' She pointed at the yellow-tipped fingers of the main ringleader, pulling a face and shuddering. 'I wouldn't want those touching me.'

The lad sneered. 'I wouldn't be offering. Not to a prissy lass like you. I heard what you did to Sid Lambert. I don't need none of that. There's plenty of girls who fancy me.'

'No accounting for taste,' said Kate as Jeannie paled.

'Hey, move on there,' called an older woman, pointing at the lads. 'Enough of your nonsense. You're holding up the queue and we want our dinner.'

The lads quickly moved on, unwilling to engage with the fierce matron. The girls quickly selected their meals, paid for them and moved to a table as far away from the lads as they could find.

'Maybe we should've gone to the girls' canteen,' said Jeannie.

'I don't see why we should,' said Kate, sitting down and placing her cutlery beside her plate before she looked at Jeannie. 'Pay no mind to those stupid boys.'

'But it's not just them,' she said, looking miserable. 'After Douglas and then Sid, no one wants to walk out with me. I'm going to end up an old maid, I know it.'

'Don't be daft. You'll find a decent lad who'll treat you right. Neither of those two were fit to carry your bags, let alone call you their sweetheart. What about that Tom?'

'No, I don't think so,' she said with a sigh. She still couldn't bring herself to look him in the eye whenever he was around. 'Lucas will come back and settle down with a wife and I'll end up looking after Ma and keeping the twins in line for the rest of my days. Not that I mind looking after Ma, of course,' she added quickly, looking guilty.

Kate raised her eyebrows. 'Has Lucas got a sweetheart?'

'I don't think so. But he's never been one for telling me anything about the girls he likes.' She frowned. 'Come to think of it, I've never known him to court a girl. He's never brought one home, anyway. But that doesn't mean he hasn't taken a girl out sometimes, does it? He just didn't want Ma getting her hopes up, I suppose.' She paused, looking thoughtful. 'I did wonder whether something might develop between Louisa and Lucas – I know it's too soon after Mattie, but... I don't know. They're becoming good friends, writing to each other. I know it comforts both of them that they can share their grief over Mattie together.' She shrugged. 'I just like the thought that it might bring them together, you know? Ma would be thrilled, I know. She's always going on about us settling down with someone nice and giving her grandchildren.' She sighed. 'At least, she was until Douglas let me down and then Lucas enlisted. Now she's always moaning that we'll leave her a lonely old woman without even grandchildren to comfort her.'

Kate shook her head. 'I wouldn't get your hopes up about those two. Surely your ma's not pushing you to find yourself another fellow, is she?'

'No, not any more,' she sighed again. 'Even if I wanted to walk out with a lad, I couldn't. Ma's nerves are so bad these days, I daren't leave her on her own for long in case she has a bad turn. I would've been running home every dinner time to check on her like you did when your ma was ill if our neighbour hadn't promised to check on her while I'm at work. There's no hope for me going out after work these days. I have to rush back or she'll end up in floods of tears, convinced I've met with an accident.'

'Are the twins still not helping?'

'They're doing a bit more – carrying in the coal and such like at long last. But they're training hard with the football team most days after work and playing in matches on Saturday afternoons.' She grimaced. 'I shall be glad when the season's over. I just hope they don't get obsessed with cricket in the summer.'

Kate laughed. 'Don't court trouble before it even happens.' Her smile faded. 'I'm sorry your ma's suffering, though. It's hard to watch, isn't it? I felt so helpless when my ma was poorly.'

'But yours was really ill,' Jeannie protested, feeling the familiar guilt in her stomach at being so unsympathetic about her ma's plight. 'Ma's not sick, apart from her arthritis. She's letting her emotions get the better of her. It's got so she's like a little child – needing someone to do everything for her because she just can't pull herself together and do what needs to be done.' She poked at her food with her fork, her appetite gone. 'I wish she'd remember she's got three other children in the house who need her. It's as though, when Lucas left, he took her will to live with him. Me and the twins don't seem to count at all.' She looked up at Kate, blinking against the tears that threatened. 'If anything, I think she blames me for not stopping Lucas from going.'

'Oh, love.' Kate patted her arm. 'I'm sure she doesn't. It's just her nerves. She'll come round. Didn't you say she was like this after your pa died?'

Jeannie nodded. He had been killed in a freak accident in a lift at the factory, leaving Ma a young widow with four children under ten. If it hadn't been for the help of the Friends at the Meeting House and Jeannie's grandparents, the family would have been broken up. Eventually, Ma had come out of the deep fog of grief and worked hard for her children. But neither Lucas or Jeannie would forget it, and to see her like this again filled her with fear. Their grandparents were all gone now and although their lovely neighbour and some of the Friends tried to help, Jeannie felt ashamed. After all, there were plenty of others who were in need because of this awful war, and really, she couldn't understand why Ma couldn't just pull herself together and make the best of things for the sake of her and the twins.

'I just want things to go back to normal,' she said. 'But, until Lucas comes home, she's not even going to try. It's as though, with him gone, no matter how often he writes to reassure her he's all right, she's just given up. She barely eats these days. I have to nag her to get out of bed and brush her hair. I had to force her to have a bath the other day. I ended up washing her like she was totally helpless – like I was the parent and she was the child.' She blew out a breath, trying not to let her emotions get the better of her. 'I'm so tired, Kate, and I can't see any end to it. Especially if anything happens to Lucas.'

Kate squeezed her arm. 'I know it's hard, love. I felt like that after Ma got ill. Then when the Floozy and her devil spawn moved in, I thought I'd die and no one would care. But, thanks to you, it all got sorted out, didn't it? I'll do what I can to help you with your ma. Auntie will as well, I'm sure. She knows your ma through the Meeting House, doesn't she?'

Jeannie nodded, still blinking back tears.

'Now,' Kate went on. 'You need to eat. You can't help yourself or your ma if you make yourself ill, can you? So come on, tuck in, girl. It'll soon be time to get back to work.'

More grateful than she could say for her friend's strength, Jeannie began to eat.

29

In the second week of March, Kate rushed into work, her face flushed with pleasure as she grabbed Jeannie just as she was tying on her apron. She was bursting to tell her.

'It's a boy!' she cried. 'Auntie got a letter just now. The postie caught us just as we were leaving for work.'

'Peg's had the baby?' Jeannie asked.

For a moment, Kate faltered before she nodded, her lips thin. 'A boy. They're calling him Matthew William,' she said.

'Oh, that's lovely. I'm pleased for Will and Peg. And Auntie Betty, of course.' They'd both taken to calling her that.

Kate forced herself to widen her smile, wishing she wasn't the only one who knew Louisa's secret. But she had promised her that she'd never tell. If she wanted Jeannie to know, she'd tell her herself. It was hard, though. She was sure that Jeannie would understand. But poor Louisa had suffered so much at the hands of her parents that she was too afraid to take the chance on letting anyone else know. Kate supposed it was probably for the best that no one but her, Peg and Will knew the truth. She assumed that

Louisa's ma and pa had worked out what their daughter was doing as well, but they certainly wouldn't say anything.

'They say he's really bonny, came out yelling his head off. Auntie says Mattie was the same.' Kate's heart had missed a beat at the thought of that. 'Mother and baby are doing very well.' She knew that was code for her to let her know that Louisa had come through her labour all right. She just hoped that her heart wasn't shattered all over again over what she now had to do. It had to be so hard.

Jeannie clapped her hands together. 'Oh, that is good news. It couldn't happen to a nicer couple. They'll be such a bonny family.'

Kate nodded, pulling her apron on quickly and sitting down as Mr Briars looked their way. 'Will says once she's finished her lying in, he's going to try and get a family portrait done at one of those photographic studios to send home.'

Jeannie's eyes misted over. 'Oh, I can't wait to see it. I wish...'

'Time to work, girls,' said Mr Briars as he stood at the end of their row of three machines. 'No time for gossip.'

'Sorry, Mr B,' said Kate. 'I was just telling Jeannie, we heard from Peg's husband this morning. She had a little boy.'

The stern supervisor softened for a moment. 'That is good news. Pass on my best wishes to your sister, lass.'

Kate grinned. 'I will.'

'Now, get on with your work. Save your celebrations for after the shift.'

'Yes, Mr Briars,' both girls said together before they bent over their work.

*　*　*

Kate caught up with Fred in the factory yard as they were heading back to work at dinner time. She left Jeannie, telling her she'd catch up with her.

'Did you hear?' she asked Fred. 'Peg and Will have a little boy. We got a letter this morning.'

He grinned. 'Yeah? Good for them. She all right?'

Kate nodded. 'Peg is fine,' she said, wishing someone could worry about poor Louisa. But, of course, it wouldn't occur to them because none of them knew the truth.

'I'll tell Vi if she hasn't got a letter. George and Ada too.' The two brothers lived a few doors from each other on Goswell Road, just round the corner from Reggie Davis's house in Silver Road but at the opposite end of the village from where Kate now resided with Auntie Betty.

'Good. Should we tell Pa?'

Fred scowled. 'We can tell him if we see him. But he won't talk to me at work and I'm not going to bother going round there and I don't think you should either. No point if all you're going to get is abuse from his fancy woman. I hear she was out carousing again last night. She's fonder of the cider than she is of her own littluns. No wonder they're like wild animals.'

'I know,' she agreed. 'I've no wish to visit them, that's for sure. You tell Pa if you want – you're more likely to see him than I am.' She didn't confess that whenever she spotted him, she ducked out of sight so that she wouldn't have to speak to him, but she suspected from Fred's expression that he already knew that.

'All right,' he agreed. 'I suppose your friend will want to be coming home now, won't she?'

Kate shrugged. 'I don't know. I hope so, but she might decide she prefers a fresh start.' She really hoped Lou would come home, but she understood her reluctance. Her recent memories of life in Street were miserable and the rare, stiff communications she'd received from her parents didn't indicate that they might have softened towards her. Kate had no idea what she would do in the same situation.

'Well, George is doing regular runs to Nottingham at the moment, so he mentioned he might try to get up to Lincolnshire while he's there to see Peg and the baby when it arrived, so he might be able to bring Louisa back if she wants to come.'

Kate nodded. 'I'll let her know.' She sighed. 'I wish I could go and see them. I miss Peg and I'd love to see the baby.'

'Talk to George. He might be able to take you with him.'

She was filled with hope. 'Do you think he could?' But as quickly as her excitement had bloomed, reality set in. 'I doubt if I can take the time off work.'

'Don't fret, lass. The factory will be shut for a few days over Easter. But they'll all be back soon enough if you can't go. This damned war can't go on much longer.'

Kate hoped he was right. But people had been saying that for years now. She wondered if they'd ever get back to how things were before the war.

They went their separate ways back to their work.

She resolved to speak to George to find out whether it might be possible for her to go with him to visit Peg – and maybe bring Louisa home. Then she'd speak to Mr Briars and hope that she might be given permission to miss work for a day or two if need be. At least now that she didn't have to give up her whole pay packet to Pa, she had a little money put by after she'd paid Auntie Betty for her keep. She had spent some of it on some new shoes – Clarks, of course – and material to make a few new clothes and wool to knit more. She'd always been ashamed that she wore such old, tatty shoes when she worked for Clarks. She'd invested in a decent pair of their women's walking shoes. They and the clothes she was making with Auntie's help should see her through the next couple of years. The rest of her wages she'd kept safe to buy Ma's headstone. But her brothers and Peg had all said they'd try to help with that as well, so she could afford to miss a day or two's pay if she had to. So long as she didn't get ill, she'd be all right.

For a moment, she worried that she shouldn't take the risk. Maybe it was better to stay at work and wait until Peg could come back to Street before she saw baby Matthew. But then she realised that, if she could find a way to go with George to get her, Lou would more likely come home and she would be there with her friend when she most needed her – when she had to say goodbye to Mattie's son and accept that she couldn't be a true mother to her baby.

Yes, I must go if I can. But how can I persuade Auntie Betty not to come? I know she won't think badly of Louisa, she will love her and the child no matter what, but Lou could not bear for her to know. So I must keep her secret and let Auntie go on thinking little Matthew William is Peg and Will's child.

30

Dear Lucas,

I am sorry that I haven't written to you for a little while. I hope that you are safe and well and that the weather is improving wherever you are. The news here is that the baby has been born. He is a bonny boy, called Matthew William after his father and uncle. I was with Peg when he was born and the moment I set eyes on him, I fell in love with the little man. He reminds me so of Mattie – and Will, of course. The brothers were so alike, weren't they?

Peg is going to be a wonderful mother to little Mattie. I envy her so. Although Will and Peg are now both Friends and don't have a Christening ceremony like we do in the Church of England, they did me the honour of asking me to regard myself as his godmother. I know such a role doesn't exist in the Quaker faith – Will explained to me that the whole congregation of Friends embrace the child and will be there to help him grow *and flourish. But as Peg grew up Church of England like me, she suggested it to him and he agreed. I was overwhelmed when they asked me and of course said I would be honoured. I'd do anything for that little boy.*

I confess I am very tired. The baby has a fierce appetite and wakes to demand feeding every few hours. We're all exhausted! Peg and Will have found help with some local Friends. The wife, who has three little ones of her own, is helping Peg to find her feet and her husband is working in the same factory as Will. It seems that the government will exempt a Quaker man from fighting if he is prepared to work in a factory making instruments of war, but not to work in a shoe factory. It seems ironic as everyone needs boots and shoes, so it really is an essential industry. I know Will does not enjoy the work here and wishes he could return to Clarks. But at least it keeps him safe at Peg's side as little Mattie starts out on his journey through life. I pray that it will be a long and happy life and that this awful war is over long before he is old enough to understand that men are being forced to kill others to satisfy the desire for power and glory of a few Godless men.

I am sorry, I must not speak so to you. It is not fair. Where you are, wherever that might be, you have no control over your destiny and must follow orders. I pray every day that you stay safe and come home soon. Forgive me. Lack of sleep and the sadness I feel at having to leave here soon is making me melancholic.

Yes, that is my other piece of news. I am to return to Street. My mother saw Mattie's ma, who told her about the baby's birth. She wrote to me and urged me to return to Somerset. Clarks are short of workers now that more young men are being conscripted – or put into prison as conscientious objectors. Jeannie tells me my old machine lies idle as the girl who replaced me wasn't up to scratch and the woman who replaced her slipped on ice up at Overleigh in February and broke a leg. They don't know when, if ever, she will be able to return to work. So I could soon be back, working alongside dear Jeannie and Kate. I hope so. I do miss them so, although nothing will ever be the same again.

While I will be glad to be reunited with them, I still feel reluctant to return to the place where Mattie and I were so happy together. I am not sure that I can bear it. But Peg and Will say that I should welcome my memories of those times. After all, to deny them would be like denying our love, wouldn't it?

They say that we grieve because we have loved. What I felt for Mattie was so sweet and true that I do not expect to ever feel like that again. So I suppose they are right. I must remember the good times and be grateful that I have known such a love. I must return to Street and know that, even though I will never see him there again, I will see him in my memories and in my heart. I know that he is in a better place and that, no matter how much I prayed for it, the good lord will not let me join my Mattie just yet.

Ah, baby Mattie has just awoken and is crying for more milk. I must go and give what help I can in these last few days before I take my leave of the family. George Davis has kindly offered to pick me up in his lorry when he next delivers a load of merchandise to Nottingham. It is about the same distance from Nottingham to here as it is from Street to Bristol. I am grateful to him as the journey by train is tortuous at best and I am sure I should get lost changing trains!

Stay safe, my dear friend. I hope that we shall both find peace in Street soon.

From your friend,

Louisa

Louisa folded the notepaper and slid it into the envelope. Her heart ached. She had come so close to confessing the truth to Lucas. It wasn't until the letter was sealed that she realised she had said that the baby was named Matthew William *after his father and uncle*. Would Lucas notice and realise the truth? She wished she could confess it to him and that she could keep her beautiful baby boy forever.

But, with Mattie's death, her fate had been set, and so had their son's. Peg and Will already loved him as though he were their own. They would give him a good life. No matter how hard it was, she had to accept that and not be selfish.

Whether she would ever recover from this fresh heartbreak, she didn't know.

31

By some miracle, George managed to get assigned an extra trip to Nottingham which would take him away from home on the Easter weekend in April. Auntie Betty was persuaded to spend time with Ada and helping her with the children, leaving Kate free to go with her brother. They set off early on Good Friday, made the delivery that afternoon and drove on to Will and Peg's where they would stay for the night. All being well, they would be back late on Saturday and could spend Easter Sunday with the family back in Street.

Kate was tired and aching by the time they arrived on the outskirts of Lincoln.

'I don't know how you can bear driving all the time,' she said to George.

''Tis better than working in a factory, lass. Haven't we seen some beautiful countryside today?'

'Nottingham wasn't so pretty,' she said. 'And I didn't notice much after the first couple of hours because my poor backside has been sore from all the jolting and my head is aching from the growl of this beast.'

He laughed. 'Spoken like the girl you are. Ada hates it as well. When we were courting, she'd sneak on board and come with me sometimes. But the romance soon wore off.'

'There is nothing romantic about a smelly, noisy lorry, brother. I'm surprised she married you.'

He winked and wiggled his eyebrows. 'She knew I was a good catch.'

Kate laughed. 'Well, I'm going to beg Peg for a pillow to sit on for the journey home.'

George parked the lorry near a row of cottages. By the time he had turned off the engine, Peg had come out of one of the houses and run to greet them. When Kate jumped down, her older sister engulfed her in a hug.

'Oh, my, it's so good to see you! I didn't think you'd be able to come.'

'I had to come,' she grinned. 'I've missed you so much and couldn't wait to see little Matthew.' Her smile faltered. 'How's Lou?'

Peg sobered too. 'It's hard for her. Her heart is breaking all over again. I'm glad you're here for her.'

George came round the front of the lorry to join them.

'Because this lump won't be much help to her on the drive home.'

He looked offended. 'Is that any way to greet your favourite brother? Now come and tell me how much you've missed me,' he said, opening his arms and catching her in a bear hug, lifting her off her feet and making her shriek with laughter.

Kate hadn't realised until she'd spoken to George about joining him on the trip to Lincolnshire that he knew about Louisa's condition. They'd had to tell him when he'd helped them to move, and Louisa to escape her parents because she'd wept much of the way and had to stop to be sick a couple of times. He hadn't mentioned it to anyone, not even his wife or brother. So he didn't show any surprise that Peg looked just as trim as usual, even though the baby was only a few weeks old.

Will came out and joined them, kissing Kate on her cheek and shaking hands with George before engaging him in man talk about the vehicle, which was a newer model than the old lorry they'd used for the move months before.

'Go on,' said Peg, softly, giving Kate a gentle nudge towards the open cottage door. 'You go in and see them. She'll be so pleased to see you.'

Kate wasn't so sure she'd be happy to see her, knowing that it meant it was time for her to return to Somerset without her baby.

In the cottage, Louisa sat in a rocking chair by the range, cradling her son. When Kate first walked in, her friend's attention was so taken up by the child in her arms that she didn't notice her. She watched her, knowing that Lou must be treasuring every last precious moment before she had to leave him behind. It broke Kate's heart to think of it and she was fiercely glad that she was there to help her on the journey back to Somerset. Peg was right. Lovely as George was, he'd be a useless lump on this occasion. If she had to, Kate would hold Louisa and cry with her all the way home if it would help her get through this.

'Lou,' she said softly.

Louisa looked up, her eyes widening and her mouth dropping open when she saw Kate standing there. 'Kate!' she gasped. 'But how?'

'The factory's shut for Easter, so I cadged a ride with George. I couldn't wait to see you.' She approached and knelt by the chair, touching the baby's cheek. 'So this is little Mattie, eh?'

Louisa nodded, her eyes filling with tears before she blinked them away.

'He's perfect,' Kate whispered.

'He is. My little angel.' A tear escaped and made its slow path down her cheek – one of many that had taken the same route, no doubt. 'It's time, isn't it? George has come to take me back to Street.'

Kate gently wiped the tear from Louisa's face. 'Yes, love. I'm so sorry, Louisa. It shouldn't happen like this. But Peg and Will are going to love him and give him a good life and you're his godmother, so you'll always be part of it.'

Louisa stifled a sob as she nodded. 'I know. I couldn't ask for better people to care for him. They've been so kind to me, more than I deserve.'

Kate put her arms around her friend and the sleeping child. 'Don't talk like that. You're not a bad person, Lou. You did nothing but love a man who was lost fighting for king and country. It's this heartache you don't deserve, love.'

'I miss him so much,' she whispered. 'I swear he came to me when I was delirious with the labour pains. I saw him as clear as I see you now. He spoke to me. I thought I'd died too as the pain faded away.'

'Oh, my word, Lou.'

'I was so happy to see him, Kate. I reached out to touch him, but then the pain came back again and Peg and her neighbour Annie were shaking me and telling me not to give up, and when I looked again, Mattie was gone.' She took a deep breath. 'Do you think he joined his spirit with our baby's?'

Kate held Louisa tight for a moment, then loosened her grip, not wanting to smother the baby, who continued to sleep peacefully in his mother's arms. She didn't know what to think. She hoped that the grief wasn't turning Louisa's mind. 'I'm sure he's watching over him and you both, love,' she said. 'And he always will.'

Lou nodded. 'I know. He promised he would.' She looked down at her child. 'It comforts me to know he'll be here with little Mattie when I'm gone. That he approves of me leaving him with his brother and Peg.' She took a shaky breath. 'Now I've seen my love, I know I'm doing the right thing and it gives me the strength to go through with it.' She looked up. 'I suppose George will want to leave early tomorrow, won't he?'

The sadness in her eyes nearly broke Kate. But she knew that Louisa needed her to be strong for her right now. She nodded. 'He will, love. Do you need any help packing?'

She shook her head. 'No. Peg said he'd be here any day, so I've been getting ready. I doubt I'll sleep much tonight anyway, so I can finish it then.'

Kate didn't comment. She understood. She would do her best to make sure Lou rested, but she didn't suppose she would be able to.

'Are you going to stay with me and Auntie Betty?' she asked.

'No,' Lou sighed. 'Ma has asked me to go home. I wasn't going to, but then I thought maybe I should try it. Until my fall from grace, we were a happy family, weren't we? I know things will never be the same again, but maybe we can learn to get along again. I feel as though I should at least try.'

Kate wasn't so sure, although she admired her friend for being prepared to try. 'Fair enough,' she said. 'But if you need to get away, our door is always open.'

She nodded. 'I know. Thank you, Kate. You've been a wonder. I don't know what I'd have done without you.'

She shrugged. 'You'd have managed somehow. But I was glad to help. It seemed only right to involve Peg and Will, seeing as how they're blood kin to Mattie.' She smiled down at the baby. 'I can see he's got the look of the Searle brothers already.'

'He has, hasn't he?' Louisa smiled, although the aura of sadness around her never wavered as she touched the baby's soft cheek. She seemed to have aged ten years in just a few months. Little wonder, considering what she'd been through. 'It will make it much easier for people to accept Will as his father, won't it?'

'No one will know, love. None of us who know the truth will ever tell anyone.'

The door opened and the others came into the parlour. Kate gave Peg and Will a grateful smile, knowing they'd stayed out in the cold with her brother for longer than they should have in order to give her time to talk privately to Louisa.

George greeted Louisa cheerfully, admiring the baby but not commenting on the fact that she was holding onto him with fierce possession. Kate saw Louisa begin to relax a little in his company once she realised he wasn't going to judge her.

Peg had a hearty hotpot keeping warm in the oven and Louisa reluctantly laid the babe in the beautiful wooden cradle Will had made for him and joined them around the table to eat. Kate was glad to see her eating, because although her belly was a little plumper and softer than before, Lou had clearly lost a lot of weight in recent months. Her face and arms were thinner.

'Will you be going back to Clarks?' George asked Louisa.

'Yes,' she said. 'I wrote to the personnel manager. They said I could start again on the first of the month.' She glanced at Kate. 'I'll be back in the Machine Room.'

'Good,' she said. 'With any luck, Mr B will put you back with me and Jeannie. I'll ask him. We've missed you.'

'How is Jeannie?' asked Louisa. 'I haven't heard from her this week.'

Kate nodded. 'She said to apologise to you. Her ma has been right poorly this past fortnight with her nerves. She's taking all of Jeannie's spare time. It doesn't help that they haven't heard from Lucas for about three weeks now.'

Louisa frowned. 'Come to think of it, I haven't either. I wrote to him just after little Mattie was born. He usually writes back within a week or so, but I've had nothing yet.' She looked around the table at everyone's concerned faces. 'I've been so preoccupied that I hadn't noticed. I hope he's all right.'

They all nodded, their gazes focused on their plates. Kate felt a chill run down her spine as she thought about how unlike Lucas it was for him not to write. Both Jeannie and Louisa had said he was a very good correspondent.

'He'll be fine,' said George. 'You'll all get a bundle of letters in one go, I'll wager.'

'They'd have told his family by now if...' Will couldn't finish the sentence. 'I'm sure George is right. You'll get weeks' worth of letters in one go.'

'Let's pray that they'll have heard from him soon, although there'll be nothing delivered over Easter, will there?' said Peg. 'If anything comes here for you after that, I'll send it on, Louisa, love.'

Lou nodded. 'Thank you.'

'Now, eat up, everyone,' said Peg, her smile not hiding her concern. 'Thanks for bringing me some apple cake,' she said to Kate. 'I've tried making them here, but it's not the same without Somerset apples. I do miss them.'

'I hope Mrs Searle made it,' said George. 'Our Kate's never been that good in the baking department.'

'Cheeky devil!' gasped Kate, smacking his arm. 'I can bake a decent cake.'

'And when have you ever tried?' Peg asked him.

He held up his hands in surrender. 'Not my place to show you women how it should be done. I'm just saying. Pa nearly broke a tooth on that ginger cake she made.'

'I was ten years old!' Kate cried. 'When are you going to let me forget that?'

He grinned. 'Never,' he confirmed.

Will chuckled, earning a glare from both his wife and her sister.

Louisa remained quiet throughout the rest of the meal. No one made any demands on her, knowing that in just a few hours, she would be facing the hardest test of her life.

When little Mattie awoke, Louisa looked at Peg.

'Would you mind?' she asked her. 'I know I should stay back, but...'

Peg reached over and touched her hand on the table. 'It's all right. Go to him. I'll warm up some milk while you change him. Then Kate and I will do the washing up while these lumps go outside and talk nonsense and drink the cider George got Will to hide in the woodshed.'

'Will's not taken the pledge, has he?' said George. 'I can't drink on my own.'

Louisa quickly picked up the baby, kissing his temple as she cradled him close. She disappeared into the other room, cooing softly to the crying child.

The lads went outside, promising they wouldn't drink *all* the cider George had brought. Peg brought a glass bottle with milk in from the pantry and put it in a bowl of hot water from the kettle that had been sitting on the range. While it warmed, Kate used the rest of the water in the kettle to fill a basin and began to scrub the dishes. Peg filled the kettle again from the tap and put it back on the range, then took the bottle out of the bowl and, having checked the milk was warm enough, fixed a rubber teat onto the neck of the bottle.

She saw Kate watching. 'Our friend and neighbour Annie has a six-month-old and she's still producing plenty of breast milk. She suggested giving us her surplus for Mattie, because if Louisa kept feeding him until she left here, people might notice if she leaked when she got home. So she stopped breast-feeding him after the first fortnight and now her milk has dried up. It was hard for the poor love, though.'

Kate nodded. 'I hadn't thought about that.'

'Nor had we. Annie's been such a blessing, and so understanding of what Louisa is going through. We were a bit worried at first that she might judge, but she never has. I'm so grateful she's here. I'm terrified of doing something wrong, but she promises me she'll see me right. If our Mattie is half as sweet and good as her little ones, I'll be happy. Now, let me take this through. I can hear him starting to yell.' She opened the door and went inside, closing it behind her.

Indeed, the baby's cries had increased in volume, but they were silenced moments later. Kate imagined Louisa feeding her son for what might be the last time and her heart ached for her. It looked as though Peg felt the same when she came back and began to dry the dishes that Kate had washed.

'Are you all right, love?' Kate asked gently.

Peg nodded, her lips thinning as she blinked back tears. 'I'll be all right. But it's hard, seeing what she's going through.' She glanced towards the closed bedroom door. 'We're so happy to have a baby at last – I'd pretty much resigned myself to being childless and wondered if maybe Will might look elsewhere.'

'He wouldn't do that,' said Kate. 'I know he wouldn't. He loves you.'

Peg shrugged. 'I know he does. But a man needs a son, and I think it was preying on his mind – especially after his brother died. He worried his ma would never have grandchildren. I think that's why he was glad to move away from Somerset, because it make him feel guilty every time he saw her looking at the children playing in the fields behind her cottage or down by the river. So when you told us about Louisa and her problem, we felt as though God was giving us a true blessing by allowing us to help her and honour Mattie and his ma by providing a true family for the baby.' She paused, her gaze on the plate she was drying with exaggerated care. 'But our happiness is marred by Will's grief for his brother and Louisa's pain at having to give her son up. It doesn't seem right that we should be granted this wonderful gift of a child at the expense of Mattie's life and Louisa's happiness.'

Kate put the last cup on the draining board and dried her hands. 'Better that you and Will do this than she be forced to hand over little Mattie to a stranger, as her parents wanted. At least this way, she will be able to watch him from afar and know that he's happy with a family that loves him.'

'We do love him,' confirmed Peg as she put the last of the dishes away in a cupboard. 'He's our world already.'

Kate nodded. 'And Louisa knows that. It's hard for her now, and it might take a long time for her to get over it and get on with her life. But, knowing that he's with Mattie's family, being brought up by his own blood kin, that means the world to her. You mustn't feel guilty, Peg. You're doing the best thing for all of you, including the baby. Don't let anything spoil it.'

Peg hugged her, taking a deep breath. 'Thank you, Katie, love. You're right. But I can't help feeling Lou's pain. She's been so strong these past months that I think she's worn herself out.' She stepped back, keeping her hands on her sister's shoulders and looking deep into her eyes. 'Promise me you'll look after her? She's going to need your friendship more than ever now.'

She nodded. 'I know. I promise. That's why I came today.'

Peg nodded and kissed her cheek. 'You're a good girl, Katie. Ma would be so proud of you.'

She felt her own tears well. 'Oh, dear lord, don't bring Ma into it or I'll be blubbing all night.' She blinked hard as Peg chuckled softly. 'What on earth would she think of all them shenanigans with Pa and the Floozy, eh?'

Peg shuddered and rolled her eyes. 'I can't believe Pa would be so stupid. I know he wasn't the best husband or father, but to fall under the spell of that witch and lie to everyone for all these years...' She shook her head. 'Well, I doubt he'll be reunited with Ma in the next life. She's an angel in heaven, I'm sure, while he'll be heading in the other direction to pay for all his sins. She's well shot of him. Let him suffer with the Floozy and her devil children.'

'You know they're our brother and sister, don't you?'

'I do, and I realise they're innocents in this mess. But their mother made sure they wouldn't invite any sympathy by letting them grow up as mannerless, unpleasant little monsters.'

Kate couldn't help but agree with her. After all, she had had to live with them until her escape, putting up with their rudeness and laziness as well as their tantrums when they didn't get their own way. She had no time for them, blood tie or not.

'Now,' said Peg. 'You pop and see how Lou's getting on while I chase the men out of the shed. They've had time to have a bellyful of cider and Will's not as used to drinking as George is. I don't want him to start singing drunken songs and disturbing everyone.'

32

The journey home to Somerset the next day was a sombre affair. George concentrated, grim-faced, on his driving while Kate held Louisa as she wept, pouring out her grief as the miles between her and her child grew. Eventually, she fell into an exhausted sleep in Kate's arms.

Kate gently woke her friend when she spied Glastonbury Tor in the distance, bathed in the pink and purple lights of the sunset. The rest seemed to have helped Louisa, for she sat up straight, her eyes calmly drinking in the sights of home as they passed through Glastonbury town and finally reached Street village. Yet the evidence of her tears was still visible in her puffy and bloodshot eyes and that aura of sadness remained around her like a blanket.

'Do you want me to take you to Auntie Betty's with Kate?' George asked. 'She won't be there – she's over at my house with Ada and the...' He hesitated, obviously unwilling to mention children or babies for fear of upsetting her again. 'It will give you a little while to rest before you need to face your folks.'

But Louisa shook her head. 'No, thank you, George. Could you take me to my parents' cottage, please? If I don't go straight there, I fear I'll never find the courage to cross the threshold.'

'All right,' said George, making the turning into the Somerton Road.

'But if you change your mind, even when we get there,' said Kate, 'you must say and we'll take you with us straight away.'

Louisa's parents must have been watching for them because they came out of their cottage the moment George's lorry pulled up. Kate took her time opening the door and getting out in order to help Louisa exit the vehicle. She studied Mr and Mrs Clements, watching for signs that they would not welcome their daughter home. After their treatment of her when her pregnancy had been discovered, Kate did not trust them to treat her well. But Mrs Clements smiled and opened her arms to her daughter the moment her feet touched the ground. Kate was sure the woman would have clung to Louisa, but her friend allowed just a brief embrace before stepping back.

'Mother,' she said, her tone formal. 'Father. It's good to see you.'

'Welcome home, lass,' said her pa, his voice gruff with suppressed emotion.

'Come on inside,' said her ma, her tone almost cheerful as she held out a hand. 'You must be exhausted after your journey.'

Louisa turned away from them as George came round the back of the lorry, her bags in his hands.

'Thank you, George,' she said to him with a shy smile. 'For everything.'

He nodded as he handed her luggage over to Mr Clements.

'Yes,' said her pa. 'Thank you for bringing her home.'

Kate was glad Mr Clements didn't mention George's part in Louisa's escape all those months ago.

'You're welcome, sir,' he replied.

Louisa hugged Kate, clinging to her in a way that she hadn't with her ma. Kate caught a glimpse of the pain on Mrs Clements's face before she pinned on a smile.

'We're much obliged to you both,' she said. 'Can we offer you some refreshments after your journey?'

'No, thank you, ma'am,' said George. 'My wife's waiting on us.'

'Of course. Well, thank you. Come on, Louisa. Let's get you settled. I've put up new curtains and made a new bedspread for your room. I hope you like them.' She continued chattering as Louisa let her lead her into the cottage.

Mr Clements stayed behind, a worried frown on his face as he watched them go through the front door.

'How is she?' he asked Kate softly.

Kate sighed. She wanted to rant at the man for putting his only daughter through this, but she could see that they had suffered in her absence and her soft heart couldn't help but feel sympathy for them. 'She's deep in grief for the second time in a year, sir. I hope you'll give her the time and space to learn to live with it.'

'We couldn't have done any different,' he said. 'Keeping it would have ruined her life, spoiled her for a decent marriage.'

Kate closed her eyes, her sympathy waning. She wanted to remind him that Mattie had wanted to marry Louisa before he went to war but he had stopped them. If he hadn't been so rigid, she could have been a widow and been able to keep her child without shame. But what would be the point? He knew all that. He would have to live with his guilt, just as Louisa would have to live without the comfort of Mattie's child in her life.

Instead, she informed him, '*It* is a little boy called Matthew William Searle.'

Mr Clements's jaw tightened and his lips thinned, but Kate didn't care if she'd offended him by answering back. 'Louisa did what was right for her child. He will grow up with Mattie's family, even if his grandmother will never know the truth of it. Your family's reputation is safe, Mr Clements. But that doesn't mean Louisa's life hasn't been ruined. Marriage is the last thing she wants now. Mattie was the love of her life.'

'We'll see,' he said, his gaze cold. 'She's young. They both were. He was a Quaker, not an Anglican like us. There was no guarantee they'd have made a decent match, given their differences. She'll find someone else soon enough. She needs to get back to work and to make the best of her life – put all this behind her.'

Kate didn't hide her contempt as she stared back at him. Surely the whole point of being Christian was to love as Jesus did – without prejudice or judgement. To deny his daughter the chance to marry her love because he didn't worship at the same church as they did was cruel and in her opinion un-Christian. But she saw no point in saying anything else.

Mr Clements tilted his head towards George, who had got back in the lorry and was waiting for Kate. 'Your brother. Does he know?'

'Of course,' she said. 'How could he not when Louisa wept all the way to Lincolnshire last year and did the same all the way home today? But don't worry, Mr Clements; he hasn't told anyone. He'll keep Louisa's secret because he's a decent man and little Mattie is now our nephew, so we'll protect him to our last breaths.'

She knew from the way he raised his chin that her barbs had hit home, but she was so thoroughly disgusted that this man was more bothered by appearances than the terrible time his daughter was going through that she really didn't care.

'Now, we must go. George's wife will be wondering where he is. Goodbye, Mr Clements.'

He nodded and turned and walked into the house, closing the door. Kate hoped Louisa wouldn't suffer because of her words. If anyone had tried to defend her to her pa when she lived at home, she would have been punished for making him look bad, even if it had been true and his own doing. She had to remind herself that Mr Clements wasn't like her pa and her friend had found untold strength over the past few months, so no doubt she could deal with her parents now.

Yes, she'd be all right. She had nothing more to lose. After all, she knew that if things didn't work out at home, there was room for her at Auntie Betty's, where she would be loved without condition.

33

On Easter Sunday, Jeannie hurried along the High Street with her brother Peter, past the factory towards the Friends' Meeting House. She hadn't wanted to leave Ma, but Ma had insisted that they must go to pray for Lucas.

'But we can all pray for him here,' Jeannie had said. 'We don't need to be in the Meeting House to do that.'

'I know that, lass,' said Ma. 'But I need you to tell the Friends we need their prayers.'

John had scoffed. 'Why would they pray for him if he's gone off to fight? Some of the elders are saying he must be banished from the community.'

Jeannie had kicked him under the table and warned him to shut up with a glare. 'And others aren't,' she said. 'I can talk to the ladies, Ma. I'm sure they're already including him in their prayers. But I don't like leaving you on your own.'

'I'll stay with Ma,' said John.

So Jeannie and Peter had set off for the service, the lad grumbling most of the way.

'I should've made you stay and brought John with me,' she said. 'At least he doesn't go on so. He'd just sulk in silence.'

'I don't want to go,' he said. 'I'd rather be playing football.'

'Oh, you and your blasted football,' she scolded. 'No one plays on Easter Sunday, for goodness' sake. So stop your complaining. It's an hour of your time, that's all. We're doing it for Ma and Lucas.'

'Bloody fool,' he mumbled.

'What did you say?' She stopped, hands on hips, her anger and frustration rising. 'Did you just call me a bloody fool?'

He halted, staring at the ground, his shoulders hunched, hands in pockets. 'Not you. Lucas. Why the hell did he run off to war like that?'

Jeannie had asked herself that same question over and over and never really come up with a satisfactory answer. 'I don't know,' she sighed, the fight draining out of her. 'I think it had something to do with Mattie dying.'

Peter still didn't look up, but he nodded a couple of times. 'We thought so too. Like I said, he's a bloody fool. Mattie won't be coming back, will he? Going after him isn't going to help.'

'I know. But grief can grip people like that, can't it? Poor Louisa couldn't bear to stay in Street. But she's coming back now. Let's hope our Lucas does the same.' She linked her arm through his, hoping to comfort him. But, being the lad he was, he immediately stepped away, looking round to make sure no one saw him arm in arm with his big sister.

Jeannie rolled her eyes. 'Come on, or we'll be late.'

They began walking again, reaching the Meeting House a few minutes later. 'Now, remember,' she said. 'We're here to pray for Lucas and his safe return. And to ask others to do the same. That's what's important. Our brother.'

'I know. Come on.'

She shook her head as he stomped up the steps to the entrance, sending a silent apology to the lord for her brother's surliness.

* * *

Inside the Meeting House, Jeannie was surprised to see Tom. She'd never seen him there before and she'd had no idea that he was a Friend. He was speaking to some of the other men who greeted Peter when he walked up to join them. She felt herself blush when she saw Tom notice her and nod in acknowledgement. Not wanting to appear rude by ignoring him, she gave him a cool nod in return before she spotted Mrs Searle and hurried over to join her. Miss Alice Clark was there too, so Jeannie greeted the women politely, but didn't ask Auntie Betty about Kate in front of their boss.

So she kept quiet, listening respectfully as the women spoke together. Miss Clark didn't take her leave of them until everyone was called to worship, so Jeannie didn't get the chance to speak to the older woman alone or to ask about Kate until after their hour of silent contemplation.

'Oh, yes, my dear. They got back yesterday. I left Kate in bed. She was worn out, the poor love.'

'And Louisa's home?'

'That she is. Back with her parents where she belongs.' She shook her head. 'I can't understand why they thought to send her away. At a time of loss, we all need our families, don't we? Kate says she's still missing my Mattie.'

'I'm sure she is, Auntie. We all miss him, but him and Louisa... well, we thought they'd be together forever.'

'Aye, lass. I can't argue with that. I'm heartily sorry for young

Louisa. I will always think of her as a daughter-in-law. I wish I could understand why my Mattie thought to go off and fight. It was so unlike him. But one day, he came to me and said, "Ma. Please don't think badly of me, but I've got to go." And that was that. Off he went, and God took him for an angel. Now me and Louisa will have to wait until the good lord chooses to take us before we can be reunited with him.' She wiped a stray tear from her eye. 'But I reckon I'll be seeing my darling lad a long while before poor Louisa. She's still so young and I've lived most of my life already. I've been praying for her, that God will send another good man to take the place of my boy. She's a good girl who deserves to be happy. Mattie wouldn't want her to be so sad and on her own.'

Jeannie touched Auntie's arm, thinking again about Louisa and Lucas. She was sure it was just wishful thinking on her part. She would love Louisa to be her sister-in-law. 'I'm sure he wouldn't,' she said. 'But I doubt if Lou is ready to let anyone take Mattie's place in her heart right now.'

'That's what Kate said. But time will heal, I'm sure.' Betty patted Jeannie's hand on her arm. 'Now, what's the news from your Lucas?'

Jeannie swallowed against a lump in her throat and nodded. 'We haven't heard from him for a couple of weeks now. Ma's beside herself with worry. We all are, but...' She shook her head. How could she explain how her fears rendered her mother incapable of doing anything? 'We need to ask everyone to pray for him.'

'I understand, lass. A mother's fear for her children can take away their reason. I expect your ma has taken to her bed again?'

Jeannie nodded, wanting to make excuses for Ma, but unable to speak. Where Betty Searle had carried on after the death of her husband and her beloved son, keeping herself busy and counting her blessings, Jeannie's ma had simply turned in on herself. When

Pa had died, even though Jeannie had only been little at the time, she remembered having to help Lucas with the twins because Ma had just given up. If it hadn't been for the help of others, Jeannie had no idea what would have become of them. But there were other families in need of help now thanks to this awful war, so much of the burden of caring for Ma had landed on Jeannie's shoulders.

Jeannie wasn't sure how much longer she could go on like this. Even with Kate's brothers keeping an eye on the twins and urging them to help her, she wasn't getting much of a break between working full-time at the factory and running the house and caring for Ma. She was so tired yet barely slept these days, and if Lucas didn't come back, she couldn't see an end to it.

Right now, she longed to be able to go and visit Louisa and welcome her friend home. But she knew she had to rush back to organise their meal, or they'd be having bread and cheese for their Sunday dinner. She'd already peeled the potatoes and prepared the vegetables and there was a plump rabbit ready to go in the oven. But the twins hadn't a clue, so she couldn't rely on them to help finish the cooking. She just hoped she could persuade Ma to get out of bed and join them at the kitchen table to eat.

'I'd better get back to her,' she said. 'John stayed at home, but he doesn't have a lot of patience, that boy.'

'You go on, lass. Give my regards to your ma and tell her I'm praying for her, Lucas and your whole family. I'll spread the word and get the others to do the same.'

'Thank you, Auntie,' Jeannie said, kissing the older woman's cheek. 'That'll be a great comfort to her.'

She turned to find her brother and saw with a sinking heart that he was talking to Tom. Taking a fortifying breath, she approached them.

'Peter, we need to go.'

'Tom's been telling me about working as an engineer,' he said, tilting his head towards him. 'I reckon I could do that. I hate working in the carton department. Making shoe boxes all day is boring.'

'Everyone needs to start somewhere,' she said. 'If you work hard and show willing, you'll get the chance for better things soon enough.'

'Your sister's right,' said Tom. 'I worked my way round a few different jobs back in Northampton before I managed to get into the type of work I do now.'

'Why'd you—'

'Peter!' Jeannie interrupted. 'Stop being so nosy. We've got to go. I've got to get the dinner done for Ma.'

'Aw, but Jeannie, Tom can help me get on. I'll earn more money as an engineer, won't I?'

She shook her head. She didn't have time for this. Tom must have read her expression because he said, 'I hear your ma's poorly. You can't hold up her dinner for the sake of a few questions, can you?'

Peter looked a bit shamefaced. 'I suppose not.'

Jeannie was relieved and was about to turn away and escape this man who made her stomach flutter whenever he looked at her when he spoke again.

'Why don't I walk back with you both so I can answer your questions without delaying your sister?'

'Yes, please!' said Peter, beaming at him. 'That'll be fine, won't it, Jeannie?'

She wanted to say no, but knew that would be unspeakably rude considering he was prepared to encourage her brother to better himself with a skilled trade. So she nodded, tight-lipped,

and felt her cheeks burning when she looked at Tom and registered his knowing look.

As they made their way past Clarks and up the High Street,
Peter bounced around Tom like an eager puppy, firing questions at
him. Tom answered each one with patience, not sugar-coating the
amount of studying Peter would have to do if he chose to become
an engineer.

'I was good at mathematics and science at school,' Peter said.
'And I'm studying at the Day School a couple of half-days a week,
although they say they might stop our lessons on account of so
many men going off to war. I hope they don't. I really like it. It's
better than making shoe boxes all day long.'

'Well, if you study hard and your grades are good enough, you
could apply for an apprenticeship.'

Peter looked downcast. 'That will take years.'

'It could. There's a lot to learn,' he said. 'But the sooner you
start, the sooner you finish. And once you do, the money's good.
And machines are our future. You'll be set for life.'

That perked the boy up. He thanked Tom before rushing off
ahead to tell his twin about the opportunities available for bright
engineers, leaving Jeannie alone with Tom.

They walked in silence for a little while, making Jeannie feel
uncomfortable. She came to a halt and turned to face him.

'Thank you for encouraging him,' she said. 'But now he's
rushed off like that, there's no need for you to keep on with me. I
know you're lodging with Mr and Mrs Persey and going to our
house is taking you out of your way.'

He smiled. 'Have you been checking up on me, Jeannie
Musgrove?' he asked, his tone teasing.

'No!' she replied, her cheeks warming again.

'So how do you know where I live?'

'I... someone said, that's all,' she said, feeling foolish. 'I just didn't want you to feel you needed to walk out of your way now that Peter's finished with his questions.'

'I don't mind walking you home,' he said. 'It's good to feel spring in the air at last and I'm in no rush.'

'Oh. All right.' She didn't know what to say. It would be rude to tell him to go away now, wouldn't it?

They carried on walking. Jeannie became aware of his limp again. She hadn't noticed it when he'd been talking to Peter. She supposed that was because she'd been looking anywhere but at Tom, not wanting her brother to notice that she couldn't seem to stop herself staring at the man. She told herself it was because she was embarrassed about him being the witness to what had happened at The Cross.

'I hope you haven't had any more trouble with that lout at The Cross,' he said after a few moments, making her wonder whether he could read her mind.

Jeannie sighed. *Of course he had to mention it.* 'No. My brother – my older brother, that is – made sure he didn't bother me again.'

'That'll be Lucas? The one who's in France?'

She nodded, remembering again that they hadn't heard from him for weeks. 'Tom, when you were in the army, did your letters get through to your family regularly?' she asked. 'Only we haven't had any news from him lately and...'

He stopped and gave her a narrow-eyed stare. 'How did you know I was in the army?'

She swallowed and gave him a nervous smile. 'I noticed your limp. Someone said you were injured fighting.'

He sighed and ran a hand through his hair. 'That's right,' he said, looking away. 'But I don't discuss it.'

'Oh!' She took a step back. 'I'm sorry, I wasn't prying. It's just what I heard. I'm so worried about my brother. I thought you might...' She paused and closed her eyes. 'I'm sorry. I shouldn't have said anything.'

She opened her eyes. He caught her gaze and held it. Jeannie didn't even dare blink. He looked fierce, like he had that night at The Cross, and it frightened her a little, even as it excited her. After what seemed an age but was probably only a moment, he lowered his gaze.

'No, I'm sorry. I shouldn't have snapped at you.'

She wanted to deny he had done anything of the sort, but he went on before she could speak.

'And I'm sorry you're worried about your brother, but all you can do is wait for a letter. Believe me, you'll hear soon enough if something awful has happened.' He gave her a smile that didn't reach his eyes. 'No news is good news,' he said, injecting a false heartiness into his voice.

His little pantomime chilled her to the bone. He must have seen her distress because his expression softened. She could see regret in his eyes now, all fierceness gone.

'Try not to worry,' he said. 'It doesn't help.'

She nodded. 'I know. But it's so hard.'

'That it is,' he said. 'But what choice do you have?'

The clock in Clarks Tower chimed the hour. Jeannie looked back in that direction, glad of an excuse to look away from him.

'I must go,' she said. 'Ma will be wondering...'

'Of course,' he nodded, not offering to escort her the rest of the way. 'I hope you get some good news soon. I'll pray for you.'

'Thank you,' she said, touched by his words.

She watched him walk away, back in the direction from which they had just come. 'Tom?' she called out after he'd gone a few steps.

He stopped and turned. 'Yes?'

'Was it hard, going to fight when you're a Friend?'

He raised his chin and tilted his head a little to the side as he thought about her question. 'Actually,' he said, 'I was a Methodist when I went to fight. It was what I saw over there that made me explore the life of the Friends. I've only just joined them.'

Without waiting for her response, he turned again and carried on walking, leaving Jeannie staring after him.

Louisa couldn't persuade her parents to let her stay home from church on Easter Sunday. They both came into her room to wake her, telling her to get ready.

'The sooner you face people, the better,' said her father. 'You can't hide away at home for ever, lass.'

'I've barely come through the door,' she protested. She had also been awake most of the night, crying. 'Can't I wait until next Sunday?'

Her mother laid a gentle hand on her shoulder. It took all of Louisa's strength not to flinch away. She could hardly bear for her to touch her.

'Louisa, dear. Don't you think that today of all days – on the day of Christ's resurrection – is a good time for you to make a new start? You should see this as your resurrection. A new life.'

She closed her eyes and turned her face away, not wanting her mother to see the revulsion she felt. 'I don't want a new life,' she said. 'I don't want anything.'

Her father blew out an impatient breath. He had barely looked at her since she arrived. 'Whether you want anything or not, lass, you will accompany us to church. People will expect it now you're home.'

Her mother sat on the bed. 'Come on now, Louisa. It's time to look forward. To get back to normal. I know it's hard, but you'll be all right soon enough. You did the right thing. Now you must make the best of things.'

Louisa wanted to scream and shout that she knew nothing of what her own daughter had been through these past months because she had chosen to drive her away rather than face the shame of her fall from grace.

'You haven't even asked me about him,' she whispered. 'He's your grandson.'

Her father went rigid. 'No, he's not,' he declared, his voice low and deadly. 'He's Will and Peg Searle's son now, nothing to do with us, and the sooner you accept that, the better. Now get up and do as you're told. You're coming to church with us and you'll act like a respectable young woman and not the sulking child you appear to have turned into.'

'I would have been a respectable young woman and been able to keep my baby if you'd only let Mattie marry me when he asked you,' she said, unable to keep the words inside.

'That was never going to happen, and you know it. He wasn't the right sort for my daughter – a fact proven by the way he disrespected you and left you in the family way.'

Louisa gaped at him. 'Disrespect? He loved me!'

Pa scowled and leaned closer to her, his voice cold even though his eyes burned with rage. 'He had no right. I told him I'd never agree to him marrying you and he deliberately seduced you in defiance of me.'

She shook her head, her tears overflowing. It would be no good arguing that no seduction had been necessary. In fact, she'd had to persuade Mattie to make love to her, not the other way around. 'You weren't ever going to accept him, were you?'

'No. You'll marry a proper Christian and you'll put this whole sorry matter behind you. Now, get ready for church and stop this nonsense.'

Both Louisa and her mother flinched when he slammed the door behind him, leaving them alone. For a moment, neither spoke. Out of the corner of her eye, Louisa saw her mother trying to gather herself. Clearly, Pa's outburst had upset her. But, just as clearly, she wasn't about to go against her husband.

'Come now, love,' her mother said gently. 'You left some of your clothes here. Shall I find you something to wear?'

'They won't fit me,' she snapped. 'I've bigger bosoms and I've still got a fleshy belly.' She swung her legs over the side of the bed away from her and stood up. 'I've something in my bag I can wear.' She looked over her shoulder. 'Don't worry, no one will notice – it's a loose coat that will cover my sins.'

She was grateful her mother hadn't suggested a restricting corset to hide her new shape. Peg's friend Annie had assured her she would lose the loose flesh around her belly soon enough if she took herself out for walks and kept active, but in the meantime she'd suggested the style and helped her make the dress and long jacket Louisa now pulled from her bag.

She paused, taking a deep breath, trying to calm herself. 'Pa's wrong, you know. I don't care that he thinks he's right. He's not. Mattie was a good man and the only one I would consider marrying. Now he's gone and I've been forced to give our son away, all because of Pa's narrow-minded views. I'll never forgive him, or you. Never.'

'You don't mean that.'

She looked at her mother, her face set. 'I do. Every word of it. I'll play your dutiful daughter today, Ma. But I'm not the girl I was before I had to run away to save my child. I'll never marry and I'll never forget Mattie and little Matthew.'

Her mother sighed and got up. 'Very well. I can see you're going to be stubborn as usual, but you'll see soon enough that we're right. I'll leave you to get ready. Maybe this week, we can go through your things and alter them as necessary before you go back to Clarks.'

* * *

The walk to church was silent and uncomfortable. Her father greeted people cheerfully as they walked down Somerton Road and into Church Road. Some were going in the same direction towards the parish church or the Baptist chapel. Others were turning in the other direction at The Cross, heading for the Friends' Meeting House, or going further along the High Street to the Methodist church or the Salvation Army hall. Louisa hoped and dreaded she might catch a glimpse of Mattie's ma, knowing instinctively that she would get a warmer welcome from Betty Searle than she had from her parents but afraid that she might break down at the sight of Mattie's beloved ma. She wondered whether Kate had yet given the older woman the pencil sketch she'd drawn of little Mattie. It had been hard to give it up, but she had a hidden sketchbook full of images she'd committed to paper of her beautiful little man. It was a small sacrifice to give one of them to his grandmother, who she knew would love him with all her heart.

They didn't see Mrs Searle, but her parents acknowledged several folk – some of whom worked for her pa in the Cutting Room at Clarks. The men all doffed their caps in respect for their foreman. Some looked at Louisa curiously, but she kept her gaze averted and didn't encourage anyone to speak to her, even the women and girls from the Machine Room who recognised her and called greetings. Instead, she simply smiled politely with her mouth and waved in their direction but kept on walking. She was relieved when the church came in sight and she knew she could sit quietly in a pew and not have to pretend to be polite.

The service was pure torture for her. In previous years, she had enjoyed the Easter Sunday service, excited that it marked the end of Lent and the beginning of spring. The church looked beautiful, filled with fresh spring flowers after the bare austerity of Lent. But she had nothing to be excited about now. Nothing to look forward to. Nothing to bring her joy.

When the vicar talked about how Jesus died so that we might be forgiven our sins, Louisa clenched her hands into fists, her nails digging into her palms hard. She closed her eyes, not wanting to see this man of God talk about forgiveness when she knew full well he would condemn her as beyond redemption for the sin of loving Mattie without going through a church-approved wedding ceremony. There would have been no forgiveness for her if she had kept little Matthew and presented him at church for baptism. They would both have become outcasts in the eyes of this so-called Christian man who preached to them now about the lord's forgiveness of sin. She wanted to stand up and scream at him that he was a hypocrite and a liar.

If there truly is a God in this church, he is not a loving, forgiving God. He is a cruel, vicious, horrible monster who took my Mattie and then forced me to give up our child. I will not worship such a God.

It made her feel so physically sick that she refused to move when her parents got up to take communion. They couldn't force her without drawing attention to themselves and they would never do that. Instead, while they were at the altar rail, their backs stiff with disapproval, she slipped out of the pew and left the church, determined never to enter that place again.

She turned away from the village, making her away across the fields towards Glastonbury, joining the road and crossing the River Brue at Pomparles Bridge. She had no idea where she was going. She barely noticed the chill wind coming across the levels. She simply had a fierce urge to get as far away from the church as she could. The ground was soft and damp beneath her feet, soaking her best shoes, but she didn't care. She paused on the bridge and looked down into the river, wishing it was deeper and swifter so that she might throw herself in, sure of drowning and being swept out to sea. But the shallow waters and sluggish flow mocked her and she knew it would be a pointless exercise. At the back of her mind, pushing its way forward through her distress and despair was the thought that, if she were to take her own life, and there actually *was* a God, then she might be denied the chance to ever be reunited with Mattie as suicide was a cardinal sin.

With a sigh, Louisa crossed the bridge and carried on walking past the Morlands factory, barely noticing the stink that hung around it even when it was closed, and into the heart of Glastonbury. She paid no attention to anyone she passed, pausing only when she reached the Chalice Well Gardens at the foot of the Tor.

She looked up towards the tower atop the Tor. She and Mattie had often climbed up to it, and would stand on the summit enjoying the views across the levels to the Mendip Hills to the north and the Quantocks to the south. They had thought they could overcome anything then, not realising the awful fates that destiny had in store for them. She wondered whether she would feel closer to Mattie up there, but knew she didn't have the energy to make the climb today. Ever since she had given birth, she had felt weak and listless.

'I'll do it soon,' she whispered to herself. 'Then maybe Mattie will come to me again.'

She knew that Kate hadn't believed her when she said he had

visited her during her labour. *She probably thinks I was mad with the pain. Well, I was. But I know it was more than that.* She hadn't told her friend what he had said to her. His words were the only thing that kept her going – both through the pain of birthing their son and now, even in her present misery. She knew she must remember what he'd told her and what he'd made her promise him. After Kate's reaction, she knew she couldn't tell anyone else. She'd not wanted to mention it to Peg and Will, knowing it would upset them. But she'd hoped her friend would understand. Now, she knew that telling her had been a mistake, so she would keep her silence and allow Kate to believe it had been the temporary delirium of childbirth that had affected her.

As she thought about this, she walked through the gardens surrounding the Chalice Well, coming to the well itself. To her relief, the place was empty of people, although she could see from the flowers and candles left around the well-head that pilgrims had been here to celebrate the resurrection this morning.

She sat on a bench by it, soothed by the soft, tinkling sound of the water coming from the ancient spring, its iron-red colour giving it the alternative name of the Blood Well. Legend had it that Joseph of Arimathea travelled to Glastonbury from the Holy Land with the holy grail and cruets containing the blood and water from Christ's body, and had lived out his life here. Some folk believed that the water from the well was coloured by the holy blood itself and that the grail was hidden somewhere nearby.

As a child, Louisa had been thrilled and a little awed by the thought of this. But in her present situation, she realised it was a foolish legend, perpetuated by people who gave lip service to Jesus's words about love and forgiveness but were in reality cold and cruel. It had been a harsh lesson, to learn that her own father could be counted amongst these men. But now she had no illusions. She could never again rely upon her pa to protect her.

She closed her eyes, her mind conjuring up pictures of her lover and their child behind her eyelids. She tried to imagine Mattie and their son together, but couldn't. She wished with all her heart that she could be assured that Mattie's spirit would guard little Matthew from heaven.

The familiar emptiness filled her heart and her arms and her head dropped to her chest as she fought to keep from weeping. She stayed like that for a long time, her mind filled with memories of being with Mattie – of the times they'd spent together and with their friends – until she heard voices and footsteps coming in her direction. It wasn't the same, being back here without Mattie – or Lucas, for that matter. She wondered where he was and whether he was safe. She would have to go round to Jeannie's to see if they had news of him. It wasn't like him not to write.

Stiff with cold, she got up and made her painful way back through the gardens, avoiding meeting anyone. She began the walk back to Street and her parents' home, her steps slow, her head bowed. She would be expected to apologise for leaving church, no doubt. But she couldn't feel sorry that she had. But, for the sake of peace today, she would say that she was and try to be a dutiful daughter for the rest of the day. She would save the battle over whether she went back to church again for another day.

But tomorrow, she would go to see Jeannie. She felt in her heart that there would be news soon. And if Lucas, Jeannie and their family needed her, she would do whatever she could to help them.

35

The letter was hand-delivered by a man in uniform. He apologised for disturbing them on the Easter Monday, but explained he'd been lucky enough to have a few days' leave and had volunteered to bring the letter to the Musgrove family on his way to his home in Middlezoy from his regimental headquarters near Salisbury.

Jeannie stared at the official-looking envelope that he was holding out towards her, fear holding her paralysed. It could only be bad news. Was Lucas dead, like Mattie? Her heart was racing and her skin felt cold. How would they cope without Lucas? Her life would never be the same again. Ma and the twins would need her more than ever. She was glad that the twins were out and Ma had stayed in bed today; just the sight of the soldier holding out the envelope would surely kill her. How could she tell Ma? Who would be there to help the twins grow into decent men? Or would they rush off to fight to avenge their brother? Jeannie was frightened to take it, sure it was the news they had been dreading, wanting the messenger and message to disappear as though they'd never been. Her reluctance must have been evident, for the man shifted uncomfortably and cleared his throat.

'It's not that kind of letter, I promise,' he said gently.

'He's alive?' she asked, searching his face. He looked kind. She was sure he wouldn't lie to her.

'Yes,' he said, nodding firmly. 'Just arrived back in Blighty.'

'He's home?'

He looked a little uncertain now. 'Not ready to come home just yet, miss. He's in the hospital at Salisbury. But he was lucky. Most of his platoon bought it, but he and a couple of others were able to get back behind our lines. Once he's recovered, he'll be sent home. He's done his bit. Might even get a medal – he's been mentioned in dispatches. He saved a man's life. This is the official notification from the regiment that he's being honourably discharged on medical grounds.'

'He's hurt?' Again, those chills of dread wracked her body as she focused in on the mention of the hospital. She reached for the letter, ripping it open, even though it was addressed to Ma. It was better that Jeannie read it and be able to break the news – whatever it might be – to her gently.

'Yes,' he confirmed. 'Took some shrapnel as well as a bullet. But don't worry, the medics did a good job. It might take a while, but he should make a decent recovery.'

She scanned the letter. It confirmed what the soldier had told her, that Lucas had been injured in battle and, after treatment at a field hospital, had been transferred back to England, where he was now a patient in a military hospital near Salisbury. While he should make a good recovery, he was deemed unfit for further combat duties and would be honourably discharged once he was sufficiently recovered to be released from hospital.

Relief flooded her. 'Oh, thank God!' she said, tears filling her eyes. 'He's coming home.'

Again, the man shifted on his feet, reminding Jeannie of her manners.

'Oh! I'm so sorry. I went into a bit of a panic there for a minute. Can I offer you a cup of tea? And there's some Simnel cake left if you'd like some?'

He held up his hands. 'No, thank you, miss. I need to get on to see my family.'

'Oh. All right. But at least let me give you some cake to eat on the way?'

'That would be lovely, thank you.'

He followed her into the house and waited patiently while she cut a generous slice and wrapped it in waxed paper for him.

'Thank you so much for coming to see us,' she said. 'I'm sorry my ma isn't well enough to meet you, but I'll tell her what you said.'

He nodded. 'My pleasure, miss. It's good to bring you better news. Too many families are getting the worst kind.'

'I know. We've been so worried about him. When do you think he'll be able to come home?'

He shrugged. 'He looked fairly good when I saw him last week, but...'

'You've seen him?' She wanted to grab his arm and make him stay to tell her every little detail, but she knew she couldn't.

'I have. I was sent over to the hospital to check on casualties who'd been sent back to Blighty. He was certainly looking better than a few of the chaps. All limbs intact, no obvious impairment.' He sighed. 'Some of the others... well, they're going to find it hard. But your brother should be all right. Just give him some time.'

She nodded, her heart aching for the others he talked of while she wanted to fall down on her knees and thank the lord for returning her brother to them in one piece. 'Can we go and see him?' She wasn't sure when she'd manage to get all the way to Salisbury, or whether she'd be able to get Ma on a train, but she needed to see Lucas, to reassure herself and Ma that he was indeed all right.

Again, he looked uncomfortable. 'Visiting hours are restricted, but it can be arranged. But... well, to be honest, miss, I got the impression your brother wasn't keen on having visitors.'

'Why ever not?' she asked, not believing him.

'It's quite common,' he explained. 'These lads have seen things you can't imagine. They've seen their pals die. The chaps in the know – the mind-doctors, if you will – well, they say it's common for lads like your brother to feel guilty for having survived when so many people around them didn't.'

Jeannie immediately thought of Mattie and how Lucas had felt guilty about letting him go off to fight on his own. If Lucas had seen other lads killed or maimed, he probably felt even worse after all that. Again, her heart ached for her brother. The soldier went on to explain how Lucas had saved himself and another lad after the whole platoon had been assumed dead.

'A lot of survivors are reluctant to face their loved ones at first. He might even tell you he won't come home. But don't worry. I'm sure he'd be pleased to see a familiar face if you can get there and he'll soon change his mind.' He gave her a reassuring smile. 'Now, I must be off.' He held up the cake she'd wrapped in waxed paper. 'Thanks for this. I'll enjoy it on the way.'

He left her with details of visiting hours at the hospital and then with a salute and a wave, he was gone, leaving Jeannie staring at the letter.

'Jeannie?' Her mother's soft voice carried down the stairs. 'Who's here? Are the twins back?'

'No, Ma,' she called back. 'They've gone to a football match in Yeovil, remember? They won't be back for hours yet.' She tucked the letter into her pocket. 'Do you want some tea and Simnel cake?'

'A cuppa would be nice. But who was just here?'

'Give me a minute to put the kettle on and I'll come up and tell you.'

* * *

An hour later, Ma was asleep and Jeannie was worn out. As she'd expected, her mother had been distressed by the news that her eldest son had been injured, but also thankful that he was alive and coming home to them. It had taken a while to calm and reassure her. It had been a relief when she had finally fallen into an exhausted sleep and Jeannie had come back downstairs.

She checked on the stew that was cooking in the range ready for when the twins got home. She had just sat down to rest for a moment when there was another knock at the door.

Kate stood there, a grin on her face. When she stepped to one side to reveal the girl standing behind her, Jeannie gasped.

'Louisa!' she cried at the sight of their friend. 'Oh, lord, I've missed you!' She engulfed her friend in a fierce hug, right there on the doorstep, unable to stop the sob that escaped her.

Lou hugged her back and the friends clung to each other, crying and laughing.

'Come in, come in. Oh, my word, I can't believe you're here. Kate said you'd be back, but I told her I couldn't believe it until I saw you for myself. I felt sure you'd decide to stay in Lincolnshire. But here you are!' Jeannie ushered them into the kitchen, looking at her properly for the first time. She put her hands on Louisa's cheeks. Her face was thinner than she remembered. 'How are you?' she asked.

Lou smiled, although her eyes remained sad, as though she'd forgotten how to be happy since they'd got the news about Mattie. Jeannie wanted to hug her again, to breathe some joy into her friend's heart. If she was still grieving after all these months...

'I'm all right,' she said. 'It's good to be back. But... well, it's never going to be the same, is it?'

'No, I don't suppose it is, love. But I'm so glad you're home. Maybe it wasn't the right thing, to go away like that?'

'Better Lincolnshire with Peg and Will than with her miserable old aunt in Exeter,' said Kate, her voice a little sour.

Louisa looked away, her glance resting on the brown envelope where Jeannie had left it on the table, ready to show the twins when they got home.

'Is that...?' She pointed at the letter. 'Is it about Lucas?' she asked, a worried frown creasing her brow.

'Oh, God,' said Kate, staring at it with dread as she covered her mouth with her hand.

'Yes, but it's not the worst news,' said Jeannie. 'Someone brought it this morning. He's been injured. Not so serious as to leave him crippled or anything, but enough that they've sent him back to England and he'll be getting an honourable discharge. The chap that came to give us this said he might even get a medal... not that Lucas would be interested in anything like that, I'm sure.'

Kate nodded, looking cautiously relieved. 'That's good, isn't it? He's coming home?'

'I think so. But not yet. He's in hospital near Salisbury.' She urged Louisa to sit in Ma's chair by the range and Kate took the one opposite while Jeannie pulled the bench from the kitchen table over to sit on. 'I wanted to take Ma to see him, but she's really not up to the journey, and I don't think I should leave her.' She rubbed her tired eyes. 'We're both desperate to see him for ourselves, but I tried to get Ma out of bed earlier. I thought that, now we know he's alive, she'd rally and make the effort. She did try, bless her. But she's been barely eating and fretting so that now her legs just can't hold her any more. I need the twins to carry her downstairs, so what chance have I got of getting her on and off a train? Then we'd have to get to the hospital, which could be miles from the station. She'd never be able to walk it.' She sighed. 'Plus I suppose the army won't be paying him for much longer and he'll need to convalesce before he can get back to work at Clarks. We'll need to watch the pennies for a while, so maybe we shouldn't be spending money on train fares.'

The girls looked sympathetic, but said nothing. Jeannie knew they'd help if they could, but what could they do?

As if reading her thoughts, Kate said, 'I wish we could help. I've got a bit put by that would help with the fare. Maybe we could watch your ma while you go?'

For a moment, Jeannie was hopeful. But then reality set in and she realised that Kate's savings were destined for her late ma's headstone. She shook her head. 'It's kind of you to offer, but I can't afford to take time away from work. Even if I left after work on Saturday, I wouldn't have enough time to visit Lucas and get the train back, and I'm not sure if there are any trains other than troop movements on Sundays.'

'George might be able to get you a lift on a lorry,' said Kate. 'They do a lot of runs to Salisbury and beyond. Someone could drop you off and pick you up on their way back.'

Jeannie thought about it. 'Would they be working at the weekend?'

Kate grimaced. 'Probably not.' She blew out a breath. 'There must be something we can do that won't mean you have to miss work.'

'I could go,' said Louisa.

'What?' both girls said at once, turning to look at her.

She nodded. 'I'm not due to start back at the factory until the first of the month, so I could go any day of the week. If George can arrange a lift, I could go so you could carry on looking after your ma and not miss any shifts. I could see him and come back and tell you how he is.' She looked at her friends, who were staring at her with astonishment. 'What? Lucas and me have been writing to each other all these months. He's my friend – Mattie's and mine. I want to make sure he's all right as well, and I want to be able to reassure you and your ma. It makes sense, doesn't it?'

'Actually,' said Kate, 'it does.'

'But...' said Jeannie. 'I wanted to...'

'The sooner someone goes and sees him, the sooner we can reassure your ma and get him home,' said Louisa. She leaned forward, resting a hand on Jeannie's knee. 'Let me do this for you, Jeannie, love. Lucas has been a good friend to me these past few months when I've been missing Mattie so, just as you and Kate have. Now I can do something for him and for you. I could go tomorrow if Kate can arrange the lift.'

'What about your ma and pa? Won't they want you home? I'm sure they've missed you.'

Louisa shrugged, looking away again. 'Things aren't the best between us,' she said. 'I left church early yesterday, I just couldn't bear it, and now Pa isn't talking to me at all. Ma just keeps looking at me and shaking her head and telling me I've got to buck up my ideas and get on with my life.' She sighed. 'He finally admitted yesterday that he never had any intention of letting Mattie marry me. It was because Mattie was a Friend... He didn't care what a good man he was or how much we loved each other.' She shook her head. 'So I've learned the truth at last. My father is a hypocrite, working for the Quaker Clarks yet stopping me from marrying Mattie because he was a Friend like them.'

'That's ridiculous,' cried Kate. 'How can he work at Clarks and be so against you marrying a Friend?'

'There are a lot of families like that,' said Jeannie. 'I know

Friends who have threatened to disown their children if they marry Anglicans as well, even though we're taught we shouldn't judge. It's daft, I know. But I seem to remember one of the Clarks marrying an Anglican and the bride had to join the Society of Friends before the family would acknowledge her.'

Kate rolled her eyes and tutted. 'And they all call themselves Christians,' she muttered. 'What about all that talk of loving your neighbours as yourselves, eh?'

'I know.' Jeannie pulled a face. 'Although I confess, I've been guilty of the same sin,' she confessed.

'What are you talking about?' asked Kate. 'You're the least likely sinner I know. You're almost too good, sometimes,' she teased.

Jeannie shook her head. 'Well, after seeing how your pa and his Floozy were doing you ill after drinking and carousing, I took against that fellow Tom when I saw him coming out of the Street Inn, even though he came to my rescue.'

Kate looked confused. 'I thought that was because you were embarrassed about the incident with Sid.'

She looked down at her slippered feet, her cheeks growing warm. 'It was at first. But then I started to tell myself he was a bad'un because he must be a drinker like your pa. He'd looked so... worked up, y'know, when he grabbed Sid. I got a bit frightened that he was a drunkard and violent with it – no better than Sid or your pa.'

'Do you still think like that?' asked Louisa, looking thoughtful.

Jeannie shook her head. 'Kate found out he was only staying at the inn until he found himself somewhere to lodge. Now he's living with a teetotal family who wouldn't tolerate a drinker in their house, so I don't think he is one. And he's started coming to the Meeting House. He told me he was a Methodist until he went to fight and now his beliefs line up better with the Quakers.'

'So he's not a drinker and he's a Friend?' said Louisa, smiling. 'Is that why you think you've become a sinner – because you misjudged him?'

She sighed, feeling embarrassed. 'Maybe.'

'And now you like him?' Kate pushed, making her feel uncomfortable.

Jeannie resisted the urge to cover her warm cheeks. 'I don't know,' she groaned. 'I mean, he's a nice enough chap, I suppose, and I did feel pleased when I realised he was a Friend and not a drinker. But he's a few years older than us.'

'He's hardly ancient.' Kate waved a hand as though sweeping this away. 'Maybe middle twenties.'

'What else?' said Louisa. 'You look like there's another "but", Jeannie.'

She shrugged, wishing she hadn't said anything. 'But I can't forget how he looked when he was grappling with Sid. He was blazing. That's the only way I can describe it. He was filled with a passion that frightened me. I thought he was going to beat Sid to death.'

Louisa shuddered. 'That would frighten me too, no matter how much Sid deserved it. Although, I confess, I was proud and pleased when Mattie defended me against some louts there one evening. Not that he had to use much violence to subdue them, the drunken idiots.'

Kate looked at Jeannie with narrowed eyes. 'Interesting,' she said.

'What?' Jeannie frowned back at her.

'Oh.' She waved a hand at her. 'It's just that you described him as passionate.'

'That's right. What of it?'

'Not angry or violent, but *passionate*?'

She felt her cheeks warm. 'Well, yes, he was, angry, that is. He gave Sid a good telling-off for treating me like that.'

'But the word you used was passion, not anger,' Kate persisted.

Jeannie shook her head, not looking her friend in the eye. 'I don't understand what you're saying.'

Louisa looked between the two of them and began to nod. 'I do,' she said. 'It's not his anger that frightened you. After all, he didn't actually hit Sid, did he? No, what's worrying you is the *passion* in his eyes when he looked at you.'

Jeannie jumped up, far too agitated to sit still. 'What? No? He... I didn't... You don't understand!'

Kate and Lou exchanged a glance. One part of Jeannie's mind rejoiced in seeing that look between her friends, knowing that Lou was finally back with them. But another part was alarmed that they seemed to be seeing far more into this than she was prepared to admit.

'He wasn't looking at *me* with passion,' she declared. 'He was filled with a passion for violence. He was looking at me as though he was asking me for permission to batter Sid, right there in front of me.' She wrapped her arms around her. 'I'm not sure I could trust a man like that. He would have enjoyed hurting Sid, I'm sure of it.'

'But, Jeannie,' said Kate gently. 'He didn't, did he? He might have threatened Sid, but he didn't batter him, only restrained him to keep you safe.'

Jeannie stared at her, thinking about what she'd said. She hadn't thought about it like that. She'd just panicked at the look in his eyes and she hadn't been able to forget it.

'Maybe you should give him a chance,' said Louisa.

She frowned. 'A chance?'

Kate nodded. 'He obviously likes you,' she said. 'I've seen him looking at you. I'm sure he wants to court you.'

Jeannie's cheeks glowed. She wanted to put her hands up and hide them, but she couldn't. 'Of course he doesn't,' she denied. 'And, even if he did, I don't have time for that sort of thing.' Even as she said it, a little voice in her heart said: *I really don't, and I shouldn't want it, but oh, how I wish...*

Even as her outer and inner voices vied for supremacy, she felt an overwhelming sadness. What with work and looking after Ma and the twins, and now Lucas coming home with God only knew what injuries, she would have even less time for courting, even if she wanted to. The thought that her chances of finding a good man and getting married and having a family of her own were getting slimmer and slimmer left her feeling empty and afraid. *At this rate, I'll end up an old maid.*

The envelope on the table caught her eye and she pulled herself together. She couldn't afford to think about anything else now. 'Anyway, none of that matters. Lucas is in the hospital and we need to find out when we can get him home.' Despite the soldier's assurance that her brother wasn't too badly hurt, she couldn't help worrying that he might have suffered worse injuries that the man hadn't mentioned. She'd heard of men coming back broken in mind and body, and she couldn't rest until she knew the extent of Lucas's suffering. She turned to Louisa. 'If you really mean it, Ma and I would be mighty grateful if you could go and see him for us. We need some reassurance that he's really going to be all right.'

Louisa nodded, getting up and taking Jeannie's hands in her own. 'Of course I mean it.'

Kate got up and joined them, putting an arm round each of her friends. 'That's settled then,' she said. 'Lou and I can go and speak to George when we leave here and see if she can get a lift. That will solve the problem of a train fare.'

'Are you sure your ma and pa won't mind?' she asked. 'I don't want to get you into trouble.'

For a moment, Lou's expression was cold and hard, but then she shook her head and laughed. 'Don't you worry about that,' she said. 'Whether they mind or not, I'm going. I'm not a child any more. The sooner they accept that I'll be making my own decisions about how I live my life from now on, the better.'

36

'You are not to go, Louisa. I forbid it.'

Louisa stared at her father, her aching heart hardening. He had barely acknowledged her since she had walked out of church on Easter Sunday, even when she had tried to apologise and explain why she'd done it. Now, two days later, he chose to speak. The last time he had used the word 'forbid' had been when he had told her she and Mattie couldn't marry when he came home on leave before heading to the trenches. That decision had cost her her son.

'I'm sorry, Father,' she said. 'But I must. I promised Jeannie and Mrs Musgrove.'

'I will not allow it.'

'Come now, Louisa,' said her mother. 'You've only just got home. You can't possibly go gallivanting around the country.'

Louisa looked at her, wondering why she had always thought her mother was a strong, independent woman. In reality, she bowed to her husband's will in everything. She knew she would find no help from her in this battle. Her mother's frown indicated that Louisa hadn't been able to hide her contempt from her. She looked away, unafraid as she stared back at her father.

'I am going to Salisbury to visit a wounded soldier, a man who has fought for king and country, to take him letters and gifts from his family. I hardly call that gallivanting.'

Her father bristled at her challenge. 'As long as you live in my house, you will do as I say.'

Louisa raised her eyebrows. Until she had fallen pregnant, she had always been a good, respectful and faithful daughter. But her experience in recent months, when her whole world had fallen apart, had shown her that none of that mattered. Her fall from grace had not only left her parents distant and disappointed in their only child; it had left her equally disappointed in them. That her father chose this moment to lay down the law left her unmoved.

'Do you understand?' he asked when she remained silent.

Taking a deep breath, Louisa nodded. 'Yes. I understand.' She turned and headed for the stairs. 'I'll pack my things.'

'What?' her mother asked, her voice shrill. 'Whatever do you mean, Louisa?'

She paused and looked over her shoulder. 'As I have every intention of going to Salisbury in order to fulfil my promise, I must leave my father's house. I'm clearly not welcome here.'

'But where will you go?'

She shrugged, unmoved by her mother's distress. Where she lived didn't matter. Nothing really mattered to her any more, other than keeping her promise to Jeannie. 'My friends will help me.'

'Louisa, no! You must stay here. What will people say? This is your home. You're our daughter.' She turned to her husband, gripping his arm. 'Tell her she must stay,' she cried.

Louisa wanted to point out that they hadn't been able to get rid of her fast enough when she was expecting. It was ironic that they had worried about what people would say to that, and now they were again concerned about the same people – not about their daughter and what she wanted or needed. She turned to her father, waiting for his judgement, beyond caring what it might be.

He stared at her, his gaze cold and hard. He must have recognised that she was unmoved. 'What has happened to you, Louisa?' he asked. 'You used to be...'

She held up a hand. 'Don't ask me, Father, because you will not like what I would say, and my words, once spoken, could never be taken back. Only know that I *am* going to see Lucas Musgrove in Salisbury, whether you approve or not. If that is unacceptable to you, then I shall gladly vacate this house and will accept that you no longer wish for me to be your daughter.'

Her mother began to weep quietly. For a moment, Louisa wanted to go to her and comfort her. But then she remembered how she had stood against her when she had needed her the most and her heart hardened.

Her father closed his eyes, as though he couldn't bear to look at her. 'Very well,' he said. 'Go to Salisbury. But I will not have you break your mother's heart. You will continue to live in this house until such time as you marry.'

Louisa sighed. She would never marry, nor would she stay in her father's house for the rest of her life. But maybe now wasn't the right time to leave. She still had to get back to work at the factory, and moving out in the same week that she had returned home would cause more gossip than she had the strength to fight against right now. But she said none of this. Instead, she simply said, 'Thank you.'

* * *

Lucas sat on the bench overlooking the hospital grounds. He had been glad to escape the ward when the staff nurse had suggested he take some air. He had been helped to dress and put on his greatcoat and a porter had been summoned to wheel him outside in a bath chair – something that irritated Lucas greatly. He was perfectly capable of walking. The few pieces of shrapnel that had penetrated his hip and legs had been minor and those wounds were healing well. But he had stayed silent, knowing that to protest would result in him being ordered back to bed. Now, he had been left to sit on the bench and enjoy the solitude for the first time in so many months.

He closed his eyes and took a deep breath of the spring air. It was cool after the warmth of the ward, but not as bad as the biting cold winds that had chased them through the trenches. He tried not to think of them too much. Some of his fellow patients clearly still did, their minds unable to accept that they were finally home and safe. The nights were worse, when some poor fellow would scream out, waking them all and sometimes setting off others. Then none of them would sleep.

Out here, he couldn't hear the screams. There were no explosions or bugles or gunfire. Instead, he felt the weak sun on his face and listened to the almost forgotten sounds of the birds in the trees around the hospital, recognising the chatter of starlings and the melodies of the robin and blackbirds as they busied themselves making their nests. Not far from where he sat was a hazel hedge, heavy with catkins. He supposed that the orchards in Somerset would be full of blossom now. For the first time since he'd been hit, he began to relax and the pain from his wounds was muted. Despite the problems he still had to face, he felt at peace. He began to doze.

He didn't know how long he slept there, but he was jolted awake by the realisation that someone had joined him on the bench. He looked to his side, expecting to see a fellow patient, or maybe even the porter, come to return him to the ward. The last person he expected to see was...

He blinked, unable to believe his eyes.

'Louisa?'

She gave him a shy smile. 'Hello, Lucas.'

He scrubbed a hand down his face, trying to wipe away the fog of sleep. When he looked again, he half-expected her to have disappeared. But she was still there. 'Sorry,' he said. 'It's hard to sleep on the ward. I must have dozed off. What are you doing here?'

'I missed your letters, so I offered to come and visit you so I could see if I've upset you.'

'No, of course you haven't. I... I've been a bit...' He paused, not knowing what to say. 'How did you know I was here? Did you come all the way from Lincolnshire?'

She shook her head. 'I moved back to Street this past weekend, just as you said I should. Your family just got the news of your injury and are desperate to know that you're all right. As I won't be starting work back at Clarks until the first of the month, I offered to come, so I could see for myself and reassure everyone at home. They all send their love. They're worried about you and can't wait to see you. But your ma isn't up to travelling right now and the others had to work.'

The familiar guilt ate at his gut. 'Is Ma all right?'

Louisa looked at him, her eyebrows raised and lips thinned – just as she used to when Mattie said something daft. 'She's been better,' she said. 'But you know she took to her bed when you didn't make it home at Christmas, don't you?'

He sighed and nodded.

'She seems well in herself,' she went on when he remained silent. 'But being bed-ridden for so long has left her weak. The twins have to carry her downstairs now if Jeannie can persuade her to come down to eat with them. But I don't think she's had much of an appetite since you've been away, either.'

Lucas sighed. 'I'd hoped she'd have sorted herself out by now.'

'Jeannie tells me she's got worse since your letters stopped coming. They didn't know if you were alive or dead until someone from the regiment came to see them with an official letter. But she will improve once you're home and she doesn't have to worry so, I'm sure.'

He looked away. 'I'm not sure I'm going home.'

'What are you talking about?' She sat up straighter, looking alarmed. 'Oh, no. They're not sending you back to the front, are they?'

He shook his head. 'No.' He shuddered at the idea. Much as he hated his current situation, he had no desire to go back to that hell.

Louisa put a hand to her chest and blew out a breath. 'Thank God. For a moment there, I was worried. So why are you saying you can't go home?' She studied him. 'The chap who spoke to Jeannie says you're whole and recovering well.'

He hesitated, unsure how to explain. 'I've got all my limbs and organs, if that's what's worrying you. It's not that. I'm just not sure I want to go back to Street. I'm thinking maybe I need a fresh start, away from all my memories.' He looked her in the eyes and held her gaze for the first time since he'd woken to find her there. He was struck by how blue her eyes were. He hadn't noticed before. She had simply been Jeannie's friend and then Mattie's girl, so he'd never taken much notice. It hadn't been until they'd started writing to each other that he felt he'd begun to get to know her.

'Like I did?' she asked softly, her pain dulling her eyes.

He nodded.

She shook her head and looked away. 'It won't work,' she told him. 'Your memories will just go with you, you know. You'll run away, but you won't be able to escape them, and you'll look around one day and realise that you should be at home, where everyone who loves you is waiting and missing you.' She took a deep breath and looked back at him. 'I didn't have a choice but to run away. But you do, Lucas. Don't turn your back on them – on us. Come home. Please.'

Her words stung and he tried to dismiss them from his mind. She didn't understand. But something jarred...

'What do you mean, you didn't have a choice but to run away?'

She shook her head, her gaze sliding away for a moment. 'It doesn't matter. I didn't come here to talk about me. I'm here to see how you are.' She looked him up and down again. 'You're pale, and your face is thinner, but your shoulders are broader and you're looking well, Lucas.' She tilted her head towards the hospital building. 'Not like some of those poor souls in there. I was scared when I got to your bed and it was empty, and then so relieved when they said you were out here.'

'I'm better off than a lot of them,' he agreed, feeling the familiar guilt burn his gut. 'At least I've got two arms and legs and can walk when they let me.' He pulled a face. 'They wheeled me out here in a bath chair. I wanted to tell them to stuff it, but that staff nurse is fiercer than my sergeant was, so I didn't dare cross her. She'd have confined me to bed for my trouble.'

Louisa laughed softly. 'Sometimes we have to pick our battles, eh?' She winced. 'Sorry, wrong choice of words. That was insensitive of me.'

He shrugged. 'My battle is over. Not that it achieved anything. But that doesn't mean I can just go home and act like nothing is different. I'm not the lad I was when I left home. That's why I'm not sure I can go back.'

She bowed her head and sighed. He couldn't see her expression, but the feeling of sadness was coming off her in waves.

'Oh, Lucas,' she said, her voice soft and delicate. 'I understand more than you realise. But you really do need to go home. Your family need you.'

'No, they don't,' he said through gritted teeth. 'They're better off without me.'

She turned and stared at him. He met her confused gaze coolly. She didn't know the half of it. 'Why?' she asked.

It was his turn to sigh. He needed to make her understand. 'I'll be nothing but a burden to them,' he said.

'Of course you won't,' she said. 'You'd never be a burden. To think they'd feel that way is just plain daft.'

'You don't understand,' he said, averting his gaze. He couldn't bear to look at her.

'Then explain it to me.' Her voice got firmer. 'Tell me why – when your ma is wasting away from the worry of you, when your sister is working herself to the bone at the factory then coming home to care for your ma and keep house and feed your brothers, when the twins are in need of a man's influence to keep them in line – you must tell me why you have a notion to stay away from the ones you love when they need you so much.'

He was surprised by her vehemence. 'The Davis brothers are keeping the twins in line.'

She raised her eyebrows. 'To an extent. But they still don't do as much as you did at home. It's all on Jeannie now and it's not fair on her. She's exhausted. She's starting to look older than her years.'

He shook his head. 'You don't understand,' he said again, wishing he had the words to make her see.

'So you said. I'm still waiting on your explanation, Lucas. I can't believe you'd be so selfish.'

His temper began to rise. 'Do you think I want this?' he demanded. 'If I go home now, I'll be less than useless.' He pulled up the right sleeve of his great coat, revealing a network of angry scars up his forearm. 'You say I look well, but these are just a few of the scars that have ruined my body.'

Louisa reached out to touch his skin, but he flinched back.

'No one cares about a few scars, Lucas. You came by them honourably.'

He pulled his sleeve back down but continued to hold his right hand out. 'You wondered why I didn't write to you lately,' he said. He turned his hand over. She looked at it, clearly not seeing what he was showing her. 'I couldn't. Shrapnel ripped the tendons and nerve endings in my wrist. They tried to repair what they could, but I can't feel this hand or use it. It's bloody useless.'

Louisa's eyes filled with tears. She put one hand over her mouth as her other reached out and grasped his before he could stop her. He didn't have the heart to pull away. He couldn't even feel the warmth of her fingers as she entwined them with his and squeezed.

'Now do you see?' he asked, his voice catching in his throat. 'I can't go back to my job as a clicker because I can't do the work with only one hand. I can't write. I can't even do my damned boot laces up. I might look whole, Louisa, but I'm a useless lump and I won't burden my family with it.'

'You can't feel anything?'

He shook his head. 'Pain sometimes. Occasional pins and needles. But nothing else.'

She pulled his hand closer and began to massage it with both of hers.

'What are you doing?'

'When Pa was a clicker, Ma would massage his hands every night so that he didn't end up with arthritis in his fingers like my grandpa did. She did the same for me after I started working in the Machine Room.' She pulled a face. 'I don't think she's going to be so inclined when I go back to work. We're barely speaking. I'll have to do it myself.' She lowered her head, focusing on his hand as she pressed and stroked and manipulated his dead fingers.

He wanted to tell her that it was pointless as he couldn't feel anything. But she seemed so intent on her task he didn't have the heart to tell her to stop.

They sat in silence for a while as she worked on his hand. It comforted him, even though he couldn't feel the pressure she was applying or the warmth of her fingers on his skin. In the distance, a church bell struck the hour.

'They'll send you away soon,' he said. 'Someone will come at half past and take me back to the ward.'

She looked up. 'You can't stay in this hospital forever and you can't go away, especially if you can't do the work you're skilled at. How will you manage on your own? Come home, Lucas, please. We'll work together and find what you can do. You're not useless. You've got another hand, a good mind and a strong back.'

'I can't.' He closed his eyes. 'I won't be a burden.'

She sighed. 'Mattie said you could be a silly beggar.' She paused for a long moment. 'Have you seen him in your dreams?'

He opened his eyes wide, all his senses on alert. 'What are you talking about?' *How does she know?*

She smiled that sad little smile that had become such a part of her since Mattie left. 'You're not the only one who nearly died, Lucas Musgrove. I was sure I was going to join my love in heaven just a few weeks ago. But he came to me in my delirium. He told me it wasn't my time. He helped me to overcome... He still is helping me, even though I can't see him or touch him. He's helping you, as well, I'm sure of it, because he loved you too. His spirit would have been by your side on the battlefield. And if he was here now, he'll be telling you to stop being a silly beggar and to get on home to your family. Maybe he's already told you that in your dreams? So when are you going to listen to us both and accept that being at home with your family is the best place to be?'

He took a deep breath, trying to calm his racing heart. He *had* dreamt of Mattie, more than once since he was injured. The first time had been right there on the battlefield as he lay bleeding under the bodies of his comrades. Like Louisa, he'd thought that he was dying and was going to join his friend in the hereafter.

'It's all right. I'm not going to insist you admit it,' she said softly.

Through the haze of confusion, some of her words came back to him. 'You said you nearly died. Have you been ill?' He searched her face for a sign of poor health, but apart from her cheekbones being a bit more prominent and the aura of sadness she carried, she looked in perfect health.

She shook her head. For a moment, he thought she wouldn't say anything, but then she sighed and took in a deep breath. 'I'm going to tell you something that hardly anyone knows, not even Jeannie. I pray it doesn't change how you regard me and that you'll keep my secret even if you don't want anything to do with me after I tell you. I've come to rely on you as a friend, Lucas, and it scares me that you might not want to know me after you know the truth. But I know Mattie trusted you and that's what I'm going to do.'

He frowned. 'Of course you can trust me. I am your friend,' he said. 'I always will be.'

She tilted her head to one side. 'Thank you. But don't make promises until you've heard me out.' She took another deep breath. He could see she was gathering her courage to speak. 'The reason I ran away to Lincolnshire was because I was carrying Mattie's child.'

He froze, shock rendering him speechless.

'My parents knew and they were intent on sending me to live with my aunt in Exeter until the baby was born and could be given away to strangers. They wouldn't let me tell anyone, especially Mattie's ma.' She closed her eyes briefly then opened them again and continued. 'But I didn't want to give my child away to someone I didn't know. Kate found me when I was in a state, and not knowing what to do, I confided in her. She suggested Peg and Will would help me and they agreed to take me to Lincolnshire with them and pretend that the child is theirs. But it was me who was expecting, not Peg. After he was born, Kate came and brought me back to Street. Peg and Will are bringing him up as their own, so his Grandma Searle will get to know him after all.'

'You named him for Mattie, didn't you?' he whispered.

She nodded, tears filling her eyes. 'Yes, me, Peg and Will agreed. He's called Matthew William. He's beautiful. Just like his pa. Leaving him was the hardest thing I've ever done. But his pa, *our* Mattie, came to me when I thought I was going to die bringing his boy into the world and he kept me going. Just like I'm sure he did when you lay on the battlefield. He said it wasn't my time. I expect he told you the same thing.'

He couldn't deny it. He *had* been ready to die, but his friend had come to him and kept him going until he found the strength to move. He nodded, saying nothing. *She understands.* As though reading his thoughts, she nodded too.

'I had no choice but to run away, Lucas. Just as I had no real choice but to come home again now, without my baby, because it was the only way that I could ensure that he would have a good life and not be tainted by the fact that Mattie and me weren't allowed to marry before he went off to fight. At least this way, I get to hear about our boy as he grows up and I'm comforted to know he's with his father's kin. I couldn't have borne it if he'd been given away to strangers.' She looked down and he realised she was still massaging his useless hand. 'I only learned when I got home that my pa had had no intention of ever letting me marry Mattie. Well, I'm leaving the church now; I can't bear to be there, even though my parents are angry and keep pressing me to go back. Pa says I must live at home until I marry. But I'll never marry, of course. Mattie was it for me. But nor can I stay under their roof for long. So I plan to leave home as soon as I can manage it. I'll be finding my way in the world and I'm going to need my friends to help find my path. I don't think I can ever forgive my parents for what they did and for what I've learned since then. As far as I'm concerned, I have no family now.'

Lucas wanted to weep at the unfairness of it all. His throat was tight as he whispered, 'I'm so sorry, Louisa.'

She shrugged. 'Thank you. But it's not your fault.'

Isn't it? He wanted to say it, but didn't have the courage. He didn't have half of the backbone and heart that his young woman sitting beside him had. 'I wish I'd known,' he said. 'I would have helped.'

She smiled at him, even as her sadness surrounded her like a cloak. 'You're a good man, Lucas. I'm glad I told you and I'm grateful that you don't think too badly of me.'

'I couldn't. I'm so sorry you've had to give your baby up. I know you loved Mattie and he would have married you if he could. It's not fair, what your pa did. But I know Mattie's brother and sister-in-law will be good parents to him, and Mrs Searle will be a loving grandma.'

'I know they will. As for my pa, no, it's not fair. I always thought my parents were good to me and loved me. But this has taught me that they can only love me on their own terms. I've disappointed them and they can't forgive me, and that feeling is mutual, believe me. But I'll survive and I'll live my life as I choose now. As will you. But, like me, you need to come home so that I and everyone who loves you can help.' She held up a hand as he opened his mouth. 'Now, don't argue. You know it's the right thing to do. You know it in your heart and now you've had both Mattie and me telling you. So, are you going to stop being a daft beggar and put us all out of our misery?'

He wanted to say no. He had no idea what he could do or what he wanted or... His thoughts came crashing to a halt as he looked at Louisa again and realised the enormity of what she'd just confessed to him. Yes, he'd been to hell and back. But so had she. Yes, his life was changed. But so was hers. Neither of them knew what the future held for them, but he remembered what Mattie had said to him in his dreams.

You have to look after Louisa for me. I'm relying on you. Don't let me down.

He hadn't let himself think about his friend's words as he'd slowly recovered from his wounds, hadn't dared to believe that he really had visited him from the afterlife. He'd put it down to the effects of nearly dying and the medicines they'd given him. But night after night, Mattie had visited his dreams and told him to go home and that he had to look after Louisa. And now Louisa had told him her secret and how Mattie had visited her in her hour of need as well. That she had come to Lucas now filled him with a warmth he hadn't felt in all the months since Mattie had enlisted. He finally understood the importance of what Mattie had been telling him about Louisa. It wasn't just that she needed comfort in her grief. She needed so much more than that and Mattie trusted him to give it to her.

'All right, I'll come home,' he said. 'We'll help each other.'

Her smile now was tinged with relief, as was his answering one. He'd been terrified of what the future held, but now he had a purpose. He had to fulfil Mattie's wish and help Louisa move on with her life – not just from one loss, but from two. If that meant letting her help him find his path at the same time, then all well and good.

'Oh, thank the lord,' she said, blowing out a breath. 'I don't know what I would have been able to tell Jeannie if you'd kept on being so stubborn.' She looked down at his hand, still cradled in her own. 'I'd have been mighty disappointed as well. I promised Mattie I'd do my best.' She sighed and looked up at him. 'I miss him so much. He said to tell you that he loved us both.'

He raised his good hand to his eyes, pinching the bridge of his nose to try to stem the tears that threatened. He'd been a damned crybaby ever since he'd been injured. It was embarrassing enough amongst other casualties who were just as bad, if not worse after some of their experiences in the trenches. But he couldn't bear for Louisa to see him in this pathetic state.

He felt her hand on his shoulder. 'It's all right,' she said, her tone gentle. 'I know how much you loved him.'

He couldn't look at her. Instead, he nodded and stared out across the grounds towards the hospital. He spotted the orderly walking slowly towards them, pushing that God-awful bath chair. He hated that Louisa would see him being carted around in it like a damned cripple, yet he felt so drained from all the emotions that were swirling around inside him that he knew he wouldn't be able to make it back to the ward on his own two feet.

She followed his gaze and saw the man approaching. 'Oh, it looks like our time is up.' She finally let go of his hand and stood up, gathering her things. He hadn't noticed she'd brought two baskets until she handed one to him. 'I nearly forgot. These are all from your family. An apple cake, more new socks, a pullover, some letters, a couple of books... and,' she looked round to make sure the orderly wasn't within hearing, 'I think the twins might have sneaked in a bottle of cider under everything. Make sure you hide it from that ward sister and enjoy it when she's not looking,' she said, her eyes sparkling with mischief. 'I'll explain to them why you haven't been able to write. But maybe you could start practising using your left hand to write now? Or is there someone you could dictate your letters to?'

'I don't know.' He knew that sometimes volunteers came in to help and some wrote letters on behalf of the chaps who were too badly injured to write for themselves. He hadn't wanted to ask as his injuries seemed so trivial compared to some of them. But he could see the wisdom of what Louisa was saying. His ma and siblings deserved to hear from him. He needed to stop feeling sorry for himself and start thinking of others again. 'I'll try left-handed. If it's not readable, I'll get someone to write my words out for me.'

He stood, grateful that he didn't sway as he had on other occasions when he'd tried to. 'Thank you, Louisa. For everything.'

She stood on tiptoe and kissed his cheek. 'You're welcome. Thank you for all your letters. They really helped me. I'm sorry I didn't tell you about the baby before now, but I was in such a state, I didn't dare in case I lost your friendship. I'd have hated it if that had happened.'

To his relief, she greeted the porter politely as he arrived and then with a wave turned and left, not waiting around to see his shame as he sank into the bath chair before being wheeled back to the ward.

* * *

Louisa sat on a wall outside the hospital, waiting for her lift back to Street. She was shocked that she'd told Lucas about little Mattie. She hadn't intended to. But she knew it was the right thing to do the moment she opened her mouth and the words had flowed out unplanned. At first, she'd been terrified. He'd looked so shocked, she'd expected him to turn on her and send her away. But he hadn't. He'd been so kind.

She was sorry about his hand, but relieved that she didn't see any evidence of worse injuries. Of course, who knew what was hidden under his clothes? She blushed as she thought it, and resolved never to think of it again. It was none of her business! She spent the next half hour as she waited there thinking about what she would tell Jeannie and her family, and how they might all help Lucas to adapt to life with a useless hand.

Although she wondered whether it was completely useless. She could have sworn that, when she told him about her baby, his fingers had twitched and gripped hers a little. It wasn't much, but maybe it was a start?

37

It was another two weeks before Lucas was released from hospital and the whole family was at Glastonbury Station on the Saturday afternoon to greet him off the train. It had been enough time for Jeannie to feed Ma up and get her almost back on her feet. Once she'd known that her firstborn was alive and would soon be home, she had rallied, much to her daughter's relief.

Mrs Musgrove still hadn't been strong enough to make the walk all the way to Glastonbury, but she insisted on going, so the twins had managed to borrow a hand-cart and she sat on some blankets like a queen while they wheeled her from their cottage, along West End and the High Street, out on the Glastonbury Road and over Pomparles Bridge. Both lads were sweating as they finally reached the station in the centre of Glastonbury, but they were laughing and flexing their muscles as they came to a halt, catching the attention of a group of giggling girls on the platform.

'Lucas won't recognise us,' said Peter. 'I'll bet we're nearly as tall and broad as him now.'

Jeannie shook her head, smiling with Ma. They were certainly as tall as him now after a mad growth spurt these past few months, but they were still stick-thin and gangly. Though, no doubt, they'd soon be more men than boys, they still had a way to go.

'Help me down, boys,' said Ma.

'Are you sure, Ma?' said Jeannie. 'Maybe you should stay on the cart.'

'I'll not have my boy seeing me for the first time in months, lolling on an old cart. I'll be standing on my own two feet so I can grab him and kiss him the moment he's close enough.'

Jeannie laughed, relieved to see her mother so positive. 'Fair enough.' She nodded to the twins, who helped her down. 'Why don't we sit on that bench over there until the train arrives?' she suggested, gently leading her mother over to it. The older woman didn't argue and they sat down together, their backs against the station building, to wait while the twins stayed with the cart and flirted with the girls.

Someone who knew her mother came over to say hello. Jeannie was thrilled by how cheerful Ma was as she greeted them, telling him that her son was coming home from the war.

'He might be getting a medal,' she told them. 'Although my Lucas is too humble to be bothered by all that. But the soldier who came to see us told Jeannie that Lucas managed to get himself and another lad back to their line, even though they were both injured. The other poor boy wouldn't have made it back on his own. I'm so proud that Lucas saved a life in the middle of all that destruction.'

Jeannie let her talk, knowing that Ma might be proud, but she was also unaware of the full circumstances. The soldier who had told her what had happened had said that the rest of their platoon had been killed and Lucas and the other lad had been buried under their bodies. No one had realised there were survivors, so they hadn't sent help. If Lucas hadn't rallied and dragged his comrade with him, they'd have both perished. The thought of what he'd gone through, left for dead like that, horrified Jeannie so she'd made the decision not to reveal the full story to the family. It would have given Ma nightmares. It worried her what effect that might have had on her brother. Did he have nightmares? She hoped not, but she would be there to help him if he did.

She knew that things wouldn't be the same when he got home. Louisa had explained about his hand, but Jeannie agreed with Lou that they would all help him to adapt. He was already making the effort to learn to write with his left hand. His letters were a bit scrappy, especially considering he'd had such a neat script before, but she could see the improvement in the few letters he'd sent in the past two weeks.

'Oh, good, we're not too late.'

Jeannie looked up to find Louisa and Kate, plus Kate's brothers standing there.

'We know you said he didn't want a fuss,' said Kate. 'But we couldn't wait to see him and welcome him home.'

Louisa nodded. They all greeted Ma politely then Fred and George went over to talk to the twins and to inspect the cart. The giggly girls got even worse as the two handsome men joined the boys, but they were ignored as the married men spoke to the boys about carts and football, and eventually they gave up and moved off up the platform.

Ma went back to talking with her acquaintances as Jeannie got up and linked arms with her friends.

'Are you excited?' asked Kate. 'You must be.'

'I am. I can't wait to see him. Knowing he's on his way home has worked miracles for Ma. She's determined to be standing on the platform when he gets off the train.'

Lou looked over at the cart as the twins bragged to the men about how they had conveyed Ma on it to save her legs. 'I hope Lucas is up for the walk home from here. He'd hate to have to join your Ma on the cart, wouldn't he?'

'I know,' she said. 'I was thinking the same thing. I brought some money for a fare, in case we needed to put him on the bus, but I don't think Ma will want to let him out of her sight and I don't have enough for both of them. That's why the boys borrowed the cart for Ma.'

'He'll be fine,' Kate reassured her. 'He won't need to use the bus. My brothers said they'd prop him up between them if need be so he can get home on his own two feet. They said a man's got to hold onto his pride.'

Jeannie smiled, her heart filled with gratitude. 'Is that why they came?'

Kate shrugged. 'Might be. Fred heard Lou tell me about how they made him sit in a bath chair to get out of the ward and how he hated it. It's a man thing, you know. While I'd love someone to push me around in a comfy chair, especially after a hard day in the Machine Room, the male of the species hate that sort of thing, don't they?'

A distant whistle alerted everyone on the platform that the train was approaching. Before Jeannie could do anything, George said something to the twins and they rushed over to help Ma up, offering their arms for her to lean on. Jeannie mouthed, 'Thank you' to George, who smiled and nodded. His kindness left her free to focus on the approaching train without worrying about Ma.

As it pulled into the station, there was a cacophony of hissing steam and creaking metal as the locomotive came to a halt. It took a few moments before Jeannie spotted Lucas leaning out of one of the door windows.

'There he is!' she cried, suddenly blinking away tears. There had been moments when she'd been sure that this moment would never come. Breaking away from her friends, she ran towards her brother as he climbed stiffly down from the carriage. He had barely straightened, his duffle bag slung over his shoulder, before she reached him, flinging her arms around him.

As she wept tears of joy and relief, Lucas hugged her tight. She didn't have him to herself for long before the station master told them to move out of the way so that others could get on or off the train, and the twins brought Ma to meet them halfway. Jeannie relinquished her tight hold on her brother so that he could sweep their mother into his arms. She tried not to notice how lean his face looked or how broad his shoulders had got, and especially not the way his right hand hung lifeless at the end of his arm. Instead, she wiped her eyes and followed as everyone gathered round to greet him. Fred relieved him of his duffle without a word as Ma wept over him and the twins rushed to tell him every little detail of their lives, sometimes talking over each other, other times finishing each other's sentences. Jeannie stood on the edge of the group, glad when her friends came and joined her.

She gripped Louisa's hand. 'Thank you,' she said, kissing her friend's cheek.

'What for?' she smiled.

'Bringing him home. I had an awful feeling that he wasn't going to come and I was so worried. I couldn't leave Ma to go and see him, and the twins would have been worse than useless. But thanks to you, he's here.'

Louisa shook her head, her cheeks a little pink. 'He'd have come home, I'm sure. But it's not going to be easy for him.' She looked over at Lucas, who was listening intently to the twins while his mother clung to his side. 'He's worried he'll be another burden for you to carry.'

'I don't care if he is, although I can't imagine him letting himself be one for long,' she said. 'He's home and he's safe. That's all that matters.'

As well as the people who had been waiting on the platform,

some of whom were now boarding the train, the numbers had been swollen by those who had disembarked with their luggage. The noise level rose as people called greetings and farewells, and the engine continued to hiss as doors were opened and slammed shut. Several porters had appeared, calling out for everyone to clear a path so they could get on with moving trunks and cases along the platform on their carts. The girls moved out of the way of one particularly well-laden one. Jeannie recognised Mr Roger Clark and his wife, Sarah walking behind it. To anyone who wasn't from Street, the couple might seem humble and uninteresting in their plain clothing and quiet demeanour. But to a Clarks employee and a Friend like Jeannie, Roger Clark and his wife were like royalty – to be respected and revered. As a Director of Clarks and the Company Secretary, he held power over everyone's jobs. As an elder of the Society of Friends, he was a godly man who led by example, exercising a great deal of influence over everyone at the Meeting House.

The couple drew level with Lucas and Ma. Mrs Clark recognised Ma from the Meeting House and stopped, asking after her health, while Lucas greeted Kate and Louisa and thanked them for coming. When the Clarks had gone, the twins helped Ma onto the cart, Lucas's duffle bag serving as an extra cushion for her. Lucas walked over and stood beside the cart, shaking his head as Ma offered to make room for him. 'I'd better get over there before Ma embarrasses Lucas by dragging him onto the cart.'

But before she could get to them, Fred and George had organised the twins to push Ma on the cart and the men stood on either side of Lucas.

'It's good to see you, friend,' said George, wrapping an arm around Lucas's shoulder. He turned to Ma. 'Don't you worry, Mrs Musgrove. We'll be right behind you, walking with Lucas.' He turned and winked at the girls. 'I'll bet Lucas is gasping for a decent cup of tea; I know I am. Maybe the girls can go ahead and get the kettle on?'

Jeannie nodded. 'Come on, girls. John and Peter, you be careful with Ma, now. No racing. Take it nice and steady, all right?'

She couldn't resist another quick kiss of her brother's cheek before she and her friends left the station, hurrying back to the Musgrove house to prepare for Ma and Lucas's arrival. Jeannie was pleased she'd thought to bake a couple of his favourite apple cakes from their winter store of fruit last night. Now she had enough to be able to offer the Davis brothers and Lou and Kate a slice as a thank you for their kindness.

'He looks better than he did at the hospital the other week,' said Louisa as they headed back towards Street. 'I knew coming home would be good for him. Your ma, too. Did you see how she talked Mrs Clark's ears off?'

Jeannie giggled, feeling almost giddy with happiness. 'I did. It's like I'm getting them both back at once.' She was still smiling as they hurried across Pomparles Bridge, leaving Glastonbury behind and entering Street village.

'Hey, look who it is,' said Kate, nudging her shoulder even as they didn't falter in their brisk pace.

'Who is it?' asked Louisa as Jeannie recognised the slightly wonky gait of Tom coming towards them. She immediately felt her cheeks warm.

'Just someone from work,' she said. 'One of the mechanics fixing the machines.'

'He's more than that,' scoffed Kate as she walked along, her arms linked with Jeannie on one side and Louisa on the other. She leaned closer to Louisa's ear. 'It's Tom. Her hero.'

Louisa's eyes widened. 'The chap who rescued you from Sid?'

'Shh!' said Jeannie, keeping her smile pasted on her face as they drew level. She was aware that they were very close to the very spot at The Cross where Tom had come to her aid and she felt both excited to see him but also still embarrassed that he had witnessed her humiliation.

'Hello, Tom,' said Kate, earning a pinch on the arm from Jeannie.

He looked over, not surprised to see them. He must have seen them coming along the road, chattering to each other, long before they spotted him. He touched his cap. 'Ladies,' he said. 'Out for a stroll?'

'Not exactly,' said Kate. 'Jeannie's brother just got back from the army hospital. We met him at the station.' She looked over her shoulder. 'He's walking with my brothers. They'll be along in a minute.'

Jeannie wondered whether Tom might be a help to Lucas, seeing as how he was injured in the trenches as well. But then she remembered he didn't like to talk about it. She didn't know whether Lucas was likely to want to talk about it either. She'd noticed a new reserve in his latest letters and had thought it might be because it was so hard for him to write left-handed. But maybe it was more than that. He'd seemed different at the station. More serious, almost detached from the high spirits around him. It might simply be that he was tired from the journey and over-whelmed to be home, and anyway, she had barely had the chance to talk to him. But something definitely seemed different about her brother.

She became aware of Tom's gaze on her and she blushed again. She really wished she didn't do this every time she saw him. She didn't have time for this nonsense. 'That's right,' she said, lifting her chin. 'We're the advance party – got to get the kettle on.'

He nodded, tapping his cloth cap again. 'I won't hold you up, then. Nothing better than that first cuppa when you get home after a long time away. Bye, ladies.' Even as he said it, his eyes were on

Jeannie. When her gaze met his, he smiled, heating her cheeks further. And then he turned and was gone, striding towards Glastonbury. In the distance, Jeannie spotted the others coming.

'Come on,' she said, turning her back on Tom and pulling the others along. 'If we don't hurry up, they'll catch us and they'll be moaning that the tea's not brewing.'

'Told you she liked him,' said Kate, her expression smug.

'So I see,' said Louisa, a soft smile on her lips. 'He seems nice.'

'Her hero,' said Kate, pretending to swoon.

'Oh, stop it,' said Jeannie, dragging her friend by the arm. 'He was just in the wrong place at the wrong time and saw me at my worst.'

Kate laughed. 'You mean he saw the damage you did to Sid with your knee. At least he knows not to mess with you. He'll definitely treat you with respect.'

'He looked like he's keen on you,' said Louisa. 'Maybe he'll ask you out.'

Jeannie scoffed, wanting to fan her hot cheeks but not daring to. She turned her head away from her friends' knowing looks. 'I haven't got time for courting.'

'Yes, you have,' said Kate. 'Now Lucas is home, you won't have to do everything now. If there's anything he can't manage, he'll make sure the twins do it. If Tom asks you out, you should go.'

She hoped they were right about things being easier now Lucas was home. She was worn out from doing everything for everyone for so long. But that didn't mean she should throw herself into a relationship. And though she liked Tom more as she got to know him, she couldn't forget what she'd seen in his eyes that night at The Cross and his coldness when she'd later tried to get him to talk about his experience as a soldier. There was far more to Tom than the polite, hardworking young man most people saw. A shiver ran down her spine. Under that quiet exterior was a boiling cauldron of emotions that Jeannie didn't think she had the strength to deal with.

'I doubt he'll ask me,' she said, though she'd never admit the disappointment she felt at that thought.

'Why not? You're pretty and smart and plenty of the lads like you.'

She laughed. 'Yeah? So why haven't any of them asked me out?'

Louisa chuckled. 'Well, it might be something to do with how you dealt with Sid's attack with your knee, and then chucking your drinks over that cheating Douglas and his bit on the side when you caught them kissing at the Crispin Hall dance. But that says more about what a lily-livered lot they are than about you, love. But it might also be because most of the lads round here know Lucas is your big brother and none of them have the courage to ask you out while knowing he'll be watching and waiting to deal with them if they break your heart.'

'Exactly,' said Kate. 'Just like my brothers scare off anyone sniffing round me – not that I mind. I'm grateful for it, to be honest.' She pulled a face and shuddered. 'I don't want any lad thinking he can rule my life, thank you very much.'

Louisa sighed. 'I wish I had a brother. All I've got are Ma and Pa telling me to smarten myself up and find a husband.' She sighed. 'But I'm like you, Kate. I don't want a man. No one will match up to my Mattie. So I won't even bother looking.'

Jeannie shook her head, picking up her pace past the shops and houses along the High Street. They would soon reach her home in West End and the others wouldn't be far behind them. 'Honestly, what am I going to do with you two? You're both sworn off men, yet you're nagging me to find one. What makes you think Lucas won't scare Tom off, anyway?'

'He won't,' said Kate. 'Because Tom is an incomer, so he doesn't know Lucas yet, so he won't be intimidated by him. Also,' she went on, 'Tom isn't a boy. He's a soldier, just like Lucas. If anything, I reckon Lucas will approve of him.'

Jeannie puffed out an irritated breath. 'I don't need my brother's approval and I didn't need Tom saving me, thank you very much. But even if I did, it wouldn't matter. He hasn't asked me out, so this conversation is pointless.'

'But he might,' said Kate. 'So you'll say yes if he does?'

'No!' she said, hoping she meant it. Most of the time, she was sure she would turn him down if he did, but then she'd see him and she'd get tongue-tied and embarrassed again and she'd be confused and excited and scared and disappointed all at the same time. 'Look, he's not going to ask. And even with Lucas home, I'm still too busy to even consider courting, so can we forget this conversation, please?'

The girls took pity on her, although they exchanged knowing glances that left Jeannie feeling irritated until she remembered how much she'd missed the three of them being together.

'Anyway,' she said, pulling them along the last few yards to her front door. 'If neither of you are going to let a man into your life, I reckon it will be more fun to stick with you girls. We can go dancing and to the pictures and do all the things we said we were going to do before our families claimed most of our time.'

'Sounds good to me,' said Kate. 'Lou, are you in?'

Louisa looked sad for a moment before she squared her shoulders and raised her chin. 'I am,' she said. 'We'll be like the Three Musketeers. What do they say?'

'*All for one and one for all, united we stand, divided we fall*,' Kate quoted as they entered the cottage. 'Yes, that sounds like us, doesn't it, girls? We're the Three Musketeers, only much, much prettier.'

Jeannie laughed, feeling truly light-hearted for the first time in many months. Her friends were here, Lucas was home, Ma was getting better. Life was good again.

38

Lucas's homecoming turned into a party as Louisa and the Davis siblings joined them for tea and cake, then neighbours popped in to say hello, as did the twins' friends. The boys were eager to hear first-hand tales of the battles Lucas had been involved in, but he wasn't inclined to talk about it.

'I'll tell you this much it's worse over there than I ever imagined it would be, lads,' he said, his drawn face and tired eyes adding gravity to his quietly spoken words. 'Pray the war is over before you're old enough to be conscripted.'

Jeannie had chased the boys out, hissing at the twins to keep them away. She'd half-expected them to take umbrage against her – they'd clearly been keen to show off their hero brother. But the haunted look in Lucas's eyes had conveyed to them and their friends more than words that maybe war wasn't the great adventure they'd thought it might be. Peter and John had shown their friends out and quietly apologised to Lucas. He'd accepted with a grave nod.

'Just don't you two go thinking about enlisting,' he said, pointing a finger at them. Jeannie couldn't help noticing it was his left hand and she felt her gut twist. 'It's a fool's game,' he went on. 'I was daft to go and I'll regret it for the rest of my days.'

She could see Ma nodding and wiping her eyes. No doubt she was as relieved as Jeannie that Lucas was going to make sure the twins didn't do anything stupid like he'd done.

* * *

It was a good hour before the house was clear of most of their visitors. The Davis siblings had all taken their leave, as had the neighbours. Now just Louisa remained, helping Jeannie wash up the cups and plates. She seemed reluctant to leave. Lucas hadn't really had the chance to talk to her, so he wasn't sure how things were at home for her. He'd thought a lot about what she'd told him and he felt a burning guilt in his gut, wishing he'd known earlier so that he could have helped her when she needed it. He was only glad that Kate's sister was married to Mattie's brother and she'd been able to get them to help Louisa. It didn't take away the fact that Louisa had lost her baby, though. That sat heavily in his heart and on his shoulders.

His family was everything to him and the thought that his ma might have had to give one or all of them up after their pa had died didn't bear thinking about. It could have come to that. Pa had been working hard to support his young family when he'd died in the accident at the factory. He'd been killed instantly when a cable snapped, sending the lift car crashing down onto him. The twins had been little – not even six – Jeannie barely eight and Lucas ten. They'd all been too young to understand how difficult it had been for Ma, having to go back out to work while caring for her children and mourning her husband. She hadn't earned nearly as much as him, of course, and the way she suffered with her nerves made it hard for her to cope with even the simplest work. Things had got really bad at home.

But they'd managed somehow, even if it meant they went to bed hungry sometimes and their clothes weren't always as clean as they should have been. Once Lucas was old enough, he started working when he wasn't at school – fetching and carrying and doing anything that would earn him a few pennies. Then he'd left school behind as soon as he could and started working full-time at the factory. Jeannie had followed his example, and with both their wages, they'd just about been able to manage when Ma hadn't been able to cope any more and had to stay at home. Once the twins had started work, things got easier with four wages coming in. Lucas had been doing well as a clicker, becoming quite skilled at leather cutting over the past few years before he'd ruined things by rushing off to fight.

Ma agreed to have a lie-down as the excitement of the day was beginning to catch up with her. One of the twins carried her upstairs. Lucas marvelled that his younger brothers were now big enough to lift her, although he felt humiliated that he was no longer capable of such a feat thanks to his useless hand. He took the opportunity to slip outside and light up a cigarette. He was sitting on the garden wall smoking when Louisa came out.

'I didn't know you smoked,' she said, standing in front of him.

He looked up at her as he took a long drag. He shrugged as he blew out a long line of smoke. 'We were issued with tobacco with our rations. I just got into the habit of it.' He looked at the half-smoked cigarette in his hand. 'It helped calm me when the bombardments were bad. This is the last of them, though. I doubt I'll carry on. If I can't work, I can't afford to waste money on smokes.'

'You *will* be able to work, Lucas, I'm sure. You just need to find out what you can do rather than fret about what you can't.'

He smiled, warmed by her faith in him. It still felt odd, being home. But she'd been right. It was the right thing to do. He would do his best to make everyone proud. 'We'll see. Are you starting work soon?'

She nodded. 'Monday morning. You should come along to the factory and talk to the folk in Personnel. They've got to give you your job back, but if you can't manage it, they'll maybe have some ideas you haven't thought about yet.'

'Maybe I will,' he agreed. The sooner he did it, the better. No point in fretting at home. 'Anything will be better than sitting about like a useless lump. I had enough of that in the hospital.' He extinguished the cigarette against the Blue Lias stone wall that matched the cottage he and his family lived in.

'Let me know how you get on?' she asked.

'I will. I'll want to know how your first day back went as well.'

She sighed and closed her eyes. 'I can't wait to get back there. Ma has been hovering and fussing and Pa is barely talking to me. The sooner I can get to work and earn my keep, the better.'

'Will you have to stay there? I thought Mrs Searle had offered to take you.'

'She has, but... well, it's hard, you know? Every time I see her, I think of Mattie.' She lowered her voice, looking round to make sure no one could overhear. 'She's so kind to me, but what if she finds out the truth about the baby? I don't think I could bear it if she thought badly of me.'

'She won't,' he said, firm in his belief. 'No one will tell her. But even if she did find out, she loves you like a daughter and she'd understand, I'm sure, especially as you've given the babe to Mattie's brother to bring up.'

Louisa shrugged, her eyes dull with pain. He wished he could take away her grief, but he didn't know how. He couldn't shake his own. 'Maybe,' she said. 'But it's not just that. Pa is adamant he won't let me leave home unless it's to marry. He doesn't want people to talk. He's set Ma off, encouraging her to find a decent match for me, like she was doing before I started walking out with Mattie.' She shuddered. 'It was horrible then, so I've no illusions that it will be any better now. I'll not entertain any of the lads they'll suggest. But they're convinced everything will be all right if I'm safely wed.' She looked away. 'I haven't said anything yet, but I will tell them. I'm not about to let them force me into a loveless marriage. Nor will I lie to any man they try to fob me off onto. Ma and Pa won't like that, but I won't be swayed. Maybe that will deter them with their relentless matchmaking – the thought of me telling people about why I went away.' Her smile was humourless. 'Anyway, I've managed to earn myself a reprieve by claiming I want to focus my energy on getting back to work, but I don't suppose it will stop her for long.'

In the distance, the parish church rang the hour.

Louisa sighed. 'It was her daft matchmaking that pushed me into Mattie's arms in the first place. Not that I regret a moment of that. But I suppose I'd better get home now. I've still to convince them I'm not going to church with them any more. We had an awful row this morning, but I'm standing firm.'

He winked at her, trying to lighten the mood. 'Picking your battles, eh? Church first, then work, then freedom.'

'Exactly,' she smiled sadly. 'I wish they understood me as well as you do, Lucas.'

He hadn't expected that and it filled him with warmth that she should think so. 'I've listened to you – or rather, I've mostly read what you've had to say – and I'm glad to listen to you now that we've both found our ways home.' He didn't mention how many times he'd read and re-read her letters. Now he understood why she'd written about the baby's name, *Matthew William, after his father and uncle*. 'It's not hard to see that you need to change your life after everything that's happened to you. I'm sure your ma and pa think they're doing what they believe is best for you.' He'd always thought Mr Clements was a fair man. He'd been a good foreman to work under – Lucas had learned a lot from him. It vexed him that the man wasn't as patient with his own daughter. 'They just haven't listened to you properly. You're not a child any more. You've suffered more loss than most in the past year.'

'So have you,' she said softly. 'But thank you. It's good to know you have listened and you understand. I hope you feel I've done the same for you.'

He nodded, but didn't say anything.

'I'm really glad you're home, Lucas.'

'Thanks. So am I. Mattie was right. I was being a daft beggar.'

He frowned suddenly, sitting up straighter as words echoed through his mind.

'What?' she asked. 'Are you all right?'

He shook his head then nodded, no doubt confusing her further. 'I'm fine. I just... I've had the oddest thought, Louisa.'

She put her hands on her hips. 'Well, don't just sit there scowling at me. Are you going to tell me or not?'

He chuckled, glad to see a hint of the old, teasing Louisa again. 'Sorry, I wasn't scowling at you. I was trying to work out what rushed into my head like that. It's something daft. I doubt it will help.'

'Why don't you tell me and I'll be the judge of that.'

He took a deep breath. His thoughts seemed to have a mind of their own, rushing through him and making him wonder whether these were independent thoughts or words being planted in his brain by Mattie's spirit.

'Right-o.' He held up a finger. 'Just don't dismiss this out of hand, all right? It's just come to me, so maybe we need to think it through.'

She wrinkled her nose. 'You're not making any sense.'

'No, I know. But the more I think about it, the more sense it makes.'

'Lucas. Just tell me.'

He nodded, breathing deeply again, wishing he had another cigarette to help calm his mind. 'Well, I'm thinking about your church.'

'What about it?'

'If you really can't bear to go back, would you consider attending gatherings with me and Jeannie at the Meeting House?'

She looked thoughtful. 'Actually,' she said eventually, 'I did think about it, even before Mattie died. I nearly went with Peg and Will to their meetings in Lincoln. But then I thought it might cause raised eyebrows.' She pulled a face. 'I pretty much hid myself away once I started showing. And, to be honest, I'm still trying to work out whether I actually believe in a god who lets so many awful things happen in the world. I'm not sure I can worship Him even if I did believe He did exist. Pa says God has a plan for all of us, but why would a so-called loving god let so many suffer?'

'I know. It's hard to imagine, isn't it?' he agreed. 'But I'll go back to meetings and try to find the light inside me again. Maybe then I'll understand.'

She nodded. 'At least I wouldn't have to listen to sermons I can't agree with if I came with you. Kate's already said she's going to join the Friends, too. She's struggled about church since her ma died, but staying with Auntie Betty has made her think about the Friends more. We talked about it with Jeannie the other day, but I haven't made any decisions yet. I'm sure Pa would be furious about the very idea.'

'But what can he do?' he asked. 'The Clarks are Quakers. They hold sway over this village. Why, there's not a family in Street that doesn't rely on jobs in their factory, including your own. What can your pa do if you decide to join them at their place of worship rather than his?'

'You're right,' she nodded, looking thoughtful. 'He can hardly cause a fuss if I choose to worship alongside his employers, can he? If he objected publicly, they'll disapprove and it could look bad for him. I hadn't thought about it like that.' She smiled. 'I'll definitely think on it and talk to the girls a bit more.' She paused, tilting her head to one side. 'Thank you.'

He raked his good hand through his hair. 'You're welcome, although your pa won't thank me, I'm sure.'

'I won't mention your name,' she assured him.

He nodded, relieved. 'Right now, I can't think straight. I'm suddenly worn out.'

'Of course,' she said, her expression softening. 'I'm sorry, I should have realised. It's been a big day for you, getting out of hospital and travelling home, hasn't it? I'd better get off, anyway. I'm later than I said already.' She touched his shoulder. 'But thank you for your mad thought. I think you might just have helped me see the path I need to follow.'

He nodded. 'It will give you the chance to get used to being around Mattie's ma as well. She'll be so pleased you're thinking of becoming a Friend.'

He watched her smile and wave as she walked away, although he noticed the smile hadn't reached her eyes, which stayed sad and wary. Before she was out of sight, he saw her pause, straighten her shoulders and raise her chin, as though preparing for the inevitable battle she faced at home. He hoped he hadn't made it worse for her by putting ideas into her head.

He sighed and got up, his bum cold from sitting on the stone wall for too long, but he barely noticed. Spending the winter in the trenches tended to harden a man to discomfort. He went back into the cottage, feeling again that rush of gratitude that he had found his way home. He just wished he'd listened to everyone who'd tried to dissuade him from enlisting. But he hadn't, and now he had to live with the consequences.

He thought again about the way Louisa had braced herself as she'd headed home. It broke his heart that she was having such a rotten time of it just because she'd loved Mattie. He cursed his friend for going off to fight, setting off a chain of events that had led them all to this point.

You're the daft beggar, Mattie, he thought. *You could have had it all – a loving wife and a bonny baby. Instead, you're rotting six feet under while she has to go on without you or the child.*

He sank into his usual chair by the range, running his good hand over his face. He was getting used to being left-handed, although sometimes he still forgot and tried to use his useless hand, making himself angry and embarrassed by his own stupidity.

'You all right?' It was Jeannie, leaning against the door jamb to the back yard.

'Yeah. Just tired. Where are the twins?'

She shrugged. 'They went out to catch up with their pals. They'll be back when they're hungry. Why don't you go up and rest? They put your duffle in your old room. Let me have any washing you need doing.'

He shook his head. 'It's all clean. They did it at the hospital for me. Not that there's much in there. I had to give back my uniform. They let me keep my boots, but they're not Clarks quality, and I had to pay a pound to keep my greatcoat. Anyway, come and sit for a minute. I need to talk to you – find out what needs doing. I'm going to have more words with the twins about them being lazy beggars.' He glared at her. 'If other people hadn't told me, I'd never have known. Why didn't you tell me?'

She glared back. 'What was the point? Not much you could've done about it. I didn't want to worry you.'

He would have argued, but he knew his sister and it wouldn't do any good. It was water under the bridge now. He was home. He'd sort his brothers out, make sure they did their bit and not leave it all to Jeannie. 'All right. But it's over and done with. I'm home now and I'll keep them in line. And I'll be going down the factory Monday morning to see what work I can get.'

'There's no rush,' she said, sinking into the chair opposite him.

'Yes, there is. Once my discharge papers arrive, I need to start paying my union subs again or we won't be entitled to any benefits if we need them. And you'll need my wages for the housekeeping. I'll pay my way, like always.'

She nodded, not saying anything. It had always been a sacrifice to pay the subs to belong to the Union of Shoe and Bootmakers, and Jeannie hadn't been happy about it given the trouble the union had started last year, but he'd been advised by a friend of their late father's that it would stand them in good stead if one of them wasn't able to work through injury or illness, and it came with death benefits if the worst happened. Their pa hadn't been a union man and had ended up in a pauper's grave, even though Clarks had given a grant to help them, and the family had barely avoided becoming destitute. It had left Lucas determined to join. It was their security. Jeannie had thought about joining, but because she was earning so much less than her brother, she couldn't afford the expense. Lucas's union membership fees had been suspended when he had 'taken the colours', but that didn't apply any more. If he didn't pay up, he wasn't covered. He needed to go back to work, whether he was ready or not. Only then would he be able to make a claim for assistance if he found he couldn't do the job.

'I'm glad you're home, brother,' she said.

He felt his throat tighten, so he nodded without speaking.

'We will manage, you know,' she said, leaning forward and touching his knee. Her fingers felt warm and reassuring. He took a deep breath, hoping he didn't disgrace himself by bursting into tears like a lass.

'I know,' he said, his voice gruff. 'Just don't fuss round me, all right?'

She chuckled. 'I won't, but you can be sure that Ma will.'

He rolled his eyes. 'More reason for me to get back to work then.'

She nodded. They were silent for a few minutes before she spoke again. 'It's been a hell of a time of it, hasn't it? First, we lost Mattie. Then you and Lou went away and we didn't know if either of you would come back.'

He frowned. 'Didn't you expect Louisa to come home?'

She shrugged. 'Everyone said she would. But... I don't know. I had a funny feeling about it. Like she'd never come back, knowing Mattie wasn't ever going to be here again.' She looked at him with concern as he scrubbed at his face, trying to keep his emotions under control. It had been hard for him to come back for that very reason, so he understood what Jeannie meant about Louisa. 'Sorry, love,' she said. 'I know you miss him, too. You were as close as brothers.'

He nodded, his gaze fixed on the range.

'Anyway, you both came back, for which I thank God. It wasn't the same without my big brother and my best friend.'

'You had Kate,' he pointed out.

'I did. I'm truly blessed to have two such good friends. But poor Kate's been through a difficult time as well. First losing her ma after she fought so hard to keep her well. Then her pa moving the Floozy in with those awful kiddies of hers. I actually saw that woman try and throttle Kate, you know. I've never been so scared and so angry – apart from when you decided to enlist, of course.'

'That Floozy woman sounds horrible,' he said, ignoring that last remark, glad the conversation had moved on from him, Louisa and Mattie.

'She is. Truly wicked. I'm only glad you suggested I write to Peg. That did the trick. Kate's a different girl since she moved into Auntie Betty's. Before that, I feared that woman would end up killing her.' She sighed. 'But I'm not going to think about that now. You're back and my friends are both home and safe. We can get back to how it used to be again.'

Lucas closed his eyes and groaned. 'Don't be stupid,' he snapped.

'What?'

'It'll never be the same, don't you see?'

She sighed again. 'I know. But I can hope that it will at least get better, can't I? These past months have been awful, Lucas. Is it so wrong of me to want to get back some of our innocent happiness?'

'You're still innocent,' he scoffed, unaccountably irritated by her desire to imagine nothing had changed.

She smacked his leg where before she'd been resting her hand like she didn't want to let go of him for fear of him leaving again. 'Don't you speak to me like that, Lucas Musgrove. I might not have seen what you've seen, but I've had enough troubles to cope with here. I've been miserable and scared for you and Ma and Kate and more angry than I've ever been, what with the twins playing up and Sid Lambert making my life a misery and...' She stopped suddenly, sitting back in her chair with a whoosh of air.

'And?' he asked gently, his irritation fading into a mix of guilt and love for his sister.

She shook her head then looked up at the ceiling. 'I've tried so hard to be a good person. I know as Friends we should devote our lives to service and helping people as much as we can.' She sighed and put her hands over her eyes, scrubbing with her palms. 'But I'm so tired, Lucas. So bone weary. I work hard and then come home to find Ma hasn't made the effort to get out of bed and that the twins have run in, grabbed some grub from the pantry and rushed out to play football and if I don't get on and cook and clean and do the washing and darning and shopping then nothing gets done and me and Ma will starve to death. It was never as bad as this before you went away, so is it wrong for me to want everything to go back to how it used to be?' When she looked at him, her eyes were full of tears.

His guilt increased ten-fold. 'Not wrong at all,' he said, reaching out and taking her hand. 'I'm sorry, Jeannie. This is all my fault.'

'Just tell me you're home to stay and you'll help me sort out Ma and the boys.'

'I am and I will.' He looked down at his useless hand resting on his thigh. 'Though what good I'll be...'

'Stop it. You'll be fine. You're in one piece and a darn sight better off than a lot of men. You'll work out how to cope with your hand. Just don't go thinking I'll put up with you feeling sorry for yourself, Lucas Musgrove, because I find I don't have the patience I used to any more.'

He gave a short laugh as something occurred to him. 'Then I'll mind myself. I don't want to get on the wrong side of you. I heard about the damage you did to Sid.' He grinned at her. 'I'm proud of you.'

She chuckled, shaking her head. 'He didn't half scream.'

He rested his head back against the chair and his laugh this time was long and hearty. 'I'd like to have seen that. I hear that fellow Tom came across you just after Sid went down. I shall have to ask him about it.'

When he looked at Jeannie, he noticed her cheeks had gone

pink and he wondered about her reaction at the mention of this Tom. He raised his eyebrows at her but she said nothing.

'The Davis brothers introduced us on the road home earlier,' he told her. 'I also hear that you and Tom might be sweet on each other.'

The pink turned to beet red. 'I don't know who told you that but it's nonsense.'

'Is it?'

'Of course it is. I haven't got time for a sweetheart.' She looked cross as well as embarrassed. 'Not that he's asked me.'

'Maybe he realises that and he's biding his time.'

She rolled her eyes. 'Don't you start. I'm not interested.'

He leaned forward. 'Really? I haven't seen you go this red since one of the Jackson brothers – Stan, wasn't it? – tried to get a look at your knickers in the schoolyard. As I remember it, you were quite sweet on him until then.'

'Well, trying to pull up my skirt in the playground in front of everyone cured me of that silliness,' she grumbled. 'I knocked him onto his backside for his trouble and never spoke to him again.'

They were both silent as they remembered Stan, who hadn't come back from the trenches but was instead in an asylum and likely to stay there.

Jeannie shook her head and stood up. 'Anyway, like I say, I've no time for a chap, so I wish people would stop going on about Tom. He's a nice enough fellow and kept hold of Sid while I got away. But that's all there is to it.'

Lucas nodded, tiredness washing over him again. He'd been warned this would happen for a while. Jeannie must have noticed his pallor.

'Go on up and have a lie-down while I get some supper together.'

'I'm not hungry.'

'Yet you'll eat,' she told him, her tone brooking no nonsense. 'If you're going to the factory on Monday, you'll need your strength, so stop arguing and go and rest up.'

After Lucas had gone up to his room, Jeannie threw together some vegetables and cooked meat into a broth to make a soup and thought about the day's events. She knew that Lucas was right – nothing was ever going to be the same. But for the first time in months, she had her brother and her best friends close once more.

It might not be the same, but at least we're all back together again – excepting Mattie, of course, bless his heart. She felt the familiar ache in her heart as she thought of him, knowing that his loss was felt so strongly by both Lucas and Louisa. *Both of them tried to run from it. Thank God they've both come home at last. Maybe now they can start to heal.*

She thought again about the two of them, wondering whether their mutual grief might bring them together. She knew she couldn't interfere, but she would dearly love Louisa as a sister and she was sure her friend would get along well with Lucas if she could just open up her heart. But if Louisa chose to remain a spinster after losing the love of her life, Jeannie would respect that. She expected it of Kate after her awful experiences at her father's hand, so why not Louisa as well?

She smiled and shook her head as she thought about Kate. She was so much happier now that she had escaped her father's house.

Jeannie couldn't help but wonder whether she'd ever get married and have a family of her own or if she'd end up a spinster alongside her friends. She had meant what she'd said to Lucas. She really didn't have time for courting, and truth be told, she was still embarrassed that she'd been so easily taken in by the faithless

Douglas. But that didn't stop her wishing she had a sweetheart. It had been nice, going out with Douglas, until he had shown his true colours with Doris, kissing the other girl at the Crispin Hall dance behind Jeannie's back.

She couldn't imagine never falling in love or bearing children. But right now, her family needed her and she knew she couldn't possibly... could she?

In an ideal world, her ma would get stronger and be able to take on more of the chores and cooking at home, Lucas's hand would get better and he could get back to his old job or a better one, and the twins would finally grow up and stop being such hard work. Then she could find a nice man – maybe Tom, if he hadn't been snapped up by someone else by then – and she could get married and become a mother. She really didn't want to spend the rest of her days stitching shoe linings at Clarks.

She gave the soup a final stir before she put the lid on the pot and left it to simmer. With a sigh, she sank into her chair by the range and closed her eyes. The twins would be back soon and peace would be shattered.

She must have dozed, because when she awoke as the twins tumbled in through the door arguing about some nonsense, Lucas was stirring the soup and Ma was sitting in her chair next to Jeannie's, smiling as she observed all her children together again after so long.

'Ma!' said Peter. 'How did you get down?'

'I walked, son,' she said, her voice stronger than Jeannie had heard it in a long time. 'Lucas went before me. I knew he'd catch me if I fell.' She looked at her oldest boy with such love that Jeannie felt her heart swell with gratitude that God had spared her brother and sent him home.

As the Musgrove family gathered around the table, Ma, Jeannie and Lucas held their hands out, smiling as the twins grumbled but joined theirs with the others, forming an unbroken circle.

'I don't usually pray aloud,' said Ma. 'But today I want to shout it to the heavens. I thank the good lord for returning my Lucas to us, for keeping a roof over our heads and food in our bellies.'

'I thought it was Clarks what housed and fed us,' mumbled John.

'Oh, hush,' Ma said. 'Of course we give thanks for the Clarks as well. But they're our benefactors by virtue of their faith and hard work. God guides them and everyone around here benefits because of it. So you be quiet and thank the lord for all the blessings he's sent into this house this day.'

'Amen,' said Lucas, then the others, before Jeannie dished up the soup and they ate their supper.

As she did so, Jeannie sent her own silent prayer of thanks. She knew that her blessings outweighed her problems and that maybe, one day, she would be even more blessed by the love of a good man. If the image of Tom appeared in her mind at that moment, she wouldn't admit it to anyone. She would bide her time and have faith that the good lord would find a way for her to find love.

AUTHOR'S NOTE

Thank you for reading about Jeannie, Louisa and Kate. I hope you've enjoyed getting to know them better. Their stories will continue in the next book in the Clarks Factory Girls series. Will Jeannie find a sweetheart or get her heart broken? Will Louisa ever be able to get over the terrible losses she's experienced, and will she and Lucas be able to help each other build a future without Mattie? Will Kate's new life be threatened by the past? Find out in Book Three!

ACKNOWLEDGEMENTS

I am grateful to everyone who has helped me as I researched and wrote *Courage for the Clarks Factory Girls*. They include the archivists at the Alfred Gillett Trust and numerous residents of Street in Somerset – many of whom have worked at C & J Clark, who shared memories and insights that all contributed to the fictional world in which Jeannie, Kate and Louisa live. Any mistakes in this book regarding life at the factory during the First World War are my own, for which I hope I will be forgiven.

Most of the characters are fictitious, but I have included some real people in the story for historical accuracy. The scenes in which they appear are purely fictional, my imaginings of what might have happened. I hope I have done them justice.

I would like to thank my wonderful editor at Boldwood Books, Rachel Faulkner-Willcocks for helping me to make this book the best it can be; Colin Thomas for the superb cover design; the super marketing team led by Claire Fenby for spreading the word about it, and the family of Boldwood authors who have cheered me along.

Finally, my thanks to you for reading *Courage for the Clarks Factory Girls*. I hope that you enjoy it. Look out for the next book in the series, with more of Jeannie, Kate and Louisa's story to come.

ABOUT THE AUTHOR

May Ellis is the author of more than five contemporary romance and YA fiction novels. She lives in Somerset, within sight of Glastonbury Tor. Inspired by her move to the area and her love of social history, she is now writing saga fiction – based on the real-life stories of the Clark's factory girls.

Sign up to May Ellis' mailing list for news, competitions and updates on future books.

Visit May's website: www.alisonroseknight.com

Follow May on social media here:

ALSO BY MAY ELLIS

,

Sixpence Stories

Introducing Sixpence Stories!

Discover page-turning historical novels from your favourite authors, meet new friends and be transported back in time.

Join our book club
Facebook group

https://bit.ly/SixpenceGroup

Sign up to our
newsletter

https://bit.ly/SixpenceNews

Boldwood

Boldwood Books is an award-winning fiction publishing company seeking out the best stories from around the world.

Find out more at www.boldwoodbooks.com

Join our reader community for brilliant books, competitions and offers!

Follow us
@BoldwoodBooks
@TheBoldBookClub

Sign up to our weekly deals newsletter

https://bit.ly/BoldwoodBNewsletter

Printed in Great Britain
by Amazon

46327278R00195